R. Barri Flowers is an award-win[...]
mystery and romance fiction fe[...]
protagonists, riveting plots, unexpected twists and turns,
and heart-pounding climaxes. With expertise in true crime,
serial killers and characterising dangerous offenders, he
is perfectly suited for the Mills & Boon Heroes series.
Chemistry and conflict between the hero and heroine,
attention to detail and incorporating the very latest
advances in criminal investigations are the cornerstones of
his romantic suspense fiction. Discover more on popular
social networks and Wikipedia.

Juno Rushdan is a veteran US Air Force intelligence officer
and award-winning author. Her books are action-packed and
fast-paced. Critics from *Kirkus Reviews* and *Library Journal*
have called her work 'heart-pounding James Bond–ian
adventure' that 'will captivate lovers of romantic thrillers.'
For a free book, visit her website: junorushdan.com

HUNTING A PREDATOR

R. BARRI FLOWERS

BIG SKY SAFE HOUSE

JUNO RUSHDAN

MILLS & BOON

First Published in Great Britain 2025
by Mills & Boon, an imprint of HarperCollins*Publishers* Ltd
1 London Bridge Street, London, SE1 9GF

www.harpercollins.co.uk

HarperCollins*Publishers*
Macken House, 39/40 Mayor Street Upper,
Dublin 1, D01 C9W8, Ireland

Hunting a Predator © 2025 R. Barri Flowers
Big Sky Safe House © 2025 Juno Rushdan

ISBN: 978-0-263-39735-2

1125

MIX
Paper | Supporting
responsible forestry
FSC www.fsc.org **FSC™ C007454**

This book contains FSC™ certified paper and other controlled sources to ensure responsible forest management.

For more information visit: www.harpercollins.co.uk/green

Printed and Bound in the UK using 100% Renewable Electricity at CPI Group (UK) Ltd, Croydon, CR0 4YY

HUNTING A PREDATOR

R. BARRI FLOWERS

In loving memory of my cherished mother, Marjah Aljean, a devoted lifelong fan of Mills & Boon romance and romantic suspense novels, who inspired me to excel in my personal and professional lives. To H. Loraine (Sleeping Beauty), the true and dearest love of my life and very best friend, whose support has been unwavering through the many terrific years together; as well as the many loyal fans of my romance, suspense, mystery and thriller fiction published over the years. A special shout-out goes to a wonderful group of talents whom I have long admired: Carol, Charmian, Hedy, Krista, Lisa, Peggy, Olivia and Sharon. And last but not least, a nod to my great Mills & Boon editors, Emma Cole and Denise Zaza, for the wonderful opportunity to lend my literary voice and creative spirit to the Heroes series, as well as Miranda Indrigo, the wonderful concierge, who serendipitously led me to success with Mills & Boon Heroes.

Prologue

Peggy Elizondo had only recently moved to the picturesque town of Bends Lake, Kansas—some four hours' drive from Kansas City in the state—where she'd landed a teaching job at Bends Lake Middle School. Fresh from receiving her secondary teacher certification from the University of North Texas, a month shy of turning twenty-two, she welcomed the opportunity to prove her worth in the classroom and beyond. As a proud member of the Kickapoo Traditional Tribe of Texas, she fully intended to connect with the Kickapoo Tribe in Kansas to stay close to her roots and, indeed, extend them. But for now, she was just happy to do her thing, which included fixing up her brand-new one-bedroom apartment on Fennkel Road and taking full advantage of the summer activities afforded her in the community.

Peggy's long and curly brunette ponytail swung from side to side while she jogged spiritedly through the eastern cottonwood trees surrounding the winding runner's trail in Blakely Park, which bordered the popular and recreational Lake Bends and seemed to have no end in sight. That worked for her, as she loved pushing herself to the limit as part of her fitness routine. Unfortunately, the same sentiment wasn't true when it came to her love life.

Once a cheater, always a cheater. Or at least she chose to abide by this old adage in breaking up with her no-good boyfriend, Chip McBride, last month after catching him in bed with another woman. Though he called it a big mistake and said he deeply regretted it and swore it wouldn't happen again, their trust had been irreparably broken. She wasn't about to allow him to hurt her again.

If she was lucky, someone else was waiting around the proverbial corner to come into her life, putting even more distance between her and Chip.

A girl can still dream, can't she? Peggy thought imaginatively, as she sucked in a deep breath and cast her big brown eyes at the abundant nature all around her. *I could really get used to this*, she told herself. She wondered if the nightlife in Bends Lake was as generous. Maybe she would put it to the test this weekend and see if she could make a connection with someone.

Only in that moment did Peggy break out of her reverie at the sound of branches snapping in the near distance, as if whispering to her. Perhaps another runner coming or going? Or maybe some, hopefully friendly, wildlife making its or their way home?

She suddenly stopped in her tracks, as if hitting a wall, as Peggy saw a tall and muscular white male seem to come out of nowhere—he'd actually stepped out from between trees up ahead—effectively and deliberately blocking her way down the path. On a quick perusal, she supposed she would consider him handsome, if not exactly her type. He was dark-haired, blue-eyed and wearing dark clothing and gloves, along with dirty white running shoes. She guessed him to be in his mid to late thirties. Only now did she notice that he was holding a firearm.

And pointing it directly at her.

How had she missed this?

The obvious answer was that he must have slipped it out of the pocket of his windbreaker jacket as she was sizing him up.

So…what? He wanted to rape or rob her in broad daylight? Take her cell phone? Steal her car? *Good luck with that*, Peggy told herself, knowing that she had jogged to the park directly from her apartment. So her Toyota Corolla was safe.

But what about herself?

She considered that he may want to actually kill her, for one reason or another.

Or any combination of the possibilities laid out in her head could be in play.

Whichever way she sliced it, Peggy recognized that her predicament didn't look good. And that was putting it quite mildly. She was in deep trouble. Fighting back the fear that gripped her like an angry parent, she tried to take control of her emotions and keep a cool head under the obvious fire that stood curiously before her without uttering a word as yet.

Maybe if she spoke to him first—tried to reason with him as a newbie in town who just wanted a chance to make a decent life for herself in Bends Lake—he would turn his attention elsewhere and leave her alone. Was that truly asking too much?

When she managed to get something to come out of her trembling lips, Peggy couldn't prevent herself from stammering, as she said, "P-please d-don't hurt me—"

The man snickered at her with what appeared to be amusement and responded sarcastically, "I won't." He waited a beat and added in a harsher inflection, "At least not in the way you may be most dreading—short of death..."

Peggy considered his words. He seemed to be reading her mind as it related to the fear of being sexually assaulted. Or beaten up. She hated the thought of being violated, humiliated or left in agony.

But if those were off the table, it left only one thing that played on perhaps her worst fears, like the fear in childhood of being accosted by a monster with very bad intentions hiding under the bed.

"Unfortunately, you *are* about to die," the man snorted wickedly in confirming his deadly intentions, as he kept the barrel of the handgun aimed squarely at her chest. "And I'm afraid there's really nothing you can do about it—any more than those who came before you... Except maybe say a prayer or whatever you think may give you some comfort in your last moments of life and whatever comes after—"

Peggy winced. So, there were other victims caught in the same deadly trap? With nowhere to turn to escape the inevitable. Fueled by that terrible realization and refusing to succumb to it, she decided that her only chance—slim as it was—of coming out of this alive was to make a run for it. Straight toward him, hopefully catching the man off guard just enough to throw him off—while screaming at the top of her lungs for someone, anyone, to hear—and using her speed to try and escape the assailant through the trees.

Only she hadn't counted on him being one step ahead of her. Maybe two. Or three, as it turned out.

Like a trained assassin, he opened fire, hitting her once in the chest. Then twice.

Strangely, she barely heard any sounds coming from

the gun. He must have used some type of silencer. Either that, or she had somehow lost her hearing in the process of being shot.

As she went down like a ton of bricks—or the target of a vicious right hook by a heavyweight prizefighter—Peggy lay sprawled on the solid ground, clutching her chest as if this would somehow alleviate the tremendous damage done to her insides. Or the incredible pain that tore through her as if she'd been struck by a Mack truck.

When her attacker stood above her, clearly gloating over what he had done, all she could manage to utter out of her contorted mouth, with blood spurting out, was, "Wh-why…d-did you d-do this…sh-shoot me…?" Not that she expected an answer. Or would accept anything that legitimized murdering her in cold blood and depriving her of the new life she had made for herself in Bends Lake.

But he did respond, after a boastful chuckle. "Because, as the Bends Lake Predator, this is what I do—for reasons you couldn't begin to understand." He furrowed his brow thoughtfully then laughed again. "Honestly, I just can't help myself…"

The Bends Lake Predator? What did he mean? Peggy tried to decipher the words, as if they were spoken in a foreign language, even as she lay dying in a pool of her own blood. A dogged perpetrator who hunted human beings as prey for whatever sick fantasies he had? Or was there some other deep meaning to the description?

Turning back to herself, Peggy couldn't help but think about her lost future and what might have been. Had it not been for her misfortune of becoming the target of a killer.

Her attacker continued, "If it hadn't been you, trust me, it would have been someone else. Actually, it has been. One after another over time…" He chuckled, even more wickedly than before, at his own warped smugness. "So sad. Too bad."

As it began to dawn on Peggy just what he meant, and how she must have somehow found herself in the crosshairs of a serial killer, he aimed the gun at her once more and fired another shot, before everything went completely black.

THE BENDS LAKE PREDATOR took a moment to gape at the pretty dead woman, imagining what her very last thought had been before her life was snuffed out for good. Maybe she was hoping for some sort of miracle to happen—manmade or otherwise—whereby she was able to cheat death and get on with her existence.

Surely that was what the others who came before her were praying for as well.

Like them, her last-ditch Hail Mary for a successful escape fell short. No one would come to stop him just in the nick of time. He made sure of that.

He did what had to be done.

And would do so again at a time and place of his choosing. Always one step ahead of the game, he relished outmaneuvering those who tried in vain to stop him. Maintaining control and confidence was in his DNA, no matter the obstacles that always threatened to stand in his way.

He tucked the Springfield Armory 1911 Ronin Operator 9 mm pistol with a suppressor away in his waistband, hidden inside his jacket, and left the corpse for others to come upon, to their horror. And his expectation.

Backtracking through the woods, making sure he was neither seen nor heard, he waited till he was a safe distance from the scene of the crime and prying eyes before stepping out into the open. Running a hand through his thick hair innocently, he effortlessly blended in with other park goers, offering a deceptive friendly grin here and there and getting one in return.

When he reached his vehicle, the Bends Lake Predator climbed inside calmly, started the engine and drove off scot-free. while, admittedly, much more treacherous than anyone could ever suspect.

Chapter One

Looks like the Bends Lake Predator is at it once again. Declan Delgado replayed the ominous words mentally from Ursula Liebert, his fellow Kansas Bureau of Investigation special agent within the KBI Field Investigations Division. She had phoned him from Blakely Park, where the body of a female runner had been discovered less than an hour ago on this afternoon in mid-August. According to Ursula, she had been shot to death at close range, reminiscent of the modus operandi of who they believed was an adult white male serial killer prowling Bends Lake like a ruthless predator on a mission. The unsub had been given the chilling moniker *Bends Lake Predator* by the press. Declan found it more than a little frustrating that the perpetrator was somehow, some way, able to adeptly evade detection, leaving no workable clues or solid forensic or physical evidence to identify him. The killer targeted women and men before cunningly sliding back into anonymity and his normal life till it was time to strike again.

If the current homicide victim panned out as one of his, that would mean that the Bends Lake Predator had murdered six people in the last six months. This didn't sit well with Declan as he drove down Belle Lane toward the park in his duty vehicle, a mineral-gray metallic Chevrolet Malibu. The KBI had taken the lead in the investigation, as part of a Bends Lake Predator Task Force operation that included detectives and crime scene investigators from the Bends Lake Police Department and Danver County Sheriff's Office. Though no one was bumping heads, per se, the serial killer was still very much at large, much to their chagrin, and apparently hiding in plain view while eyeing new potential targets to take out.

I hate that he's clearly got the upper hand right now, so long as the unsub keeps from slipping up, Declan mused, before he cursed back the thought. But that could only last for so long. His penchant for wanting to see each and every investigation successful in terms of slapping handcuffs on the perp or eliminating them as a threat if there was no surrender had been there ever since he joined the KBI nine years ago. Before that, he had worked for the Kansas City, Kansas, Police Department as a homicide detective after receiving his bachelor's degree from the School of Criminal Justice at Wichita State University.

After losing his parents at an early age in the state's capital city of Topeka and being bounced between relatives while trying to keep his head above water when he could very easily have fallen in with the wrong crowd, Declan managed to buck the trend of some he'd grown up with. He had fought hard to stay on the right side of the tracks, determined to do something good with his life and make a difference in the lives of others.

Declan's thoughts turned to currently being an unexpected widower at the relatively young age of thirty-six. How could anyone be prepared to deal with losing one's wife the way he did three years ago, when Elise's Dodge Hornet had been hit head on by a speeding, out-of-control drunk driver? They had barely been married for four years, after a whirlwind romance saw them go down the aisle. But fate had found a way to stomp all over his life, while cruelly taking away hers.

To make matters worse for Declan, in ways he hated to admit—but couldn't run away from even if he wanted to—was that he had been involved with Elise's older sister, Stella Bailey, prior to meeting and hitting it off with Elise, an attractive divorcée. He had ended things with Stella before he started dating Elise—or even knew they were siblings for that matter—believing that there was no real future with her gorgeous but ambitious and career-minded sister. But he didn't exactly ingratiate himself with Stella when Declan asked Elise to marry him. While she seemed to want her younger sister to be happy in all ways possible, that same sentiment didn't necessarily apply to him, which Stella made plainly obvious by giving him the cold shoulder from that point on.

Elise's untimely and tragic death had only strained things between them that much more, as though Stella somehow blamed him for what happened to her sister. Or at least it appeared that way to Declan, as she cut him out of her life altogether like a surgeon would a deadly cancer in the body—as if he'd never been a part of it in the first place—giving him essentially no say in the matter. Out of respect for her, albeit it against his own wishes, he abided by Stella's apparent desire not to have anything to do with him anymore.

I can only wonder what might have been had things worked out between me and Stella before I ever got into a relationship with her sister, Declan told himself as he drove into the park. Maybe he should have been more patient with Stella. Given them a fighting chance, even if they were on different career paths, though both in law enforcement. Or would he have only prolonged the inevitable, which wouldn't have been good for either of them?

He even wondered if—in some strange quirk of nature—Elise might still be alive today had he not married her and, by virtue, inadvertently set the fatal chain of events in motion. After all, Elise had been on her way to their house after a quick trip to the supermarket to pick up some things for dinner. But had she been single and uninvolved with him, she might have taken a different route or not even have lived in Bends Lake at all that fateful day.

Don't even go there, Declan admonished himself as reality set in. No matter how he tried to play it, no amount of guilt was justifiable in trying to rewrite history with what-ifs.

He parked in the lot, cut off the ignition and checked the leather holster on his side for the loaded SIG Sauer P226 9 mm semiautomatic pistol before getting out of the car. At six foot two and a half, he was probably in the best shape of his life thanks to regular workouts at the gym, on an outside basketball court and elsewhere. After making his way inside the park, Declan flashed his identification to get beyond the yellow crime scene barricade tape and officers on hand, where he then conferred with the KBI Crime Scene Response Team, which was collecting and preserving evidence, photographing the scene and performing more of their duties.

Declan spotted Ursula Liebert, who saw him at the same time, and they approached each other. Ursula was tall and slender, with light blond hair in a blunt cut that fell just below her shoulders. The thirty-two-year-old special agent and her pregnant British wife, Melody, were expecting their first child soon. It was something he envied, given that his own dream of having children had been dealt a serious blow. He'd lost Elise before they even had a chance to get to that point in their marriage. No one he'd dated since then—and there hadn't been that many—gave him any reason to believe that equation would change anytime soon. And prior to his relationship with Elise, things had never even come close to progressing into that type of discussion when Declan was seeing Stella, before they went their separate ways.

"Hey," Ursula said evenly, snapping him out of his reverie as she stood before him.

"Hey." Declan met her clear blue eyes. "What's the latest?" he asked, wanting details over and beyond what had already been relayed to him about the apparent homicide.

"Victim's a Hispanic or Native American female in her early twenties, shot three times at close range, fatally… We're still trying to identify her." Ursula paused. "Dressed in jogging clothes. I'm guessing she was doing just that before she was ambushed by someone—"

Declan pinched his nose while musing. "Who discovered the body?"

"Another jogger… Yasmine Yoshiko. Apparently, she was caught up in her own thoughts when spotting the victim, nearly tripping over her body lying on the trail. She called 911 right away."

"Did she happen to run into anyone else along the way—or after the fact?" Declan had to ask.

"According to Ms. Yoshiko, she had just begun her run and hadn't seen anyone coming or going on the trail up to that point."

"Lucky her." Declan knew that if she had come face to face with the killer, particularly if the unsub was the serial predator they suspected him to be and she could identify him, Yasmine Yoshiko would also most likely be dead right now. "We'll see what surveillance cameras in the park or local area can give us."

"Hopefully something," Ursula said with a sigh. "Along with whatever the CSRT discovers beyond the shell casings found near the victim."

Thoughtful, Declan scratched his pate below short dark hair. "So, where's the body?"

Ursula wrinkled her nose. "Right through those trees—" she pointed at the rows of eastern cottonwoods "—just as the trail curves. The medical examiner has arrived and is with the deceased now."

"Let's have a look." Declan followed her to the crime scene, where he regarded the victim lying awkwardly on her back as she was being tended to on the dirt trail. She was slender and wearing an orange running tank, brown athletic shorts and white-and-orange sneakers. Her brunette ponytail was lying to the side, soaked in her own blood. There was a bullet wound in her forehead and two wounds in her chest.

The Danver County medical examiner and coroner was Dr. Aaron Wilson. African American, he was in his mid-forties and of medium build, with gray-black hair in a short Afro. Crouching, he lifted sable eyes behind horn-rimmed glasses to Declan and acknowledged him naturally. "Agent Delgado."

"Doc Wilson." Declan nodded at him, wishing circumstances hadn't called for them to become better acquainted of late, then cut to the chase. "Where do things stand in your assessment of the situation?"

Flexing his large hands covered with nitrile gloves, the medical examiner took a breath and responded, "Well, pending the official autopsy report, I can tell you that the decedent was shot three times at close range, with the shot to the head likely the one that killed her. Though two shots to the chest would ultimately have had the same effect..." He glanced at the victim. "No early indications of defensive wounds, suggesting she didn't even have a chance to put up a decent fight before dying where she lay."

"What's your preliminary estimate on the time of death?" Declan asked, presuming it had to be close to the time she was discovered by the other runner. Still, he wanted to have an official general timeline on the victim's whereabouts prior to her demise to consider how this could have been used against her.

Without seeming to give it much thought, Wilson answered matter-of-factly, "I'd say the decedent died instantly once the fatal shot occurred, likely within the last couple of hours..."

Which gave her killer just enough leeway to flee the scene of the crime and find a safe haven away from the murder, Declan told himself as he watched the medical examiner and coroner get to his feet and order his team to lift the victim's body onto a stretcher to take her away.

THE FOLLOWING MORNING, Declan sat on a leather swivel chair in his office at the KBI office on Washington Street in Great Bend, Kansas. Great Bend was the county seat of Barton County and around twenty miles or so from the crime scene in Bends Lake. He had just gotten word from the Firearm and Toolmark Section of the forensic science laboratory in the building, after the ballistics evidence had been transferred there from the Evidence Control Center. It confirmed what he had expected. The bullets that killed the as yet unidentified woman in Blakely Park matched the cartridge cases left at the scene and were linked to the same

Springfield Armory 1911 Ronin Operator 9 mm handgun and bullets used in five other murders committed by the Bends Lake Predator. In spite of the correlation and cross referencing of the ballistic evidence when loaded into the Bureau of Alcohol, Tobacco, Firearms and Explosives National Integrated Ballistic Information Network, the actual murder weapon had yet to be recovered for analysis.

It is obviously still in the possession of the unsub, Declan thought perceptively. Waiting to be used again on one or more unsuspecting victims while the nameless killer remained on the loose. And was as dangerous as ever.

This told Declan that—their capabilities in law enforcement within the Bends Lake Predator Task Force notwithstanding—they could use some help from the feds in solving the serial killer case. Or more specifically, the type of assistance that a well-respected profiler might be able to give them in getting a better grip on the perp and his way of thinking.

Stella Bailey came to mind. He knew she was certainly at the top of her game when it came to criminal behavioral analysis, having kept track of his sister-in-law's efforts in this area from a safe—if not uncomfortable—distance since she relocated to Detroit, Michigan.

Would she be up to returning to Bends Lake to work with him and the team, in spite of their frosty and all but nonexistent relationship since—and even before—Elise's death? At this point, even getting Stella to consult remotely would be welcome, given her expertise in criminal profiling.

Or was either option too much to ask? Or for that matter, did he even have the right to expect anything, considering the tragedy that made the divide between them greater and, he sensed, damned near impossible to repair?

Only one way to find out, Declan told himself deter-
minedly. He felt desperation—but just as much a desire to
try and make things right between them on at least some
level after three years—as he got on the phone with the
FBI's field office in Detroit.

STELLA BAILEY SAT in an ergonomic chair at the L-shaped
desk in her office on the twenty-sixth floor of the Federal
Bureau of Investigation's Detroit field office on Michigan
Avenue. The FBI behavioral analyst's sharp brown eyes
were gazing at the notes on her laptop. Or more specifically, the profile she had developed on the Montana mass
shooter who had used an AR-15 semiautomatic rifle to kill
ten people at a crowded shopping center last month in Cas-
cade County before escaping the carnage. This led to the
unsub being positively identified as Leonard Fetterman,
a vengeful estranged husband. His wife, Stefi, along with
the man she was dating, were among the victims. Fetterman was ultimately taken into custody without incident,
seemingly feeling that the deadly act more than justified
the means for him and whatever came next.

Stella sighed. She never failed to be amazed at the audacity of some perps in believing they had a right to take
the lives of others. And worse, that they were able to outsmart everyone else in the process. Till their misdeeds and
overconfidence caught up with them in the end. She was
more than happy to play a role—big or small—in taking
such despicable offenders down as a criminal profiler, having worked on cases across the United States and even on
loan abroad on occasion, when called upon. Ever since she
graduated from the University of Kansas in Lawrence with
a master of arts in psychology nearly a decade ago, Stella
knew it was her calling to use this educational pursuit to

dig into violent criminal behavior and the deviant minds of the perpetrators. Which was why she'd joined the FBI as a special agent, after successfully completing the grueling Special Agent Selection System process. Her position was boosted as she made her way to the Bureau's Behavioral Analysis Unit, with a focus on criminal investigative analysis and identifying what made offenders tick—as both a prelude to their downfall and after the fact, in order to use their characteristics to help identify and capture other dangerous criminals. She had used her knowledge to write two successful books on criminal profiling and was currently under contract to write a third book.

Beyond that, Stella felt that it had always been in her DNA to be there for those she cared about on a more personal level. Starting with her sister, Elise. Both were biracial, with a beautiful Nigerian American mother and handsome white father. Elise, two years younger than Stella, had sadly passed away before her time three years ago, which somehow seemed like forever and only yesterday at the same time.

After Elise's death, Stella's heartbroken parents, Ngozi and Lester Bailey, had moved from their hometown of Bends Lake, Kansas, to Detroit, Michigan, to escape the memories and have a fresh start—both taking jobs as professors at Wayne State University. Though she had moved around for her career, Stella would eventually follow suit when taking a job at the Bureau's Detroit field office in hopes of trying to fill the void in her parents' lives in the absence of one of their precious daughters.

But what about the giant void in her own life? At thirty-three years of age, she had been left to fend for herself, without her sister—or a meaningful romance, with no one in the picture to cozy up to at night at the moment. Not that she hadn't gone out on the occasional date that went nowhere. Or didn't want someone special in her life. After having that once years ago, only to lose him when she least expected it, she had come to believe that maybe it just wasn't in the cards for her to find true and enduring love. So instead, work had pretty much become her focal point these days.

At least that's something I can always count on, for better or worse, Stella told herself, though she was also committed to doing her best to be there for her mother and father. She broke out of her reverie as her boss, Valerie Izbicki, entered the office. The petite forty-six-year-old assistant special agent in charge had been in the post for the past two years, and Stella was certain it was only a matter of time before she was promoted to the position of special agent in charge in one field office or another.

"Hey," Stella said tentatively, eyeing her while running a hand through her long, layered black hair.

"Hey." Valerie smiled thinly, her short blond shag a good fit for an oval face and green eyes. She had on round glasses and touched them. "So, I've got a new assignment for you…"

"Okay." Though barely past her last assignment and the one before that, Stella wasn't about to complain, having gotten used to going wherever she was needed as part of the job. "Where to this time?" She considered that she may be able to lend her expertise remotely in making good use of today's advanced video conferencing capabilities.

"Actually, it's Bends Lake." Valerie waited a beat as if to gauge her reaction. "Your hometown, right?"

"Yes." Stella smoothed a thin brow, ill at ease as the painful memories came to the surface.

"The request came from the Kansas Bureau of Investigation," the assistant special agent in charge pointed out.

"The KBI?" Stella asked.

"They're investigating a serial killer on the loose there. You may have heard about it through the grapevine?"

"Actually, I hadn't," Stella confessed. Apart from deliberately avoiding keeping tabs on the happenings in the town she grew up in, she had been preoccupied with other cases, including a serial killer of children she'd profiled recently in Michigan's Upper Peninsula. Still, she cringed at the thought of a serial killer at large in Bends Lake, even while hesitant to return there for her own reasons.

As if sensing her reluctance, Valerie said, "Normally, we would assign an analyst based at or near the FBI Kansas City field office, but you were specifically requested by the KBI special agent working the case, Declan Delgado, so I figured you'd want this one. If not, tell me now, no questions asked..."

Stella's first instincts had been to take the opening she was being given and pass on the assignment with a firm no. Or, at the very least, request that she offer her analysis from afar, knowing her physical presence would not be truly needed if the digital files were sent to her.

But then that would mean she was acting on emotions rather than in her professional capacity. Was that how she wanted to play this? She imagined that Valerie was purposely putting her to the test, to see her limits. And probably the same was true with the KBI agent requesting her presence.

"Declan's my brother-in-law," Stella informed her boss matter-of-factly, assuming that he hadn't volunteered this information when requesting her services.

"Seriously?" Valerie fluttered her lashes, as if totally in the dark about it.

Stella nodded. "He was married to my sister, Elise, who died in a car accident three years ago."

"Sorry to hear that." Valerie's brow creased. "I can only imagine how difficult it must have been for both of you."

I doubt you could imagine just how difficult it truly was on multiple levels, Stella told herself. Still, she wished she had mentioned it before now, but there never seemed to be a good reason to do so. Now that the cat was out of the bag, she needed to deal with it.

"I'll return to Bends Lake and do what I can to help with the investigation," Stella told her without giving it much more thought. That would come later.

Valerie nodded without probing further and said, "The KC field office in Kansas City, Missouri, will be sending over a couple of FBI special agents to join the task force as well, as part of the Bureau's cooperation on the case."

"Okay." Stella wondered if she might know the assigned agents, having been based at that field office at one point.

"You leave this afternoon."

All Stella could think to say in response was "Then I guess I better go pack a few things."

"Good luck," Valerie said, as if she would need it, and left the office.

Stella glanced at a framed photograph on her desk and picked it up. It was of her and Elise, who was beautiful, with long blond hair in a razored shag style and big hazel eyes. The pic was taken when they were in their early twenties and the future seemed endless.

Until it wasn't.

She grabbed her nylon hobo bag and headed home.

Chapter Two

Stella drove her blue Ford Edge SUV back to the town-house she lived in on Orleans Street. It was filled with contemporary furnishings, had hickory hardwood flooring and plenty of windows with natural sunlight streaming through the venetian blinds.

After packing her bags with probably more than she needed for what Stella expected to be a relatively short trip, she called her parents and informed them that she would be headed to Bends Lake for a few days on business.

As expected, they were surprised but fully supportive of her returning home to come face to face with Declan again—whom they had kept in touch with as part of seeking to keep the memory of Elise alive. For her part, Stella viewed the personal aspect of the visit with an awareness that there were uncomfortable questions that needed to be answered, one way or another.

She got on a Delta flight and was seated by the window, where Stella stared out at the clouds, meditative, and for good reason. Or bad, depending on how she looked at it.

Seven years ago, she had dated Declan Delgado for a few months, hitting it off right away with the handsome Hispanic KBI special agent and finding him seemingly on the same wavelength in most instances. It ended all too soon in Stella's mind. Unbeknownst to her, he had turned his attention to Elise, who fell hard for Declan and vice versa, with him eventually asking her to marry him.

Elise, who had been in a brief marriage to her college sweetheart, Roland Goldoni, said yes, dashing any hopes Stella had still harbored for resuming a relationship with Declan. This reality prompted her to transfer to a different field office for work, believing that distance between her and the newlyweds was best all the way around, while wanting Elise to get everything she deserved in a husband the second time around.

They had only been married for four years when tragedy struck like an earthquake, leaving Declan a widower and Stella without her beloved only sibling. She distanced herself from the man Elise gave her heart to, feeling it was too painful to maintain anything resembling close contact. She hadn't been back to Bends Lake since Elise's funeral three years ago, and Stella wasn't quite sure what to expect. Or not to, for that matter. *I don't want to overthink this*, she thought, thin fingers running through her hair while barely realizing it. Or presume that Declan handpicked her to profile the unsub for all the wrong reasons.

I have a job to do, and that's what this is all about, Stella told herself. All that was important at the moment was to see if she could provide the task force with enough insight into a serial killer and hope it was enough to help bring him to justice. Surely Declan did not have ulterior motives in wanting to see her again?

After arriving at Great Bend Municipal Airport, Stella rented a silver Mitsubishi Outlander and drove to the nearby town of Bends Lake, which she had once called home. She took in the familiar scenery—and unfamiliar in some areas—including mature maple tree-lined streets; Cape Cod, boutique, manufactured and historic homes; new construction and rich farmland.

In turning right on Burtiford Avenue, Stella knew that had she turned left, she would have come upon Bends Lake Hospital, where Elise had worked as an occupational therapist. Passing by Bends Lake High School, which Stella once attended, along with Elise, a touch of sadness swept over her at the thought that Elise would never get to attend her twenty-or twenty-five-year reunion.

A couple of minutes later, Stella checked into the Kotton Hotel on Lake Way. She took the elevator up to her fifth-floor suite. After going inside, she scanned the place and saw that it had a separate nice-size living area with plush beige carpeting and a window wall behind cordless blinds, along with contemporary furniture. The amenities included a flat-screen television, microwave, mini fridge and granite wet bar.

Stella took a walk through the spacious corner bedroom with a queen bed and another television and an en suite bathroom before stepping out on the balcony that overlooked Lake Bends and gazing at the forty-five-acre lake that had a fishing dock, boating, swimming and an adjoining nature trail. She recalled spending time on and in the water with Elise and their friends.

No sooner had she gone back inside and started to unpack her belongings—including the Glock 19 Gen5 9x19 mm compact duty pistol, which she put away in the bottom drawer of the walnut dresser—when there was a knock on the door. Deciding she was presentable enough while still wearing her casual flight attire and flats, Stella walked to it, thinking someone from the hotel might be checking to see if she needed anything.

Only when she opened the door, Stella laid her eyes on the tall and firmly built person who was, she hated to admit, still as handsome as ever. Honestly, she had once wondered if she would ever see him again.

Declan Delgado.

"Declan…" Her voice shook as she tried to get his name out while gawking at his square-jawed face and deep brown eyes with enticing gray flecks. His coarse black hair was in a high and tight style. He was dressed in a navy blazer over a light blue button-down shirt, dark pants and black loafers.

"Hi, Stella." His own voice was smooth, calm and collected. "It's been a minute."

"Actually, more like three years," she replied sarcastically, though suspecting he knew as much, considering the circumstances. How did he know where she was staying?

"Yeah, time flies." He brushed his Roman nose thoughtfully, then read her mind as he said, "I was told where to find you by my contact at the Bureau—and when you would arrive."

It took Stella a moment to regain her equilibrium. "I see."

He grinned askance. "Thanks for coming."

"I wasn't given much of a choice," she told him tartly, even if this wasn't exactly true. "My boss has a bad habit of cooperating when our assistance is requested in investigations."

"Guess some habits, good and bad, are hard to break," he quipped, museful. "Appreciate it, nonetheless."

Don't make a big deal out of coming home and seeing him again, Stella scolded herself. She needed to put professionalism above all else. Softening her tone, she said, "I'll do whatever I can to help with the case."

"I was counting on that." Declan eyed her with a straight look. "With your expertise in criminal profiling, I'm sure you'll be able to shed some light on the unsub we're after and just what we're dealing with here." He waited a beat before asking, "Mind if I come in?"

For whatever reason—actually, she could think of one or two but kept them to herself—Stella didn't think that was such a good idea and responded accordingly. "There's a coffee shop downstairs. Why don't I meet you there instead? Just give me a few minutes to freshen up."

"Not a problem." His jaw tightened. "See you then."

Stella watched him walk away for a moment, before closing the door and leaning her back against it broodingly. She couldn't fault Elise for wanting to be with Declan as his wife, as Stella knew full well the many admirable qualities he possessed as a man. Any more than she could fault him for choosing her sister to be his bride. Elise was beautiful, smart and a good catch for any pursuer—having moved back to Bends Lake upon getting her master of occupational therapy degree from the University of Kansas. She would also have been a wonderful mother, had fate not intervened.

Stella could only imagine what else might have been in store for her sister, had Elise been able to live a full life. *I'm sure that Declan's also wondering the same thing*, she told herself. Even if he had moved on with his life—and romantic interests, undoubtedly. She sucked in a deep breath and headed toward the bedroom.

After washing her face, putting her hair up and quickly changing her clothing, Stella grabbed her small leather handbag and left the room while feeling a little nervous at the prospect of getting together with Declan again.

DECLAN WAS ADMITTEDLY on pins and needles as he sat at a table in Kendre's Coffee Café, sipping on brewed coffee, while awaiting Stella. Truthfully, he hadn't even been sure she would come back to Bends Lake, if it meant they would have to have a conversation on everything from breaking up to marrying her sister and Elise's death. He half—maybe more than that—expected Stella to find a way out of the assignment.

Yet here she was, meaning that they both would need to come to terms with some things, apart from whatever Stella could bring to the Bends Lake Predator investigation.

Declan watched as she walked toward the table, looking every bit as gorgeous as the day he first laid eyes on her. A diamond-shaped face with a beautiful complexion was taut, with attractive small brown eyes, a button nose and full lips proportionately situated. Long raven hair was in a high ponytail with curly layered strands bordering her face. She was now wearing a white satin top, brown knit trousers and low-heeled black pumps.

"Hey," Declan said, offering her a soft smile.

Stella responded evenly, "Hey."

"I took the liberty of ordering you a latte," he told her as she sat on a wooden chair. "I assume that's what you still like in coffee?"

"Yes, it is," she confirmed. "Thank you." She lifted the mug and took a sip.

"No problem." Declan tasted his own coffee. *At least it's nice to know that some things never change*, he thought. "So, how have you been?"

Stella sipped more coffee thoughtfully. "Busy," she responded simply. "My life has been anything but boring."

He could take that in more ways than one but decided not to ask just yet about her love life, feeling it was probably inappropriate. Still, imagining her with another man was uncomfortable, even if he had absolutely no right to resent Stella moving on with her life in whatever way she saw fit.

Declan brushed that thought aside. "Yeah, I suppose that working as a special agent for the Bureau, and especially profiling different villains as part of the process, can be a demanding job."

"It can be," she conceded, then turned the tables on him. "How are things with you these days?"

"Also busy, chasing the bad guys and trying my damnedest to not let them slip through the cracks," he responded, while thinking, *Wish I could say I'd found someone new to share my life with, but that isn't the case*. Not that this was something he figured she had any interest in at this stage.

Stella regarded him. "You mean like the so-called Bends Lake Predator?" She paused, adding, "I did a cursory glance at your investigation through news accounts while on the plane."

"Yeah, that would certainly be at the top of my current caseload," Declan told her. "So far, the unsub's managed to stay on the deadly offensive while adroitly avoiding capture. I'm hoping that the more we can get into his psyche, the better the chance of identifying and nailing him before he kills again—"

"I understand." She flipped one of the cute curls from her brow. "I'm ready to learn more about the unsub and where the investigation is at this point."

"Good to know," he said, putting the mug to his lips. "As it is, we're about to give an update on the case and look forward to your assessment of the serial killer."

"You'll have it," she promised, "with the obvious caveat that characterizing an offender can only go so far in getting to the root of the criminal behavior. Not to mention, any unsub is capable of changing his or her patterns of conduct at any time."

"Understood." Declan liked being able to speak with her again, even if on a professional level. If he had any say in it, they would go beyond that while the opportunity presented itself. He leaned forward. "Look, I know the Bureau is footing the bill for the hotel—but, just so you know, you're more than welcome to stay at the house while you're here. There's plenty of room…" Was he really trying to put pressure on her to let bygones be bygones?

"Thanks for the offer." Stella looked at him for a moment. "But I think it's probably best all the way around that I stay put during the short time I'm in town. So if it's all right with you, I'll pass."

"Of course." Declan hid his unrealistic disappointment. "Whatever works for you." He wouldn't push it. "Well, if you don't mind riding with me, I'll drive you to and from the police department."

She flashed a tiny smile. "I'm fine with that."

"Okay." He would take every small victory that came his way in the slow thaw of the wall of ice between them, if he was reading this correctly.

IN A CONFERENCE room at the Bends Lake Police Department on Sorenten Street, Declan stood in the front, eager to get started. He glanced at the three individuals standing beside him and said affably, "I'd like to welcome to the Bends Lake Predator Task Force FBI special agents Stella Bailey, Keene Haverstock and Arielle Mendoza. Agents Haverstock and Mendoza are from the Bureau's Kansas City field office, and Agent Bailey is a well-known FBI behavioral analyst out of Detroit, who just happens to be my sister-in-law." He swept over that quickly, wanting to be transparent while also dismissing it as irrelevant to her involvement in the case. "Their participation in the investigation will hopefully bring us closer to wrapping up the case and holding the unsub fully accountable for everything he's done in Bends Lake—"

He shook hands with the three, starting with Keene Haverstock—who was in his midforties, tall and muscular, and had a gray high-fade haircut—followed by Arielle Mendoza—an attractive and curvy Latina in her early thirties with brunette hair in a pixie wedge. Declan finished with Stella. He wrapped his large hand around her small hand with thin fingers and felt a tingle of memory course through him as they locked eyes. Had she felt it too?

If so, it must have stung, as Stella released their hands almost as quickly as they grasped one another. Declan accepted her resistance to—or defense mechanism against—anything that suggested more of a personal relationship between them than strictly coworkers. He understood the delicate lines that neither of them wanted to cross given their prior connection.

As the special agents stepped away and found somewhere to sit, Declan motioned for KBI special agent Ursula Liebert to join him in getting to the main crux of the meeting. After grabbing the stylus pen from the rectangular conference table, Declan gazed at a large touch screen display and placed on it a collage of six photographs of individuals taken while they were still alive and well.

He glanced at Stella and then, largely to give her everything he could to work with, said, "In the past six months, these six persons have been shot to death in Bends Lake by an unknown assailant. Three men. Three women. It still remains to be seen if this was calculated. Or happenstance."

Declan clicked on one picture, which then occupied the

screen all by itself. It was of an attractive white female with curly red hair in a collarbone blunt cut and blue eyes.

"Erica Reilly, a thirty-nine-year-old caterer, was gunned down outside her home on Vale Lane, as the first victim linked to the unsub we're calling the Bends Lake Predator—on account of his brazen display of violence and ability to slither away like the poisonous snake that he is and make himself scarce from detection and apprehension, while leaving no positively identifying DNA or fingerprints at the crime scene."

He selected the next image of an Asian male with a black faux hawk hairstyle and brown eyes, and said, "Victim number two was Henry Minnillo, a twenty-five-year-old software engineer, shot and killed after visiting a friend at the Leighwood apartment complex on Roiten Road." Declan went to another picture—this one an African American female who had platinum hair in a fluffy Afro and black eyes. "The next victim was thirty-six-year-old Gwendolyn Gunderson, a cabaret singer who was shot to death shortly after a performance at a jazz club on Twenty-third Street."

Declan let that sink in for a moment before switching to the fourth person to become a victim of gunfire. He glanced at the gray-haired white male with green eyes and said, "Billy Rottenberg, forty, a construction supervisor, was shot and killed outside a building his company was constructing on Jenkins Lane." Declan immediately moved on to the next image of a young Hispanic male with long and stringy brown hair and dark eyes. "The fifth victim was nineteen-year-old college student Erique Ruiz, who was shot when he was walking along Warline Road, blocks away from Bends Lake University."

Switching to the most recent victim, who had attractive

brown eyes and long brunette hair, he said, "Yesterday morning, Peggy Elizondo, a twenty-one-year-old Native American middle school teacher, was gunned down while jogging in Blakely Park." Declan sighed, expressing his discontent. "All six victims were shot at point-blank range three times—the last shot of which was a kill shot to the head. Needless to say, the unsub shows no signs of slowing down. Not till we force the issue, one way or the other—"

With that, Declan stepped aside, turning the stylus over to Ursula, who flashed him an even look and quickly brought up on the monitor a firearm. "All six of the murder victims were shot to death with a Springfield Armory 1911 Ronin Operator 9 mm pistol—much like the one you see on the screen," she said smoothly. "The bullets were fired from a gun barrel with six lands and grooves that had a right-hand twist. Based upon the lack of sound as reported by witnesses and others nearby, we believe that the gun was likely equipped with a sound suppressor." She put one on the screen as an example. "Though the actual murder weapon is not yet in our possession, we're confident that this is only a matter of time. Just as it is before we identify the culprit and put an end to his reign of terror in Bends Lake, where he appears to be targeting victims randomly...or who happen to have the misfortune to come within his crosshairs..."

Declan had moved over to sit beside Stella as Ursula continued. "Speaking of the unsub, security camera footage near two different crime scenes indicates a serious person of interest as our chief suspect." She put the video images on a split screen. "Though the unsub's head is covered by a hood from the hoodie that's worn, along with dark clothing and dirty running shoes—we believe the suspect is a tall white or light-skinned Hispanic male with short dark hair, likely in his mid to late thirties or early forties. He appears to be in pretty good shape, based on body type and the way the unsub has been able to make haste in distancing himself from the scenes. Based on surveillance videos obtained from the vicinities where the murders occurred, we believe that the suspect may have been driving a dark SUV during his escape." Ursula took a breath and said keenly, "The task force will flush him out into the open, whatever it takes, and stop this madness…"

Declan was inclined to agree, even if they weren't there yet. He regarded Stella, who had been taking everything in, and said to her interestedly, "So, what are your thoughts?"

She met his gaze and responded contemplatively, "I have a few ideas, and I'm ready to share…"

"Have at it." He nodded, thinking again about the surge of electricity he felt when their palms touched earlier. "We'll be happy to take whatever you have to offer in trying to get the bead on our unsub."

"Okay," Stella said equably and rose to her feet.

THOUGH SHE HAD been in this situation before, Stella still had butterflies in her stomach as she stood at the podium. Was it truly a case of nerves? Or was it because she was there on behalf of Declan, whom she had spent the last three years trying to avoid, more or less? *I wonder if it was only my imagination when we shook hands and our skin touching somehow seemed to reverberate throughout my body as it had once before years ago?* she asked herself.

Stella broke away from the notion, absurd or not. She collected her thoughts for the moment at hand, deliberately avoiding Declan's steady gaze, as she went over mental notes and then said measuredly, "Though this perspective is subject to change once I delve deeper into the unsub's psyche—" which she hoped might not be necessary if they could nail the perp first "—based on what you've laid out on this Bends Lake Predator, my initial thoughts are that, as opposed to there being no rhyme or rhythm to the killings per se, I believe that, in fact, there is some rationale to what the unsub is doing…"

She took a short breath and went on, "For most serial killers, there is almost always a method to their madness, so to speak—even for what appears to be at face value random homicides—that may not be as discernible as we'd like in law enforcement. As it is, I worked on a similar type of serial killer case in Lansing, Michigan, last year where the victims were being gunned down, one by one in seemingly unrelated attacks…only to find out that there was something akin to an unorganized connection beneath the surface…"

I'd better get back to the point before I lose them, Stella told herself, glancing at Declan, who seemed glued to what was coming next. She swallowed and said evenly, "The fact that there have been three women and three men murdered is, in and of itself, indicative of a pattern of behavior. It tells me, for one, that the unsub is not gender specific in who he targets. Meaning that he is equally bent on killing women and men in order to satisfy his thirst for murder. This, of course, makes it difficult for law enforcement to zero in on one demographic for victimization to try and narrow down the killer's lane. Similarly," she needed to say, "the twenty plus age range of nineteen to forty for the victims means that the unsub is less interested in targeting a particular age group than he is in going after those who fit other situational characteristics—such as opportunity, location, time of day and a surefire getaway path—for the kills. This, again, complicates things when trying to narrow the focus for prevention and apprehension—"

Declan cut in as he asked her, "What's your take on the diverse racial and ethnic breakdown of the victims? Is there something to make of this in the unsub's head in terms of messaging or intent? Or is it entirely happenstance?" His voice rang with skepticism on that last note.

Stella didn't need much time to consider her answer, even if there were no absolutes in criminal profiling. She met Declan's eyes and responded coolly, "I seriously doubt that anything the unsub has done to this point is by chance. I believe that the variance in murders by race and ethnicity is not at all a reflection of some deep-seated prejudices against any groups in particular, when you consider the range of the victims' racial and ethnic background. My guess is that the choice to go after these individuals was meant more to confuse the authorities as to his motivation and keep them guessing, while making it more difficult to track down the unsub."

"Yeah, I feel the same way," Declan told her, giving a nod that they were in sync on this. "Which seems to fit in as well with the other range of victim characteristics..."

"True." Stella sighed and made sure she kept from slouching, a tendency she had at times, as she continued. "But that doesn't mean that the unsub's wide latitude and intentional guesswork in his killing ways makes him untouchable. No matter how deliberate his actions are, he's bound to make mistakes that will prove to be his undoing—similar to other smart serial killers like Albert Fish, Ted Bundy, John Wayne Gacy, Lonnie David Franklin Jr. and Richard Ramirez, to name a few. Most will not simply disappear into scary folklore, such as the infamous Whitechapel serial killer, Jack the Ripper.

"Now, in characterizing the Bends Lake Predator, beyond his physical appearance, I see him as a loner, but not necessarily alone. He may even be happily married with children, while still conducting his criminal activities without anyone in his inner circle being the wiser." She inhaled a breath. "Based upon the unsub's chosen method of killing, he's not one for wanting to get his hands dirty by committing the murders in more personal ways—such as by stabbing or strangling, which would make it easier to collect his DNA or fingerprints." Stella looked at her fellow FBI special agents, neither of whom she'd known when she worked at the KC field office herself. "The unsub would rather shoot his victims to death and get out of there as quickly as possible, while blending in with his surroundings. But his comfort with using a firearm also tells me that he could have honed his skills at a shooting range. Or could have a current or previous career in law enforcement or the military—or some other occupations that involve the use of firearms…"

Stella eyed Declan and couldn't tell if potentially implicating someone in law enforcement made him uneasy. Or not. Surely, he and others on the task force had already come to this same possibility, with catching the killer a top priority—wherever it took them.

She finished her initial assessment of the unsub by saying confidently, "I believe that the man you're looking for is a predatory killer—in that the murders are largely about the hunter preying upon his targets like a lion out for blood, as a recreational pursuit—and it appears, is just as bent on killing for hedonistic reasons, or in other words, a kill for the thrill mentality." Stella paused then gave a blunt warning, "Unless you can put a stop to the homicides, it is all but certain that they will continue for the reasons stated."

She left the podium on that note, knowing that she had given them food for thought as part of the overall investigation. It would fall upon Declan and the teams' collective laps to use this to paint a better portrait of the unsub as the hunt to capture him went on.

Chapter Three

"You did a great job in giving us a pretty good profile of the unsub," Declan told Stella as he drove her back to the hotel. He added silently, *and that's an understatement for how excellent an analysis it was.*

"Did you expect otherwise?" she asked, glancing at him.

He chuckled. "Not in the slightest. You obviously know your stuff, which is why I asked for you in particular, leaving nothing to chance in getting someone from the Bureau to size up the perp we're after." *And maybe there was another reason for wanting you back in Bends Lake—to try and repair our damaged relationship, if at all possible,* Declan told himself behind the wheel. But this probably wasn't the best time to bring that up.

"Just checking."

"And I'm happy to reassure you that we appreciate your input," he offered. None more than himself if it helped this case be solved as quickly as possible.

After a moment or two, Stella asked him tentatively, "So, what did you think about the possibility that the unsub could be a former or present member of law enforcement— present company excluded?"

"Hmm." Declan mused, his gaze fixed on the road. He

had considered this avenue himself, even if it pained him to think that the serial killer could be someone from among their ranks. "Well, honestly, I would've been surprised if you hadn't tossed that one out there to chew on."

"Seriously?" She angled her face. "I didn't want to step on any toes, but between the gunshot deaths and the relative ease on the unsub's part in avoiding certain roadblocks to his freedom, such as forensic evidence and other solid leads, it's kind of hard not to contemplate that the Bends Lake Predator could work in an occupation with enough know-how to evade detection up to this point."

"I don't disagree with you," Declan told her sincerely. "Trust me when I say that everyone on the task force is committed to finding the unsub, whoever he is, including if he carries a badge and firearm. That being said, we have no indication, thus far, that the perp is a member of law enforcement—in spite of the use by some of Springfield Armory 1911 Ronin Operator 9 mm pistols, on and off the job. But until the unsub is behind bars, I'll always keep an open mind. Even if my gut tells me that the killer is not one of us…"

"So long as your mind remains open, that's fine by me," Stella said. "My assessment as a criminal profiler is to be as inclusive as possible when characterizing the unsub. I don't mean to step on any toes."

"You haven't." Declan faced her with a reassuring grin. "It's all good. Keep doing your job and let the chips fall where they may."

"All right." She ran a hand through her hair. "If I come up with anything else that I believe might be helpful to the investigation, I'll be sure to let you know—either here or when I'm back in Detroit, assuming you haven't cracked the case by then."

In more ways than he wanted to admit, Declan found himself hoping she would stick around for a while—maybe even after the investigation had ended—if only to have an opportunity to reconnect. Or was she even open to the possibility of such on a more personal level?

After they reached the hotel, Declan felt it incumbent upon himself to offer her a more comfortable place to reside than her present accommodations. "Just want to put out there that the offer still stands, if you want to come to the house and chill—"

Stella seemed to consider the notion for what it was worth, before retreating, as she replied, "I'll stick it out here, but thanks, again…" She favored him with a half-hearted smile—or was it a smirk—before getting out of the car. "See you later," she said simply and closed the door.

Declan watched her walk away and couldn't help but wonder if they had taken two steps backward for every step forward. Or was he overanalyzing this? He owed it to her and Elise to not jump the gun when trying to sort out his feelings for Stella. Or wonder what hers were for him at this stage.

He drove off, knowing that there was still a murder investigation that commanded his attention. Even if he found himself wanting to spend time with Stella, getting to know her all over again. Never mind that it took two to tango, and she didn't seem that inclined to accompany him to this dance.

JUST TALK TO HIM, the voice in Stella's head told her, as she glanced over her shoulder while Declan was driving away. Yes, there was still a wall due to circumstances that neither of them had prepared for. But to evade getting to the root of it—like a cavity—was probably not a good idea. After all, wasn't confronting Declan at least part of the reason why she agreed to return to Bends Lake?

Inside her room, Stella finished unpacking, as if she planned to be there for a while, and then went to grab a bite to eat at the hotel's restaurant, before returning to the room to map out her schedule for providing more insight on the serial killer to the task force and then taking some personal time to reflect on her return home.

An hour later, Stella had changed into a purple tank top, blue shorts and white athletic sneakers and was using the elliptical exercise machine in the hotel's fitness center. She loved working her body to stay fit. This included jogging, swimming and karate, the latter having come in handy for self-defense, both on and off the job, from time to time.

Afterward, she hopped in her car and drove around, re-acclimating herself to Bends Lake, while thinking about Elise and how everything that seemed so right in her life went so wrong in a split second. At least she had been given a taste of happiness, riding it like a prized stallion for as long as she was allowed to before disaster struck.

Much like my own life, when I thought I had it all—until it was taken away from me, Stella told herself mused about her short romance with Declan before he turned his attention elsewhere, breaking her heart in the process.

What's done is done, she thought, refusing to wallow in self-pity. Declan made his choice in Elise, and Stella felt that they both had to live with it, having moved on with their lives with her sister dead and buried.

She headed back to the hotel room, wanting to go over the file that Declan had sent her on the Bends Lake Predator, in case she missed something that might require an adjustment in her characterization of the unsub.

URSULA LIEBERT WOULD not have wished what the parents of Peggy Elizondo were going through on her worst enemy. Having seen up close and personal the devastation of losing a family member to gunfire when her brother Gabriel was shot to death during an armed robbery more than a decade ago, Ursula knew all too well what Naveen and Julianne Elizondo would have to deal with. They were forced to reconcile themselves with the reality that Peggy was gone and never coming back. The fact that the young school-teacher's death was a senseless act of violence, perpetrated by a serial killer, made it all the more painful.

Ursula was behind the wheel of her official vehicle, a Chevrolet Malibu, while en route to the Winstone Apartments on Fennkel Road, where Peggy lived. Her parents had come to collect Peggy's things. The medical examiner had released the victim's body to the local mortuary, from which her parents planned to bring her back to Eagle Pass, Texas, for a proper burial.

I can only hope that we find the unsub responsible for Peggy's death and give her folks some peace of mind, Ursula told herself, knowing that the stakes grew higher with each death attributed to the Bends Lake Predator. It was up to her and Declan, along with the rest of the task force, including its newest additions from the FBI, to capture the perp before there was more bloodshed, if possible.

Having Declan's sister-in-law, Stella Bailey, on hand could only be a plus to the investigation. Ursula had actually read one of her books on criminal profiling and got a lot out of it. Maybe the pretty behavioral analyst's interesting interpretation of the man they were after could actually lead to uncovering his identity and his subsequent arrest. Declan, who was obviously fond of his late wife's sister, even if he tried hard not to show it too much, certainly seemed to think so.

Ursula was fully on board with whatever steps they took to achieve their objectives. She pulled into the parking lot and left the vehicle before heading to Peggy's third-floor apartment to convey more sympathies to her parents. And provide an update on the status of the case, though knowing full well that there wasn't much more to tell.

Other than that, sadly, the unsub was still very much at large.

DECLAN SAT ON the bench at Rory's Gym on Quail Road, lifting weights to maintain his muscles as a prelude to running on the treadmill, one of his exercise routines before or after work or on the weekends. It was a good way to get the heart pumping and stay in shape.

Not to mention occupy his thoughts for a bit while the stress and strain of an active murder investigation was underway. Then there was seeing Stella again, bringing up old memories as if they were only yesterday. Instead of preceding his relationship with her sister.

We can't go back, Declan told himself as he stepped onto the treadmill in his workout clothes of a T-shirt, sweat shorts and training sneakers. Could they? He would settle for just having Stella back in his life as a friend. And someone with whom he shared a painful loss.

Half an hour later, after showering and changing his clothes in the locker room, Declan said goodbye to a couple of others in law enforcement and headed out the door.

It took ten minutes before he was pulling up to his circular driveway on Rochel Lane. He and Elise had purchased the century-old, renovated, two-story farmhouse with four bedrooms and three bathrooms, sitting on four acres of rural land that offered a great view of the Cheyenne Bottoms wetland, during their first year of marriage. They believed it would be a great place to settle down and raise a family. Declan winced at the thought that this was no longer possible, with Elise in a grave.

Exiting the car, he made his way inside the house and took in the place with its old-school charm, rich hickory architecture and modern updates that brought it into the current century. This included a state-of-the-art security system, custom blinds for double-hung windows throughout, reclaimed hardwood flooring, high-end appliances, a great room, dining room and gourmet kitchen with a rustic island and glazed porcelain tile. There was an eclectic mix of traditional and retro furniture.

Upstairs were all four spacious, well-appointed bedrooms, one of which had been converted into a home office. Aside from the primary suite with an en suite bathroom, there were two other rooms for guests that had their own private bathrooms. One of the rooms, Declan imagined, had Stella's name on it, should she change her tune and decide to spend the balance of her stay in the house he and Elise had tried to make a home in Bends Lake.

After grabbing a frozen pepperoni-and-cheese pizza out of the freezer of the stainless-steel refrigerator, Declan put it inside the electric range oven before he headed up the spiral staircase. He put away his firearm and freshened up, then went back downstairs, got a bottle of beer from the fridge, opened it and took a sip as he waited for the pizza to cook.

Later, while sitting at the island on a solid wood stool eating, Declan found himself wishing Stella had taken him up on the offer to stay at the house. He could have used the company, feeling that the place was too big for one person, but believing it to be too good of an investment for now and into the future to sell it unwisely.

Still, it was tough being there right now, knowing that tomorrow would mark three years to the day that Elise died. Declan imagined that Stella was thinking the same thing— giving them both something to mourn, while trying their best to get on with their lives and whatever the future held.

THE NEXT DAY, Stella walked across the damp, well-manicured lawn of the Bends Lake Cemetery on Outon Lane till she came upon the gravesite of Elise. Cringing as she gazed at her sister's granite headstone, it pained Stella to think that someone so energetic and enthusiastic about the future she had planned with Declan could be taken away so cruelly and likely without Elise even knowing what hit her in the broadside collision.

It could just as easily have been me to die, had I been the one Declan chose to make a life with in marriage, Stella told herself, fighting back tears. Her emotions were mixed at the prospect of having become his wife. Had she fought harder to keep Declan, it could not only have altered the course of history for herself—which could have meant an entirely different fate than what befell Elise—but could have prevented her sister from dying so young and being deprived of the long life she deserved.

When Stella heard some rustling behind her as someone was approaching, she turned around and saw Declan standing there. In his hands was a bouquet of crimson roses.

"Hey." His voice was solemn. "Had a feeling I might see you here."

Stella blinked. "I wanted to visit Elise's grave on the third anniversary of the day she died." She doubted she needed to explain this but did so anyway.

"Me too." He laid the flowers against her headstone. "I try to come as often as possible, whether Elise is aware of it on some level or not. Just seems like the right thing to do."

"I think she would like that," Stella told him honestly. It was a way to keep her sister's memory alive for the man she was wed to. For her own part, Stella kept Elise alive in her heart, even from afar. "It's still hard to believe Elise is no longer with us."

"Yeah, I feel the same way," Declan said, gazing at the gravesite. "She deserved so much better than to have it all end that way."

Stella concurred and told him so. She added mournfully, "Not a day goes by that I don't think of her." *Or what might have been had both of our lives taken a different turn*, she thought, glancing at the flowers and turning to Declan.

"Can we talk?" His eyes narrowed thoughtfully.

She cocked a brow and asked curiously, "You mean here…?"

"Actually, I was thinking more of a restaurant," he replied evenly. "Can I buy you lunch?"

Her first thought was to object, pulling away from him. But then she realized this was something that needed to happen—no matter how tough it could be for her. Or him, for that matter. Bottling up emotions was never a good thing. Even if she had managed to do so for the past three years, perhaps against her better judgment.

"All right," Stella told him tonelessly. "I'll follow you there."

He nodded and they both took one final look at Elise's grave in a united show of love and respect.

Chapter Four

Stella wasn't quite sure what to expect—including from herself—as she sat in the booth across from Declan at Teresa's Grill on East Maple Street. *Just hear him out*, she told herself, as Stella tried to concentrate on the menu. And allow Declan to hear what she had to say and go from there.

She settled on salmon cakes and a spinach salad and watched as Declan ordered the margherita flatbread, garlic braised short ribs and a side garden salad. Both went with black coffee and water.

After a moment or two, Declan sighed and said, "Let's just clear the air, if we can…" He tasted the coffee musingly as Stella waited with bated breath. "I'll start by saying what I probably should have a long time ago. If I had known when I met her that Elise Goldoni was your sister, I would never have started dating her, much less married her. But that knowledge didn't come till I had fallen head over heels for your sister—after things between you and I had ended…"

"And whose fault was that?" Stella challenged him, allowing her bitterness at essentially being dumped to overshadow her acknowledgment that their relationship was over when he met Elise, for better or, more likely, worse. "You didn't exactly fight for me…for us—"

Declan furrowed his brow. "I wasn't sure at the time that there was anything worth fighting for."

Her lashes fluttered. "Oh really?"

"Let me clarify that… I cared for you a great deal and wanted things to work out between us. But—" he halted his words, looking down and then back at her "—it seemed to me that you were just too dedicated to your career to want to be in a real relationship."

Stella spurted out, "And you weren't just as dedicated to your own career?" She refused to make this easy for him. Why should she? "That's pretty lame. Most people can actually have their careers and solid romances at the same time. It's called life. I was certainly ready and willing to try and meet you halfway." She clutched the coffee mug. "But you never gave us a chance…"

"If you want to know the truth, I guess I thought we were on the same page, more or less, with respect to where things stood between us," Declan muttered, jutting his chin.

Her eyes flashed hotly at him. "I think we were reading different books," she countered sarcastically. "I was never opposed to making compromises if it meant being in a stable relationship."

"Fair enough." Declan pursed his lips, sitting back. "I misread things, in sticking with that school of thought. My fault. As for the work ethic, you're absolutely right, I'm just as career driven as you are—if not more. I guess I didn't see things as clearly as I should have at the time in failing to look in the mirror at myself while judging you. I'm sorry." He took a long pause, staring at his coffee. "That's probably too little, too late—but I needed to get it out there anyway. You deserved better than what you got from me…" His voice dropped an octave. "Maybe Elise did too—"

Stella favored him with a straight stare. She hadn't seen

that coming—him owning up to his role in their break up. In truth, she was probably every bit as responsible in not giving it her all to try and work things out.

But she was equally tuned in to his confession that he hadn't been everything that Elise had wanted as a husband. What exactly was he saying?

Before Stella could get to the root of it, the food was served.

Now Declan felt as though he was in the hot seat, having owned up to bowing out of their relationship, perhaps prematurely, when it seemed as if they were at a crossroads. Or, at the very least, not entirely on the same page as it related to what—and whom—they wanted out of life. Had he jumped the gun back then? Should he have stuck it out longer to see if they might have worked things out— thereby changing the course of both of their histories? Not to mention Elise's?

I can't undo what's been done, he told himself as they ate in silence. Decisions were always made, at every step of one's life, by doing what seemed best at the time. Should this be any different?

His thoughts turned to Elise. He could almost read Stella's mind speculating about his words regarding her sister deserving better than she got from him. Knowing he owed Stella an explanation, Declan held up slicing his knife into the tender short ribs and gazed across the table as he said, "About Elise—just so you know, I loved your sister and always wanted to do right by her." He stopped musingly, eyeing the coffee that had been refilled into his mug. "But, like you said, I was into my job, probably more than I should have been—too much. Maybe if I had worked less and spent more time with Elise, I might have been driving

with her that day and somehow averted what happened—"
Even after three long years, he could hardly bring himself
to say the words: *car accident*.

Stella furrowed her brow as she used her fork to cut into
a salmon cake and said insistently, "You can't blame yourself. The accident wasn't your fault, any more than it was
mine. Elise was simply in the wrong place at the wrong
time. No amount of second-guessing will ever change that."

"Maybe you're right," he conceded, nibbling on the margherita flatbread. "It's still hard not to, though. Elise should
be here right now, living out her dreams."

"Yes, in an ideal world." Stella drew a thoughtful breath.
"But she was able to make the most of the time she had.
Being married to you made her happy, and Elise wouldn't
have traded that for anything in the world." She paused
again. "Neither would I, knowing how much you meant
to her."

"Elise meant as much to me," Declan said sincerely. He
was glad to see that Stella had been able to get past the
bitterness of their own failed relationship to show sisterly
love for Elise. That meant everything to him. And by ex-
tension, it told Declan that things were not as far apart between them as he'd feared. "I've missed having you in my
life, Stella," he couldn't help but admit, knowing that they
were friends first, before the romance followed.

"Me too," she surprised him by saying. "I think we both
needed some time to reflect on everything before breaking the ice—"

"You're right." Declan didn't dare say he wished they
had broken the ice sooner, settling for the moment at hand.
He ate some of his salad and watched as she chewed a piece
of salmon cake, then asked out of curiosity—or perhaps

it was more than that, "So, are you seeing anyone these days…?"

Stella finished eating and replied succinctly, "No." She met his eyes. "But before you assume it's a work issue—it's not. More like the right person simply hasn't come along. I'm not interested in putting myself out there and falling flat on my face…"

Declan felt a pang in his chest while wondering if that was a backhanded way of getting back at him for short-circuiting things between them prematurely. Or was he misinterpreting her words for all the wrong reasons? "That's perfectly understandable," he told her, tasting his water.

"What about you?" she asked him, peering across the table. "Anyone special in your life?"

Declan lowered his chin. "Not since Elise," he answered candidly.

"It's been three years." Stella drew a sharp breath. "My sister would not fault you for moving on with your life. Actually, knowing her as I did, she would have insisted upon it—including in the romance department."

He didn't doubt that for one moment, as Elise was the type of loving person who encouraged him to live life to the fullest—even if it now meant finding that special someone to share his life with. Ironically, Elise wished too that would find her true soulmate one day.

Declan gave her a crooked grin and said evenly, "I'll keep that in mind."

She smiled. "You should."

"I will," he promised. "Like you, though, as soon as that right person comes into my viewfinder, I'll know and can act accordingly, if we're in sync—"

Even in saying this, he couldn't help but wonder, if things had worked out differently with Stella, whether she might well have been a perfect fit into that puzzle of his life and times. Had that time come and gone?

Or perhaps, in some strange way, the universe had found a way to reunite them—with the possibilities of moving forward in the palms of their hands?

STELLA CHECKED IN with her parents after going back to the hotel, knowing that they were sorrowful on the third anniversary of Elise's death.

As Ngozi and Lester Bailey appeared on the screen of her cell phone, both in their sixties, Stella offered them a soft smile, having always had their support in both her personal and professional lives, in good times and bad. Just as had been true for Elise with their parents.

"Hey," Stella said to them in an even tone.

Her father, sporting a salt-and-pepper quiff hairstyle, pushed up the square glasses over his blue eyes and said animatedly, "Hi, honey."

Her mother, still as beautiful as Stella remembered from when she was a little girl, with dark brown eyes and long, straight gray hair with the ends curled, asked carefully, "How's it going there in Bends Lake?"

"So far, so good," Stella answered truthfully, as she pondered the get-together with Declan and smoothing out unresolved issues. "I'm doing what was asked of me by the Bureau and waiting to see what happens."

"I hope your input will help them find the person they're after," Ngozi said.

"Me too." Stella looked at their faces before saying, "I went to Elise's gravesite today." She took a reflective breath. "I just miss her so much."

"I know you do." Ngozi's eyes watered. "She's always with us."

Stella felt her own eyes moisten. "I ran into Declan there—"

"How's he doing?" Lester asked equably.

"He's hanging in there," Stella answered. "Just trying to get on with his life as best as possible."

"We all are," her mother said, pausing. "So glad that you two have had a chance to talk. Elise would've wanted that."

"I know," Stella conceded. She and Declan had come clean with Elise about their prior involvement. Her sister, while shocked, had taken it in stride, as Elise believed that what had been bad for them had opened the door for her and Declan to come together. Even if initially unnerved at the prospect, Stella had come to realize deep down that she and Declan hadn't been ready to move ahead with their relationship. Elise, on the other hand, had come into Declan's life at the right time, and vice versa, and was entitled to run with it and find the happiness he gave her till the very end.

It was hardly anything that Stella could begrudge either of them, and she never would. She was glad that the tension in the air had softened between her and Declan. Maybe there was still a chance that as two single adults there might be something there for them to explore down the line.

After ending the call with her parents, Stella grabbed a bottle of water from the mini fridge. She drank a generous amount before settling onto the mid-century modern sofa with her laptop to catch up on some work.

BENDS LAKE POLICE OFFICER Jeremy Ponte was sitting in his Tesla Model Y patrol car on the side of the road, on the lookout for reckless speeders. In the ideal world, he would be sitting on the beach in Maui, Hawaii, retired and sipping pineapple margaritas with his girlfriend, Cassidy. But the real world required that, at thirty-six, he still needed to make a living to be able to afford the lifestyle and luxuries that made her happy—perfectly reasonable as they were.

His train of thought was interrupted when dispatch reported an armed robbery at a convenience store on Allen Street. The unsub was described as a dark-haired, white male in his thirties who fled the scene in a blue Buick Enclave SUV.

With the crime scene only a few blocks away, Jeremy was more than ready to do his part to try and track down the culprit. That became a bit easier when a traffic surveillance camera spotted a vehicle matching the description of the getaway car and a license plate reader was able to capture the plate number. More importantly, it appeared to be headed his way.

No sooner had that thought entered his bald head when Jeremy's gray eyes watched as the Buick Enclave with the right license plate number whizzed by him on Fortlene Road like its occupant was late for a party. After activating his police lights, he took off in full pursuit of the suspect while radioing for backup. He would try and cut off the vehicle before it could blend in with traffic.

Feeling an adrenaline rush, Jeremy put on some speed, not wanting to let the perp out of his sight. Unfortunately, the armed robbery suspect seemed to have a different idea, as he sped up in a blatant attempt at getting away.

The song and dance between them came to a screeching halt, quite literally, as Jeremy watched the unsub's vehicle spin out of control during a sharp turn onto Ellington Road and then hit a barrier in a construction zone. The driver managed to stagger out of the car, clearly dazed.

Jeremy, with a six-five sturdy frame, was quick to exit the patrol car. After turning on his body-worn camera and removing the Glock 22 .40 S&W service pistol from his tactical holster, he approached the suspect, just as a firearm fell out of the man's zip-up jacket.

Kicking what he recognized as a Springfield Armory 1911 Ronin Operator 9 mm handgun away from the suspect, Jeremy promptly placed him under arrest for speeding and other traffic-related violations, for starters.

DECLAN SAT IN a wooden chair at a metal table across from the armed robbery suspect in an interrogation room at the Bends Lake Police Department on Sorenten Street. Identified as thirty-five-year-old Todd Kavanaugh, he was slender with dark hair in a cropped cut and blue eyes. He also had a criminal record that included robbery and a DUI.

Under normal circumstances, Declan might have left this to the local law enforcement. But his interest in the suspect was piqued as a result of the firearm that fell from his pocket after crashing the stolen vehicle he was driving during a police chase, while coming away from it disoriented but otherwise uninjured.

The Springfield Armory 1911 Ronin Operator 9 mm pistol was the same type of handgun used to commit six homicides by the unsub known as the Bends Lake Predator.

Could this be the murder weapon?

We'll know soon enough, Declan thought as he sized up the robbery suspect, wondering if he might be a serial killer as well. His pistol was being examined by the KBI's Firearm and Toolmark Section to determine if the fired bullets and spent cartridge cases recovered could be linked to the handgun used by the Bends Lake Predator to take out six individuals.

After staring at the suspect for a long moment, who was identified by both the victim and surveillance video, Declan said evenly, "Armed robbery is a serious offense in Kansas, which I'm sure you know, having been down this road before. Yet, here you are…facing some heavy time behind bars."

Kavanaugh, who had yet to lawyer up, giving Declan free rein to interrogate him, wrinkled his nose and muttered defiantly, "I guess I'll just have to deal with it."

"I guess you will," Declan shot back. "Could be that this is the least of your problems…" He sat back, glaring at the suspect in feeling him out. "Tell me about the 9 mm handgun you used to rob the Brakers Store on Allen Street?"

Kavanaugh hunched his shoulders. "What's there to tell?"

Declan pursed his lips. "For starters, you might want to tell me where you got the gun—" which was already found to be unregistered and possessed illegally by the suspect "—and, more importantly, what other crimes were committed with the firearm." *We know that it had been fired more than once*, Declan told himself.

"I used it to rob a couple of other stores, okay?" Kavanaugh responded tartly. "I borrowed the gun from a friend."

"Does the friend have a name?" Declan pressed and thought, *If one isn't guilty of committing multiple murders, maybe the other is.*

Kavanaugh waited a beat before responding, "Lenny Vergara." He sighed. "He has nothing to do with this—"

"He has everything to do with it," Declan begged to differ. "Besides the gun being an illegal weapon and used in the commission of a serious crime, a Springfield Armory 1911 Ronin Operator 9 mm pistol just like it has been used by a serial killer in Bends Lake in recent months. I wonder if you or this Lenny Vergara know anything about that…?"

Kavanaugh looked nervous as he licked his lips and insisted, "Hey, I never killed anyone..." He hesitated. "I can't speak for Lenny."

"Guess he'll have to speak for himself." Declan peered at the suspect and was about to grill him further on this, when Ursula entered the room.

She glanced at Kavanaugh and said to Declan tonelessly, "Can I have a word?"

He nodded, got to his feet and told the suspect, "Be right back."

In the hall, Ursula made a face and said, "We got the results back on the 9 mm handgun Kavanaugh possessed."

"And?" Declan asked her.

"It wasn't a match," she said matter-of-factly. "This isn't the same weapon that was used by the Bends Lake Predator to shoot to death six people."

Declan jutted his chin in hearing the not-so-shocking news. "It was worth a try," he said soberly. "Unfortunately, Kavanaugh won't be walking away, as there are several other charges he'll have to answer to."

"Right." Ursula met his eyes. "In the meantime, we'll keep at this, till we find our man."

"And we will," Declan told her with conviction, trying to ignore the disappointment that Todd Kavanaugh wasn't the culprit.

Chapter Five

That evening, Stella sat on a faux-leather stool at Hedy's Club, a bar on Sixth Street. Around the lounge table were Declan and Ursula, along with FBI special agents Keene Haverstock and Arielle Mendoza. They were sharing a pitcher of beer and a large bowl of assorted nuts.

After listening to the discussion about armed robbery suspect Todd Kavanaugh, who turned out not to be the unsub they were seeking to track down, Stella weighed in by pointing out perceptively, "I could have told you that Kavanaugh wasn't our serial killer." She had watched the suspect being interrogated in another room but was only there to observe, unless her opinion had been sought.

"Oh really?" Declan cocked a brow amusingly and tasted his beer. "What did you see or not see in Kavanaugh?"

"Well, if you truly want to know, I could tell by his demeanor and the way he responded to your questions that being an armed robber and a violent serial killer were not one and the same in this instance. That being said, the charges against the suspect are serious," Stella had to say, as she scooped up a few nuts. "Then there was the fact that the one who Kavanaugh claimed actually owned the gun could well have turned out to be the perp—had the Firearm and Toolmark Section not proven otherwise in eliminating it as the Bends Lake Predator's Springfield Armory 1911 Ronin Operator 9 mm pistol. So, in other words, you were certainly right to check out Kavanaugh in the investigation, considering."

Declan feigned a sigh of relief. "I feel a lot better now." He chuckled and lost it on a dime. "Unfortunately, that doesn't bring us any closer to nailing the serial killer perp."

"I disagree," Ursula said, holding her mug. "Confiscating Kavanaugh's Ronin Operator pistol gives us one less illegal firearm on the streets while also eliminating one that might've belonged to the unsub."

Arielle grabbed a handful of nuts and said, "That's true. Makes our job a little easier in the process of trying to track down as many registered as well as unregistered handguns that fit the bill."

"Okay, I stand corrected." Declan laughed. "We're making progress, slowly but surely."

Keene's gray eyes lit up as he drank beer, then said after belching, "All of us from the Bureau are happy to lend a hand in catching the unsub—however long it takes." He gazed at Stella. "Having a top profiler come in to assist is huge."

"I couldn't agree more," Declan said, a lift in his voice. "Stella definitely knows her stuff. Always has."

Stella blushed, flattered by the compliment, especially coming from him. She sipped her beer and said, "Look who's talking. Must be something about being familial. Or maybe it's in the water—infecting us all," she added merrily, to try and keep it from sounding too personal. Even if it felt that way.

UNBEKNOWNST TO THEM, at a nearby table in the bar sat the Bends Lake Predator, who was coolly nursing a gin and tonic. Caught up in his own dark thoughts, he relished having the power of life and death—all at his whim. He wondered who would be next to take a bullet—make that a few bullets—from his reliable Springfield Armory 1911 Ronin Operator 9 mm pistol. He pretended that it could be anyone in there at the moment.

Maybe the guy with the uneven black hair at the table over there.

Or perhaps the good-looking biracial woman with long dark hair who the man was talking to.

Or even one of the other three people who shared their table.

He couldn't quite make out what they were talking about. And was only mildly curious.

He thought the pretty, dark-haired woman had looked his way. Or was it only his imagination?

Either way, he quickly shifted his own gaze. The last thing he wanted was to attract unwanted attention.

Not when he needed to remain anonymous in order to continue carrying out the executions that fueled his dark desires, separating somewhat from the other part of his life that required he conform to societal rules, to one degree or another.

Finishing off his drink, he refrained from having one more for the road.

The Bends Lake Predator ran a hand through his hair and stood up, casually walking away and in the opposite direction from the group of five still seated around the table talking shop.

As DECLAN DROVE Stella back to the hotel, he found himself wishing they could go to his house instead. Maybe have a nightcap and just talk. That was perhaps what he missed most in their earlier time together—feeling comfortable enough with each other to talk about whatever came to mind.

Or at least till the time arose that neither of them cared to talk much about what they truly wanted out of life and if it was possible to achieve it together.

I'll have to put much of the blame on myself, he truly believed, part of him wishing they could go back in time for a redo. With the other part knowing that, in so doing, he would be taking away the short period of happiness he and Elise had given each other.

Declan glanced at Stella and wondered what was going on inside her head. Apart from the insight she had displayed by correctly profiling Todd Kavanaugh, which could only serve them well when they finally caught up to the serial killer at large. She was probably thinking about how soon she could get out of Bends Lake and return to the life she had created for herself in Detroit. The thought of losing her once more was a hard pill to swallow.

He broke the silence by saying candidly, "Looks like we still have our hands full with the Bends Lake Predator investigation."

"What else is new?" Stella turned to him. "Let's face it, Declan, you enjoy this sort of thing—even if it is serious business."

"When you put it that way…" He laughed.

She chuckled. "You said it, not me." Her hand brushed against his knee. "As it relates to your case, trust me when I tell you that the perp is feeling the heat much more than you or I. Killers—especially serial killers—may present a deceptively cool and calm veneer, but they are quite the opposite inside and forced to constantly think and rethink

what they are doing and just how long they can get away
with it. You've got this, Declan—eventually."

"You're right," he told her, his level of confidence returning. "Particularly with your help—and the rest of the
task force," Declan decided to add for her sake.

She smiled. "Duly noted."

When he pulled up to the hotel, Declan said, "Here we
are."

"Thanks for the ride," she told him.

"Anytime." He meant this in every way.

After a long moment, Stella leaned into him and kissed
his mouth. It was sweet and painfully short as she pulled
back, touched her lips and uttered, "I probably shouldn't
have done that. Sorry."

"Don't be," Declan came to her rescue, finding the kiss
to be to his liking. He considered following her lead by
initiating another kiss, but wouldn't press his luck. "It was
nice," he told her nonetheless as flashes of history danced
in his head.

Stella blushed. "Good night, Declan."

He grinned. "Good night."

After she exited the car, gave an awkward wave and
headed toward the hotel, Declan watched for a moment or
two before driving off, giving himself more possibilities
to contemplate.

WHAT WAS I THINKING? Stella asked herself once she was
back inside her hotel room. Wasn't making a move on Declan—or maybe that was an exaggeration, kissing him—
inappropriate on so many levels? Hadn't they been there
and done that before, ending in disaster? Would it be any
different this time around—even with Elise no longer there
to come between them, through no fault of her own?

Long-distance relationships did not work, and Stella was not inclined to go down that road. Not even for old times' sake.

And seriously, how much had really changed in their lives? Both were still very much involved in their careers. Was there enough wiggle room in between to have a successful relationship?

There you go overthinking things, Stella scolded herself, as she started to undress. However she tried to interpret it, it was just a kiss and hardly that. And she didn't get the impression that Declan was put off in the least. She wasn't sure if that was an opening that was begging them to both walk through. Or merely a moment of weakness that they needed to avoid at all costs in the future.

After taking a shower and slipping into a pink silk chemise, Stella responded to some messages on her cell phone before heading to bed.

The last thought on her mind prior to falling asleep was, not too surprisingly, Declan Delgado.

THE NEXT DAY, Declan used some time off to get in a quick workout on an outdoor basketball court in his neighborhood on Jecklin Avenue. He enjoyed stepping away from his official duties by shooting some hoops with active local youth. It was a way to recharge the batteries and do what he could to try and keep them on the straight and narrow, rather than them steering off track and having to answer to him or other law enforcement down the line.

He was going one-on-one with a seventeen-year-old kid named Aurelio Valderrama. A Latino, like himself, Aurelio was two inches taller, in at least as good shape, with brown eyes and black hair that had a textured crop top and an undercut. He worked part-time at a local delicatessen when not attending classes at Bends Lake High School, where he was a junior. After graduation, his dream was to attend Declan's alma mater, Wichita State University.

Tossing the ball to him, Declan challenged, "Let's see what you've got!"

Aurelio laughed arrogantly. "Sure you wanna find out?"

"Probably not," Declan kidded as the ball was tossed back at him. He bounced it once, threw it to Aurelio and said seriously, "But I'll take my chances..."

With that, they went at it, trading baskets and fouls, while working up a good sweat. Declan had no problem keeping pace, even while secretly admiring his opponent's seemingly endless energy and deft moves on the court.

By the time it was over, though, Declan had prevailed by a point, while knowing it could easily have gone the other way had Aurelio's last jump shot not bounced in and out of the basket.

Still, Declan couldn't help but be boastful when saying, "Good game. Better luck next time."

Aurelio chuckled as he bounced the ball on the court. "I'm not the one who'll need the luck," he argued. "See you later..."

"Count on it," Declan told him and headed in the opposite direction, toward his house. He looked forward to getting another crack at the younger opponent, while expecting the same result.

After grabbing a bottle of water from the fridge and downing it in one long gulp, Declan thought about how empty the place seemed these days. He imagined that Stella could certainly fit the bill in addressing that issue with her presence. Even temporarily. But was that even realistic, given the missteps in their history and the current trajectories of their lives?

What was that old adage about hope springing eternal? Declan mused wistfully, pushing past the obvious obstacles to taking up with Stella again. Who knew what the future could hold, if the will and want were strong enough both ways?

He got cleaned up before going into his home office, where there was a walnut adjustable sit-and-stand workstation, mid-back faux-leather computer chair and large window overlooking the wetland. After sitting down, he went to his laptop to review the Bends Lake Predator case and where they were in the investigation.

STELLA DECIDED TO bypass the fitness center to go outside for some fresh air and a power walk through the nature trail. She was mindful that the serial killer on the loose tended to target victims who were by themselves, no matter the location or time of day. And though the odds were against being singled out by the unsub, to be on the safe side, she carried her Glock 19 pistol in a concealed carry holster beneath her black workout tank.

Having been near the top of her class in pistol marksmanship while training at the FBI Academy in Quantico, Virginia, Stella assured herself she could more than hold her own when encountering an armed assailant. Especially one who may be overconfident, allowing her to turn the tables when least expected.

Hopefully, it will never come to that, she told herself, having no desire to confront the perp, even in broad daylight. She would push that onto Declan and other law enforcement tasked with taking down the Bends Lake Predator.

After a cool down and good stretch, Stella walked back to the hotel. She was moping around in the lobby, while wondering if she should reconsider Declan's offer to have her spend her remaining time at the old farmhouse he and Elise purchased, when a female's voice called out to her, "Stella…is that you…?"

Turning to her left, Stella regarded an attractive, slender woman about her height and age, with bold aquamarine eyes and a long, wavy blond balayage hairstyle. She was dressed in casual clothing and slingback sandals.

As Stella strained for recognition, though there was some familiarity, the woman said, "It's Gayle Reese—we went to high school together…"

Studying her further, it came back to Stella. "Gayle," she uttered. Though they didn't exactly hang out with one another at Bends Lake High School, she did remember her now, them having been in some of the same classes and on the swim team. Stella recalled that she had brunette hair in high school. "How are you?"

"I'm good." Gayle's tone flattened, but then she gave Stella a hug. "Been a while."

Hugging her back, Stella said, "Yes, it has." She was sure they hadn't seen each other since shortly after graduating and going their separate ways. Stella thought that she might have heard through the grapevine years ago that Gayle had run off with a guy she met for parts unknown. Had she moved back to Bends Lake? Or, like herself, was she only here for a visit? "Are you staying at the hotel?"

Gayle licked her lips. "I wish." She batted fake lashes. "I'm actually working at the gift shop."

"Really?"

"Yeah, for a couple of years now—or ever since I moved back to town from Atlanta, following my divorce."

"I see." Stella was saddened to hear about the divorce—something she never wanted to experience—but was glad to know that Gayle had apparently gotten back on her feet. "Sorry the marriage didn't work out," she offered sincerely.

"So am I. It happens." Gayle sighed. "I just wish I'd gotten out of a bad relationship sooner, but didn't have the courage to go there till it finally came upon me."

Stella offered in response, "You did what you needed to, when it was the right time."

"Yeah." Gayle ran fingers across her hair. "I take it that you're a guest at the hotel?"

"Yes," Stella answered evenly. "Just for a few days on business," she added, leaving it at that for the time being. "I'm living in Detroit right now."

"Nice." Gayle smiled briefly then furrowed her brow. "I heard about your sister—I'm so sorry..."

"Thanks for that." Stella flinched, as if it happened just yesterday. "It was hard to fathom this could have happened to Elise, but time has allowed me to come to terms with it."

"I'm glad to hear that." Gayle flashed her a thoughtful look. "Well, I'm just finishing up my break, so I better get back in there. Maybe we can catch up later—"

"I'd like that," Stella told her, even if she wasn't sure she would have much time for socializing. Maybe she would make the time, in trying to get back in touch with her roots, with Elise no longer around to bounce things off of. And Stella wasn't certain how much she could trust herself in rebuilding things with Declan that could stick, in spite of the familiar comfort zone that seemed to be drawing them closer to each other like magnets.

Chapter Six

Diane Wexler was into her third lap in the custom swimming pool of the multimillion-dollar home she shared with her husband of nearly twenty-five years, Kendall. It was her absolute favorite pastime—she could easily swim for hours—but was by no means the only joy of her life. Another bright spot was her daughter, Estelle, who, at twenty-one, was only beginning her journey in life and the craving for independence at that stage.

Estelle's path was much like her own when Diane had been a free spirit. Till she had to grow up and had to assume responsibilities and face realities that brought her to this point in time. Would she change some things if she could do it all over? Probably—okay, so yes, definitely—when looking at her mistakes squarely. But then, who wouldn't make the necessary modifications along the way if given a second chance?

No regrets, remember? Diane reminded herself, counting her blessings, all told. She emerged from the pool, her magenta one-piece swimsuit clinging to her shapely body like a second skin above long, lean legs. Though forty-one years old, she prided herself in often being able to pass for someone ten years younger.

She grabbed a beach towel from the patio wicker chaise longue, used it to dry her face and soak up water from her long V-shaped layered blond hair, then headed across the flagstone walkway toward her two-story brick estate.

But before she could go inside, Diane was thrown off guard as her blue-green eyes caught sight of a male figure who emerged from the side of the house. He was wearing dark clothes and dark leather gloves. There was a gun in his hand.

As she tried to come to grips with the person and her familiarity with him—not to mention overcome the fear that threatened to engulf her like a blaze—the assailant fired a shot at Diane's rib cage, shattering it. The force propelled her backward toward the pool. Clutching her chest while assessing the damage and pain, she was shot again; this time it ripped through her stomach.

When the next bullet hit her directly in the face, Diane immediately lost consciousness, before she fell backward into the pool, her life over.

DECLAN GOT THE call about a woman found dead in a swimming pool by her housekeeper at a home on Lavador Lane. She had apparently been shot multiple times, grabbing the attention of the KBI as it related to their ongoing investigation.

While en route to the scene, accompanied by Ursula in the passenger seat, Declan remarked in an understatement, "Looks like our killer may be at it again—albeit in an interesting location, given his standard modus operandi…"

"Or it may not be the unsub's work at all this time," Ursula cautioned him thoughtfully. "Six months ago, the KBI came to this location after there was a reported domestic violence incident. The suspected victim was the wife, Diane

Wexler, with her husband, a wealthy real estate investor, Kendall Wexler, thought to be the aggressor. But she refused to press charges and that was that. Whether things escalated into the current situation remains to be seen."

"Six months ago, huh?" Declan went back to how she began. "About the same time that the Bends Lake Predator started murdering people. Could be some symmetry there—"

"Possibly." Ursula gazed out the window. "We're about to find out."

"Or not," Declan said, leaving enough wiggle room to move in a different direction, if warranted. He glanced at her, museful. "So, when's the due date for your baby?"

"Our precious little girl should be making her way into the world on Halloween," she answered.

"Should be a real treat and no tricks," he said lightheartedly.

"Definitely." Ursula laughed. "Both Melody and I are counting down the days."

Declan smiled. "As you should."

"Hey, you'll get to experience the joy yourself someday, Delgado," she told him with confidence.

"Hope so." He wasn't so sure about that, but saw some light at the end of the tunnel as Declan pondered the prospects and whether or not Stella might fit into the equation.

They pulled up behind a patrol car outside the Wexler's estate, got out and then headed toward the two-story brick house as Declan took note of the white Lexus NX 350 and blue Volkswagen Jetta parked in the driveway.

The front door opened, and they were met by Bends Lake Police Officer Judith Hansen, a tall thirtysomething woman with short red hair. After Declan identified himself, flashing his badge, and Ursula did the same, Judith, whose

uniform was wet, said solemnly, "The victim's been identified as Diane Wexler by her housekeeper, Rhonda Kishi,
who discovered her body in the pool shortly after showing up for work. According to her, the victim swam daily
in the afternoon—which would indicate that she hadn't
been dead for long."

Declan angled his face and said, while feeling bad for
both the victim and housekeeper, "Was there anyone else
at the house when you arrived?" His first thought was the
husband.

"No one that I saw," the officer answered, adding, "I
went through the place after calling it in. The killer had
vacated the premises—if the person entered the house at
all. There was no sign of forced entry."

"Interesting," Declan said, scanning the place. This
would suggest that the unsub had accessed the swimming
pool area from outside the house—and thus would have
been privy to perhaps both the victim's routine and point
of entry.

Ursula said to the officer, "Can you take us to the body?"

Judith nodded. "Right this way…"

They followed her across bamboo flooring and an ex-
pansive main level with expensive furnishings and lots of
windows covered by plantation shutters, as Declan surveyed the layout and possible escape routes for a killer, till
exiting out a sliding back door.

Near a pool house, Declan spotted a fiftysomething
woman with short dark hair wearing a housekeeper's uniform.

"I'll go talk to her," Ursula volunteered.

"Okay," Declan said, and turned toward the swimming
pool.

Lying next to it was a white female, identified as Diane

Wexler. She was wearing a swimsuit, her wet body covered in blood from what looked to be two gunshot wounds and her face shattered from a single bullet shot at close range.

"I pulled her out of the water and tried administering CPR—to no avail," Judith said, her lower lip quivering. "It was too late. She was already gone."

"You did what you could," Declan told her sympathetically. "Unfortunately, someone wanted to make sure that any such efforts would be in vain."

The Danver County medical examiner and KBI Crime Scene Response Team arrived and began their respective duties in dealing with a homicide and the quest for assessments and gathering crucial evidence.

Declan and Ursula listened as the medical examiner, Aaron Wilson, grimaced in going through the motions in his preliminary thoughts on the deceased.

"Same old, same old," he indicated sadly while flexing his nitrile gloves. "The victim was shot twice in the chest at close range and was likely finished off with a shot to the face." His brow creased. "It looks as though the decedent never really had a chance."

"Not by the looks of it," Ursula agreed.

Just like the others, Declan told himself, as the early indicators were that this had the trademarks of their serial killer at work. Even if the circumstances demanded that they keep an open mind.

They heard some noise and then saw a tall and sturdy man in his early forties, with brown hair in a taper cut and blue eyes, step out of the house, wearing business casual clothing and black leather derby shoes. He rushed toward the victim, who was still being attended to, calling out her name in sorrow.

Declan stepped in front of him, stopping his advance in compromising a crime scene. "Are you the husband?"

"Yes, Kendall Wexler." He grimaced. "I got the call from Rhonda, saying to get home…that Diane had been shot—"

"She was," Declan said candidly, while not knowing if he was truly shocked or just playing the part of a grieving husband. "I'm afraid your wife is dead."

Wexler's shoulders slumped. "Who would do this?"

"I was hoping you might be able to help us with that." Declan made eye contact with Ursula and turned back to him. "Why don't we go inside?"

Wexler glanced at his wife's body and hesitated before nodding. Declan followed him and Ursula caught up, as they were both interested in what the man had to say.

Standing in the center of the open concept great room, Wexler ran a hand through his hair and said sharply, "I have no idea who would have done something like this."

That's what all abusive spouses say, Declan told himself sardonically. He peered at the suspect. "Did your wife have any enemies?" he had to ask.

"No, none that I'm aware of," Wexler responded tersely. "She was liked by everyone."

Except for at least one person, Declan thought, and regarded the husband. "How were things in your marriage?"

Wexler's brows knitted. "What exactly are you asking?"

"Was your wife—or you, for that matter—involved romantically with anyone else?" Declan threw out bluntly.

"Absolutely not," Wexler insisted. "We were both faithful in our marriage."

Maybe you were and maybe you weren't, Declan thought, knowing that infidelity and homicidal tendencies often went hand in hand. "Had to ask," he told him laconically.

As Wexler took this in, Ursula asked pointedly, "Do you

mind telling me where you were when you received the call concerning your wife?"

Wexler looked at her. "I was at my office on Wymore Road."

"Can anyone vouch for that?" she asked.

"My administrative assistant, Mollie Chenoweth," he answered matter-of-factly. "Mollie was the one who actually took the call initially and passed it on to me."

Declan regarded him and asked, "When did you get to the office?"

Wexler scowled. "I'm not sure I like your insinuation."

"Not insinuating anything—just yet," Declan retorted. "Your wife was murdered, and it's our job to investigate it. That begins with the person closest to her and with the best knowledge of the layout of the property—"

Wexler drew a breath. "I got there at nine o'clock," he asserted. "And never left the office till I learned what had happened."

"So you say." Ursula narrowed her eyes at him suspiciously. "Question—did you ever hit your wife again after the incident that happened six months ago?"

Wexler's head snapped back as if he had been punched. "That was all just a big misunderstanding," he argued. "Things weren't perfect between us, as with any marriage, but I've never hit Diane. And I sure as hell wouldn't have killed her!"

Declan kept the heat on, wanting to cover the bases, just in case he was trying to play them. "Mr. Wexler, do you own a firearm?"

Wexler batted his eyes. "Doesn't everyone in this day and age?"

"It wouldn't happen to be a Springfield Armory 1911 Ronin Operator 9 mm pistol, would it?" he asked him directly, knowing this would make him an automatic suspect in the Bends Lake Predator case.

Wexler shook his head and responded, "No, it's a Korth 2.75 inch Carry .38 Special, 357 Magnum, 9 mm Luger revolver. I keep it locked away in a safe. Diane didn't want a gun in the house at all, but I insisted upon it for our protection." Lines deepened on his forehead. "Little good that did."

Declan and Ursula exchanged glances, then she asked Wexler, "Does anyone else live at the house?"

"Only my daughter, Estelle," he replied, "when she's home. Right now, she's attending college at the University of Oxford in England."

"Good school," Ursula remarked.

"Yeah," Wexler concurred.

Declan knew that Ursula's wife had graduated from Oxford University, and both took pride in it. Having noted that the house had a security system, he asked Wexler, "I'd like to take a look at your surveillance video."

Wexler said agreeably, "You're free to. But you won't find anything there. When I heard what had happened, I accessed the security cameras from my cell phone. There was no one inside the house. The camera showing the pool area was turned off by Diane while she swam." He paused. "We don't have a camera on the perimeter, leading to a wooded area behind the house. I'm guessing that the intruder came in that way… See for yourself—"

Wexler removed the cell phone from the pocket of his pants and played the video for them, then handed the phone to Declan. He examined it alongside Ursula, and as Wexler had indicated, there was no movement inside the house, which seemed to rule out robbery as a motive. No footage either of the assailant by the pool or the property's perimeter. Was this by design? And was there any reason, in particular, to target this individual?

"We'll need to take a look at your security video from the last twenty-four hours from all vantage points," Declan told Wexler.

"Sure, no problem." He was handed back the phone. "Whatever you need. Whoever did this to Diane, I want you to catch them."

"We all want the same thing," Ursula made perfectly clear.

Declan said to him, "We'll need to see your firearm, for verification."

Wexler complied, handing over his Korth Carry Special revolver to Declan. Studying it while wearing a latex glove, it was obvious to him that it wasn't the handgun choice of their serial killer. But this did not necessarily exonerate Diane Wexler's spouse from being her killer.

When Wexler's alibi checked out, he was given free rein to contact his daughter and make arrangements for his wife's burial as the investigation continued.

HOURS LATER, Stella was walking alongside Declan downtown on Sorenten Street, not far from the Bends Lake Police Department, as he gave her the scoop on the latest murder to rock the town.

"After initially entertaining the thought that the victim might have been killed by her husband, Kendall Wexler," Declan was saying, "the preliminary ballistics report on the shell casings found and bullets removed from Diane Wexler's body links them to the same Springfield Armory 1911 Ronin Operator 9 mm handgun used to shoot to death six others. Or, in other words, this is most likely the work of the Bends Lake Predator."

As Declan furrowed his brow, Stella said with sincerity, "I'm so sorry for the victim that she had to die this way."

"Yeah, me too." Declan brushed against her shoulder. "Especially considering that she left behind a college-age daughter to have to try and pick up the pieces, along with her father—to carry on with their lives."

It made Stella think about Elise and the children she never got to have. How might her sister have ever been able to cope with such a tragedy, had it befallen her in losing a child? *No doubt the same as I'd feel—and Declan*, Stella told herself. She turned to him and said, "Based on what you told me about the way things went down with the murder—including the lack of surveillance video of the unsub and his likely escape route—it's clear to me that this killing, above all others, was carefully planned. The killer must have known, or figured out, the layout of the property and also may have stalked the victim to know her routine before acting on his dark impulses and successfully vacating the premises."

Declan ran a hand along his jawline and said, "I was thinking the same thing. He definitely knew what he was doing in seemingly going against the grain of the random-like nature of the other murders. It's possible that he and Diane Wexler were acquainted, in one manner or another, and she somehow managed to get on his bad side."

"True. It's also possible that any perceived acquaintance-ship was all in his head," Stella threw out, "and along with it, a snub in his mind that motivated him to pay her back by adding her to his list of victims—while maintaining as much of his modus operandi as possible, so there was no mistaking who was behind the attack."

Declan frowned. "Now that the unsub has potentially chosen to make his killings more personal in nature—

though opportunistic homicide is still possible—it makes it a little more complicated in figuring him out."

"Serial murderers are always complicated, to one degree or another," Stella told him knowingly. "This one is no more or less complex. The unsub has proven to be clever enough that any moves he makes are likely calculated for his own devious purposes and perhaps to keep the authorities guessing. It never works, when all is said and done. His strengths will ultimately be the same dynamics that bring him down."

Declan nodded and favored her with a grin askance. "I like the way you think."

She smiled at the thought. "Do you now?"

"Yeah, always have." He stopped walking as they approached a food truck. "Hungry?"

"Yes, I think I could eat something," Stella told him, running a hand across her ponytail.

"Same here. What's your pleasure?"

She studied the menu on the truck and went with a grilled chicken wrap and watched as he ordered a Philly cheesesteak taco.

As they waited for the food to come, Stella's cell phone rang. She pulled it from the side pocket of her linen pants and saw that it was her boss, Valerie Izbicki.

"I need to get this," Stella told Declan.

"Go ahead," he said. "I'll bring you the wrap when it's ready."

"Okay." She stepped away from him and answered the call. "Hey."

Valerie responded, "Just wanted to check on you and see how things are going."

"They're going," Stella told her dryly. "Actually, the serial killer case is still alive and well. In fact, it seems that the unsub just added another victim to his number of homicides," she hated having to say.

"Hmm...that's not good," the assistant special agent in charge said. "I take it that you've weighed in on the unsub?"

"I have." Stella watched as Declan was paying for their food. "It's still a work in progress as the unsub appears to be changing some of his tactics. Of course, if I'm needed elsewhere..." She let the words trail off while hoping to remain in Bends Lake for a bit longer to continue to mend fences with Declan.

"No, stay put for now," Valerie told her. "Do what you need to and give them your expertise to help nail this killer."

"Thanks. I'll do my best," Stella promised her.

She responded, "Keep me posted."

"I will."

After Stella disconnected, she saw Declan standing there. He asked, "Everything all right?"

"Yeah," she told him. "I was just giving my boss an update on where things stand in the investigation."

Declan was thoughtful. "I see." He handed her the grilled chicken wrap. "Hope you'll be able to stick around a little longer. I was just starting to get comfortable seeing you again."

"Me too." Stella gazed at him. "Unfortunately, it can't last forever," she warned honestly. She immediately wanted to take back the words, knowing that her career choices were what split them up before. Was it inevitable that history would repeat itself?

"I know." Declan glanced at his Philly cheesesteak taco and met her eyes. "But that doesn't mean we can't make the most of every moment you're here."

"I agree." She bit into her wrap while thinking, *Too bad*

most of those moments will be spent investigating a serial murderer. "On a lighter note, I ran into an old friend from high school at the hotel."

"Is that right?" He dug his teeth into the taco. "Is she here visiting too or…?"

"Actually, she works at the gift shop." Stella nibbled on the food. "We weren't really all that close in school. Still, it's a small world."

"Tell me about it," Declan said. "I've had my fair share of encounters over the years that remind me just how small the world truly can be."

Stella smiled, while wondering if that comment was directed in part at their own unexpected reunion and what it could mean in the scheme of things. "True," she said thoughtfully.

Suddenly, Declan reached toward her with a napkin and said, "You've got some sauce there that needs a little cleanup."

He pressed the napkin to a corner of her mouth, causing Stella to blush. "Thanks."

"Don't worry about it."

"Neither should you," she tossed back at him when spotting a bit of cheese that had landed on his chin, which she took the liberty of wiping away with her finger and showing him.

Declan laughed. "Guess we're both messy eaters," he joked.

"I think it's more like we're keeping our priorities in order," she told him with a chuckle, bringing back vivid thoughts of this natural repartee between them once upon a time.

They finished eating and headed back to the police department.

THE BENDS LAKE PREDATOR drove around inconspicuously in his SUV. He wouldn't exactly say he was hunting for new victims. But then again, if the opportunity arose that landed the right person in his crosshairs, he wasn't the least bit afraid of acting upon it.

On the other hand, he took more of an interest in some people than others—making the kill even sweeter. Diane Wexler came to mind. Their paths had crossed, and when she had rebuffed his attempts to kick things up a notch, it told him everything he needed to know about her. And it wasn't pretty.

His plan had been executed flawlessly. She barely knew what hit her. Unlike the others, he didn't have the luxury of stretching things out before it was time for her to die. Not when the housekeeper would show up at any moment, had he chosen to dillydally.

And so, he put the attractive woman of the house out of her misery, short and sweet—before getting the hell out of there.

Another triumph to relish as he contemplated the authorities scratching their heads in frustration over his ability to run rings around them and get away with it.

Too bad. So sad.

The Bends Lake Predator laughed hysterically, knowing the sounds were trapped inside his vehicle. He continued to drive while staying well within the speed limit. The last thing he needed was for the cops to pull him over and find that he was in possession of the Springfield Armory 1911 Ronin Operator 9 mm pistol he used to take seven lives.

But were that to happen, he was always ready. Having the advantage of being able to read their minds before they could read his thoughts was all he needed to get the jump on any unsuspecting cop who got in his way.

Which happened to be equally true for anyone he encountered who was a step slower than him, for his better and their worse.

Chapter Seven

The next afternoon, Declan was in his KBI office, analyzing the autopsy report on Diane Wexler. It confirmed what he suspected and had been posited by Aaron Wilson. The victim died from a point-blank gunshot wound to her face, with two shots to the body contributing to the death—occurring before she fell into the swimming pool. Not surprisingly, the death was listed as a homicide.

Before he could chalk this up as the seventh murder committed by the Bends Lake Predator, Declan got on the phone with the forensic science lab's Firearm and Toolmark Section, where the spent shell casings and bullets removed from the victim were being analyzed.

He was connected to Josephine Okamura, a forensic scientist, to get the official word on the submissions to the evidence control center, after the preliminary findings.

Declan asked, "What's the scoop on the ballistics?"

Josephine, who had been with the KBI for the past decade, responded affirmatively, "It's a match. The recovered shell casings, bullets and bullet fragments definitely fit together and came from the same Springfield Armory 1911 Ronin Operator 9 mm pistol."

"Just as I thought," Declan told her.

"Now if we can get our hands on the weapon itself and positively link it with the ammo…"

"We can find the unsub and solve the case," he finished for her.

"Exactly," Josephine expressed.

Declan could not agree more. The trick was to make this happen as soon as possible and try to save more lives in the process. He disconnected and headed out the door to brief the field investigation division's special agent in charge, Kimberly Ullerich.

Stepping inside her corner office, he saw that she was on the phone while sitting on the edge of her walnut desk. In her early fifties, the slender Kimberly had strawberry blond hair in a cheekbone-skimming bob and was wearing oval glasses over blue eyes.

When she disconnected, Declan wasted no time in providing an update on the serial killer investigation. He finished with "We're going at this from every angle—till we hit pay dirt in bringing in the unsub…"

"That's good." Kimberly nodded, but her mind was clearly elsewhere. "I know you and the team will get it done. At the moment, though, we have a more pressing issue on our plate…"

"What is it?" Declan was attentive.

"We just got a report of a young child being abducted by her own mother. The estranged father had full custody of the eight-year-old girl." Kimberly frowned. "If this is as it seems, we need to find her before something bad happens that no one can undo—"

"Got it," Declan said, as he pondered the worst-case scenarios that no custodial parent should ever have to go through. His current case, unsettling as it was, could be put on hold just long enough to help bring this girl home.

STELLA SAT IN the coffee shop across from Gayle as both sipped black coffees. They spoke about their high school years and in general terms about nothing in particular.

"So, are you still swimming?" Stella asked curiously, even as a sad thought danced in her head of Diane Wexler being pulled out of a pool.

"Yeah, I try to swim in Lake Bends whenever I have the time and the weather's nice," Gayle answered. "How about you?"

"Yes, I still swim every chance I get." Stella glanced at her coffee, conceding that time wasn't always on her side for the pastime, with the constant demands of her job occupying her seemingly nonstop.

Gayle regarded her and asked inquisitively, "What do you do for a living?"

Stella waited a beat and then answered evenly, "I'm a special agent and profiler for the FBI." *That usually throws people for a loop, for whatever reason*, she told herself.

"Seriously?" Gayle's eyes popped wide. "I know we lost touch a long time ago, but I seem to recall you once expressing an interest in becoming a writer—"

Stella had to laugh. "Actually, I'm a writer too."

"Really?"

She told Gayle about her books on criminal profiling and added that she had also written some articles in leading journals. Stella even admitted to harboring a secret wish to try her hand one day at writing a novel—perhaps a romance or crime thriller.

"I have aspirations of my own," Gayle told her, tasting the coffee. "One of these days, I'd like to open my own shop—selling antiques and collectibles…"

"I say go for it, when the opportunity presents itself," Stella encouraged her, believing everyone should follow their dreams, if possible. Before fate ever had a chance to deal a fatal blow.

"Is there anyone in your life these days?" Gayle eyed her, seeming to take note that there was no ring on Stella's finger. "Or are you going solo, as I am right now, while I focus on myself for a change…?"

Stella immediately thought of Declan and their rekindled camaraderie. Wasn't exactly a romance, but did give her hope that there was still a place in her life for a real relationship. "Nothing to report at the moment," she said ambiguously. "Right now, there's no one I can say is in my life where we're both able and willing to look at the big picture."

Gayle lifted the mug to her lips and said philosophically, "Whatever will be, will be, for both of us…"

"I agree." Stella brought up her own mug and drank from it thoughtfully. When her cell phone rang, she lifted it from the pocket of her knit trousers and saw that the caller was Declan. "I need to get this," she told Gayle, who nodded in understanding.

After Stella addressed him, Declan said in a serious tone, "There's been a reported parental abduction. I'm heading over to the house of the father, who had full custody of the girl who was apparently taken unlawfully by her mother— his estranged wife. I was hoping you'd like to come along and assess what we might be up against in bringing the child home safely."

"Of course," Stella readily agreed. "Whatever I can do to help."

"Great. I can pick you up in ten minutes—if that's okay?"

"It is. I'll see you then." She disconnected and then told Gayle, "Something's come up. Have to go."

"I understand," Gayle said. "My break is just about over anyway."

They both stood and Stella told her smilingly, "Thanks for the coffee."

"Thank you for the company," Gayle responded. "It was fun reminiscing, and more."

"Same here." Stella met her eyes affably. "Catch you later."

Leaving the coffee shop, where they parted ways, Stella raced to her room for a quick refresh and was back downstairs. She waited outside for Declan to arrive, while hoping that the alleged child abduction could end peacefully.

"MAYBE THIS WAS just a simple misunderstanding," Stella tossed out from the passenger seat. "Where it concerns stressful matters of marital separation, oftentimes the parent who has custody can overreact if the other parent's visitation hours are off by even the slightest."

"That's not how I'm reading this," Declan responded from behind the wheel of his Chevrolet Malibu. He considered the Kansas laws pertaining to parental kidnapping that applied to children under the age of sixteen who were taken away or enticed to leave by a noncustodial parent and held or concealed from the custodial parent in the process. "From what I understand, the girl was apparently taken without the permission of her father, who was concerned enough for her safety to report it."

"Okay, so maybe I was being overly optimistic and idealistic in thinking in terms of the importance of the nuclear family and finding ways to keep it intact." Stella drew a breath. "Obviously, that's not always possible in the real world—especially when children are involved, and one parent or the other uses them as leverage, as a means to an end."

"We'll see which way the pendulum swings here and act accordingly."

For his part, Declan couldn't imagine exploiting his own child or children to save a marriage. Or as some kind of retaliation for a relationship turned sour. He knew that Stella, who would make a great mother, felt the same way. All they needed was to find it in themselves to go down that road of parenthood and all it stood for, even if they had to do that with different partners.

They arrived at a sprawling cattle ranch on Praglin Street on the outskirts of Bends Lake. Parked outside the two-story main house was a black Ford Explorer and a gray Chrysler Pacifica.

The moment Declan and Stella stepped from his vehicle, they watched as the door of the house opened and a tall and husky man in his mid to late forties came out, approaching them. He was wearing ranch clothes and a brown Stetson cowboy hat above short salt-and-pepper hair.

He regarded them with hard gray eyes and said in a steady voice, "I'm Jeb Stottlemire."

Declan said, "KBI special agent Delgado."

Stella identified herself, "FBI special agent Bailey."

Jeb shook their hands, and Declan asked him, "You reported that your daughter has been abducted?"

"Yeah. India, who just turned eight, was taken by her mother—and my ex-wife—Naomi Stottlemire," he responded tartly.

"Under what circumstances?" Stella asked him.

Jeb sucked in a deep breath and answered, "She showed up at India's elementary school on Boone Lane—before I could get there—and just took her. Because Naomi's her mother and lied about being given permission to pick India up, the school staff allowed it to happen."

"And you have full custody of your daughter?" Declan wanted to make it clear.

"Yeah, I do. Because of Naomi's history of drug abuse and suicidal behavior, the court recognized that India needed to be in a safe environment twenty-four seven." Jeb jutted his chin. "That would be in my custody. Now Naomi pulls a stunt like this!"

"Do you have any idea where she might have taken your daughter?" Stella asked him, glancing at the livestock grazing. "Perhaps back to wherever she lives?"

"Don't you think that was the first place I looked?" Jeb snapped. "Since our divorce last year, Naomi has been staying with her mother at a house on Olive Road in Bends Lake. According to her, Naomi never came home the night before—or since—and supposedly has not contacted the mother." He took off his hat and ran the back of his hand across a perspiring forehead. "I've tried to reach Naomi on her cell phone, but she won't pick up." His nostrils widened while eyeing Declan and Stella. "I'm worried about India. I fear what Naomi might try to do to her—"

So do I, Declan thought, meeting Stella's eyes, before he asked, "Has your ex-wife ever given you reason to believe that she might harm your daughter?"

"Not specifically," Jeb replied, putting his hat back on. "But she took India while unauthorized to do so. Even if I believe she loves our daughter in her own way, when Naomi does something as reckless and selfish as this, it makes me believe she's back to using drugs—antidepressants, cocaine and marijuana…"

"What type of car does Naomi drive?" Declan gazed at

the missing girl's father, knowing that this was the easiest way to track her down through surveillance cameras.

Jeb replied, "A red Nissan Kicks."

As Declan took note, Stella said to Jeb, "We'll do everything we can to locate your daughter and ex-wife. Do you have recent photographs of them?"

"Yeah, I can pull them up from my cell phone," Jeb told her.

The images were sent to Stella's cell phone, and she, in turn, sent them to Declan's phone. He took one look at them and could see that Naomi Stottlemire was much younger than her husband. In her early thirties, she was blue-eyed and had straight blond hair in a blunt cut. India looked more like her mother than her father with long blond pigtails and big blue eyes. Physical similarities notwithstanding, Declan believed that the girl could be in danger.

By the time they left the property, he had put into motion the issuance of an Amber Alert, along with a request for the assistance of the KBI Child Victims Unit and Danver County Sheriff's Office's Exploited and Missing Child Unit. Stella had notified the FBI's local field office about the parental kidnapping and the Bureau's Child Abduction Rapid Deployment Team, in case they were needed, as she and Declan were well aware that the first few hours of a child's abduction were critical in locating the child unharmed and returning him or her home safe and sound.

Declan was on the road when he glanced at Stella and asked, "So, what's your read on Naomi Stottlemire and the likelihood that she would harm her daughter, for whatever reason? Especially if renewed substance abuse is part of the equation?"

After taking a moment or two to consider, Stella responded coolly. "Operating on limited info on the marital

issues that resulted in a divorce and awarding Jeb full custody of India, my guess is that this is more an act of desperation by Naomi in wanting to be a greater part of her
daughter's life—albeit an ill-advised move to be sure—
and she probably has no wish to hurt her daughter." Stella
took a breath, then said, "But even with the best of intentions, if Naomi was operating with drugs in her system,
she may not be or may not have been thinking clearly in
the decision to abduct her daughter from school. If this is
the case, Naomi could still pose a real danger to India—
one way or another—the longer they remain at large…"

"I'm thinking the same thing," Declan had to concur.
"Which means we need to find the mother and daughter…
and fast—"

Stella said, "Given the timeline, physical descriptions
of the two and description of the car Naomi's likely to be
driving, she couldn't have gotten far. Assuming that was
her intention."

"Something tells me she didn't think this through, regardless of her state of mind when Naomi Stottlemire
nabbed her daughter. Let's just hope for her sake—not to
mention India's and Jeb's—that this can end peacefully."

"I'm with you there." Stella touched his pant leg. "We
all want the same thing."

Declan had little doubt that they were on the same page.
At least as law enforcement professionals. On the personal
front, the jury was still out.

ABOUT AN HOUR LATER, the good news came. A sheriff's
deputy spotted Naomi Stottlemire's Nissan Kicks with the
help of a license plate reader on Lakmon Road in Bends
Lake. The driver, identified by her license as the suspected

parental abductor, was pulled over with her daughter, India, in the backseat and unharmed.

Naomi Stottlemire was placed under arrest, facing parental kidnapping charges, and the child was reunited with her father.

Stella, who was in the passenger seat of Declan's vehicle, breathed a sigh of relief. "Thank goodness India wasn't hurt in all this."

"I couldn't agree more." Declan briefly faced her while driving. "Let's just hope that her mother gets whatever help she needs and the girl doesn't have to suffer too much as her parents deal with their issues."

"Unfortunately, divorce and broken homes are part of life, whether we like it or not," Stella told him candidly. "Children are always the ones left to pay the price whenever parents decide to split up, though in some cases the dissolution of the marriage is actually in the child's or children's best interest."

"True." He drove closer to her hotel. "I doubt that would ever be the case when you get married—if children were ever in the picture."

She regarded his profile. "You think?"

"Don't you?" Declan bounced the question back at her. "From where I sit, it would always be in your children's best interest for the parents to stay together and work through any problems that come their way."

"Thanks." Stella felt her heart skip a beat in imagining such a scenario as marriage and family. "I could say the same for you. If you and Elise had been given a chance to have children, I'm sure they would have benefitted in each and every way."

"I agree." Declan paused. "It just wasn't meant to be with us," he reckoned. "Maybe I'll get a second crack at it."

"Maybe," she told him and mused, *Maybe I will experience such joy for the first time at some point.*

After he pulled up in front of the hotel, Declan eyed her and said flatly, "I don't suppose you'd like to invite me up for a drink?"

Stella turned to him and fluttered her lashes with interest. "Would you like to come up for a drink?" she asked daringly.

"Thought you'd never ask." He chuckled. "I'd love to."

She smiled with anticipation, even as Stella wondered just what she was getting herself into, while welcoming it nevertheless.

DECLAN STEPPED ONTO the balcony and gazed out at the lake. It was perfect at this time of year, but not nearly as perfect as he saw Stella in so many ways that he had not given proper attention to when they were together. Was it too late to acknowledge this?

He looked at her as she stood beside him, checking out the boaters. They were both holding cups of sparkling rosé wine. After taking a sip, Declan said, "I remember us taking a boat out there once." It belonged to a fellow KBI special agent, who had since retired.

"Me too." Stella smiled, tasting the wine. "It was fun."

"Yeah, it was." As were most things they did together back then. Declan found himself yearning for the good old days, even if they preceded his great relationship with Elise. But enjoying the company of Stella took nothing away from being with her sister. Or vice versa.

After they went back inside the room and put the emptied cups down, Declan studied Stella up close, liking everything he saw. He suddenly decided this was as good a time as any to do what he'd wanted to since practically the day they had laid eyes on one another again after three years. Or, at the very least, since they last kissed.

"Stella…" Declan touched her dainty chin. "You mind if I…" His words trailed off like a gust of wind, and as she made no attempt to stop him, he tilted his face ever so slightly and planted a nice kiss on her soft lips. Tasting the wine, he was more than happy to keep it going, and she seemed just as agreeable.

When Stella pulled away, touching her mouth, she eyed him ill at ease and asked tentatively, "What are we doing, Declan? Is this some sort of trip down memory lane for old times' sake? Or what?"

It was a good question, and he believed she deserved an answer that they both could live with. Holding her shoulders, Declan answered equably, "The memories of us together are great, by and large, Stella. But I don't see this as some sort of rekindling of yesteryear, per se. Instead, I prefer to view it as creating new memories and whatever they entail moving ahead…"

She held his gaze. "I like that."

With that, he cupped her cheeks, and they started kissing again. Though it felt perfectly natural to Declan to kiss Stella, and he found himself aroused and wanting to take this further—all the way to her bed—he resisted the impulse. If they were to pick up where they left off years ago, he wanted to do it right and safely, in both their best interests.

When the kiss ended, Declan sighed and said reluctantly, "I'd better go."

Stella nodded thoughtfully. "All right."

"See you when I see you," he told her at the door, and gave her one more quick kiss, then left before he could change his mind.

En route to his home, Declan felt good about the possibilities between him and Stella. Even if he understood realistically that there would be challenges that neither of them could run away from, even if they wanted to.

He pulled up alongside a basketball court and saw Aurelio Valderrama and a group of other young adults shooting hoops. When Aurelio spotted his car, he ran over to the passenger side, and Declan rolled down the window.

"Hey," Aurelio said, wearing a black sweat headband.

"What's up?" he asked him.

"We're short one guy." Aurelio rubbed his nose. "We could use another player. Are you game?"

Though Declan had more important things to do, the competitive spirit in him couldn't resist the request. "Give me ten minutes to change."

"Cool." Aurelio flashed his teeth. "See you then."

He headed back to the court, and Declan drove off as his mind meandered between playing basketball, his current investigation and the sweet taste of Stella's lips when they kissed.

Chapter Eight

The next morning, Stella went jogging with fellow special agent Arielle Mendoza on a trail at Rendall Park on Velle Road. Both carried their official firearms as concealed weapons for personal protection in the event that they should be accosted by someone wishing them harm.

Strength in numbers, Stella told herself as they jogged through bur oak trees. Still on her mind was the kiss that, this time, Declan initiated. Not that she needed much convincing. She enjoyed the affection between them that seemed as natural as waking up to start a new day. What was yet to be determined was if these new memories he believed they were making had real legs. Or might they too wind up being untenable for the long run, as was the case the first time they tried to delve into something— only to fall flat?

"So, I'm thinking about applying for work in the Bureau's International Operations Division," Arielle said, with the sound of field sparrows chirping happily in the background.

Stella lifted a brow. "Really?"

"Yeah." Arielle wiped her brow with the back of her hand. "I'm currently unattached, fluent in Spanish and pretty well traveled. I'd love to work in South America or Europe in counterterrorism while taking in a different culture."

"Sounds great." Stella smiled at her. "If you feel strongly about this, I say go for it."

Arielle nodded. "Maybe I will." She sighed. "Do you plan to remain at the Detroit field office for a while?"

Stella stared at the question. A few days ago, she would have said definitely. Now she wasn't so sure after reconnecting with Declan. She would need time to consider other options that might materialize. She took a breath and told Arielle candidly, "I'm keeping an open mind on my future—wherever it leads me…"

Arielle grinned. "Nice way to look at things."

"I think so," Stella agreed. Just as she was contemplating this and the possibilities, they were stopped dead in their tracks when they came upon the body of an adult white male lying flat on his back in a pool of blood. She guessed him to be in his mid to late thirties and in good shape, with dark brown hair in a crew cut and a short, boxed beard. Wearing jogging clothes and black running shoes, he was lying just off the trail and, judging by the distinctive deep wounds to his chest, had been shot at least twice.

Instinctively, Stella and Arielle went for their firearms, not knowing if the shooter might still be lurking. They looked this way and that for any sign of danger, before deciding that the perp had apparently fled the scene and did not pose an immediate threat to their safety.

"Check him out," Arielle said, ill at ease nonetheless. "I'll cover you…"

"Okay." Stella put away her Glock 19 pistol long enough to crouch down and feel for a pulse. Albeit faint, she did detect one. "He's alive!" Her voice raised an octave with hope that the man could get through his victimization and come out okay on the other side. "Hang in there," she pleaded with him, though it was clear that the man was unconscious and hanging on for dear life.

"I'll call it in," Arielle said anxiously, tucking her gun back inside its holster and taking out her cell phone.

Stella nodded, her brow etched with worry as she regarded the man, knowing that both she and Arielle were thinking the same thing.

Apart from the fact that there appeared to be no gunshot injury to the head or face, the shooting bore all the trademarks of the Bends Lake Predator's modus operandi.

BEFORE HE ARRIVED at the crime scene, Declan had already begun calculating if the shooting that was reported by Stella and Arielle could actually have been the work of the unsub who had shot to death seven locals. Was this victim meant to be number eight? But had somehow managed to survive for now?

Guess I'll have to wait and see if the bullets pumped into the victim and spent shell casings that crime scene techs have already retrieved prove to be a match to the murder weapon used by the Bends Lake Predator, Declan told himself. He pulled into the parking lot with other law enforcement vehicles and an emergency medical services vehicle.

"You okay?" he asked Stella a couple of minutes later as Declan met up with her in the park. He noted that she was wearing jogging attire, which showed off her attractive, lean physique.

"I'm fine," she told him, her tone even as she faced the victim. "Wish I could say the same for him—identified by his driver's license as thirty-seven-year-old Blake Michaud III."

Declan regarded the man, who looked in pretty bad shape, as he was being placed on a gurney by paramedics. "Is he going to make it?"

"Don't know," Stella answered frankly. "He took two bullets to the chest, causing lots of damage." She sucked in a deep breath. "Based on their initial assessment, the EMTs seem to believe he has a fighting chance to survive—"

"That's the best we can hope for," Declan told her cautiously, and glanced around the wooded area. "Did you or Arielle—" whom he saw was conferring with police officers nearby "—see or hear anyone?"

"No." Stella shook her head. "Whoever shot him had apparently used a silencer and likely already had an escape route planned in advance."

"Hmm…" Declan made a face. "We'll have to see if any witnesses come forward. Or if surveillance cameras can help narrow down suspects."

Stella ran a hand across her forehead. "Even better would be if the victim can give us anything on his attacker to work with."

"Yeah, there is that," Declan agreed, as they both watched Blake Michaud III being carted off while fighting for his life.

"THE BULLETS AND shell casings were a definite match with the ones fired from the Springfield Armory 1911 Ronin Operator 9 mm pistol that resulted in the deaths of seven people," Josephine Okamura told Declan on a video chat in his office a few hours later.

Leaning forward, he fixed the thirtysomething forensic analyst's narrow face on his laptop. It was surrounded by a brunette French-girl-chic hairstyle, and she was wearing geometric eyeglasses as Declan reaffirmed, "So, this attempted murder of Blake Michaud III was apparently a targeted shooting by the same unsub…?"

"No other way to look at it," she doubled down. "Same old, same old. Unless there's more than one shooter who used the same firearm."

"Not likely." Declan didn't believe for one minute, based on everything they knew, that there were two or more serial killers involved in the homicides. "The Bends Lake Predator has struck once again. Only this time, the unsub fell short—along with one bullet shy—of his customary outcome." *At least as of this moment, with the latest victim still clinging to life*, Declan thought.

Josephine touched her glasses and quipped, "The unsub must be losing his mojo. Or something else came up to break the pattern…"

"Yeah, maybe," Declan muttered, while wondering which applied. And if it was a troubling sign that could make the perp even more dangerous.

He was still somewhat perplexed on that front, though Declan had some thoughts on this as he wondered what Stella's take as a criminal profiler would be on what seemed to be a missed opportunity to get the job done by the unsub.

Declan briefed Kimberly Ullerich in her office on the latest development. She lowered her chin and said musingly, "Could be the break we've been looking for, assuming the victim survives and is able to reveal details on his would-be killer—"

"My sentiments exactly," Declan told her, thinking that a description of the unsub by a survivor could go a long way toward nabbing him. "I'll share this with the task force and see if we can begin to close in on the unsub."

Kimberly nodded. "Do that and let's find a way to bring him to justice before he goes after someone else…"

He left the field office for the Bends Lake Police Department for a task force update on the latest happenings in the investigation.

STELLA SAT BETWEEN Ursula and Arielle in the conference room as Declan started to brief them on the case. Or more specifically, the state of things with the most recent shooting victim and its relationship to the serial killer probe.

While holding the stylus pen at the front of the room, Declan regarded the touch screen display and said with a pained look on his face, "This morning, a thirty-seven-year-old, single businessman named Blake Michaud III was the victim of an attempted murder at Rendall Park." Declan put on the screen a recent photograph of the short-haired man, who was smiling and wearing a blue suit. "By chance, he was discovered seriously injured on a running trail by special agents Stella Bailey and Arielle Mendoza. Michaud had been shot twice in the chest. Ballistics confirmed that spent shell casings found at the scene and the bullets were a match and came from the same Springfield Armory 1911 Ronin Operator 9 mm pistol used to shoot to death seven other people. Such as the one you see on the screen."

Declan put up the image of a Ronin Operator 9 mm handgun as he said, "Paramedics rushed the victim to Bends Lake Hospital, where emergency surgery was performed. Though this was successful, according to staff, Michaud remains in critical condition, but it is believed that he will pull through. When we get the go-ahead, of course, we'll want to talk with the victim and see what he can tell us about the shooting—and most importantly, the shooter. In the meantime, an armed guard has been stationed outside Michaud's room, in the event that the perp tries to finish what he started."

After clearing the screen, Declan put up a montage of the dead victims, along with Blake Michaud III as the sole survivor of the Bends Lake Predator serial killer, and said with an edge to his voice, "This makes eight individuals who fell into the crosshairs of the unsub—with only one fortunate enough to have escaped death, as of now. Undoubtedly, this was made possible by the unsub mysteriously diverting from his usual MO by not shooting Michaud in the head…" Declan favored Stella with a direct look and said knowingly, "Perhaps Agent Bailey would like to address this?"

Yes, I would, Stella told herself, having expected this and given it some thought. She stood up and walked over to him, where she whispered in his ear, "I'll give it my best shot."

Declan smiled softly and gave her a friendly pat on the shoulder, then said in support, "Any thoughts you have would be appreciated."

She nodded and then eyed everyone else and waited a beat before telling them in a clear voice, "When I first came upon the victim while running at Rendall Park, noting the similarities of the shooting to victims who were shot dead by the serial killer, my first thoughts were that the unsub may have been spooked by my presence, along with Arielle's, and was forced to flee the scene prematurely, at the risk of being exposed and having to deal with that."

Stella sucked in a calming breath and continued, "I still think that's a good possibility in explaining why the unsub didn't shoot the latest victim in the face or head. But there's also good reason to believe that the serial killer's gun could've jammed. Or run out of ammo, as a mistake on his part in not checking ahead of time." She kept her shoulders even. "Bottom line, from my perspective, is that it was the unsub's full intention to murder the victim in the manner the killer was accustomed to—but his plans were thwarted through one means or another—saving the life of Blake Michaud III. And possibly endangering others, as the unsub may attempt to make up for this mistake by finding a replacement victim, sooner than later—"

"Would you like to have dinner with me at my place tonight?" Declan pulled Stella to the side as the task force members dispersed after the briefing. With the latest victim still sedated and not expected to be in a position to be interviewed till morning, now seemed an opportune moment for Declan to see if she was ready and willing to move past her hesitancy in revisiting the house he lived in with Elise—but was now void of the energy she brought to it. He believed Stella could do the same, and more, if she only gave it—them—a real chance.

"Yes, I'm up for that." She met his eyes steadfastly. "I think Elise would probably feel that it's high time."

Declan grinned. "I agree." He felt relieved that she was on board. Where they went from there would be up to them. "How does seven sound?"

"Perfect." She smiled. "Shall I bring anything?"

"Just yourself will do," he answered smoothly. It was more than enough to make for a pleasant meal.

Stella nodded. "All right."

Declan watched her walk away, and he spoke for a few minutes with some members of the task force who were still in the room, before heading out himself. He was admittedly excited about being able to cook for Stella, as not only a respite from their official duties, but another step toward one another.

After dropping by a supermarket on the way home to pick up some items for dinner that he believed would appeal to Stella's tastebuds, Declan was back in his car and on the road. While his thoughts meandered between the investigation and Stella being back in his life, he could only wonder if there was some symmetry there that could only lead to good things, when the dust settled.

STELLA WAS TRULY a bundle of nerves as she drove toward Declan's house for the first time since returning to Bends Lake, having avoided it like the plague for probably all the wrong reasons. *It's time that I put the demons to rest*, she told herself while studying the road. Elise was gone and so was her marriage to Declan. *But I'm still here and so is he. We both deserve just as much happiness in life, should it come our way*, Stella mused as the familiar landscape came into view. Even if that happiness could be short-lived, with geography still an issue. At least as things stood at the moment.

Stella thought briefly about coming upon the victim of an attempted murder during her run—at the hands of the unsub known as the Bends Lake Predator. Being with the Bureau, she'd encountered violence before. But it was usually in the line of duty. She had been shaken somewhat in becoming a witness after the fact to a man shot twice and left for dead. The fact that it appeared he would survive the ordeal, and possibly be able to help them apprehend his attacker, gave her solace, even if Stella knew this could only be complete when the investigation had run its course.

She pulled up next to Declan's vehicle, while marveling at the property he owned and the wetland, having practically forgotten what a great piece of land it was—including the farmhouse itself.

Stella ran a hand through her long hair, which was loose. She took one look at her attire—a mocha puffed-sleeve midi dress and slingback sandals—and decided it was satisfying enough for the date. Was that what this was? Or was it simply a meal between two acquaintances who had to eat?

Before she reached the front door of the house, it opened and Declan filled the door nicely. Freshly shaven and his hair still wet from showering, he was wearing a light blue linen button-up shirt, beige slacks and brown loafers.

She met his eyes. "Hey."

"Hey." He grinned at her. "Glad you remembered how to get here," he joked.

Her eyes batted playfully. "Guess there are some things you never forget."

"Guess you're right." Declan flashed a thoughtful look. "Come in."

The moment she stepped inside the house, Stella felt the memories come flooding back as though from only yesterday, while she took it all in—knowing that Elise had left her mark on the decor and loving her sister for that.

"Make yourself at home," Declan cut into her thoughts, "and I mean that sincerely."

"I will." She smiled as her nostrils picked up the scent of food. "Smells good."

"Should taste even better," he bragged. "I made grilled halibut with tomato vinaigrette, sliced red potatoes and herbed ricotta biscuits—serving it with white wine."

"That does sound delicious," she had to admit, having forgotten just what a good cook he was when they dated.

He seemed to read her mind as he said, "Being on my own, I don't really invest much time in cooking very much these days—but I can still bring it when duty calls."

"Never doubted it." She chuckled. "So, what can I do to help?"

"You can relax." He angled his face. "Or if you really want to help, you can open the wine and fill the wine-glasses."

"I'll go with the latter option." She grinned, feeling that this was the least she could do to be a small part of the process.

"So be it," he agreed. "I'm sure you remember where the glasses are kept?"

Stella laughed. "I think I can find them."

They sat on retro faux-leather chairs in the dining room across a mid-century modern solid wood table from each other.

"My compliments to the chef," Stella had to say honestly, after sinking her teeth into the mouthwatering grilled halibut.

"Thanks." Declan grinned sheepishly. "Good to know that I haven't lost my touch."

"Not even a little," she assured him, and stuck a fork into a red potato.

"Well, there's more where that came from," he told her in a teasing manner before sipping wine.

"I'll bet." Stella wondered if there was a double meaning there, as a wave of desire swept over her like a sudden rise in body temperature. Was he feeling this too? If so, what should they do about it?

By the time the meal was over, that speculation was put

to rest. They brought their goblets of wine into the great room, finished them off and started to kiss like crazy.

Feeling light in her head and on her feet, Stella uttered between his lips brazenly, "I want you, Declan."

He unlocked their mouths and, while peering into her eyes, responded intently, "Are you sure about that?"

She hesitated for a moment, meeting his hard gaze. "Yes," she uttered unwaveringly.

Declan lifted her chin and said fervently, "Then I may as well be honest when I tell you, Stella, that I want you more, if that's possible."

"Not sure it is possible…" she confessed blushingly, laying her cards on the table. They had been building up to this moment, slowly but surely, since the time she returned to Bends Lake. And there was no denying it. "At the very least, I'd say that we're on pretty much equal footing here," Stella offered, meeting him halfway.

Declan grinned excitedly. "I can live with that."

Her teeth shone. "So can I."

"Then let's live…together—"

They moved back toward one another and kissed more passionately, causing Stella's body to tingle wildly all over, before she forced herself to ask him in a responsible way, "Do you have any protection?" If they were ever to procreate, she wanted it to be planned and with mutual consent in bringing precious children into the world.

"Yes," he assured her and took Stella's hand. "Come with me…"

They mounted the stairs to the second floor, where Declan led her to the primary suite, a large room with traditional furniture and a king sleigh bed that had a patchwork quilt on it. He opened a drawer in a rattan nightstand and removed a pack containing a latex condom. It was all Stella

needed to see to up her desire to be with him a notch—
maybe a few notches—as they began to quickly undress
and allow nature to take its course.

Chapter Nine

Stella was all in as she traced every square inch of Declan's rock-hard body in the nude, bringing about an awareness of familiarity. She felt a tad self-conscious as his eyes studied her nakedness from head to toe, till turning his gaze to meet her own, and Stella could see the raw desire in them. It put her at ease and, at the same time, solidified her own wish to be with him.

It feels so right, Stella told herself as, while still standing, they moved up to one another and started to kiss in an all-consuming way that was giving them all the buildup needed to take things to the next level.

When Declan pulled away from her, he gave Stella a once-over again and declared, "You're so beautiful—all of you!"

"Umm..." was all she could think to say in a blushing response, before Stella told him candidly, "That makes two of us."

"If you say so," he said huskily. "We both deserve this as beautiful people hot for each other!"

"Show me," she uttered, barely able to hold her composure in wanting to be with him.

Without ado, Stella found herself being swept into Declan's powerful arms and carried to the bed. He laid her down on the sateen sheet, put on the protection and slid beside her.

As Stella reached for him, eager to feel his weight upon her and the sexual relations in motion, Declan said smoothly, "Not just yet. I want you to lay back and enjoy this…"

She watched with interest as he used his deft fingers and firm mouth to stimulate her from head to feet and toes, bringing Stella to the brink. She read the hunger for her in his eyes, matching hers for him. When she could stand it no more, she voiced lustfully, "Declan, make love to me—right now!"

He got the message, loud and clear, responding, "If you insist."

"Yes, I do," she uttered vivaciously.

"Then say no more!"

On that note, Declan smoothly positioned himself between her splayed legs, and Stella winced with pleasure as he gave her a hearty kiss and drove deep inside her. She dug her nails into his broad shoulders, and they clung together as the heat rose a few notches at the start of their lovemaking.

Almost instantly, Stella felt her climax roar through her body like a wildfire and she cried out, quivering with the tremendous impact.

Only when she had calmed down did Declan plunge further into her, their bodies slick with perspiration, and shortly thereafter had his own potent release. Simultaneously, a second orgasm ensued for Stella, as they rode the rapids of intimacy till thoroughly satiated.

Afterward, while side by side and catching their breaths, Declan chuckled and said, "Wow! That was amazing!"

She laughed. "You think so, do you?"

"Don't you?" He looked at her.

Stella blushed. "How could I not?"

Declan rested a hand on her knee. "Some things in life are worth the wait."

"I agree," she told him as a case of déjà vu flashed in her head. Then she added, without giving it much thought, "Other things can't happen soon enough." *Did I just say that?* Stella asked herself as she met his eyes. Since when had she become so forward where it concerned such intimate and sincere thoughts?

"Right on that score too," he concurred. "What's meant to be is meant to be—no matter the obstacles that may get in the way."

Stella chewed on his philosophical words, wondering if they were truly meant to be, as if they'd been waiting their turn. Or was what just happened more indicative of pent-up needs than a gateway to the future and coming attractions?

AFTER A BRIEF PAUSE, they went at it a second round. Only this time, Declan was able to take his own sweet time in exploring Stella's perfect body—from her gorgeous face to firm, medium-size breasts to shapely legs and feet—and intoxicating scent, without the encumbrance of needing to keep his libido in check till she had been satisfied.

Instead, they got to bridge the gap between being totally aroused with each other and fulfilling that need by reaching a peak of pleasure—like climbing Kansas's Mount Sunflower—before tumbling back down to earth, left still wanting more.

That came during the wee hours of the morning—with more satisfaction both ways—after which Declan held Stella as if never wanting to let go, as she fell asleep. The truth was, she had proven to be much more than he could have asked for in rediscovering each other.

But he wanted to ask for more of her. A lot more. Problem was, he didn't quite know how to do this. Not without the risk of losing her again. *Do I really want to put either of us through that a second time?* Declan asked himself, knowing there wouldn't be an Elise to come into his life the way she had, should he fail. Nor would he want to pursue anyone else, with Stella such a good fit. A very good one, in fact.

But did she feel the same way beyond their feverish night together?

Declan allowed this to weigh on his mind before drifting off to sleep. He awakened in the morning and watched Stella as she slept peacefully. He wanted to see this vision time and time again, if it were possible—with them sharing the same bed. Again, he wondered if this was asking for too much.

When she opened her eyes and stared at him, Stella said, smiling, "How long have you been awake?"

"Long enough to enjoy watching you in your beauty sleep," he said coolly.

She chuckled. "Hope I wasn't snoring?"

"You weren't." Declan regarded her thoughtfully. "Why don't you stay here for the rest of your time in Bends Lake?" he suggested.

Stella met his gaze. After a moment or two, she asked tentatively, "Is that what you really want?"

"Yeah, definitely." Declan made no bones about it, but he still didn't want to put any undue pressure on her or scare her off. "Look, you can use a guest room, if you like, and have the run of the place, which is a lot more comfortable than a hotel—even though you do have a nice view from the deck." He paused. "Say yes," he prodded gently.

"Okay, yes," Stella acquiesced. "You win, I'll move out of the hotel."

Declan grinned. "Good." He glanced at her outline beneath the sheet, imagining her beauty in the nude. Just then, his cell phone rang. He stretched his long arm and grabbed it off the nightstand and saw that the caller was Ursula.

"Better get that," he told Stella, who nodded, as he said over the phone, "Hey."

Ursula got straight to the point when she said, "Blake Michaud is awake and apparently able to talk."

Declan reacted positively to the news. "That's great."

"I'm heading to the hospital right now."

"I'll meet you there," he told her and disconnected, then relayed the information to Stella.

"I'll go with you," she said, and started to get up.

"Not necessary," he told her succinctly. "The victim may not have much to offer. Stay here and rest up a bit more—after not getting much sleep last night."

She batted her eyes. "And whose fault was that?" she teased him.

"Guilty as charged." He colored as intimate thoughts crossed his mind, and he was perfectly okay with taking responsibility for their blazing sexual activity—even if she had proven to be more than able to hold her own.

Stella laughed with a yawn. "Me too."

"I'll accept that." Declan climbed out of bed. "I'm going to go take a quick shower. I'll leave the spare key on the island in the kitchen." He leaned over and gave her a sweet kiss. "Catch you later."

STELLA WATCHED DECLAN'S firm backside as he stepped inside the en suite bathroom. She had a mind to join him, but thought better of it as he had a job to do without being distracted or otherwise slowed down by her while in pursuit of a wicked serial killer.

Leaning her head back against the fluffy pillow, Stella closed her eyes for what was supposed to be a moment, after getting little sleep. Only when she opened them, she realized that just enough time had passed that Declan had showered, dressed and left her a little note to say how much he enjoyed her company and hoped to have more of it.

I feel the same way, she told herself, stretching her legs and flexing her toes.

Stella's thoughts turned to the night of unbridled passion with Declan. It tapped into every nerve in her body and reminded her of what she'd been missing in her life since their relationship ended. But there was no second-guessing. She believed that most things happened for a reason, and that was probably true for how things fell apart for them previously.

As for this time around, she was keeping her options open as to what she should read into it. Hot sex was not enough in and of itself to consider uprooting her life. Or Declan's, for that matter. But the chemistry between them could not be denied. Nor her sense of belonging as she lay in his bed, still picking up his invigorating manly scent.

Being invited to spend the remainder of her stay in town at the house made perfect sense to Stella. As a practical matter, it would make it easier for them to spend time together when operating under one roof—no matter how much time they had to work with. And should things progress between them to a whole new level, they could take it from there and see where it went—if, in fact, they were meant to go somewhere special.

She forced herself to roll out of bed, shower and get dressed before Stella poured herself a cup of coffee that Declan had made fresh. After drinking it, she headed back to the hotel to pack her bags for a return trip to the house that was beginning to feel a lot like home. Only she had a home in Detroit—and parents who also had begun a life there.

Was upending that a wise move? Or even possible, career-wise?

Don't get ahead of yourself, Stella told herself as she parked in the lot and went inside the hotel, determined not to blow a good thing with Declan. Assuming he felt the same way about her, and they could both agree on exactly what they wanted—or even expected—from each other.

AFTER A STOP at the field office, Declan headed toward Bends Lake Hospital, bringing back memories of Elise working there in the field of occupational therapy. She was great at what she did, and he was proud of her for following through on a dream. Just as he had in pursuing a career in law enforcement.

Now he was pursuing Elise's sister, whom Declan had met first and never was able to quite get out of his mind with the connection they had. Maybe it was all meant to come full circle, even if they had to get through some detours in the process of life.

Only time would tell.

For now, he was more than willing to play the hand both had been dealt and see how far they could get in the final analysis.

Declan reached the hospital and met up with Ursula inside the ICU waiting room. He asked her, "Have you spoken to Michaud?"

"Not yet," she replied. "The doctor's with him now."

I hope he can shed some light on the unsub that will lead

to identifying him, Declan mused. "Has any surveillance video surfaced on a possible suspect?"

"We're still working on that." Ursula relaxed her shoulders. "Maybe whatever Michaud can tell us will provide some clarity that can correspond with any security camera footage that comes into play."

Declan nodded in agreement. Both turned as they were approached by a fortysomething, slender male with red hair in a short fade cut and a Balbo beard. He was wearing doctors' scrubs.

"I'm Dr. Hunt," he said.

"Special Agent Delgado," Declan told him.

Ursula followed with "Special Agent Liebert."

Hunt nodded at them. "You can go in to speak with Mr. Michaud now—but only for a few minutes. Though he managed to survive two bullets shot at close range, he still sustained some damage and is very weak, a bit disoriented and faces a long period of recovery."

"Got it," Declan told him, while eager to speak to the victim.

They went inside the room and saw what was expected with the typical machines, tubes and wires. Blake Michaud III was lying on the bed looking miserable, though no doubt he was glad to be alive after his ordeal.

After they identified themselves and flashed their IDs, with both standing on one side of the bed, Declan said straightforwardly, "Can you tell us what you remember about your attack?"

Blake winced and said in a strained voice, "I was jogging in the park, minding my own business—when this guy came out from the trees, blocking my path…"

"And then?" Ursula prodded him.

He drew a breath and continued, "The man had a gun in his hand. He pointed it at me and said coldly, 'You're going to die.' I said, 'What?'" Blake's brow furrowed. "He replied, 'I'm the Bends Lake Predator. See you in hell—maybe...' That's when he shot me..."

Declan was glad that the unsub confirmed what had already been established—if only for the record. But it still didn't explain why only two shots instead of three, per the unsub's MO.

Just as Ursula started to ask the victim about this, Blake licked dry lips and said, "I remember that he pointed the gun at my face and pulled the trigger. But the gun was empty. I wasn't sure if he would reload or what—but passed out at that point, not knowing if I would ever wake up again..."

"You got lucky," Declan told him bluntly, sure that he had already made that calculus—even if he probably wasn't feeling it at the moment, while recovering from his injuries.

Blake muttered, "Yeah, I suppose."

Ursula leaned toward him and said, a catch to her voice, "I have to ask, do you have any enemies—or know of anyone who might want to do you harm...take your life—?"

Blake considered the question for a long moment then responded surely, "I don't know anyone in my business or personal life who wants to kill me." He sighed. "Believe me, if I did, I would tell you."

Declan had no reason to doubt him. Even if his pursuit of success in the retail sector could be cutthroat, his rivals shouldn't resort to murder—unless there was more to the man than met the eye, including unrelated to work. "Can you describe the man who attacked you?"

Blake twisted his lips thoughtfully before replying, "Honestly, I didn't get a good look at him—it all happened so fast—and my mind's a bit fuzzy...but I can try," he said.

After they got the description, Declan asked Blake if he would be up for talking to a forensic sketch artist, and he agreed. They got the doctor's permission and set things in motion for what Declan hoped might result in pinpointing the unsub's identity.

STELLA CHECKED OUT of her room, put her bags in the car and went back inside the hotel to say goodbye to Gayle Reese, having spotted her earlier at work.

Stepping inside the gift shop, Stella saw Gayle chatting amicably with a tall and fit thirtysomething male. He had black hair, styled in a number three buzz cut, a high forehead and a designer stubble beard. Dressed in casual clothing and oxfords, he stopped talking in following the flight of Gayle's gaze and regarded Stella curiously with eyes that were solid blue.

"Hey," Gayle said to her, smiling.

"Hey." Stella smiled back.

"This is my cousin, Lochlyn." Gayle angled her face at him and back. "This is Stella. We went to high school together. Ran into each other here at the hotel, where she's staying."

Stella met his eyes. "Hi."

"Hello." He grinned. "That was obviously after I had graduated from Bends Lake High, having attended a few years before Gayle started. Sorry we missed each other."

Stella took that as harmless flirtation and said, "We all have our time period in school and can only make the most of it."

"Very true," he said evenly and studied her. "So, where do you live these days?"

"Detroit." Stella assumed he was still local, so didn't bother to ask otherwise.

"Cool." Lochlyn smiled and regarded Gayle. "Well, I'll leave you two to talk. Are we still on for tennis this afternoon?"

"Yes," Gayle told him. "I'll be at the court as scheduled."

"Okay. See you then." He looked at Stella. "Nice to meet you."

"You too," she said.

Lochlyn headed off and took a cell phone out of his chinos, tapped it and put it up to his ear as he left the gift shop.

"Cousin, huh?" Stella said as she faced Gayle while they stood by a display of souvenirs.

"Yeah. Lochlyn's really been more like a big brother to me over the years, not having a biological one," Gayle remarked. "He helped me deal with going through the divorce, having been there himself."

"Glad he was there for you." Stella was thankful that she'd never had to go down that road as she wanted a marriage that would last a lifetime, if possible. "Anyway, just wanted to let you know I've checked out of the hotel."

"Oh?" Gayle's eyes widened. "Sorry you're leaving."

I'm not actually, Stella thought, but didn't feel they were quite close enough right now to dish out the details of her love life and its potential. "Me too," she told her sincerely. "Let's keep in touch."

Gayle nodded. "Absolutely."

They exchanged phone numbers, and Stella left as Gayle went to help a customer.

When she got back to Declan's farmhouse, Stella resolved to get past any weird feelings of being in a place her sister once occupied as woman of the house. She missed Elise dearly but needed to live in the present, with an eye toward the future. Which may or may not include Declan.

Settling into one of the guestrooms, which was bright

and cheery with its own en suite bathroom, Stella felt more comfortable, at this point, having her own space while there. Even if she wound up in Declan's bed at night, if the passion they shared was sustainable.

She unpacked her things then took out her cell phone and called her mother for a quick catch up, nonchalantly mentioning that her stay in Bends Lake had been extended, without elaborating further.

Chapter Ten

That afternoon, the search was on for a serial killer suspect named Joaquin Kalember. The thirty-nine-year-old ex-con became a person of interest in the case after shooting victim Blake Michaud III described his attacker to forensic sketch artist Helene Davidovich.

Using sketch recognition software, Declan and the team were able to match the forensic sketch to a close enough degree to Kalember's mug shot. A known sex offender with a history of violence and predilection for child pornography, Kalember had been fingered by Michaud. His body type also conformed to the description provided by the victim. Furthermore, Kalember was caught on surveillance video near the park where the crime occurred, giving Declan even more reason to think he could be the person they sought. Declan wanted to bring in the suspect for questioning.

When Bends Lake police officers spotted Joaquin Kalember driving a dark blue Kia Sportage SUV that was registered to his name on Heptor Street, the car was pulled over and the unarmed suspect taken into custody without resisting arrest.

Now that Kalember was off the streets, before he was

interrogated, Declan wanted to have all his ducks in a row. He secured a search warrant for the suspect's residence and cell phone, hoping to find direct evidence that linked Kalember to the shootings.

Wearing ballistic body armor, Declan and Ursula, bolstered by personnel from the KBI's Special Operations Division, the Danver County Sheriff's Office's Criminal Investigations Division and a K-9 unit from the Bends Lake Police Department, converged upon the Wylson Mobile Home Park on Pletcher Road, where they executed the warrant.

With no one present, the order was given by Declan to break the door down to the manufactured home. They stormed inside the cramped place with two bedrooms and well-worn furnishings, and a search ensued for a Springfield Armory 1911 Ronin Operator 9 mm handgun and ammunition. Along with any other relevant indicators of the suspect's complicity in the serial murders that had terrorized the residents of Bends Lake for more than six months.

"Find anything?" Declan eyed the team at work.

"Nothing that ties Kalember as yet to the Bends Lake Predator's crimes," Ursula answered, a sound of disappointment in her tone.

"Keep at it," he directed her and the others on hand, while moving about himself, wearing nitrile gloves.

By the time the search was completed, inside and out, no murder weapon was found. Or ammo.

The suspect, though, was found to be in possession of child sexual abuse material and illegal narcotics, including cocaine and fentanyl pills.

While Kalember would have to answer for these serious offenses, Declan's current objective was to get the suspect in front of him as it pertained to the serial killer case.

Half an hour later, he was sitting across the table from Joaquin Kalember in an interrogation room. Declan took a moment to size up the suspect, who looked fairly similar to the composite sketch rendered by the forensic artist. Of course, she was only as good as the description given of the shooter. Though the suspect's mug shot was spot on, Declan could still detect slight differences, as Kalember's face was a bit narrower, nose a little longer and chin not quite as protruding. The suspect's close-set blue eyes were bloodshot, and his short dark hair was in a modern mullet.

Declan gazed sharply at him and said, "You're in serious trouble, with the child porn found at your house and on your cell phone, as well as the drugs confiscated from your residence—but right now, I want to talk about an attempted murder in which you've been implicated…"

"What?" Declan watched the color drain from the suspect's face as Kalember argued, "I don't know what the hell you're talking about…"

Leaning forward, Declan drew his brows together and said flatly, "The victim described to a sketch artist the man who shot him yesterday morning at Rendall Park. This matched your mug shot. Surveillance video spotted you leaving the area around the same time. I have to say, this doesn't look good for you, Kalember," he told him in no uncertain terms.

Kalember, who was not cuffed—but in no position to take Declan on, if it came down to Declan needing to defend himself from the suspect—ran a hand across his mouth then responded ill at ease, "I met a woman at the park to sell drugs to, then we went our separate ways—that's it! If someone described me to a sketch artist, he was wrong. I didn't shoot anyone—"

Declan peered at him dubiously. "I need the name of this

person you say you sold drugs to—and where I can find her to verify your story." As the suspect pondered ratting out the drug user, Declan added, "Believe me, it's in your best interest—and hers—to cooperate. Otherwise, you could be facing an attempted murder rap…" *And that's only the start of the homicide-related charges that could be coming your way*, Declan thought.

Kalember seemed to get the picture and spilled the beans regarding his drug transaction. For Declan, even if he would have loved to coax a confession out of Kalember, given the lack of an attempted murder weapon—to say nothing of being unable to link the suspect to the seven actual murders committed with the same Ronin Operator 9 mm pistol—the evidence simply wasn't there to support the contention that Kalember was the Bends Lake Predator.

Declan was left with no real choice but to accept this for what it was. As Blake Michaud was admittedly fuzzy about his recollections, he was apparently off in his description of his attacker. Or, if accurate, it was someone who looked like Joaquin Kalember, but he wasn't the one who tried to kill Michaud.

Meaning that the true killer was still on the loose—and as dangerous as ever—while the hunt for him had been temporarily sidetracked.

Though Kalember's alibi had yet to be confirmed, as far as Declan was concerned, his troubles—which could have him put away for a long time—did not include a failed attempt to gun down Blake Michaud in a manner that had already been successful with seven others.

At the Wylson Mobile Home Park, the Bends Lake Predator watched through the window of his manufactured home as law enforcement was still coming in and out of Joaquin Kalember's place. Why had they hauled him in? Had one of the neighbors tipped off the authorities that Joaquin was dealing drugs?

Or worse, rumor had it that he was into child porn.

Whichever way he sliced it, the Bends Lake Predator had no sympathy whatsoever for anyone who crossed the line the way Joaquin was thought to have. He fully deserved whatever he had coming to him.

By comparison, his own misdeeds were much more acceptable to the serial killer. In his way of thinking, those who took bullets from his hand needed to die. He had the ultimate power over their lives and deaths—and chose to pull the rug from beneath them by taking away anything and everything they stood for in practically the blink of an eye.

Knowing that their fate was sealed—just as sure as being diagnosed with a terminal illness—he watched the light go out of their eyes as the reality of losing any control over their own destiny set in morbidly.

Except for the execution that went awry. It had been his every intention to end a life at Rendall Park. Instead, his firearm failed him at the very moment of eliminating the target. Without having the ammo to finish the job and with footsteps approaching, he was left with no choice but to leave his prey and hope the two bullets pumped into the man's chest would still get the job done.

But this failed.

The runner survived and was apparently on his way to making a full recovery.

Damn him.

The Bends Lake Predator cursed his rotten luck in this instance. He knew it would be all but impossible to finish the job.

And so he would have to make up for it with someone else, for he would not be denied. Two for the price of one.

He continued to gaze out the window at the activity underway and couldn't help but crack a grin at the thought that the authorities had the Bends Lake Predator right under their collective noses and, sadly, weren't the wiser.

Their terrible misfortune would be his gain once more.

STELLA DID NOT necessarily consider cooking to be her strongest suit, but she'd learned just enough from her mother and Elise to be able to create a decent meal if she put her mind to it. Being used to takeout, quick meals and restaurant dining during her busy life as an FBI behavioral analyst, she decided to step up her game by making dinner as Declan's houseguest. After making a stop at the supermarket, she had gathered the ingredients she needed to make a corn pudding casserole, barbecue chicken breasts baked in the oven, fried green tomatoes and zucchini bread. It was the least she could do in carrying her own weight— even if she was uncertain just how long her stay would be here, with neither of them looking much beyond the moment at hand.

While preparing everything in the kitchen, Stella's thoughts wandered to the news she'd received from Declan that the sketch of the attacker as described by Michaud had not panned out. The mug shot of suspect Joaquin Kalember, which resembled the facial composite, turned out to be misleading, as Kalember's alibi checked out.

Meaning that Blake Michaud's assailant was still out there.

This disturbed Stella as she, like everyone else, just wanted this to be over with by nailing the serial killer. But it would be longer now before he could be apprehended for his crimes.

At least in going after Joaquin Kalember, they were able to serendipitously uncover his penchant for child pornography and dealing in illegal drugs—both of which were intolerable—taking him off the streets for their trouble.

Stella's mind turned back to the task at hand, as she put the finishing touches on the meal and grabbed the bottle of white wine from the fridge they had opened the day before.

By the time Declan had arrived home, having given her a heads-up, she had already set the table and was ready to eat.

"Hey!" Stella told him coolly when he walked through the door. She hoped that a good meal might take his mind off the disappointment of not being able to put the brakes on his investigation with an arrest.

"What's this?" Declan looked genuinely surprised. "You cooked dinner?"

"Yes." She laughed. "I wanted to return the favor."

He lifted a brow whimsically. "Okay."

She told him, for context, "I seem to recall cooking for you once or twice back in the day."

"Yeah, I remember." He chuckled. "Glad to see that you were comfortable enough here to go for it."

Stella blushed. "I'm getting there," she confessed, maybe more than she cared to admit. "Why don't you wash up, and I'll put the food out, and you can tell me just how tasty it is."

"Sounds like a plan," he said, grinning at her in a way that reminded Stella of just how good-looking Declan was, along with how sexy. Both had served him well and made it relatively easy to fall for him again.

Fifteen minutes later, they were sitting at the dining room table eating. Stella watched tensely as Declan dug into the corn pudding casserole and said, "Looks like I'll have some competition in the kitchen. This is amazing!"

"Glad you like it." Her teeth shone. "Runs in the family," she told him, paying homage to Elise and her parents.

"I can see that." He smiled at Stella then lifted a slice of zucchini bread and bit into it. "Bloodline has its place, but your abilities in and out of the kitchen succeed on their own merits."

"Nice of you to think so," she said, not about to argue the point.

"I know so," he doubled down, and sipped wine.

Stella told him candidly, "Your merits are just as rock solid."

"I suppose." Declan nodded. "Must be why we get along so well."

"Among other reasons," she said coquettishly.

"True," he concurred musingly while forking a tomato.

Stella sank her teeth into a piece of chicken, and they talked about the latest twist in the serial killer investigation.

"I thought we might have had him dead to rights," Declan griped. "But it was not to be."

"These things happen," she said in defense of Blake Michaud and his faulty depiction of the unsub who tried to kill him. "We both know that trying to describe an attacker after being under duress at the time of the attack is wholly unreliable—especially after the disorienting trauma of being shot twice in the process."

"Spoken like a true profiler," Declan said with a laugh. "I take your point, though. Michaud was off on his description, and that's the way it goes. The fact that he survived at all, and that the unsub fell short of his intentions, was a major victory in and of itself."

"I agree." Stella dabbed a napkin to her mouth. Though

she wondered what this meant in the long run with an un-hinged serial killer still out there and possibly looking for retribution after failing to complete another kill, she had to say, "At least the composite sketch resulted in nabbing someone who was into child porn and drug dealing."

Declan responded in concurrence, "That was definitely a good thing."

"I think so," she said, taking each victory as it came in the often unpredictable world of law enforcement.

They went to bed, where Stella took the bold initiative of exploring Declan up and down, wanting to reacquaint herself with him in every way—and enjoying everything he had to offer, which was plenty.

In turn, he gave her just as much pleasure, and more, while they made love for hours—till sheer exhaustion and full sexual satisfaction overcame them, and they fell asleep in each other's arms.

But before she drifted off, Stella felt that she was fall-ing in love with Declan all over again, as if that raw emo-tion had been hidden even from herself over the years and was now coming back with a sweet vengeance. Even if she wasn't quite sure how to process it. Or how he would.

DECLAN HAD BEEN enjoying an erotic dream, where he and Stella picked up where they left off in the real world in his bedroom, when he was jarred awake by a ringing sound. Opening his eyes, he still heard it and quickly re-alized that it was his doorbell ringing. He grabbed his cell phone from the nightstand and saw that it was 10:00 p.m. There was also a text message from Aurelio Valderrama that read succinctly:

Need to see you. On my way over. Important.

As Declan assessed this, the doorbell rang again. He saw Stella rousing awake. "Is that your bell?" she asked in a sleepy voice.

"Yeah. Got a text from a local kid I play basketball with. He's at the door." Declan sighed musingly. "I need to see what this is all about."

Stella lifted on an elbow. "Do you want me to come with you?"

"Not necessary," he answered, knowing that she was naked beneath the cover and sheet and seeing no reason for her to put on clothes just yet. "I won't be long."

Declan kissed Stella on the mouth and rolled out of bed. He grabbed a pair of jeans and a T-shirt off a gray accent chair in the corner of the room and quickly donned them before heading downstairs in his bare feet.

While contemplating what could be so urgent that Aurelio needed to show up at his door, Declan considered that he and his younger sister lived with a single mother—with the father having long been out of the picture. As far as Declan knew, the kid hadn't gotten into trouble beyond the normal teenage issues of drinking and vandalism—neither of which had landed him in the juvenile justice system. But the pressures were always there among peers to delve into other behaviors that could land him in hot water. Was that the case here?

When he opened the door, Declan stared at Aurelio, who looked nervous and was wearing his typical basketball attire. He was holding a brown paper bag.

"Hey—sorry to just show up like this," Aurelio stammered. "But thought it was best to talk in person."

"This better be good," Declan said stiffly, though intrigued nonetheless. "Come in."

Once inside, Aurelio gazed down at his sneakers and

looked up at Declan tentatively and said, "I have something you need to see…"

He handed him the bag, and Declan said curiously, "What is it?"

Aurelio took a breath. "Just take a look."

"Okay." Declan opened the bag and saw that there was a handgun inside. He glanced at Aurelio and back at the weapon, studying it as he asked the kid uneasily, "What are you doing with this?"

Before Aurelio could respond, Declan's heart skipped a beat as he recognized the firearm as a Springfield Armory 1911 Ronin Operator 9 mm pistol with a suppressor. Just like the weapon used by the Bends Lake Predator serial killer to shoot eight people—seven fatally.

Chapter Eleven

After Stella got dressed and joined them, as Declan had a feeling this was something she needed to hear, he introduced her as Special Agent Bailey—figuring that Aurelio was wise enough to draw the correct conclusions that they were romantically involved. Besides that, Declan knew that discovering he had company at night was the least of the kid's concerns at the moment, as Aurelio had some major explaining to do.

Stella made coffee, and they all sat on kitchen island stools before Declan peered at Aurelio and asked tersely, "So, tell us about the gun—"

Aurelio clutched the mug, tasted the coffee and said unevenly, "Okay. Half an hour ago, my girlfriend, Bella Sorvino, and I were just talking inside my mom's Honda Prologue outside our house on Tutler's Way when this SUV drives past us. We didn't think anything of it, till the SUV stopped up ahead and a dude got out. He was carrying that—" Aurelio pointed to the bag on the island "—and walked over to a garbage can and tossed it inside, got back in his car and drove off like he was in a hurry."

Declan exchanged glances with Stella and asked him suspiciously, "You want to tell me how you ended up with the bag?"

Aurelio sipped more coffee nervously and answered, "Guess I was curious. While Bella waited in the car, I went to see what he had thrown away. That's when I saw the bag and took it out. I saw the gun inside and thought about tossing it back in the trash. But knowing you're with the KBI, when you're not knocking down shots in the park, I decided to bring it to you. Bella thought I should too."

Declan nodded. "Smart choice." He sipped coffee thoughtfully. "Did either of you touch the handgun?"

"Not a chance!" Aurelio made a face. "We weren't about to get our fingerprints on it and then have to explain that to you guys—knowing the dude probably had his reasons for getting rid of the gun..."

Stella smiled over her mug of coffee. "Another wise move by you and your girlfriend."

"Yeah," he muttered, putting the mug to his lips.

Declan agreed, giving them one less thing to deal with here if Aurelio and Bella were truly innocent of any wrongdoing—and he had to believe that was the case, considering that Aurelio was astute enough to bring the firearm to him.

He gazed at Aurelio and asked, "Can you describe this person you saw carrying the brown bag?"

"Definitely a white dude and tall. He was wearing dark clothes." Aurelio hunched broad shoulders. "Since it was nighttime, couldn't see his face when he turned our way for a second, but he didn't seem to see us. I think he had dark hair."

"What about the SUV he was driving?" Stella asked, sipping her coffee. "Can you describe it—make, model, color—anything would help..."

"Hmm...black, dark blue...something like that." Aurelio scratched his head. "It was too dark to get a good look at it before he took off."

Not surprising under the circumstances, Declan thought.

"We'll see if any surveillance cameras near Tutler's Way can give us a more detailed description of the SUV during that timeframe."

Aurelio looked at him and asked grimly, "You think he shot someone with the gun?"

"That's a pretty good possibility," Declan answered logically. The question in his mind was whether or not it was the same Ronin Operator 9 mm pistol used by a serial killer who attempted another murder. "We may need to speak with your girlfriend later," he advised Aurelio, as standard procedure—even if Declan was certain he was on the level in his account.

Aurelio nodded. "Bella's kind of freaking out about it…" He paused. "Guess it has to do with her brother being accidentally shot while deployed with the US military in Syria."

"She has nothing to worry about," Declan tried to assure him. "We only want to get to the bottom of why someone chose to get rid of the gun—and in that location."

"Okay, I'll tell her that," he said.

Declan stood. "Thanks for bringing this to me. We'll take it from here."

Aurelio got to his feet. "Just doing my civic duty," he asserted.

"Good for you," Stella told him with a smile.

After Declan showed Aurelio out, he went back to Stella, who was examining the firearm inside the bag and asked him, "Do you think this is the handgun we've been looking for?"

He contemplated the question and responded with a gut feeling, "Probably. What better time for the unsub to get rid of the murder weapon and distance himself from it?"

"True." Stella finished her coffee. "We'll find out soon enough."

"Yep," Declan agreed, and was optimistic that it could be an important step toward the unsub's downfall. He gazed at her as his thoughts turned toward their being cozy in bed after hot sex, before Aurelio showed up. Now neither of them was likely to be getting much more sleep this night.

THE FOLLOWING AFTERNOON, Declan briefed the team on the latest development in the investigation. He made some general remarks, meant to offer a positive view that they were definitely on the right track in solving the case, and then asked forensic scientist Josephine Okamura to share her important news on the firearm brought to him by Aurelio Valderrama and turned over to the forensic science lab's Firearm and Toolmark Section for evaluation.

Josephine used a stylus pen to display a firearm on the large touch screen, as she said measuredly, "This Springfield Armory 1911 Ronin Operator 9 mm pistol armed with a sound suppressor, that Special Agent Delgado confiscated and sent to the evidence control center, proved to be a positive match for the bullets and spent shell casings linked to seven local murders and one attempted murder. Though the pistol was empty, a firearms examiner was able to test fire rounds to show that its gun barrel with six lands and grooves and a right-hand twist lined up perfectly with the bullets and casings involved in the homicides."

She took a short breath and said, "In other words, this is *definitely* the weapon used by the unsub referred to as the Bends Lake Predator to shoot the victims… The gun is still being processed for possible prints and DNA and has also been entered into the NIBIN to establish a link to any other crimes that might have been committed using the firearm—"

Declan offered her a smile and said, "Good job."

She nodded and said softly, "Hope you get him."

"You've put us on the right path," he told her. When she stepped away, Declan professed to the task force, "This was one of the things we've been waiting for to break this case wide open." He pointed at the Ronin Operator handgun still displayed on the monitor. "We have the murder weapon. And the bullets and shell casings fired from it. We also have the unsub on his heels, whether he knows it or not. Two teenagers spotted him getting rid of the handgun and saw the unsub drive off in a dark SUV, which corresponds with other info we have. We're currently collecting surveillance videos from the area that may help us to zoom in on the make and model of the SUV and identity of the driver—or, at the very least, a more accurate description. Until then, we need to remain diligent in our pursuit of the unsub so that he can't know a moment's rest from the chase..."

Declan let that settle in as Ursula said a few words, with Stella to follow in assessing the latest move—or blunder— by the Bends Lake Predator.

STELLA WASTED NO time in giving them her honest impression of the unsub and his ridding himself of the primary piece of his killing machine puzzle—and what it may mean. She glanced at Declan and Ursula, then said to the team levelly, "Honestly, I believe that the unsub is running scared right now. By dumping the Springfield Armory 1911 Ronin Operator 9 mm pistol in the trash, it tells me that this was his way of trying to cut his losses, if you will, by separating himself from the handgun with which he was unable to kill his last target. In the process, the unsub may believe that this will somehow throw the investigators off track just enough to keep them at bay."

Keene Haverstock asked her, "So, are you saying that this is basically just a head fake on the part of the unsub and that he has every intention of carrying out more hits on targets, whether they're random or not?"

Good question, Stella told herself, and one she was fully prepared to respond to. She favored the FBI special agent with a serious look and responded bluntly, "I think it's highly likely that our unsub has no intention of fading into the woodwork. Like most serial killers, they fancy themselves as smarter than the rest of us. The Bends Lake Predator is no different." She furrowed her forehead and uttered ominously, "He will almost certainly strike again—with a new firearm and new prey—unless we can get to him first…"

Arielle Mendoza stated affirmatively, "That's why we're all here, right? It's what we do. We can't let him win. No matter his warped sense of self-importance."

"We won't," Declan stressed. "With the Ronin Operator handgun now safely in our possession, even if it's replaced by another weapon, the unsub has given us a major opening, and none of us will back down even a little bit until we make him pay for this—one way or another."

With this positive energy in the face of a relentless serial killer, Stella had to say, "Arielle's right. Whatever the unsub can do, we can do better. As I said, he's spooked right now, which, as Declan alluded to, can work to our advantage."

Stella eyed him and got a confident, if somewhat guarded, grin in return. She was glad to see that they were all on the same page in their renewed commitment toward bringing the Bends Lake Predator to his knees. She only wondered if and when other innocents might have to pay the ultimate price in the meantime.

AFTER THE BRIEFING was over, Declan drove to the basketball court, where he saw Aurelio shooting hoops alone.

He wanted the teen to hear the news from him first on the gun he found.

After parking at the curb, Declan joined him on the court, still wearing his work clothing and shoes. Aurelio tossed the ball to him and said routinely, "Hey."

"Hey." Declan shot the ball flatfooted and drained it through the net. "Thought you might want to know about the firearm you brought me."

Aurelio dipped his chin. "Yeah. What did you find out?"

Meeting his gaze, Declan said straightforwardly, "The gun has been used in a string of local homicides."

"Seriously?" Aurelio raised a brow. "Are we talking about that serial killer on the loose...the Bends Lake Predator?"

"Yes, that's the person we believe the gun belonged to." Though Declan hated to lay this on him, he deserved to know the truth, given his inadvertent involvement in the investigation. "Needless to say, we're trying to locate the suspect and bring him in."

Aurelio tracked down the ball and asked warily, "So, am I—or Bella, for that matter—in any danger...?" He shot the ball, and it bounced off the rim. "I mean, I don't think the dude ever saw us." His eyes widened with realization. "But, oh man, what if he did? And now wants to come after us...?"

It was a valid question to Declan, and while he certainly couldn't rule out that the unsub could target Aurelio or Bella, it seemed like a low probability, all things considered. "My guess is that if the perp had spotted you and your girlfriend—and viewed you as a threat—you'd probably be dead right now," he said bluntly. Still, in erring on the side of caution, Declan told him, "You might want to play ball inside the gym for the time being."

"Okay." Aurelio dribbled the ball. "So, when are you going to catch this guy?"

Declan frowned. "I wish I could give you the answer to that, but I can't," he admitted, knowing that the investigation was ongoing and the unsub still out of their reach. "You can be sure, though, that all hands are on deck to capture him."

"All right." Aurelio clutched the ball to his chest.

"Come on, I'll give you a ride home," Declan said, as it was on the way to his own house and would allow him to make sure Aurelio got there safely.

Aurelio agreed, and during the ride, Declan surveyed other homes in the area and wondered if the unsub lived in any of them and in anonymity. His sense was that the Bends Lake Predator, being clever as he'd proven to be, had most likely driven a safe distance from his own residence. And chosen a spot at random to dump the handgun while hoping it would disappear forever. Along with his deadly association with it.

THE BENDS LAKE PREDATOR crouched among the sawtooth oak trees surrounding the single-track, three-mile loop trail. He had waited patiently and impatiently at the same time for his prey to arrive in his sights. Honestly, he was itching to pick up where he left off, now that he had discarded the 9 mm pistol and replaced it with another handgun that was equally lethal.

He thought back to when he had made the decision to trash the Ronin Operator gun. After failing to take out his last victim, he believed that the missed opportunity was bad karma. Not wishing to press his luck—or increase the luck of his prime targets—he made the smart move of relieving himself of the anvil that seemed to be weighing him down.

With that firearm dead and buried in the garbage and destined for a landfill, never to be seen again, he was now free to get back down to business. In throwing off his pursuers, he could start fresh as a killing machine and keep them guessing as to when, where and how his victims would be snuffed out like a candle.

It occurred to him that someone could have seen him when he tossed the gun in the garbage can. Had there been someone in that Honda he passed by? Or was that only his imagination?

In the end, he'd decided that it was too dark for anyone to get a good look at him. Or his SUV. So he made haste and got the hell out of there. No harm. No foul. Right?

He sucked in a deep breath, enjoying the warm humid air. Not to mention the air of invincibility he had come to enjoy like a man who couldn't be touched.

The Bends Lake Predator's reverie stopped on a dime when he spotted two mountain bikes headed his way.

It's time, he told himself, cool as ice, as he stood erect but remained hidden till the very last moment. When escape would be all but impossible.

One error in judgment was enough. He wasn't about to let another golden opportunity slip through his grasp.

There would be two, this time around, who wouldn't come out of this alive.

He checked the gun, equipped with a silencer, and made sure that it was loaded and as ready as he was to do some serious damage to his unsuspecting victims.

Chapter Twelve

That morning, Ursula received a call that two people had been found dead on Bends Lake Trail, a zigzagging single-track trail popular among adventurers and exercisers for hiking and mountain biking. So what else was new? Still dealing with an ongoing case involving a ruthless serial killer, now it appeared as though the KBI would need to assist the locals in an entirely different investigation into what appeared to be homicides.

Unless there was some symmetry between the crimes? She considered the possibility that, as Stella had alluded to, the Bends Lake Predator had upped his game in preying upon others dramatically as his warped way of coming back with a vengeance after the failed attempt to murder Blake Michaud III.

Either way, it was the type of added stress that she didn't need. Not with a baby on the way. Even if Melody would be the one giving birth, Ursula was still in lockstep with her wife in going through the process. But she was also just as committed to her work in law enforcement.

I knew what I'd signed up for when I chose this career path, Ursula told herself as she drove the Chevrolet Malibu to Bends Lake Trail, right off Seemore Lane. She could only take whatever came her way—much like Declan and the other KBI special agents—and do her job.

When she arrived at the trail, Ursula showed her ID and was let past the cordoned-off crime scene, where she spotted Declan speaking with a Bends Lake PD homicide detective. Ursula recognized him as Zack Yamamoto, a tall and slender Japanese American in his late twenties with black hair in a curtain cut.

Looking beyond them, she saw a white male and a light-skinned biracial female lying on the ground. Their heads, with helmets on them, were surrounded by pools of blood. Both were slender and appeared to be in their thirties, wearing athletic attire and cycling shoes. Ursula regarded two mountain bikes on the ground, almost as if props. She knew that this was anything but the case as she approached the two men and geared herself up to face the music, melancholy as it was bound to be.

DECLAN FROWNED AS he peered at the dead man and woman, who had been identified as Trevor LeBlanc and Michelle Hewlett. They had been shot in cold blood at close range.

"No sign of a firearm to indicate a murder-suicide," Detective Zack Yamamoto told Ursula. "But there are spent shell casings on the ground." He ran a hand through his hair and grimaced. "Looks like they were ambushed…"

"By whom?" She wrinkled her nose. "Who would do such a horrible thing?"

"That's what we need to find out," Declan said tersely. "Given the angle of the wounds to the back of their heads, it appears as though the killer was lying in wait and was skillful enough to drop them from behind." He thought about the Bends Lake Predator, wondering if he was sharp enough to change his tactics to this degree. Declan imagined that Stella would have some thoughts on it when she learned the unsettling news. But as of now, they had to keep an open mind that the cyclists may have had enemies that were only after them, and therefore could be totally separate from their serial killer investigation.

Zack, who was looking at his cell phone, said, "I may have something on that…" He got between Declan and Ursula. "A hiker named Josette Edmonds has come forward, saying she saw a strange man running from the area. Without knowing if he was running from something, instinctively, she used her cell phone video to capture him before he disappeared into a wooded area. With the press already reporting on the fatal shooting, Ms. Edmonds has sent us the video she took. Here it is…"

Declan watched as a tall and fit white male, wearing dark clothing and a hoodie with the hood over his head, dashed through the woods like a roadrunner before vanishing from sight.

"Hmm…" Ursula uttered musingly, turning to him. "Are you thinking what I'm thinking?"

"How could I not be?" Declan answered honestly. "The general physical characteristics look an awful lot like those of the Bends Lake Predator—"

When the medical examiner arrived and a preliminary examination indicated the point-blank range execution of the man and woman, Declan hoped that the crime scene investigators could come up with damning evidence in the pursuit of justice. Though he wasn't ruling out that the victims could have been targeted specifically for the kill, Declan had a feeling that this was the work of a serial killer run amok.

FOUR HOURS LATER, Declan sat in his car. He had learned that Michelle Hewlett and Trevor LeBlanc were Canadians, staying at a log cabin near Bends Lake Trail. They had only been there for three days, having flown in from Winnipeg, Manitoba, to Great Bend, Kansas, where the couple rented a GMC Yukon for a weeklong adventure.

One that ended tragically.

Declan saw no evidence that it was a robbery gone bad, as all their belongings were still inside the cabin. Nor was there any indication that the couple had been otherwise targeted by someone from their hometown, following them to Kansas in order to commit cold-blooded murder.

As far as he could tell, Declan believed that Hewlett and LeBlanc may have been chosen randomly to be killed—though, the culprit could have tracked their pattern of apparently riding their mountain bikes at the same time every day.

That, along with the video of an unsub running away from the scene, gives more credence to this being the work of their serial killer, Declan told himself as he opened his laptop. The changing modus operandi notwithstanding—with the victims each shot twice in the back of the head—it had all the indications of thrill killings, which seemed to reflect the mindset of the serial killer at large.

He reached out to the Firearm and Toolmark Section of the forensic science lab to get the scoop on the bullets and shell casings used in the double homicide.

When Josephine Okamura appeared on the screen, she smiled softly as Declan said, "What do you have for me?"

She was all business as she brought him up to speed on the news he sought, finishing with an edge to her voice, "So there you have it."

"Indeed, and thanks," he told her and disconnected before starting the car and heading for another important briefing.

In the conference room, where Declan had reconvened the team for the second time in two days, he went right to the heart of the matter. Using the stylus pen, he put the images of the victims of the double homicide side by side on the screen and said soberly, "Sometime this morning, Michelle Hewlett, a thirty-three-year-old veterinarian, and Trevor LeBlanc, a thirty-seven-year-old dentist, were gunned down while riding mountain bikes on the Bends Lake Trail loop."

Declan paused while gazing at Hewlett, who was nice-looking with a black wavy bob and big brown eyes; then he turned to LeBlanc, who was square-jawed with blue eyes and blond hair in a pompadour style. "The two Canadian adventurers were vacationing in Kansas, with plans to travel to Tennessee to visit the Great Smoky Mountains National Park next on their agenda—when it appears they were ambushed by the killer, who shot both victims twice in the back of the head."

Flipping to an image of a firearm, Declan said, "According to ballistics, the four bullets used to shoot the pair and spent shell casings came from a Taurus GX4 9 mm Luger pistol—like the one shown on the screen—with a gun barrel that has five lands and grooves and a left-hand twist." He took a breath and continued, "We have reason to believe that the shooter may be the same unsub responsible for the shooting deaths of seven other individuals and the attempted murder of a man."

Declan played a video while explaining, "This video was shot by a hiker shortly after the murders were believed to have occurred. It shows an unsub who shares characteristics of the Bends Lake Predator suspect—" He turned off the monitor. "The change of tactics is likely a maneuver borne out of necessity. Or to throw us off guard in believing we're dealing with an entirely different killer. Though all possibilities remain on the table, my current thinking is that we are dealing with the same unsub..."

After Declan turned it over to Detective Zack Yamamoto to give a few more details on the police department's investigation, Stella took to the podium to reiterate her stance on the unsub and the propensity for altering his modus operandi.

She eyed Declan, and he flashed her a show of support as Stella said smoothly, "The double homicide probe is just getting started—and could well be the work of a separate murderer. As we all know, there are many people capable of committing such violent acts in our society. I tend to concur with Declan that there is a strong possibility that the murders of these two individuals were perpetrated by the so-called Bends Lake Predator."

Stella brushed aside a strand of hair that had fallen onto her face and continued, "A killer's MO is never set in stone. Yes, there tends to be predictable patterns of behavior, but this is always subject to change as conditions warrant. In this instance, the use of a Taurus GX4 9 mm Luger pistol rather than another Springfield Armory 1911 Ronin Operator 9 mm handgun may be as simple as accessibility for the unsub. And choosing to shoot them both twice in the head, instead of once in the head and two other times in the chest or stomach, may be little more than a strategic move to confound the authorities—with the unsub confident in achieving the intended result of killing the victims."

She sighed and said, "Lastly, murdering two for the price of one may well have been a make-up murder, if you will—

an extra murder to take the place of the missed opportunity in the attempted murder of Blake Michaud III. In the unsub's warped mind, he feels the need to be in control of all aspects of his serial actions—even to the point of satisfying his homicidal impulses with a substitute killing, in addition to the preplanned murder of someone who happened to come into his line of vision."

THAT EVENING, Stella and Declan joined a few other members of the team at Hedy's Club, where they sat around a table, drinking beer.

Declan wiped froth from his mouth and said tonelessly, "Never a dull day in our line of work."

Keene Haverstock nodded, then added sardonically, "What fun would that be?" He added on a serious note, "Not that there's anything fun about nine people dead and a tenth person who's damned lucky to be alive."

Declan drank more beer. "Tell me about it."

"If it turns out to be true that Michelle Hewlett and Trevor LeBlanc were killed by a serial killer, then this unsub is some piece of work," Zack Yamamoto remarked.

"I'd say that's putting it mildly," Arielle Mendoza said, lifting her mug. "I wouldn't necessarily say that he's a psychopath, but he's definitely playing his hand with a deranged mindset, if you ask me. Or maybe I should defer to our visiting behavioral analyst…"

Stella smiled, tasting her drink while feeling all eyes on her, as though she could provide easy answers for why one becomes a serial killer. If only it was that simple. She would try to make some sense of it anyhow. "I'll give it a shot," she told them lightheartedly. "Our unsub is definitely a deviant, which I'm sure we all agree with, and is likely a psychopath. As it relates to psychopathy, which correlates on many levels with sociopathy—I'll just say that both are antisocial personality disorders that tend to be characterized by arrogance, no value for human life other than one's own, having little to no remorse for the criminal behavior and getting turned on by the power wielded in creating fear and helplessness among victims." Stella chuckled, feeling a bit embarrassed. "I think I probably said too much—I'm boring everyone to tears."

Declan smiled. "I wouldn't go that far," he said sincerely. "Your insight has been evident since you got to town. It's done wonders to give us some perspective while trying to deal with this monster."

"I'm totally with Declan there," Keene said, drinking beer. "Guess that's why the Bureau pays you the big bucks, Stella."

Arielle joked, "Actually, I think those come more from the royalties from her books."

Stella blushed and laughed. "Will you guys stop it? I'm just doing my job like everyone else. But I wouldn't trade it for anything." She gazed at Declan, who stared back at her, and in that moment thought, *Except for maybe finding true love and settling down into a lasting relationship and happy home*. She wondered if that was forthcoming. Or had that ship already sailed past her?

"It's been really nice having you here," Declan told Stella that night.

"Oh, really?" She chuckled. "Bet you say that to every naked criminal profiler you have in your bed."

Now he laughed. "Not quite," he professed. "Haven't had any other profilers in here. And wouldn't want any. You're a hard act to follow, Stella. Trust me when I say that."

She looked him in the eye with a straight face and said,

"Actually, I think I do trust you…and whatever it is that's happening here—"

"Good." He held her gaze with sincerity. "I feel the same way."

"And what way is that?" she challenged him.

Declan froze. Not because he was at a loss for words. Quite the contrary. He knew precisely what he felt in his heart and soul for her. She had come back into his life at just the right time—and given him a whole new reason to believe in love again. And a future. Where the problem came in was exactly how they could navigate that future, given the different trajectories of their lives and careers at the moment. Could they meet somewhere in the middle? Or would they only wind up repeating the mistakes of the past? And in the process lose everything they could have in the precious years ahead?

"What's the matter?" Stella broke through his reverie, an uneasy catch to her tone. "Cat got your tongue?"

Declan grinned crookedly, realizing he needed to give her something that let Stella know in clear language that he was in this for the long run—without getting too far ahead of himself. Or beyond her own comfort level, as they both lay naked in bed.

Declan breathed in air and said deliberately, "What I'm trying to say is that you can count on me to be there for you—and to not allow this bond we've established or re-established, if you will, to slip away again." He paused. "Once we get past this investigation and can put all the focus on us, we can delve deeper into where we are and where we go from here—" *I hope that will suffice for now*, he told himself as they cuddled.

"All right." Stella's voice was soft. Her body even softer. "We'll do this your way."

Declan was pleased that she was amenable to allowing things to play themselves out, with a positive outcome something they both strove for in the end. He held her even closer, kissing the side of Stella's head and then her bare shoulder while deep in thought.

Chapter Thirteen

When the KBI received a call the following day from someone indicating they might have important information about the murder of Diane Wexler, Declan was quick to check it out, wanting to leave no stone unturned in solving the crime. The caller, who identified herself as Gillian Estrada, was said to be a good friend of Diane's.

He drove to a posh two-story residence on Lavador Lane and parked behind a yellow BMW M2 Coupe before heading up to the house.

The front door opened when he reached the covered porch. Standing before him was a striking, well-dressed, slender Hispanic female in her early fifties, with shoulder-length layered curly hair and hazel eyes behind heart-shaped glasses.

"I'm Gillian Estrada," she said softly.

"Special Agent Delgado."

"Thank you for coming." She shook his hand and told him, "Please come in."

Declan followed her inside. Similar to Diane Wexler's nearby residence, it exuded the trappings of wealth with mahogany handcrafted furniture on beige hybrid flooring and numerous floor-to-ceiling windows. A Siamese cat strode across the floor nonchalantly.

Declan gazed at the homeowner and asked curiously, "You mentioned that you may have some relevant information on the Diane Wexler homicide investigation?"

"Yes…" She touched her glasses nervously. "Mind if we sit down?"

"Not at all." He sat on a blue armchair and watched her do the same.

Gillian clasped her hands and, after taking a moment, uttered, "I was devastated to hear about Diane's death. Was on a cruise when it happened and didn't receive the news until I got home."

"So, you two were close?" Declan asked, remembering that she had indicated as much.

"Yes, we hung out, when afforded the time to do so. But since she was married—if not always happily—and I was definitely happy as a divorcée, there was that getting in the way." When the cat jumped up on her lap, Gillian petted it and said thoughtfully, "Diane and I attended a fundraiser about three months ago. There was a guy who worked for the firm that provided security services who tried to hit on Diane. She politely rebuffed his efforts, but he still seemed to take it the wrong way. Honestly, it was creepy." Gillian took a breath and let the cat go. "Maybe it ended there—Diane never indicated otherwise—but after learning that she had been murdered, possibly by a serial killer, this man came to mind as someone I wanted to bring to your attention…just in case—"

Declan reacted with interest. "I'm glad you did," he told her. "Did you or Diane happen to get this man's name?"

"I think it was Sam," Gillian said.

Sam is a pretty common name, Declan thought, but it was still worth checking out. "Can you narrow it down to exactly when and where the fundraiser took place?"

She nodded. "I can get that information for you."

"Okay." He regarded the cat that had jumped back on her lap. "If there's anything that can connect this Sam to Diane's death, we'll find out."

Gillian said, "Thank you. Diane was such a gentle soul. She didn't deserve to be taken away like that—leaving behind her daughter and husband."

"I couldn't agree more," Declan concurred, reminded of the tragic loss of his own wife prematurely. Even as he had to come to terms with the strong feelings he now—and probably always, if the truth be told—had for her sister. He felt blessed to have had them both in his life at the right times.

DECLAN AND KEENE walked into the McIntosh Security Agency on Rottenham Road and approached the front desk in the small lobby.

Standing in front of a computer on a granite counter was a sixtysomething lean man with fine slicked-back white hair and a matching horseshoe-shaped mustache. He eyed them behind round glasses and asked, "Can I help you?"

After they identified themselves, Keene said, "And you are?"

"Vince McIntosh. I own the agency."

Declan said, "We need some information on one of your employees who was on hand three months ago at a fundraiser in a building on Kayllen Avenue."

"Okay." Vince regarded them for a moment. "What does this pertain to?"

"It's a murder investigation," Keene said sharply.

"Murder?" Vince flashed a look of shock. "Of who?"

"We'd rather not say for the time being," Declan told

him, preferring to limit what they divulged while probing into one of his personnel.

With a frown on his face, Vince asked, "What's the name of the employee?"

"We only have Sam to go with," Declan answered, hoping that would be enough.

"The only Sam we had on the payroll then as an armed security guard that would've been at the fundraiser was Samuel O'Shea," Vince said matter-of-factly.

Keene peered at him. "You said, 'had on the payroll'?"

"Yes. We let him go a couple of months ago, after receiving complaints from some of our clients of harassment and other behavior inconsistent with company standards," Vince explained, jutting his chin.

That sounds about right, Declan mused, considering Gillian Estrada's account of a man named Sam who stepped outside the line in pursuing Diane Wexler's affections, to no avail. But did this amount to murder? Not to mention a notch on the belt of a serial killer?

Declan regarded the security agency owner and asked intently, "So, what does this Samuel O'Shea look like?"

"Let me pull up his data," Vince said, and began typing on the computer's keyboard.

Within moments, he had printed out an image of Samuel O'Shea. Declan and Keene studied it. The thirty-eight-year-old former security guard was listed at six feet, three inches tall and had short dark hair, a square face and blue eyes. He seemed to fit the general characteristics of the unsub they were after in the string of murders, which merited moving forward in speaking with O'Shea as a suspect.

"We need an address for Samuel O'Shea," Keene said, peering at Vince.

"No problem," he responded, but added defensively,

"There were no red flags in Sam's background check." Vince sucked in a deep breath. "I hope you're on the wrong track here."

"Only time will tell," Declan said straightforwardly. Even if there was no criminal record, he had a sense that O'Shea was a legitimate person of interest and asked, "What model of handguns do your security officers carry?"

"We're equipped with Ruger LC9 semiautomatic pistols," Vince answered tonelessly. "Why do you ask?"

Because I wanted to see if they were Springfield Armory 1911 Ronin Operator 9 mm pistols, Declan thought, *like the one used by the unsub in Diane Wexler's murder*. He said, though, "Just a routine part of the inquiry."

Vince nodded and handed them Samuel O'Shea's last known address, before they headed out of the security agency.

"So, what do you think?" Keene asked once they stepped outside, his jaw set. "Would this guy truly carry a grudge for three months after being snubbed—leading to murder? Not to mention the other murders tied to the unsub?"

"Why not?" Declan answered thoughtfully. "Who's to say the victims weren't all targeted because of some real or imagined snubbing or related in some way vendetta? Beyond that, the unsub could well have used some of the other killings as a smokescreen—with Diane Wexler being his primary target." *Or maybe I'm stretching the scenarios too far and wide*, Declan mused, as he second-guessed himself, while keeping open the possibilities.

"Point taken," Keene said. "Let's go pay Samuel O'Shea a visit and see what he has to say about this."

Declan nodded pensively as they headed toward his vehicle.

STELLA JOGGED ACROSS the grass on Declan's property while admiring the view of the Cheyenne Bottoms wetland and migrating birds. She was envious that he got to enjoy this amazing wetland year-round, as well as visit the nearby Quivira National Wildlife Refuge whenever afforded the time.

Yes, I suppose I could get used to this in a hurry, Stella told herself while moving at a leisurely pace. Just as Elise had when it was her time to be with Declan. But her sister was in a different place now. *And I'm still here, looking for the same things in life: love and happiness*, she thought.

Stella was sure that Declan felt the same way. And he had intimated that they were on the same page where it concerned their affections for each other. Even if the word *love* had yet to be spoken out loud by either of them. But it seemed like this was a mere formality that they would confront once the serial killer case had run its course.

I have to exercise patience till then, Stella told herself, having had years of practice doing just that. Still of concern to her, though, was the reality that she had a life—and parents—in Detroit. Not to mention, the demands of her profession that could take her far away from home at a moment's notice.

So deal with it when the time comes, she thought with determination, not wanting to let the possibilities of a solid relationship pass her by once more.

When she got back to the house and did her cool down, Stella drank a bottle of water and then called her parents. It seemed like a good idea to inform them of where things stood between her and Declan these days.

"Hey," she said cheerfully when they both appeared on the cell phone screen.

"Hi, Stella." Her mother smiled brightly. "Nice hearing from you, as always."

"Hi, honey," her father said evenly. "How's the investigation going?"

Stella filled them in, stressing that it was still ongoing, but they were making progress to some degree. They understood that these complex cases took time to unwind, unlike in a police procedural movie. But still, her parents wondered when she might be coming home to Detroit, where they liked to get together at least once a week for a family dinner.

After a moment or two, Stella gazed at them and said in a calm voice, "So, I've started seeing Declan…"

Lester Bailey cocked a brow. "Really?"

"Yes," she reiterated. "We talked and smoothed things out. The rest just fell into place."

Ngozi Bailey put a big grin on her face and declared, "Well, it's about time. You two have obviously been connected for years. There's nothing wrong with that. Elise would definitely choose you to make Declan happy, if she could no longer be around to do so."

"I agree," her father said, nodding with approval.

Stella's eyes lit up. "Thank you both." She was delighted to have their support. Now came the harder part. "I'm not sure how this will work out as far as my job and what the future holds. I'll just have to go with the flow and see what happens."

Her father said, "We understand. Do what's best for you—and Declan. We only want you to be comfortable with whatever decisions you make, honey, and we'll always be with you, geography aside."

"Absolutely," her mother concurred.

"Love you guys," Stella uttered, nearly brought to tears, while counting her blessings for having them in her life.

After disconnecting, she gave her boss, Valerie, a call to update her on the latest news with respect to the Bends Lake Predator case. Then Stella sat on a stool at the kitchen island and opened her laptop. She looked at the proposal she had been working on for her next series of books—apart from having one more book currently under contract—while hoping her agent would approve, even while pondering how to best balance her work and private life looking ahead.

DECLAN AND KEENE walked onto the porch of a single-story ranch-style home on Zeldon Road, hoping to have a word with Samuel O'Shea.

Declan took note of the maroon Volvo XC60 parked in the driveway, after having established that a black Cadillac Escalade SUV was registered under the name of Samuel L. O'Shea.

When the front door of the house opened, a slender Native American woman, perhaps in her seventies, with a gray pixie and wearing round glasses, stood there. She asked simply, "What do you want?"

After flashing his ID, Declan responded, "We're looking for Samuel O'Shea."

"He doesn't live here anymore," she said succinctly.

"And you are?" Keene asked her.

"Mary Arbuckle."

He peered at her. "We have O'Shea living at this address."

Mary batted her eyes. "I bought this house two months ago…and don't have a forwarding address for him." Her eyes shifted between them. "Feel free to look around inside, if you want."

Declan considered this, but made a judgement call that O'Shea had moved, for whatever reason, after being canned by the security agency. But to where? And could this have anything to do with his harassment of Diane Wexler? Or even more ominous reasons—such as staying on the move as a serial killer?

"That won't be necessary," Declan told her with an affable grin. "Thank you for your time."

As they headed from the house, Keene asked, "What are you thinking about O'Shea?"

Declan responded candidly, "I'm thinking we need to talk to him—and fast! If O'Shea is indeed our unsub in the murder of Diane Wexler—along with the other related homicides—there's no telling what he may do next. And to whom…"

"I'm with you there." Keene ran a hand through his hair. "The unsub—maybe O'Shea—has seemingly been steps ahead of us with each killing. It's time we gain some serious ground here…"

"Yeah, it's way overdue," Declan said firmly, as they tried to step it up a gear in pursuit of the latest person of interest.

An hour later, Declan was at his desk at the field office, still digesting the case's various and often typical twists and turns, when he got a video call request from the KBI's forensic science laboratory technician, Ike Osorno. Accepting the call, Declan watched as his face appeared. Ike, who was in his midthirties, had red hair in a brush cut and a goatee.

"What's up?" Declan asked.

With a deadpan look, Ike said, "About the Diane Wexler murder, I have some news for you." He paused. "The Crime Scene Response Team was able to pull a latent print from near the sliding back door."

"Okay…" Declan uttered impatiently.

"We ran it through the FBI's Next Generation Identification system's Advanced Fingerprint Identification Technology and got a hit!" Ike's face lit up with enthusiasm. "It came back with the name Samuel L. O'Shea."

"O'Shea?" Declan was thinking out loud as the name smacked at him like a slap in the face, along with the fact that he'd already been someone they were currently looking into as a person of interest.

"Yeah," Ike said. "Looks like this Samuel L. O'Shea has a lot of explaining to do."

"I have a feeling it's not something he'll be able to talk his way out of," Declan declared. Especially when piecing together some of the assorted parts of the puzzle. Not the least of which was Diane's expressed concerns about the former security guard. And apparently for good reason. "Good job, Ike."

"Thanks." He grinned. "Bring him in."

"We definitely intend to," Declan assured him, and thought, *But first we need to locate the suspect.*

After he ended the chat, an arrest warrant was issued for Samuel L. O'Shea, who, unless it was somehow proven otherwise, had to be considered armed and dangerous.

Chapter Fourteen

"I've seen this face before," Stella uttered with a decided edge to her voice, as she stared at the printout Declan brought home of the man suspected in the death of Diane Wexler, as well as the string of other murders.

"You have?" Declan regarded her. "Where?"

"At least, I think I have," she said, studying the image of Samuel O'Shea further as second thoughts crept into her head like a migraine. "He looks an awful lot like my high school friend Gayle Reese's cousin, Lochlyn—minus the stubble beard he had on his face. We met briefly at the gift shop in the hotel on the day I checked out." She took a breath, hating to think that someone in Gayle's family could, in fact, be a killer. Much less, a serial killer. But then again, stranger things had happened. Stella knew from experience as a criminal profiler that anyone was capable of anything—even while presenting a normal facade.

"Hmm…" Declan jutted his chin as they stood in the great room. "His name is actually Samuel L. O'Shea. The *L* could be short for Lochlyn."

Stella agreed and said intuitively, "It probably is."

"Did you learn anything about him?"

"Not really," she said regretfully. "Only that he attended

and graduated from Bends Lake High School years before I did. And likes to play tennis."

"He may also have a predilection for serial murder," Declan voiced ominously, "if this Lochlyn and Samuel L. O'Shea are one and the same—and currently at large and wanted as a person of interest in at least one homicide. I think we need to pay your high school friend a visit and see what she has to say about her cousin…and depending on that, where he might be located—"

Stella nodded. "All right." Hard as it was to have to confront Gayle about this, it was so much harder to know that a homicidal predator was running loose and, most likely, still hunting for victims.

WHEN THEY WALKED inside the gift shop, Declan took note of the attractive female behind the counter, with long blond balayage hair, as Stella had described her old high school chum, and wearing horn-rimmed eyeglasses. Were she and the suspect related? If so, Declan had to wonder if she had been privy to Samuel L. O'Shea's wrongdoings. And whether she had been covering for him, to her own detriment.

Gayle looked up as they approached her and, after smiling at Stella, said evenly, "Hey. Thought you'd left town?"

"Not quite." Stella glanced at Declan and then gave her a poker-faced look. "I actually only moved out of the hotel."

"I see." Gayle looked from one to the other and asked her, "So, what's up?"

Stella responded seriously, "This is KBI special agent Declan Delgado. If you have a moment, he has some questions for you."

And if you don't have a moment, you'll have no choice

but to make one, Declan thought surely, as Gayle said, ill at ease, "Uh, okay. What questions…?"

Declan pulled the printout of Samuel L. O'Shea from the pocket of his navy wool blazer and showed it to her as he asked straightforwardly, "Do you recognize this man?"

After pushing her glasses up, Gayle studied the picture for a beat then answered, "Yes, it looks like my cousin Lochlyn…" She turned to Stella and asked, "What's this about?"

Stella blinked and responded coolly, "Is Lochlyn's full name Samuel L. O'Shea?"

Gayle nodded. "He's always gone by his middle name, Lochlyn. At least with family and friends." Her voice shook. "What has he done…?"

Declan took over from there, sparing Stella from having to spill the beans. He said flatly, "O'Shea is suspected of murdering a woman named Diane Wexler…"

Gayle's eyes widened. "What?"

After repeating the gist of his words, Declan told her, pulling no punches, "Your cousin is in big trouble. Apart from that murder, we believe he may also be responsible for a number of other homicides perpetrated by a man with the nickname the Bends Lake Predator—"

Gayle put a hand to her mouth in disbelief and shook her head. "It can't be."

"We hope you're right about that," Stella told her gently. "Which is why we need to bring Lochlyn in and see how he responds to the accusations."

Declan said, "O'Shea no longer lives at the address his former employer gave us on Zeldon Road." He peered at her. "Do you know where he's currently staying?"

"I didn't realize he'd lost his job." Gayle frowned and her voice lowered an octave as reality seemed to set in. "Lochlyn's been living in a mobile home on Pletcher Road for the last two months."

Declan reacted to the street name and asked, "That wouldn't happen to be the Wylson Mobile Home Park, would it?"

"Yes, that's the one," she responded without hesitation.

It quickly came to Declan's mind that it was the same mobile home park where a previous suspect in the serial killer investigation, Joaquin Kalember, lived. What were the odds? Might the two be in cahoots?

Declan recalled that Kalember's alibi had held up in the attempted murder of Blake Michaud III. And though Kalember was charged with possessing child porn and illicit drugs, he had been dropped as a suspect in the Bends Lake Predator case.

Whether that was premature or not remains to be seen, Declan told himself. He fixed Gayle's face and said warningly, "It wouldn't be very smart of you to tip off O'Shea that we're coming after him. That's called obstruction of justice or accessory after the fact. Take your pick."

Gayle grimaced. "I'm not about to interfere in your investigation, Agent Delgado," she insisted.

"Good." For now, Declan was willing to give her the benefit of the doubt that she played no role in the suspected criminality by her cousin. Relatives were often the last to know what killers had been up to, when uninvolved themselves.

Gayle gazed at Stella and said firmly, "If Lochlyn is guilty, he needs to answer for it."

Stella nodded. "Sorry about this."

"Me too," she told her, voice cracking.

Declan was sorry as well—but for the victims of a serial killer and anyone else who could still find themselves in his crosshairs.

THE SUSPECT'S SUV was nowhere to be found in the Wylson Mobile Home Park, and there was no indication that Samuel L. O'Shea was inside his manufactured home as it was surrounded by a KBI Special Operations Division's High Risk Warrant Team, an FBI Special Weapons and Tactics team, Danver County Sheriff's Office's Criminal Investigations Division detectives, and the Bends Lake Police Department K-9 unit.

In advance, knowing that O'Shea might be on the move, Declan had obtained a warrant to search the premises, making sure they were doing everything by the book. He was hoping to find any additional evidence to link the suspect to Diane Wexler's murder or any of the other homicides tied to their serial killer.

With no response from inside, Declan eyed Ursula, then in a case of déjà vu, he gave the nod to go into the mobile home by force. He had his SIG Sauer P226 9 mm semi-automatic pistol out and was wearing a tactical vest for protection in case of an ambush. They stormed the place, using a battering ram to enter the premises.

There was no one present inside the brown-carpeted, sparsely furnished, two-bedroom home—but they found a stockpile of weapons and ammunition. Among the firearms was a Mossberg MC2sc Optic-Ready 9 mm pistol, a Smith & Wesson CSX 9 mm pistol, and a Military Armament Corporation 1911 Double Stack 9 mm handgun. Rifles confiscated included a Sauer 505 Synchro XT bolt-action rifle, a Beretta BRX1 bolt-action rifle and a Mossberg Patriot Predator SF rifle.

"Seems like O'Shea was preparing for war," remarked KBI special agent Noah Rudd, a tall thirtysomething African American man with a black flattop hairstyle.

"Yeah, I can see that," Declan had to agree as they went

through the place, which based on the disarray, appeared as if O'Shea had left in a hurry. Had he been given a heads-up that they were coming his way? Or was it more instinctive for the suspected killer to be wary at every turn in how he operated and came and went—for obvious reasons? Until proven to the contrary, Declan decided that Gayle hadn't gone against her word in warning her cousin that they were onto him and in hot pursuit.

"Look what we have here," Ursula said, walking into the room. Wearing a nitrile glove, she was holding a firearm. "A Taurus GX4 9 mm Luger pistol…complete with a sound suppressor—"

Declan raised a brow and said matter-of-factly, "Like the one used to shoot to death Michelle Hewlett and Trevor LeBlanc."

"My thinking precisely," she agreed, and plopped the weapon in an evidence bag. "Let's see what ballistics has to say about it."

"In the meantime, there's no reason to believe that O'Shea isn't still packing with another firearm from his arsenal," Declan told her astutely. "Making him just as serious a threat to the public as before till we can bring O'Shea in."

Ursula bobbed her head. "Right."

A BOLO alert was issued for Samuel L. O'Shea, who was considered armed and dangerous, and the black Cadillac Escalade SUV he was believed to be driving.

Declan could only hope they could get to him before anyone else had to die.

STELLA WAS STILL reeling over the notion that Gayle Reese's cousin Lochlyn—aka Samuel L. O'Shea—was now the number one suspect in a string of deaths. Though she didn't know Gayle all that well, Stella honestly believed that her high school classmate had no knowledge of O'Shea doubling as a serial killer in their midst.

Not exactly the type of secret you keep to yourself in order to protect a cousin—at the risk of being dragged into the investigation as an accomplice to taking the lives of others, Stella thought as she sat alongside Declan in his Chevrolet Malibu. He was silent with his own thoughts as the case was heating up following the raid on O'Shea's mobile home that turned up possible evidence to implicate him in one or more homicides.

They were en route to Bends Lake Hospital, where the lone survivor of the Bends Lake Predator, Blake Michaud III, was still recovering from his serious injuries. But felt well enough that he requested a meeting with investigators on the case.

Stella was curious as to what he had to say, after the description he'd given of his attacker proved to be incorrect, though it was understandable, given his state at the time and the stress he was under.

Declan broke the silence when he said from behind the wheel, "We'll get through this, you know…?"

She wondered if he was referring to the investigation or the ups and downs of their relationship. Both seemed apropos to her. She nodded. "I know."

He flashed her a slight smile. "We make a great team— whichever sport you choose."

She couldn't help but smile at the sports metaphor. "You think?"

Touching her hand with his free hand, he said prophetically, "Wait and see."

"I will," she promised, taking him at his word that better days were ahead, once this was all behind them.

After arriving at the hospital, they went to Blake Michaud's room and found him sitting on an armchair, eating ice cream. Stella imagined that he looked much better than the last time Declan had visited him.

"This is Special Agent Bailey," Declan introduced her, after reiterating his own identification.

"Thanks for coming," Blake said, looking from one to the other as he put the ice cream bowl on a table.

Nodding, Declan asked him, "How are you feeling?"

"Better than the last time you were here. Doctors tell me I'll be released this week. I'm counting the minutes till that happens so I can get back to my life."

"Good." Declan tilted his head. "Do you have new information to share?"

"Yeah," Blake answered thoughtfully. "I heard that you have a new suspect in the case?"

Declan confirmed, "We do."

"I saw his picture on the TV screen." Blake shifted in the chair. "It was him—Samuel O'Shea—the guy who shot me—"

Declan glanced at Stella and back to him keenly. "You're sure about that?"

"Yes, I'm sure," Blake replied without prelude. "I know my initial description of the attacker was off. But I was under medication and somewhat disoriented at the time—and wasn't able to think clearly."

"And you can now?" Stella questioned him.

"Yeah. I've had nothing but time to go over it—him—in my head. That's the face—and the eyes—I saw... He's the one who shot me and left me for dead!"

"Okay," Declan told him. "That's helpful to the investigation."

Stella felt the same and asked curiously, "Had you ever seen the shooter before the encounter...?"

Blake stared at the question for a long moment, then responded contemplatively, "It's possible—but no time, in particular, comes to mind."

She considered if O'Shea could have stalked him for whatever reason as a target—before shooting him with the clear intent to kill. Or was the victim, like apparently most of the others, simply at the wrong place at the wrong time?

Declan squared his shoulders and told him, "If anything else comes to mind about your attacker, let us know."

"I will." Blake drew his brows together. "Hope you get the creep—before anyone else has to go through what I have."

"I understand where you're coming from," Declan said sincerely.

Stella added, "We both do." He may have been the lucky one, in comparison to the other victims of the Bends Lake Predator, but she knew that survivor's guilt—or survivor syndrome—was a real affliction as a facet of post-traumatic stress disorder. And a serious burden, in and of itself, for anyone who walked away from a serial killer. She hoped Blake would get the treatment he would need to deal with it, once released.

In the interim, he had provided them with another important piece of the puzzle in pointing the finger at Samuel L. O'Shea as the Bends Lake Predator.

Chapter Fifteen

The next morning, Declan sat at his desk in the field office, assessing the information they had on the still-at-large suspect, Samuel O'Shea. There were plenty of reasons to believe that he was the serial killer they were trying to capture. O'Shea had managed to evade them through clever maneuvers, handpicking victims when most vulnerable and likely with a preplanned escape route, skillful circumventing of solid evidence to tie him to the crimes and just plain old luck that worked to his benefit.

But your luck's about to run out, O'Shea, Declan told himself, feeling as certain of that as he had in the investigation up to this point. They would soon have the elusive predator in custody. But soon couldn't come soon enough.

Especially when Declan would much rather be focused on Stella and just how far they could go from here, if both were willing to let down their barriers against getting hurt. He had a good feeling that this was well within their capabilities—and a strong desire to build something special together.

Refocusing on the matter at hand, Declan looked at his laptop and did a deep dive on Samuel O'Shea to see what made him tick, to the extent that this was possible. He saw that O'Shea had a checkered past as far as his employment history, having worked in construction, sales, wilderness-related jobs and, most recently, security. He'd been married once, to Tonya O'Shea, though it ended in divorce three years ago after an apparently contentious relationship between them. The ex-wife had since remarried and relocated to the Big Island of Hawaii.

Declan took note of O'Shea's stockpile of weapons, some of which had been legally purchased. Others were illegally owned firearms. The latter included those he was suspected to be using to perpetrate serial homicides.

I wonder what handgun he's carrying at the moment, Declan contemplated with concern, fearing the suspect could use it before being located and taken into custody.

After conferring with Kimberly Ullerich, the special agent in charge, and getting her full support, he convened the task force for an important update on where things stood in the investigation.

Standing at the front of the conference room, Declan lifted the stylus pen and turned to the touch screen display. He put O'Shea's image on the monitor and said measuredly, "Thirty-eight-year-old Samuel Lochlyn O'Shea, a former security guard, has emerged as our chief suspect in the Bends Lake Predator investigation. Between raiding his mobile home and coming away with crucial evidence and other key evidence that's come to light, it's pretty apparent that O'Shea is the serial killer we're after—"

Declan talked a bit more about this and then turned it over to forensic technician Ike Osorno, who scratched his goatee and said evenly, "We were able to collect a DNA sample from the top of the trash can on Tutler's Way, where the Springfield Armory 1911 Ronin Operator 9 mm handgun linked to the Bends Lake Predator was discov-

ered. The sample was put into the Federal DNA Database
Unit's National DNA Index System as part of CODIS. It
was initially an unknown forensic profile—till a DNA
profile collected during the raid of Samuel O'Shea's mobile home proved to be a match. In other words, it was
O'Shea's DNA that was on the garbage can top, tying him
to the firearm…"

Once that had sunk in, Ursula came forward and Declan
handed her the stylus, after which she brought up a firearm on the screen and said calmly, "The search of Samuel
O'Shea's residence resulted in some interesting finds—
including a stockpile of weapons and ammo. Among the
firearms seized was the Taurus GX4 9 mm Luger pistol
with a suppressor that you see on the monitor. We handed
it, along with the ammo collected, over to the forensic science lab. They compared this to the bullets and spent shell
casings shot through a Taurus GX4 pistol's gun barrel with
five lands and grooves and a left-hand twist used in the
murders of Michelle Hewlett and Trevor LeBlanc—and it
was a perfect match." She drew a breath. "It was the handgun that was used in the double homicide—with O'Shea
pulling the trigger…"

Declan gave a few more remarks afterward, finishing
in a confident voice. "The walls are now closing in on
Samuel Lochlyn O'Shea. Though he remains at large, all
roads out of Bends Lake are being surveilled, and he's effectively boxed in. This doesn't mean he isn't still a serious threat. O'Shea is believed to be armed and dangerous.
Not to mention desperate enough that he's as much unpredictable as he had been predictable in his deviant pattern
of behavior. That makes him all the more a wild card as
we search to find and end the serial killer's reign of murder and mayhem…"

WHEN SHE WAS asked to give a closing assessment of Samuel O'Shea, Stella was more than willing to do her part in putting forth a sense of the mindset of O'Shea. Or at the very least, interpreting his calculus for avoiding capture while managing to stay active to feed his homicidal tendencies.

She only wished that Gayle hadn't been a party to her cousin's willingness to become a serial killer—right under her nose. Stella understood, though, that most such skillful killers had a facade, by design. They were able to pull the wool over the unsuspecting eyes of those they purported to be closest to. Why should this time be any different? O'Shea was obviously more than content—not to mention indifferent to how this would impact Gayle in the long run—to exploit her kinship to appear normal himself, while being anything but in his pattern of behavior. It would ultimately take courage and strength by Gayle to overcome Lochlyn's ultimate betrayal and move on with her life as best as possible.

Stella inhaled softly and, after gazing at Declan's handsome face and seeing a twinkle of affection in his eyes, said to the team, "Samuel O'Shea's been exposed for the serial killer he has become. For the better part of his serial killing, he's been totally in his element, living like the cat that ate the canary. But now that he can no longer hide behind the cloak of anonymity and the satisfaction of having a leg up on the rest of us, he is likely calculating his next move to keep his freedom. At the same time, deep down inside, in the vein of the majority of serial killers—O'Shea had to know that his days as a killing machine were not unlimited. By no means, though, does that mean he is ready to throw in the towel. Out of desperation, O'Shea will likely try to find a way to escape the dragnet, even against the odds. That makes him a ticking time bomb that could ex-plode with more killings or other aberrant behavior—if not defused through an arrest or otherwise prevented from doing more harm to others…"

She looked at Declan again and carried on thoughtfully, "I should add that, as with most serial killers, O'Shea could surrender if cornered with no way out. Or he might well go out in a blaze of glory—figuring he's better off dead than spending the rest of his life behind bars. It'll be his call." *Though O'Shea's pursuers might have some say in the matter,* Stella told herself, if there was another way that wouldn't put others at risk. Still, she was well aware of the value in keeping him alive to learn from as a crimi-nal profiler.

"I couldn't agree more with you on how this could end," Declan told her as they started to disband. "I can't get in-side O'Shea's head, as you probably can, but there's a third option for bringing this to a conclusion. And that's taking the decision-making out of O'Shea's hands."

"Hmm…" Stella lifted a brow. "You mean capturing him by surprise, before he could react, one way or another?"

Declan gave a thin smile. "Exactly. That is, getting the jump on him with such force and determination that he doesn't know what hit him. Not till it's too late. Hopefully, this would result in O'Shea being taken into custody alive, so that he lives a very, very long time in prison, where he belongs."

"That would certainly be the best-case scenario," she said, nodding. "First, we need to find him and go from there."

"Yeah," Declan concurred. "That shouldn't take much longer. Now that we're onto him, there are only so many places he can duck and hide."

Stella felt the same way. But that still represented quite a few nooks and crannies for O'Shea to try and skirt the law in. In her thinking, this was still one too many when dealing with a cold and calculated serial killer.

DECLAN WAS SITTING in a booth across from Stella at the Bends Lake Coffee House on Rocklear Street, sipping on a breve coffee as his mind wandered between the imminent arrest of Samuel O'Shea and forging ahead with what he hoped would be a love for the ages. He wanted the latter more than anything, though the former carried a lot of weight too, in terms of getting it—the serial killer headache—off their backs, once and for all.

Stella, who was drinking a red-eye coffee, broke his reverie when she asked, ill at ease, "Do you think Gayle could be in danger, as long as O'Shea remains at large?"

Declan jutted his chin musingly. "Doesn't seem like he would go after her, as someone he appears to care for. Beyond that, being on the run while the authorities try to close in on him doesn't exactly leave O'Shea with much wiggle room to target Gayle, whatever his reason might be." Declan tasted the coffee. "Of course, I could be wrong. It's possible that O'Shea could turn on the one person who had his back. At least till she discovered his dark side."

Stella narrowed her eyes and said, "I think I should go talk to her."

Declan raised a brow. "You really think that's a good idea?"

"I know we don't know each other all that well, and I can only imagine what she may be going through at the moment—but having connected at all again, I kind of feel I should reach out to Gayle and offer my support as a friend, as opposed to an FBI special agent." Stella sipped the espresso. "At the very least, I could warn her to be on guard, just to be on the safe side."

"Good idea," Declan said, though they were already keeping tabs on Gayle Reese's workplace and residence, in case O'Shea tried to contact her out of desperation. Right now, though, Declan was more concerned for Stella's health and security. He didn't want to see her end up falling into a serial killer's crosshairs, even if she was more than capable of defending herself as a member of the Bureau. But trying to keep her out of harm's way for personal reasons was probably not the way to go. Not when Stella seemed determined to be there for her high school chum—which was the type of consideration and loyalty that endeared Declan to her, among other qualities she possessed. He eyed her over his mug. "I'm sure Gayle will appreciate you being there for her, under the circumstances."

"She should," Stella concurred. "But honestly, I'm probably thinking just as much about myself and how important it is to have someone there when dealing with a break in family bonding."

"I understand," Declan told her, sitting back. *All too well*, he thought, knowing he hadn't been entirely in Stella's corner as much as he should have when Elise passed away. At the time, he was too caught up in his own grief to lean enough into hers. It was a major regret, and he only wished he could turn back the clock. The good news was that they now had an opportunity to move the clock forward, where he hoped to more than make up for lost time.

STELLA HAD NO qualms returning to the hotel where she'd first stayed when coming back to Bends Lake to work on a serial killer case. At the time, she'd wanted to have as little to do with Declan as possible. Certainly not on an intimate level. But this had all changed. Now she wanted to have everything to do with him as a man who had stolen her heart, body and soul.

As it related to Gayle, Stella wasn't quite sure if she would be welcomed back or not. Neither of them could have expected that Gayle's cousin Lochlyn would become the central character in a serial killer investigation that had brought multiple law enforcement agencies together with one common goal. That being to stop the fatal shootings and hold the person responsible fully accountable.

It seemed to Stella that Gayle felt the same way, recalling her words to that effect: *If Lochlyn is guilty, he needs to answer for it.*

And he will have to at that, Stella told herself with conviction as she watched Gayle approach her in the hotel lobby.

"Hey," Stella said equably.

"Hey." Gayle's eyes were red, as though she had been crying. "I'm glad you wanted to see me. I wanted to see you too."

They sat on plush dark red accent chairs angled toward one another, after which Stella asked sympathetically, "Are you all right?"

Gayle's voice cracked when she answered, "As much as one could be after learning that a cousin who you thought you knew was apparently someone you didn't really know at all. At least not in ways that I could ever have imagined…"

"That could happen to any of us," Stella pointed out. "None of us can read the minds of people who choose to keep their darkest thoughts to themselves."

"I suppose." Gayle shifted her body uncomfortably. "But it still hurts."

"I know." Stella regarded her for a moment or two, thoughtfully. "I have to ask—has Lochlyn tried to contact you?"

"No," she replied without delay. "And I wouldn't want him to, as I'm not sure what I would say to him. Or, for that matter, what he could possibly say to me to justify the truly awful things he's being accused of doing."

"All right." Stella was relieved to know that O'Shea had at least accorded Gayle that much respect in not drawing her any further into his web of terror than he already had. If only by association and bloodline. Even so, desperation could still call for desperate measures from the wanted serial killer. "If by chance Lochlyn does try to reach out to you, Gayle, you need to let me know, and I'll do everything in my power to have this end peacefully—with Lochlyn turning himself in." She realized this was easier said than done, as O'Shea appeared bent on remaining on the loose—while continuing to be a viable threat to anyone whom he might come into contact with.

"I will." Gayle leaned forward to place her hand on Stella's. "Thank you."

Stella nodded. She wanted to say it was her job to run interference. But it went beyond that in this instance. Gayle deserved to see this through with the least amount of damage for her to digest. Just as Declan once did when he lost his first true love—before the time would come to be given another chance at it, which was something Stella embraced with equal optimism.

LOCHLYN WAS WEARING a Kansas City Royals baseball cap tilted low on his forehead, making it harder to identify him. He kept a low profile while on the run from the law after they raided his house, confiscating most of his firearms, and put out a warrant for his arrest. He was angered at the thought, while watching from afar as his cousin Gayle was talking to her friend from high school, Stella.

Having been intrigued by her as someone who reminded him of his ex-wife, he'd coaxed out of Gayle that Stella was an FBI special agent and criminal profiler. Only after he had put two and two together did Lochlyn realize that he had seen the attractive Stella before. It was at Hedy's Club, where she was sitting with, he suspected, other law enforcement personnel. He imagined that they were probably discussing the Bends Lake Predator case.

His own alter ego.

He homed in on Stella chatting with Gayle. *Just what are you saying to my cuz?* Lochlyn asked himself, nostrils flaring. Or vice versa. Was the FBI agent trying to turn his cousin against him?

Lochlyn sucked in a deep breath, controlling his anger, while realizing he couldn't risk being made by any law enforcement who might be lurking around and allowing his presence to be known by either of the women. He had to get out of there without drawing any undue attention.

He peered at Stella once more and told himself, *You and your colleagues may think you've won the battle, but don't get too comfortable in that belief. This isn't over. Trust me.*

We'll see each other again, Special Agent Stella Bailey, Lochlyn promised, but on his own terms. Not hers. Or those of the other law enforcement personnel who wanted to take him down then gloat about it afterward, patting themselves on the back. But he wasn't about to go down easily. It wasn't in his DNA. He was not quite through with his self-proclaimed mission of elimination.

He took one last look at the special agent and his cousin,

then quietly found a side exit and slithered out of the hotel unscathed, while deep dark thoughts circulated in his mind with pleasure and promise as he walked away.

Chapter Sixteen

A license plate reader picked up the black Cadillac Escalade SUV that was registered to Samuel L. O'Shea cruising down Brownstin Lane, not far from the Nineteenth Street intersection. As a squad car trailed the suspect's vehicle, Declan converged on the scene in his Chevrolet Malibu, along with other law enforcement. They were all on the same page in wanting to stop the suspect in his tracks, once and for all.

Only then can we all breathe a collective sigh of relief in getting a stone-cold killer off the streets, Declan told himself, as he reached Nineteenth Street ahead of the Escalade, where a blockade had already been put in place to stop oncoming traffic and prevent the suspect from advancing farther.

Exiting his own vehicle, Declan met up with Stella, who came with Arielle and other law enforcement, including sharpshooters. Everyone wore ballistic vests, not knowing how this thing might end, but prepared for O'Shea to engage in a gunfight rather than be taken in alive.

"You ready for this?" Declan asked Stella, though knowing the answer.

"I think we all are," she told him matter-of-factly. "Let's

just get it over with—hopefully with O'Shea laying down his firearm peacefully."

"Wouldn't that be nice?" Arielle chipped in, not sounding too optimistic.

"Yeah." Declan kept his mind open either way, as he spoke to the SWAT team commander Jay Yonamine, a hulking fortysomething man with a short brown military haircut. "Let's do this."

Jay nodded, eyed others in place and ready for whatever came their way, then declared, "It's game time!"

Game time it is, Declan told himself, as he turned to see the suspect's SUV approaching.

It was quickly surrounded by law enforcement vehicles, shielding armed personnel, including Declan and Stella.

"KBI. Get out of the vehicle—slowly and with your hands up!" Declan ordered the suspect. "Now!"

The suspect appeared startled, but obeyed, opening the door and stepping outside carefully. He put his hands atop his head, as though he'd been through this scenario before.

"Don't move!" Jay's voice boomed from behind an FBI van.

Declan peered at the suspect, studying him as though a specimen in a laboratory. He was white and looked to be in his midtwenties, tall and lanky, with blond hair in a half-up ponytail and a brunette chin strap beard.

"It's not O'Shea," Stella said, a catch to her voice.

"No kidding," Declan responded sardonically, while in complete agreement. Yet it was definitely the suspect's SUV. "So where the hell is Samuel L. O'Shea? And why is this man driving his Cadillac Escalade?"

"Good question," she uttered.

They wasted little time in seeking answers, as the SUV driver was ordered onto his knees before it was deemed safe enough for law enforcement to rush him. He was checked for weapons—and found to be unarmed—pulled to his feet and handcuffed behind his back.

Only then did Declan put his SIG Sauer firearm back in its holster and approach the man. "I'm Special Agent Delgado. Who are you?"

The man blinked blue eyes and responded, "Martin Poole."

Declan favored him with a hard stare. "What are you doing with this vehicle?"

Poole hunched a shoulder flippantly. "Uh, driving it."

"I can see that," Declan said tersely. "Question is why?" He considered whether this was a ploy by O'Shea to buy himself some time. "Did Samuel O'Shea, the owner of the SUV, put you up to this to send us on a wild-goose chase?"

"I don't know anything about that," Poole claimed, seemingly beating around the bush.

"What do you know?" Declan glared at him. "This isn't a game. The man the Cadillac Escalade is registered to is wanted for murder. If you're an accomplice—"

"I'm not." Poole licked his lips nervously. "Look, I stole the SUV, okay? I saw a man ditch it and run off, as if wanting to have nothing more to do with it. I checked it out and saw the key was left in the ignition. I needed a ride, so I took it. That's all."

Declan regarded him dubiously and said, "Describe the man who ditched the Escalade—"

Poole described Samuel O'Shea to a T. Though there was still reason to believe Poole's story could be made up, it was just as plausible that he was telling the truth. Declan watched as Arielle came up and asked Poole, "Did you see him get into another vehicle?"

Poole shook his head. "No, he just ran down the street."

Declan asked, "What street was that?"

Poole replied anxiously, "Trowridge Avenue, a few blocks from Brownstin Lane."

Not too far away, Declan thought. But far enough to give O'Shea some latitude to seek other transportation to remain on the lamb.

"Take him away," Declan said, scowling at Martin Poole, who, at the very least, would be charged with auto theft. Even if he happened to have stolen a vehicle that belonged to the Bends Lake Predator, who had managed to outsmart them again.

Declan saw this as only a short-term victory for O'Shea, while conceding that short was relative. Meaning that it still gave the suspect enough time to cause more trouble—if they didn't catch up to him soon. But at least they had O'Shea's SUV in their possession, which would undoubtedly provide more evidence to tie him to the vehicle and, by association, the homicides the suspect was believed to have committed.

LOCHLYN WAS ONLY too happy to have outsmarted the authorities. Once he knew that they had latched on to his Cadillac Escalade, rather than switch the license plates but risk being stopped anyway, he chose to unload the SUV instead and find another vehicle to drive and in which to make his escape.

The fact that he spotted, while hidden in a wooded area, the Escalade being driven by someone looking for a free ride, played right into his hands. Lochlyn would use the subterfuge of pointing the KBI in the wrong direction to stay one step ahead of them, while continuing his deadly agenda as the Bends Lake Predator.

After which he would find a way to get out of Dodge,

so to speak, and seek greener pastures to resume killing as he saw fit.

Lochlyn was on the move, his eyes darting this way and that to keep abreast of his surroundings and any signs that the authorities were onto him. He wished he could say goodbye to Gayle as the one person who seemed to give a damn about him. But circumstances stood in the way. That certainly wasn't true where it concerned his ex-wife. And definitely not Diane Wexler, who wouldn't give him the time of day and paid the price. Not even his last employer, who gave him the boot unjustly, leaving him high and dry.

But who needed any of them? He was always one to carve his own path. Why should this be any different? Why would he want it to be, when he always landed on his feet at the end of the day?

Lochlyn spied a bald-headed elderly man in front of a home on Youngston Street. He was about to enter a white Lincoln Navigator Reserve.

Perfect for me, Lochlyn thought, grinning as he took a black Wilson Combat SFX9 9 mm Luger handgun that had a silencer out of his jacket pocket. He moved briskly toward the man before he could enter the car.

Sticking the gun into the old man's shocked face, Lochlyn said simply, "We can either do this the easy way or the hard way." Then he grinned as the man seemed to be considering his options and told him with a sardonic chuckle, "Actually, I think I like the easy way for me and the hard way for you..."

Lochlyn pulled the trigger, hitting the man in the head twice in rapid-fire action, watching unemotionally as he fell down like a collapsed building.

Too bad, so sad, Lochlyn thought heartlessly, as he took

the dead man's keys and claimed the car as his own before getting behind the wheel, starting it and driving off, while leaving behind another victim.

AFTER RECEIVING THE call about a fatal carjacking on Youngston Street, Ursula went to the scene, alongside Special Agent Noah Rudd, who drove. Both were suspicious about the timing of the crime, which coincided with the hunt for Samuel O'Shea, who had ditched his Cadillac Escalade and was on the run.

Ursula was still smarting that O'Shea had outmaneuvered them yet again in his latest move to dodge accountability for his lethal criminality. They had to put a stop to his lunacy, once and for all. But had the serial killer struck again in the meantime?

When they arrived at the scene, both special agents rendezvoused with the first responder, Bends Lake Police Officer Jeremy Ponte, who said bleakly, "We've got an eighty-one-year-old dead male, identified as Sheldon Ferreira. He was apparently about to enter his vehicle, when the carjacker took him by surprise."

Ursula eyed the frail victim, who was lying face down in his own blood, two bullet wounds visible in the back of his head. She spotted the spent shell casings near the curb and wondered if the man had tried to put up a fight for his life—possibly triggering the shooting. Or had he thought it was a losing cause and succumbed to the fateful moment at hand?

Noah regarded the victim and, furrowing his brow, commented, "Looks like an execution-style killing."

Jeremy said, "I was thinking the same thing. I have a feeling the victim didn't necessarily know what was coming, but still found himself on the wrong end of a gun and helpless to defend himself."

"Any witnesses?" Ursula asked him.

"Yeah." Jeremy jutted his chin. "A 911 call reported a man driving off in the victim's white Lincoln Navigator Reserve."

"Hmm," Noah muttered thoughtfully. "We'll get the license plate number and put out a BOLO alert for the vehicle and driver."

Ursula looked around. "I'm guessing that some of the homes on this block and nearby have surveillance cameras that may have caught the unsub on foot prior to the carjacking—or afterward when driving off with the stolen vehicle."

"We're checking that out," Jeremy told her.

"Good." Ursula took out her cell phone and contacted Declan, knowing that they were possibly dealing with another murder courtesy of Samuel O'Shea.

Declan told her bluntly, "At this point, I wouldn't put it past O'Shea to go after anyone who got in his way or had something he desperately needed—like another means of transportation."

"Neither would I," she admitted. "We'll see if we can make the connection to O'Shea."

After they ended the call, Ursula and Noah did some door-to-door interviews before the medical examiner and Crime Scene Response Team arrived to perform their respective duties on the latest homicide to hit Bends Lake.

INSIDE HIS HOME OFFICE, Declan and Stella were standing at the workstation, reviewing surveillance footage that showed a man who closely resembled Samuel O'Shea driving the Lincoln Navigator Reserve registered to Sheldon

Ferreira, a widower, who had been shot to death by the carjacker.

"It's him," Declan stated with near certainty. "O'Shea is stooping to the lowest depths in his penchant for violence and escaping justice."

Stella, gazing at the laptop in front of them, said, "Not surprising, really. It's almost like now that the curtain of anonymity has been pulled back, he feels emboldened enough to own up to shooting people in broad daylight. He's pretty much daring us to catch him if we can."

It was a dare that spoke to Declan. He took it personally, within the context of a KBI special agent, wanting to be the one to slap the cuffs on the serial killer, if possible. "We're more than happy to oblige," Declan said, an edge to his voice. "We know what O'Shea is driving, and there's no escaping Bends Lake—so the clock's ticking, and his time is definitely running out."

"Seems to be the case," she concurred. "Problem is, until such time, who else will be dragged into his horror show— and maybe never again see the light of day...?"

It was a question that Declan asked himself, more than once, disliking the answer more the longer this thing went on. He could only be optimistic in replying, "No one if we're lucky."

She cocked a brow. "And if we aren't?"

He swallowed, touching her soft hand. "Then O'Shea could still set his sights on others, with all bets off on the outcome—"

But Declan refused to go there, with his gut telling him that this was about to come to a head, one way or the other.

Stella looked at him and switched the subject, as she said, "I thought we could do takeout for dinner this evening."

"What did you have in mind?" He was amenable to taking a break from making each other meals—even if he never tired of feeding her and watching as she ate, whenever the opportunity arose.

"I have a taste for Chinese food. Harry's Wok House isn't far from here."

Declan told her, "I know the place. Been there once or twice."

She nodded and said, "I can order and we'll pick it up—along with a bottle of wine."

He smiled and imagined tasting the wine on her lips with a kiss. "Sounds good to me."

"Okay." Stella gazed at him and took out her cell phone.

Declan turned back to his laptop, where he had a video chat request from Josephine Okamura. After accepting it, he gazed at her and said, "Hey."

She smiled, touching her glasses. "I wanted to let you know that we were able to analyze the bullets that killed Sheldon Ferreira and the spent shell casings found at the crime scene…"

He peered at her. "All right."

Josephine stated evenly, "Aside from being a match, they came from a Wilson Combat SFX9 9 mm Luger pistol—and were shot through a gun barrel with five lands and grooves and a right-hand twist."

"Hmm…" Declan mused about the latest firearm that was used by Samuel O'Shea to carry out his homicides. A search of his Cadillac Escalade had come up empty insofar as he hadn't left behind any weapons after dumping the SUV as part of his effort to evade capture. But O'Shea's DNA and prints were present throughout the Escalade, tying it directly to him and the serial murders he perpetrated while using the vehicle to come and go from crime scenes. "I'll make a note of your findings on the hand-gun, Josephine, as we piece together our case against the suspect."

"Thanks." She smiled. "Happy to do my part here."

Declan nodded and ended the chat. He saw that Stella was off the phone and said to her, "Are we all set for some Chinese takeout?"

"Yes." Stella grinned. "Hope you're hungry?"

"I am." Declan moved up to her. "Especially for this…" He cupped her cheeks and gave Stella a nice long kiss.

"Umm…" she cooed, touching her lips. "I meant food."

"Yeah, that too." He laughed. "Let's go pick up our dinner."

AFTER DECLAN DROVE into the parking lot of the strip mall on Lewellen Drive and parked, they got out of the car and he said, "While you're grabbing the food, I'll head over to the store and get the wine."

"Sounds good," Stella said, eyeing the Bends Lake Mini Mart, two places down from Harry's Wok House. "I'll meet you outside."

"Okay." Declan caressed her cheek, sending electrical sparks throughout Stella's body, as was often the case when he touched her.

They separated and she went inside the Chinese restaurant, where she picked up the order of vegetable spring rolls and fried chicken wings.

While paying, Stella hardly noticed the man wearing a hoodie who entered the place and moved in her direction. Only when she caught sight of him in her periphery did she turn his way. It took Stella only an instant to recognize Gayle's cousin Lochlyn, aka Samuel L. O'Shea.

His countenance dark with deviance, Lochlyn said

menacingly, "Nice to see you again, Stella." He laughed crudely. "Or maybe not so much—for you, anyway..."

Stella was just about to offer a sarcastic comeback for the serial killer suspect, but held her tongue when she saw him remove from his pocket the Wilson Combat SFX9 9 mm Luger pistol that Declan had alluded to during the drive that O'Shea had used to commit murder during the carjacking.

She managed to control her emotions as Stella said coolly, "You don't have to do this, Lochlyn."

He chuckled and snorted, "I'm afraid I do, Special Agent Bailey. After poisoning Gayle against me, you've left me little choice. Now, let's walk out of here together, so I don't have to shoot both you and that pretty young thing at the counter for the bargain—"

"All right." Stella got the message, loud and clear. She certainly had no wish to see anyone else hurt by this monster. That included herself. But she knew that all bets were off, so long as he held a gun to her chest, having already shown a willingness to pull the trigger, time and time again.

At gunpoint, Stella led the way as she and her accoster exited the restaurant, not knowing if she would ever see Declan again, to tell him how much she loved and felt loved by him.

Chapter Seventeen

Declan had just paid for a bottle of Cabernet Sauvignon and was leaving the checkout counter when his cell phone rang. He pulled it out and saw that the caller was Ursula then answered equably, "Hey."

"The Lincoln Navigator Reserve stolen by Samuel O'Shea was spotted by an automated license plate reader surveillance camera on Lewellen Drive," she told him. "It looked to be headed for the Mackton Center strip mall…"

"What?" Declan reacted as a sense of dread swept over him like an ominous shroud. His heart skipped a beat as he uttered, "I happen to be there right now, at a store. Worse is that Stella's here too, inside a Chinese restaurant picking up an order."

Ursula sighed into the phone. "You don't think O'Shea is coming after her—?"

"I sure as hell hope not," Declan responded, but his pulse quickened as he told himself instinctively, *I honestly can't rule that out. Can I?* "But it's entirely possible," he had to admit. "Maybe O'Shea somehow tracked Stella and feels he has a score to settle now that he was ratted out by his cousin Gayle Reese—with Stella the common denominator."

"That doesn't sound good." Ursula groaned. "We're zeroing in on the location even as we speak—and we'll take O'Shea down." She paused. "Go get Stella."

"Yeah, I will." Declan sucked in a deep breath as he headed out of the store as though his life depended on it. In actuality, it was Stella's life that was in jeopardy. The mere thought of losing someone else he was in love with made him weak in the knees. Or worse, totally heartbroken. He couldn't bear not being able to have the type of relationship with Stella that they had both deprived themselves of experiencing the first time around.

I owe it to you, Stella, to make things right, once and for all, Declan told himself as he left the store. He was glad that he had instinctively brought along his SIG Sauer P226 pistol. Unfortunately, Stella had not armed herself with her Glock 19 9x19 mm handgun. She had trusted him to protect them both. *I can't let her down—my love*, he thought, with fierce determination, even as Declan had a dreadful feeling that he might have already been too late to act.

WHY DIDN'T I bring my pistol? Stella asked herself, in a classic case of second-guessing when the chips were down, as was the case in her current predicament. Too late now. She had little choice but to deal with the situation as it was— knowing that Samuel O'Shea fully intended to kill her, if he got his way, much like the others whose lives he ended by gunfire.

After he had used his free hand to unnecessarily frisk her for weapons, seeing that her form-fitting knit top and straight leg jeans left little room for a concealed firearm, O'Shea said smugly, "Had to check. Wouldn't have wanted you to catch me napping by whipping out your gun from somewhere and actually shooting me with it." He laughed mirthlessly.

They had moved away from the Chinese restaurant, and Stella had dropped her takeout order, figuring that food was the least of her concerns right now. She suspected that Declan may have left the store and was privy to what was going on. But what if that wasn't the case? Would it be too little, too late for him to intervene?

"Where are we going?" Stella asked her assailant, if only to buy time and contemplate how she might be able to gain the upper hand.

"Away from here—and KBI special agent Delgado," O'Shea said arrogantly, holding the Wilson Combat SFX9 9 mm Luger pistol fitted with a silencer to her back. "I followed you from the hotel after I saw you talking to Gayle—and to a house with Delgado there. It wasn't difficult putting two and two together. Just needed an opportunity to separate you from the special agent—to make you pay for sticking your nose where it wasn't wanted…before getting out of Bends Lake for good."

Stella could see that they were headed toward the Lincoln Navigator that O'Shea had carjacked, which was parked at the far end of the Mini Mart. She looked at the culprit over her shoulder and, recalling his accusation that she had poisoned Gayle against him, uttered pointedly, "Just for the record, I never stuck my nose anywhere. Whatever issues you have with Gayle, you have no one to blame but yourself. As far as her cooperation, she really had no choice, since you were wanted on suspicion of numerous murders. So why not just give up, Lochlyn—instead of only compounding your troubles by killing me?"

Stella doubted she would be able to reach any degree of compunction inside him as a serial killer bent on carrying out his maniacal agenda, but hoped—if nothing else—to rattle him just a little. Especially as she sensed that they were being watched and something was about to go down that could mean the end of her life…or the beginning of a future.

O'Shea laughed sardonically. "Oh, you'd like that, wouldn't you? Sorry, not going to happen. I'm not about to throw in the towel. I'm having too much fun running rings around the KBI, FBI, PD, you name it." They reached the stolen vehicle, and he opened the passenger door. Aiming the gun at her, he gave her a once-over and said musingly, "By the way, you remind me so much of my ex-wife… Should've killed her when I had the chance." His forehead furrowed. "Oh well… Looks like I've found the perfect substitute—in you…"

Stella swallowed thickly while assessing his illogical perspective. "Taking my life will never make up for letting your ex-wife off the hook," she argued, doubting it would make any difference at this point.

"We'll see about that," he hissed, then ordered with a sneer, "Get in, Agent Bailey. We're going for a little drive to put some distance between here and your boyfriend—otherwise, I'll have to shoot you right here and now and be done with it…"

"Okay, you win," Stella pretended to give in. "I'll do whatever you say." She furrowed her brow at him. "Isn't that what you've come to expect from all your victims before shooting them to death? To totally submit to your will and their fate?"

O'Shea chuckled. "Yeah, that's about the size of it. Never fails." He laughed again and stopped on a dime. "Inside…" He pointed at the passenger seat.

Just then, they both heard a noise, causing O'Shea to look away from her for just an instant. *It's now or possibly never*, Stella told herself. Swiftly grabbing the wrist of his gun hand, she twisted the barrel away from her face—then turned to a karate self-defense technique she had learned. With her fist, she hit him with a *choku zuki*— or straight punch—in the face, as hard as she could. She quickly followed with a *mawashi zuki*—which was a round hook punch—to the jaw and then gave him a *hiza geri*, or knee kick to the groin.

Her quick moves caught him off guard as O'Shea howled in pain and fury, while trying to regain control of his gun hand. As Stella fought to stay alive, Declan appeared seemingly out of nowhere and twisted O'Shea's wrist in a way that forced the Wilson Combat SFX9 handgun out of his hand, falling to the ground. But not before O'Shea managed to get off a shot that went harmlessly into the air.

Afterward, Declan hit him with a hard uppercut to the chin and another blow to the right cheek before stepping aside as a wobbly O'Shea was summarily surrounded by heavily armed law enforcement, who overcame his feeble efforts to resist, taking him into custody.

Ursula, putting her firearm back in its holster, gazed at Stella and asked, concern in her tone, "Are you all right?"

"Yes, thank goodness." Stella smiled at her. "A little unnerved but otherwise unharmed."

"Great." Ursula regarded Declan. "The system worked."

"Yeah, it did," he acknowledged, giving her an appreciative nod.

As Ursula stepped away, Stella hugged Declan shamelessly. "Thanks for coming to my rescue," she uttered softly.

"Believe me, I didn't have any other choice," he spoke matter-of-factly. "I wasn't about to let O'Shea claim another victim—least of all you."

"That's nice to know," Stella cooed. "The thought that

this could have turned out very differently—" She choked back the words.

"It didn't." Declan touched her cheek. "Neither of us were ready for this—us—to end. Not in that way."

Stella grinned knowingly. "No, we weren't."

"Have to say, you did a great job in getting O'Shea's attention." Declan gave a laugh. "You put some moves on him that took away any perceived advantage he thought he had."

She chuckled. "Karate is always a nice go-to when all else fails."

"No arguing with that." He took her hand and said cheerfully, "Why don't we go and reorder that Chinese meal, so we'll have something tasty to eat with the wine I purchased."

She chuckled. "Sounds like a good idea to me."

THE FOLLOWING DAY, after giving Samuel Lochlyn O'Shea a night to mull over just what he'd done and would have to answer for, Declan sat across from the captured Bends Lake Predator suspect in an interrogation room at the Danver County Detention Facility on Krepton Road. O'Shea was wearing an orange jail jumpsuit and shackles. He winced, no doubt still smarting from Stella's impressive karate self-defense and Declan eagerly coming to her aide after the suspect's attempt to kidnap her and worse.

Quite frankly, Declan wasn't sure what they would get out of the purported serial killer—him having been read his rights against self-incrimination—but they wanted him on the official record for whatever he wished to say. That, however, would likely be limited, as O'Shea sat next to his court-appointed attorney named Loralee Santana, who was fortysomething with blond hair in an A-line bob cut and wore oval eyeglasses.

Declan mused about Stella watching the interrogation on a video monitor in her capacity as an FBI behavioral analyst—as opposed to a damned near murder victim—in assessing O'Shea's state of mind as the case against him moved forward.

Peering at the suspect, Declan said sharply, "The Wilson Combat SFX9 handgun you were carrying has been positively linked to the bullets and shell casings left behind in the murder of Sheldon Ferreira. We also have your DNA and prints taken from Ferreira's Lincoln Navigator Reserve that you carjacked. How's that for starters?"

O'Shea shrugged dismissively. "So, tell me something I don't already know."

Declan set his jaw. "Well, since you mention it, here's something you probably weren't aware of… A new witness has come forward with video that places you directly at the scene of the murder of Peggy Elizondo in Blakely Park," he decided to share with the suspect. In fact, the witness, a professional photographer by the name of Ulysses Espelita, had taken the video randomly and from a distance and only recently reviewed it, making his shocking discovery.

Loralee looked at her client. "You're not obligated to respond to this allegation," she cautioned.

O'Shea rolled his eyes. "Whatever."

Declan pushed forward, sensing an opening till proven otherwise. He asked the suspect point-blank, "Maybe you'd like to get off your chest what motivated you to shoot to death ten different people—male and female—with the full intention of killing two others?"

Loralee again intervened. "I would recommend you not answer that."

O'Shea leaned toward his attorney and whispered in her

ear. Loralee whispered back, before O'Shea glared at Declan and responded glibly, "Do I need a reason?"

"You tell me." Declan's chin jutted. "What would possess you to become a serial killer?" He was sure there was some method to his madness, whether the suspect cared to divulge this or not.

O'Shea licked his lips and responded boastfully, "The same thing as other serial killers. I needed to take out my frustrations, for this reason or that, and found some ready-made targets to go after in giving me the release I needed. What can I say?"

"I don't think you should say anything else," Loralee told him, her agitation evident.

Declan gave him an out by stating, "We can stop this anytime you like."

O'Shea cracked a grin. "If I had my way, it would never have stopped. Why would I, if you people were too inept to stop me from killing?"

I don't doubt for one minute that he had every intention of continuing the murders indefinitely, if allowed to, Declan told himself. He watched as the suspect's lawyer looked as though she wanted to tape his mouth shut, but could only sit back and stew while O'Shea dug his own hole and fell deeper into it.

Declan glanced at the video camera and fixed the suspect's smug face as he asked him coolly, "So were most of these ready-made targets, as you called them, randomly chosen? Or was there some personal vendetta against all of them—such as with Diane Wexler?"

Loralee pushed up her glasses and warned her client, "I really advise you to end this—now!"

O'Shea waved her off and said contemptuously, "Diane was the only one I had a score to settle with. The others were simply there to pick off when the mood hit me and opportunity came my way." He narrowed his eyes at Declan. "I have to tell you, though, Special Agent Delgado, I would've truly enjoyed killing Stella if I'd been able to finish the job. Because she messed things up between me and my cousin Gayle—and gave me flashbacks of my ex-wife—Special Agent Bailey deserved to die."

Declan chose to bite his tongue rather than to allow the serial killer to bait him into crossing the line in defense of Stella, while watching as Loralee admonished her client.

She finally snapped, "This interview is over!"

Declan nodded with a deep sigh, having heard all he needed to from Samuel Lochlyn O'Shea to know that he was going down for his many crimes, and there was no way he'd ever see freedom again.

After ending the interrogation, Declan signaled to a guard to escort the suspect back to his cell.

"Samuel O'Shea… Lochlyn…is the quintessential narcissist," Stella told Declan as they stood on his land gazing at the Cheyenne Bottoms wetland. She was still coming to terms with her attempted abductor and confessed serial killer's interrogation an hour ago, which came to an abrupt halt once his attorney finally got her wish to put a lid on it. But the damage had already been done, as O'Shea's ego simply got the better of him. With just enough encouragement from Declan. "The man's inflated sense of self-worth is right there with the likes of fellow serial killers Ted Bundy and Henry Lee Lucas, among others, who see themselves as super smart and cunning to the point of controlling the narrative, even while behind bars."

Declan bristled. "As long as O'Shea can never again harm any others on the outside, he's free to boast about his homicidal tendencies and dark thoughts in that regard. I'm just glad that he was unsuccessful in making you another fatal victim of his sick penchant for murder…"

"You and me both." Stella grinned at him. She was forever grateful that what they had established with each other had not been cut short through forces beyond their control. "In an odd way, Lochlyn—as despicable as he is—was able to bring us back together, after it seemed as though the window had closed for good."

"You're right about that. Fate, however one chooses to look at it, somehow intervened in bridging the gap between us." Declan regarded her thoughtfully. "I couldn't be happier that it happened."

"Neither could I," Stella made clear, and wondered where they would go from there. If anywhere.

"So…now that the case has been solved for all intents and purposes, I suppose you'll be heading back to Detroit and the life you've built there…?"

She batted her lashes at him. "Is that what you want?"

He paused, putting his hands on her shoulders. "Only if I can come with you."

Stella inhaled quietly, meeting his gaze. "What are you saying?"

Declan peered intensely into her eyes, making Stella feel the heat throughout her body, as he answered deliberately, "I'm saying that I'm in love with you—deeply so—and I want us to make a life together, in Detroit, Bends Lake or anywhere else."

She uttered, "I want that too…" He took her quivering hands, and she felt the steadiness of his calming them.

"Good." Declan flashed her a boyish grin. Suddenly, he dropped to one knee and removed a small box from the pocket of his cashmere blazer. He opened it to reveal a yellow diamond ring. "Stella Meredith Bailey, I'm asking you to become my wife and give us both a second shot at finding the happiness we both deserve. Please say yes and make my dream come true of being the best husband I can for you—and hopefully having the opportunity to be the best father for our children, knowing you'd be the best mother…"

Stella flushed with happiness as she waited a beat to allow the incredible moment to sink in, before gazing into his eyes and crying, "Yes, yes, yes, Declan Scott Delgado—" she thought it cute to use their middle names in their romance words to each other "—I will definitely marry you, as I love you with all my heart!"

"So happy to hear you say that, Stella!" Declan's face lit up. "Music to my ears."

Stella's teeth shone brightly. "I love the melody too," she cooed, and held out her ring finger with expectation as he removed the ring, with its pavé diamond platinum band, and slid it onto her finger in what was a perfect fit. "Now get up and kiss me, Declan, to make our engagement and future together complete!"

Declan laughed. "With pleasure."

He rose to his feet in leather Chelsea boots, cupped her cheeks and laid a powerful kiss on her generous mouth that quite literally had Stella melting into his arms as Declan wrapped them joyously around her—both undeniably ecstatic about the life, love and family they had to look forward to.

Epilogue

A year later, Stella Delgado sat at the Bends Lake Bookstore on Picktor Drive, signing copies of her hot new book on criminal profiling. It never failed to amaze her how the subject matter seemed to strike a chord with the public as much as criminologists and law enforcement. The fact that this book included a chapter on the infamous Bends Lake Predator, aka Samuel Lochlyn O'Shea, piqued the interest of locals to an even greater degree.

After brazenly confessing to committing ten murders, attempting to murder two others, carjacking, possessing illegal firearms and related charges, O'Shea was sentenced to life behind bars without even the slightest possibility of parole. He would serve out his long days and short nights at the El Dorado Correctional Facility, a maximum-security prison located on State Highway 54, just east of the city of El Dorado in Prospect Township, Butler County, Kansas.

To Stella, O'Shea was getting his just reward for choosing to become a serial killer and showing no remorse, which was par for the course for most serial killers in society. Giving his surviving victims some peace of mind—herself included—made solving the case that much more satisfying.

Stella prepared to sign another copy of the book, already a bestseller. She gazed up at the handsome face of her husband of six months. Declan was, as always, her biggest supporter and the one person she loved spending every moment with. Stella's transfer to the Bureau's Kansas City field office allowed Declan to remain a dedicated KBI special agent, in spite of being more than willing to quit his job. He had, in fact, made serious inquiries about taking a position with the Michigan Department of Attorney General's Criminal Investigations Division.

And she loved him for it. But she knew this was exactly where they belonged. Returning home felt right to Stella, for both the memory of her sister and building a solid foundation to start a family. Her parents were fully supportive, inviting them to Detroit anytime they wished to visit.

"Hey." Declan's smooth voice broke her reverie. "Think I might be able to get a signed copy of your book to cherish, Mrs. Delgado—just as I do its author?"

Stella flashed him a brilliant smile. "Why certainly, Mr. Delgado. It would give me no greater pleasure than to put my autograph on your copy."

"Terrific!" Declan tilted his head. "And I mean that in more ways than one."

Stella took that for everything it was worth, and that was plenty. After she signed the book and finished by writing, *Yours Forever and Ever, Love Stella*, Declan broke into an emotional, slanted grin and uttered without prelude, "Back at you, my darling!"

He punctuated this by leaning over the table and shamelessly giving her a short, but always ever sweet, kiss.

* * * * *

BIG SKY SAFE HOUSE

JUNO RUSHDAN

To all veterans. You are heroes.

Chapter One

Nora Santana caught sight of a red and gold envelope glittering in the snow on her doorstep.

An icy chill skittered down her spine that had nothing to do with the nip in the December evening air. She stopped on her walkway, clutching her keys tight in her gloved hand, and glanced around.

The block was quiet. All the single-family homes were spread far apart, sitting on lots that exceeded three acres. Which was what she preferred. It made it easy to see any neighbors or someone who didn't belong on her property, yet still be close enough for someone to hear her scream for help if the need ever arose.

The neighborhood was decorated for the holidays, with every house adorned in cheerful lights and festive displays. Her home, the only one at the end of the cul-de-sac near the woods, was dark and lonely. It stood out for all the wrong reasons.

She hated this time of year, ever since she was sixteen and escaped.

Survived.

Nora stared at the envelope, her pulse fluttering. The fresh snow on the walkway and stairs was pristine, devoid of any footprints, as if someone had meticulously erased them. The peculiarity struck her as odd.

Taking one last look around, she climbed the four steps of her porch and picked up the envelope and read the typed message.

To Nora
From Your Secret Santa

It was probably left by one of her neighbors, she told herself. A gift card from Mrs. Moore would be her guess. The older lady was fond of Nora. Each Christmas, the sweet woman tried to get Nora to celebrate the holiday, but always failed. In the past, her kind neighbor had dropped off peppermint fudge, gingerbread sandwich cookies and eggnog Bundt cake. Nora had brought all of the treats into the real estate company where she worked and shared them with the other agents, Amanda and Joe, since there was no one else in her life. Last week, Nora had several lengthy conversations with her neighbor about the holiday and finally mustered the courage to politely ask the older woman not to make anything else for her this year. Mrs. Moore had looked disappointed, but she had agreed.

Nora tucked the envelope in her pocket.

Although Christmas was still two weeks away, her widowed neighbor planned to spend the holiday with her son in Helena. She was going to leave in a few days to enjoy her grandkids.

Nora had started marking her time in Bitterroot Falls, Montana, with Mrs. Moore's gifts.

Four years. This was the longest she'd stayed in one place since…

She shuddered, stomach churning.

Razor-sharp images slashed through her mind—an onslaught of memories. Of stark fear. Pain. Bone-chilling screams.

The sensation of pins and needles flared in her fingers, crawling into her hands and up her arms. Her pulse spiked, heartbeat drumming in her ears. Nora squeezed her eyes shut and took deep breaths to stave off a panic attack. Inhaled, exhaled, and repeated until it passed.

Nearly a decade ago, her life had been irrevocably changed, the future she'd imagined smashed into a billion little pieces. She shoved the searing memories from her mind, back into the buried vault that she never dared touch.

Opening her eyes, she unlocked her front door and stepped inside the house. Immediately the rhythmic beeping of her alarm sounded, alerting her that she had thirty seconds to disarm it before the security company called. Kicking off her boots, she closed the door, flipped the dead bolt and slipped on the chain. She moved to the system's panel on the wall and entered the code. The alarm went silent. Then the small red light flashed, showing the system was set for the night.

Fatigue seeped through her. The day had been longer than she'd expected with multiple house showings. After Halloween, the real estate market typically slowed down to a crawl, but she had two motivated sellers. They were both eager to offload their properties before the new year. Also, a family in the process of relocating to Bitterroot had a severe case of the Goldilocks syndrome. Every house they toured was either too big or too small, too outdated or too new. The picky family only wanted something that was just right.

Her stomach growled. She trudged to the kitchen, then set down her laptop bag and purse on the countertop of the eat-in island. Her left shoulder ached terribly, even though it had been seven weeks since her injury, when she was shot. A victim in a mass shooting on Main Street.

She was still struggling to get back full range of motion. *You're better. Every day it hurts less and you can do more. Be thankful you're still breathing.*

The physical therapist explained the tenderness would continue for a while but assured Nora a full recovery and return to normal would happen.

Nothing in her life had been normal in a long, long time even before the shooting. At least she was able to jog again, though running in the snow was more taxing on her body. She stretched through the discomfort.

Pain was a good reminder that she was alive. That she could endure anything.

She took the red and gold envelope from her pocket and tore it open. Maybe it was a gift card to the local café, The Beanery. Not that Mrs. Moore should've gone through the trouble after Nora had made it clear that she didn't want to celebrate the holidays. Her neighbor knew Nora spent way too much money in the café—or used to anyway. She hadn't been back to Main Street since the gunman had opened fire in broad daylight.

Nora pulled the card out of the envelope and froze.

Intricate drawings lined the border, images repeating over and over. Santa Claus, an angel and a devil. Typed across the center of the card were three lines that read:

No more running.
Hide and Seek is over.
Time for a new game.

Nora's skin crawled as her stomach tangled into sickening knots.

No, no, no.

He found me.

After years of hiding, of trying to be invisible, her worst fears were crystallizing.

The room spun. She struggled to focus. To breathe. The serial killer, who had murdered her friends ten years ago, who had almost taken her life, too, had finally found her.

Now he was going to make good on his promise.

To finish what he'd started.

The card in her hand was shaking because she was trembling. Everywhere. She dropped the note onto the counter. Clenched her hands together in a tight fist. Rubbed her knuckles with her interlocked fingers.

Breathe. Think.

Her cell phone rang, and she jumped. Snatching the phone from her coat's pocket, she glanced at the screen. A random number she didn't recognize.

Another telemarketer. She was in no mood to deal with it. "Hello," she answered, sharply, prepared to keep the conversation short.

"Sweet Nora. It's been far too long." The voice was deep. Eerie. Electronically modified.

Dread flooded her system, and her pulse ratcheted higher. It was him. He'd not only found her and had her address, but also her private cell number. She opened her mouth to speak, but her throat tightened, growing so dry as though filled with sand. No words would come out.

She sagged against the counter.

"Nor-a, Nor-a," he said in a singsongy way, the all too familiar cadence setting every nerve in her body on edge. "Let's play Santa Says."

Panic fired up inside her, burning and roiling. Rage bubbled to the surface. "Drop dead!"

Laughter, dark and devoid of humor, rolled over the phone line. "No one dies tonight. My game. My rules. Santa says, don't call the police. Or. Else."

Hot bile spurted up the back of her throat and she swallowed it down. "Or else what?"

"Or else we'll have to play a different game. A painful game. A very bloody game."

A decade of grief knocked her sideways as the horrific screams of her friends filled her ears. This monster had tortured them before he killed them. Stabbed each of them several times before ending their misery.

Tears burned the backs of her eyes, and her stomach churned. Shaking her head, she squeezed the bridge of her nose and stared down at the note on the counter. She needed to breathe. Needed to think.

"Oh, sweet Nor-a. Don't look so sad. Playing Santa Says will be such fun."

His words echoed in her mind. *Don't look so sad.*

She snapped her head up and glanced around. The house was locked up tight, with the alarm on, yet she wondered if he was somehow watching her.

Unzipping her purse, she snatched the Beretta that was inside. Clutched the cold metal against her chest. She felt a grim reassurance mixed with the sobering realization that ultimately it wouldn't save her. The nature of his games, the structure of his rules, all designed for her to lose and for him to win.

She spun around, rushing to the kitchen sink. Easing back the curtains, she peeked outside. Darkness stretched across the lawn to the perimeter of Mrs. Moore's home. Moonlight reflected off the glistening sheet of untouched snow. Colored string lights hung from the eaves of the house. No large shrubs or trees for anyone to hide behind.

"Nor-a." The electronic modification only amplified the creepiness of his voice. "You won't need a gun for Santa Says. Put it down on the counter."

She stilled, blood pounding in her ears. Her thoughts coalesced into the horrifying reality of her situation. He *was* watching.

Spying on her.

"Where are you?" she asked, the Beretta shaking in her hand.

"Close. Much closer than you realize. But not close enough for you to use the gun."

Terror pulsed like a feverish drumbeat in her veins. She rounded the island and hurried to the back door. It had a steel frame with two large panels made of tempered glass. She'd never put up curtains. Since the door faced the woods rather than a neighbor's house, she hadn't thought she needed them.

Frost streaked the windowpanes. Nora scanned the yard, searching for any signs of him. Nothing. Not a single footprint marred the blanket of pristine snow, though that meant little.

She watched and waited for any movement.

Still nothing.

But a sudden prickle along her arms and back made her stare even harder into the darkness. Her fingers gripped the edge of the doorframe, and her other hand tightened around the gun.

A shadow flitted in the moonlight between two evergreens at the tree line.

She held her breath, her gaze glued to the spot. *There.*

Movement again.

The shadow stepped out into view. Black clothing. A ball cap on his head. His face shrouded in darkness. He waved at her, and she shivered.

"Hello, Nora."

Her teeth chattered, but not from the cold. A rolling tremor had started in her jaw and now slithered through her body.

How long had he been watching her? Hours? Days? *Weeks?*

The entire time she'd been on display in the back part of her house. In her bedroom upstairs that also overlooked the woods. Where she got dressed and walked around with no clothes on. While he was watching her. Planning his next move—this moment.

Fear clogged her throat and paralyzed her muscles.

"Put the gun down on the counter," he said.

Playing his game, on his terms, meant that when he was done toying with her and it was over, she'd die.

There was only one option.

One choice.

Fight back with everything she had until her last breath. Nora grabbed the door handle, aching to run outside and unload every single bullet into him.

Maybe that was what he wanted. For her to turn off the alarm. To leave the safety of the house. To chase after him all the while he was taunting her.

"Santa says do it now," he said.

She backed away from the door.

"Good girl. Go to the counter and set down the gun."

Instead, she ran to the other security panel mounted on the wall.

"What are you doing?" he demanded.

Keeping the Beretta in her hand, she looked back

through the glass, hoping he could see her face, and pressed the panic button on the security panel, holding it for three seconds.

The alarm activated, blaring. The police would soon be dispatched.

"I warned you!" he said, over the screeching alarm. "Now I'll make you suffer!"

She tightened her grip on the gun and stepped up to the back door.

The shadowy figure stood there, breathing heavily over the line, waiting for a response from her that she refused to give.

She was done giving him her fear and her pain and her weakness. Done playing by his rules.

No more.

"Mark my words, *Noriyah*. You'll regret this!"

She'd changed her name, her hair, stayed away from her family and friends over the years. She'd taken every precaution. All for what?

He found her anyway. Again.

The killer disconnected the call and backed away into the darkness of the woods.

No relief came to her. This wasn't over. Far from it. This was only the beginning of a new deadly nightmare.

He was going to keep coming after her until one of them was dead.

Nora swore to herself that it wasn't going to be her.

Chapter Two

"Conference room, now," his boss said, stopping in the doorway of his office.

Bo Lennox looked up from his computer screen at Chance Reyes, a growl of irritation rising in his chest. "What's up?"

Tall, tanned, and with a relaxed, posh air that made him appear far younger than he was, Chance looked like he belonged at a fancy law firm—he was an attorney after all—or hobnobbing at a country club. "We have a potential new client. I want you and Autumn to sit in on the interview," Chance said, referring to Ironside Protection Services' newest team member, a forensic psychologist and former FBI consultant turned investigator.

Dr. Autumn Stratton was sharp, had a keen way of pinpointing a perp and had proven she also had guts. Although she was still learning the ropes at IPS, she'd become an essential part of the crew.

"Just us two?" Bo asked.

Chance gave a curt nod.

Since his boss wasn't bringing the other two guys on the team—Takoda Yazzie and Eli Easton—to the meeting, Bo wondered about the nature of the case and whether Autumn's expertise was truly necessary or if this was an opportunity for her to gain more experience.

More importantly, why had he been picked?

"I just finished a case," Bo said. It had been a security nightmare. "I was only planning to be in the office for a couple of hours to close out this paperwork." He'd been hoping to take some downtime. Go skiing. Mountain climbing. Kick back with a beer in front of the fire and unwind. "Why not grab Eli or Tak?"

"Because the client asked for you."

Bo straightened. "Me?"

"Yeah," Chance said. "She requested that you sit in on the meeting."

She. "Okay."

After slipping on the sport coat that he kept in the office for meetings such as these, Bo grabbed a notepad and pen and hurried behind Chance to the conference room near the front of their office spaces. Autumn was already sitting inside speaking with Nora Santana.

Bo faltered to a stop. He remembered her. How could he not? The young woman was unforgettable.

She turned toward the door. The second her gaze lifted to lock with his, he forgot how to breathe. How to think.

Then she smiled at him, and he was certain that was what it must've felt like to be struck by lightning.

She wasn't pretty, nor was she simply beautiful. She was a knockout.

Caramel complexion. Delicate features and sensual lips. Petite, dainty frame.

A soft powder blue cashmere dress molded to her shapely body. Long dark hair hung past her shoulders in wavy curls, framing a face that was too alluring. And her eyes. Amber was too tame a color to describe her eyes. Flecked with gold in the light, they reminded him of a lion. Or perhaps it was the quiet fierceness to her.

"I believe you know Bo Lennox," Chance said, taking a seat.

She started to rise from her chair, prompting his feet to move.

He schooled his features as he approached her side of the table. "Ms. Santana." He shook her hand, surprised by her tight, firm grip.

"Please, call me Nora," she said, and he had to fight a quiver zipping down his spine because her voice was soft, yet husky, awakening every sense. She sat back down. "We should be on a first-name basis. After all, you have already seen me naked."

Lowering his gaze, Bo stepped back. "I'm sorry about that." Once again. He glanced at Chance, who had arched an eyebrow, and then at Autumn's shocked expression. "It was an accident. I interviewed her at the hospital after the mass shooting."

Seven weeks ago, a sniper had opened fire on Main Street, killing two people and wounding two others. In the incident, Nora was one of the injured, struck in the left shoulder. The shot had been clean, exiting out the other side. No serious damage had been done. No bone had been hit. She'd been lucky.

"Bo walked in while I was in the middle of changing out of my hospital gown and the timing had been perfect."

"Off," he corrected. "Bad timing."

A flush suffused her cheeks.

He lowered his head and edged toward the door.

Bo had assisted Chance and Winter Stratton—Autumn's sister that worked as an agent with the DOJ Division of Criminal Investigation—with the case, right along with the rest of the team. Bo had been the one to question Nora about the events and to see if she had any information that might help them identify the shooter.

At the emergency room, she'd been in a cubicle when he'd drawn back the curtain without thinking. He'd glimpsed flawless light brown skin, mouthwatering curves straight out of a fantasy and then a startled expression on her face before he apologized and quickly excused himself.

The only fortunate thing about his intrusion that day was that he'd stopped Nora from leaving the hospital prematurely. She'd been scared and he'd assumed it had been the shock from the shooting. After the doctors treated her and stitched up the wound, they wanted to monitor her for forty-eight hours. Bo had to persuade her to stay.

She hadn't known anything valuable about the sniper, but he'd used the circumstances to spend a little time with her, even driving her home once she was discharged.

"Nora," Chance said, "why don't you tell us what you think we can do for you?" His boss looked at Bo and gestured to a chair.

Bo shook his head. "I'm good." He leaned against the door jamb.

Nora shoved hair back behind her ear. "I'm not sure where to start."

"At the beginning is a good place," Autumn said, seated next to her.

Nora nodded. "Ten years ago, when I was sixteen, a group of us, me and three other friends, were targeted by a murderer. The press dubbed him the Yuletide Killer."

"Was he caught?" Chance asked.

"No. He murdered my three friends. I was the only one who got away." Her voice thickened with emotion. "The only one who survived."

"Take your time. There's no rush." Autumn put a hand on her shoulder. "When you say that you got away, do you mean you were taken and escaped?"

"We were having a sleepover at Jessica's house in the basement. Her parents were out of town for a couple of nights. The killer broke in. Slaughtered Dana, Alice and Jessica. I was in the bathroom when I heard their screams. I hid in a crawl space, where Jessica stashed things that she didn't want her parents to find. I stayed down there for hours. Terrified. Not making a sound until the police found me."

As she recounted that tragic moment, tears welled in her eyes, her body trembling. The weight of her pain was etched across her face and it radiated off her. His heart ached to ease her suffering. The urge to reach out and comfort her was overwhelming, but he resisted.

"A few days later, he came back for me," she said. "He almost got me into a van while I was walking to Savvy's house."

"Savvy?" Bo asked.

"Savannah Watts. Everyone called her Savvy for short. She was my best friend. Lived around the corner. The man got a hold of me, but I managed to scream, drawing attention. Some guys were out shoveling snow from the sidewalk and ran over to help me as I fought not to be thrown into the van. I knew that if he got me inside that I was as good as dead."

"You have good instincts," Bo said. "Not letting him move you to a secondary location."

"Pa, my stepdad, always told me that. He was a cop."

"Wise advice that saved you," Chance said.

Nora grabbed the cup of coffee from the table and her hand shook as she drank a swallow. "The guilt, the shame that I had because I had lived when the others hadn't, was a lot. I went to stay with relatives in Wyoming and I finished high school there and started college. But then he found me. Tried to kill me again." She pulled down the collar of her sweater dress and moved her hair back, revealing a scar on her neck.

Everything inside Bo went cold. Rigid. The killer had gotten a rope or cord around her neck, tight enough to leave a permanent scar.

"I fought him. My roommate in the dorm, Jane, walked in," Nora said. "She came back early from a party. Screamed for help. If not for her, he would've finished me that night. But he stabbed Jane as he fled. Killed her instead. Because she had interfered with his fun. That's what he said to her as she was dying." Nora covered her neck and clutched the cup in both hands. "I was already taking self-defense classes and learning martial arts at a place called the Underground Self-Defense School. That's how I was able to fight him off at all, but I was still new to it. The woman who owned the school, Charlie, helped me change my name—from Noriyah Howard to Nora Santana—and start over."

Chance leaned forward. "Charlie Sharp, in Laramie?"

"Do you know her?" Nora asked with surprise.

Bo's boss was from Laramie, and he was the type of guy who made it his business to know everyone.

"I do," Chance said.

"I cut all contact with family after that, thinking that if I disappeared completely, he would never be able to find me. I bounced around various places, keeping up my training in self-defense and learning how to shoot. Eventually, I wanted to come back home to Montana. I have a younger half sister, Rosa, and an older stepbrother, Spencer, who I was close to. I've missed so much. When scrolling through their Facebook pages isn't enough, sometimes I drive over to Cold Harbor, where I'm from, to get a glimpse of their lives."

The small town of Cold Harbor was located in the rugged mountains, nestled deep within a remote region. It was approximately a three-hour drive away from Bitterroot Falls. Bo had passed through the mining town once or twice.

"I sit outside the church and watch them file out after service," Nora said, the loneliness in her voice gnawing at him. "Spencer and Savvy are a couple. Married for years and have a baby. Rosa got hitched, too. I've never met her husband or my niece."

"Is that how he found you?" Chance asked. "By going back home?"

"No," Bo said. "It was the shooting on Main Street. Right?"

Nora met his gaze, her eyes widening, and she nodded.

"Her face and name, right along with Ty Long's," Bo said, "the other guy who'd been shot, were all over the news." News that had received national coverage.

That day, Bo had escorted her out of the hospital to his vehicle so he could take her home. Nora had recoiled from the cameras, declining to answer any questions from the swarm of reporters that had descended on Bitterroot Falls. At the time, he'd assumed she'd been shy and simply wanted her privacy. Not that it had been an act of self-preservation.

If only he'd known the real reason for her aversion that day, he would've done a better job of protecting her.

"Things were quiet while I recovered." Nora put a hand to her shoulder and rubbed the spot of her injury like it suddenly ached. "I'd hoped he hadn't seen me on the news, but the coverage was everywhere. Almost constant for days. I guess my luck ran out because when I got home from work last night, there was a note on my front stoop," she said, bringing up pictures on her phone.

Bo walked closer to the table and peered over at the screen as she scrolled through.

A red and gold envelope. A note card. Autumn took the phone and zoomed in. Hand-drawn colorful images.

Santa was holding an open book of deeds.

An angel with a halo.

A red devil with a tail and heavy chains draped over his shoulders.

The words in the middle of the card were chilling. *No more running. Hide and Seek is over. Time for a new game.*

"After I got inside the house and opened it, I received a phone call. From him. I could tell he was watching me. I found him in the backyard, hiding in the tree line of the woods at the rear of my house." A visible shudder ran through her. "I pulled out the Beretta I carry in my purse. He wanted to play Santa Says—told me not to call the police and to put my gun down. Instead of playing his twisted game, I notified the police. That's what brought me here. The cops couldn't help me. There were no prints on the card and the man in the woods hadn't done anything illegal. No proof it was even the killer."

"Did you recognize his voice on the phone?" Bo asked.

"He used a voice modulator. The same as he's always done in the past. I've never seen his face. Not ten years ago, not that night in my dorm room and he stood too far away last night. Detective Logan Powell recommended that I hire Ironside Protection Services."

Not too long after Chance recruited Bo and the other IPS

guys from a combat-ready unit at Malmstrom Air Force Base, Logan Powell and his now fiancée Summer Stratton moved to Bitterroot Falls as well. Then her sisters, Autumn and Winter—the "season sisters" as Chance called them—had followed shortly thereafter. These days they were always together, joining the IPS team for dinners, celebrations, Sunday brunches, just to have drinks and hang out. They had each other's backs through the good and bad. Cared for one another.

They'd formed a sort of family. As a foster kid, always bouncing through the system when he was younger, not having any roots or relatives, Bo relied on this newly found family more and more. Not only relied on them but appreciated them. Trusted them.

If Logan had sent Nora to IPS, then the police really couldn't do much, if anything at all, to keep her safe.

"It creeped me out to stay at my house last night now that he knows where I live. I felt…" Nora wrung her hands. "Exposed there, too vulnerable. I spent the night at the hotel in town. The Bitterroot Mountain Hotel. That was hard too because the sniper had been on the hotel rooftop the day he shot up Main Street. I hadn't been back to that part of town since it happened."

"You've been through a lot recently," Autumn said. "Traumatic experiences. I'm sorry you had to revisit that area before you were ready."

"I didn't sleep at all last night. I kept checking the locks on the hotel room. Moved the dresser to block the door. But still, I couldn't relax enough to get any rest."

Bo tore his gaze from her, wanting to comfort her in some way.

Chance clasped his hands on the table. "It was smart not to stay at your house. The hotel was safer."

"Not safe enough. I found something *inside* my car this morning. Waiting for me on the passenger's seat." She picked up her messenger bag from the floor, flipped open the front flap and took out a red and gold box with a shiny red bow on top. "Do you smell it?"

They all gathered closer to the box.

Bo inhaled deeply, bracing himself for a rancid stench. It was the opposite.

"What is that?" Autumn asked.

"Cologne," Bo said.

Nora nodded, her bottom lip trembling, and his entire focus fell to her mouth. Those full, rosy lips. He wondered what it'd be like to kiss her.

"Whenever he's gotten close to me," Nora said, "that's what he smelled like. My car reeks of the scent. Of him. I drove with the windows rolled down, but it's still in there."

"The smell is woodsy." Autumn took another whiff. "Spicy. Like fire and cloves and something else."

"There's more." Nora lifted the lid of the red and gold box, revealing the contents.

A piece of coal. Sugar plums. A gold ring with a tiny accent diamond—possibly a wedding band.

And another card with the same design around the border. The typed words read:

Your punishment for not listening.
A new game.
SHARKS and MINNOWS.

"Nobody is to touch anything," Chance said. "Not until Logan takes a look at it and checks it for prints. Nora, do you recognize the ring?"

"It looks familiar." She shrugged. "But I can't place

it." Exhaling a shaky breath, she wrung her hands once more. "My first instinct was to disappear again. Change my name. Start over someplace else. But I'm tired of uprooting my life. I don't want to run anymore, always looking over my shoulder. Living in constant fear that this very thing will happen. Please, help me."

"You need protection and a safe house to stay in until we can figure out who this guy is and stop him," Chance said. He looked up at Bo. "Your place is designed for this sort of thing and you have the most experience with personal security."

Bo shook his head. "No. I can't." He backed up to the doorway as all eyes in the room focused on him. "I'm not right for this one."

They all had the necessary skills as well as safe places. In fact, Chance had the most secure property. His house was located on a ranch he had turned into a compound, with lots of guys who worked there to keep watch. Not that Chance was available to handle this one. A big case was taking him out of town later that night.

"Nonsense." Chance leaned back in his chair. "You're perfect and available to start today."

"Tak or Eli would be better suited. Don't worry, Ms. Santana," Bo said to her, not looking at her mesmerizing eyes, or her lush mouth, or her face that was too wholesome, too pretty. "You'll be in good hands with someone else at IPS."

He shuffled out of the room and stalked back to his office.

No sooner had he plopped into the chair behind his desk and released a heavy breath than Chance strode into his office and shut the door.

"I realize you just wrapped up a tough case, but that's

not like you." Chance folded his arms and studied him. "What's going on? Give it to me straight."

Unfiltered blunt talk was one of the things he enjoyed about working for IPS and specifically Chance. Nonetheless, this wasn't something he wanted to discuss. "I don't want this one. Ask E or Tak. All right?"

"No, it's not all right. 'I don't want to' is not an acceptable response. I hate to pull rank here, but I will. I don't ask, I assign. The client requested you, so you're on this unless you give me a solid reason to reconsider."

Bo weighed his options but didn't see any way around telling him the truth. "I can't work on her case because I'm attracted to her. Okay?" Embarrassment burned through him at having disclosed so much.

Chance grinned. "Is that all?"

Quite a lot if you asked Bo. More than enough to recuse himself. "It'd be a distraction. This job demands we don't let our attention stray." Not even for a minute. She needed someone laser-focused on keeping her safe, not juggling conflicting agendas—protecting her and getting cozy with her.

"Can you keep it in your pants?"

Bo stiffened. "Yes." He prided himself on self-restraint, but every time he looked at Nora, he wanted to touch her. Get closer to her. Kiss her. Keeping it in his pants wasn't the problem. Being near her was. It was impossible for him to focus clearly on anything other than Nora Santana when he was in the same room as her. "But it's not worth the risk."

"Not your call to make," Chance said. "It's mine. The client requested you and I think you're the best fit. Your personal interest in her will only make you more invested in doing your job."

Bo shoved back from his desk and stood. "I disagree." She deserved someone who would be one thousand percent focused on the mission and nothing else. "Distractions cause mistakes. The wrong error could cost someone their life." He wouldn't jeopardize hers.

"This type of situation requires the client to trust the person assigned. You already have a rapport with her. One she values. That makes this case yours. Like it or not."

Eli and Tak were both engaging and friendly. Capable. Nora simply hadn't had an opportunity to get to know them. A small thing easily rectified. Either man would easily earn her trust. Do the job without endangering her.

"No," Bo said.

Straightening, Chance arched both eyebrows.

Bo never turned down any assignment. Not for any reason. He certainly didn't get into a debate with his boss unless there was an ethical basis, and Chance was more than his employer. The guy was a close friend. Family.

"You feel so strongly about this that you're prepared to quit?" Chance asked, his expression stern.

A knock on the door stopped Bo from answering.

Nora stood on the other side. She opened it and poked her head in the office. "Can I speak with Bo for a minute? Alone?"

"Certainly," Chance said and stepped outside. "I'm going to call Logan and then I'll be in the conference room." He shut the door and disappeared down the hall.

"I know you don't want to take my case." She wrapped her arms around herself. "But I'd like you to reconsider. In ten years, I haven't felt secure anywhere or at ease with anyone. After the mass shooting, you came to the hospital to question me, and you were so patient and kind. Then when you followed up to see if I'd remembered anything else and offered to take me home because I had no one else I could call, it was the first time—in a very long time—that I felt safe. Do you remember the day I left the hospital with the press swarming around the building?"

Bo nodded.

Hard to forget. Nothing as big as the mass shooting had warranted a flock of reporters from national outlets as well as news podcasters to descend on their small town of Bitterroot Falls.

In many ways, the sniper had victimized Nora twice, by shooting her and then creating such mayhem that it caused her identity and whereabouts to be exposed in the media.

"As we were leaving the hospital, walking through the parking lot, surrounded by reporters hounding me, you cut through them like a blade, got them out of my face and whisked me into the car. Even the ride home to my house was peaceful. The way you comforted me—made me feel protected, simply by being there when you didn't have to—meant a lot to me."

Bo stood behind his desk, stunned and silent. He'd only been doing his job, careful not to cross any lines after the emergency room incident. Making an impression hadn't been his intent, but he was glad he'd made a difficult time a little easier for her.

"The Yuletide Killer told me over the phone the police wouldn't be able to keep me safe. He was right. After Logan Powell referred me to Ironside Protection Services, I almost threw the card in the trash and hightailed it out of town." Emotion thickened her voice. "Please, help me." She stilled, as though doing her best not to shatter into pieces. Tears clung to the corners of her eyes, but they didn't fall as if she were holding them back with an act of sheer will. "Please."

He couldn't ignore the beaten, weary look to her—fragile instead of fierce. Bo didn't like that. She had been through hell and he wondered how much more she could handle. He found himself needing to soothe her.

This was the perfect case for IPS. Just not for him. "We will help you," he said, the words slipping from his mouth before he'd considered the repercussions. "They will. One of the others."

"The reason I didn't throw the card away was because I remembered you worked here. I don't know if IPS can do anything for me, if anyone can, but I'm willing to take a chance on you, Bo. Either you handle my case personally," she said, holding his gaze hostage, "or I'll be forced to run again. Eventually face the man who's been terrorizing me for a decade, dead set on killing me, all by myself. I have a bag packed in my trunk, a full tank of gas, a loaded Beretta and two thousand dollars in cash to avoid leaving a trail if you turn me down and I need to run. So, what's it going to be?" Hiking her chin up, she stood a bit taller, stiffening as if she was bracing for bad news. "Are you going to take my case? Or am I on my own again?"

Something inside his chest cracked open, and every drop of sound reasoning spilled away from him.

Chapter Three

Any expectations Nora might've entertained had been cast aside in favor of hope. A small seed of hope, grown out of desperation.

Sitting in the passenger's seat of Bo's full-size pickup, she glanced over at him while he drove to his place, studying the side of his face that wasn't obscured by his tan cowboy hat. Smooth mahogany skin. Ruggedly handsome with a strong jaw. Clean shaven. Ridiculously muscled body that was apparent even with the layer of a winter coat.

His expression was unreadable, his posture rigid and his demeanor bordering on aloof. It was making her reevaluate her previous impression of him at the hospital when he interviewed her. Then he'd been professional, pleasant and not much of a talker other than asking questions—reserved yet not reluctant to be in her presence.

Why had she blabbered in his office, saying all that stuff about feeling safe and at ease with him?

Well, because it had been true. Still, replaying it in her head with the silence between them thickening and expanding, it had been a misstep on her part.

Running was easy. Fighting was intuitive, and she'd trained hard in self-defense to sharpen her skills after being attacked in the dorm. But stopping the killer who was hunting her—winning—that was hard.

She'd done this on her own for so long. She was tired and unsure if she could go up against that monster again by herself and prevail. A wave of hopelessness mixed with helplessness washed over, threatening to pull her under. She had to fight the urge to burst into tears. Continuing to do this alone meant running forever. Or dying. Neither choice was acceptable, but she didn't want to drag an unwilling soul into this nightmare.

Mirrored shades hid his eyes. Nonetheless, she could tell he still didn't want to work with her. Yet, for some reason, he had relented.

"Maybe this was a mistake," she said, reconsidering. "Getting you to take this assignment." More like pressuring him into it.

His jaw worked up and down like he was chewing the tension between them.

"You don't have to do this. Really. Starting over somewhere else, with a new name, would probably work." It had been working quite effectively until the mass shooting had caused her face and name to be blasted all over the news.

"No." The single word came out as a grunt.

He didn't say anything else to assuage her guilt. Nothing to quash her doubts.

"Are you sure?" she asked, giving him another out. Running and hiding, barely living, wasn't what she wanted. But she would do whatever was necessary. She was a survivor.

He gave a firm nod. "A done deal."

Whatever the cause for him to agree and take her case, she was grateful. "How is this protection thing supposed to work? I can't be trapped in a safe house. I have a job and commitments. I promised to do the food pantry and soup kitchen tomorrow." She must've sounded high maintenance and demanding. Not the impression she wanted to give him. "I don't want that sick murderer to steal what little life I've made for myself, Bo. I've done nothing wrong and don't want to be the one locked up in a prison."

His smile was so kind that it stole her next breath. "I respect that. I've seen you around town volunteering for all sorts of things. I know it's important to you."

"You've seen me around?" *Noticed me?* "Before the shooting?"

"Yeah."

"Why haven't you ever talked to me?" Not really a fair question. She'd seen him around plenty of times and had never once bothered to introduce herself, much less have a real conversation.

Bo shrugged. "I see a lot of people around. Can't talk to everyone." He cleared his throat. "Anyway, we'll review your schedule, and you'll go about your day-to-day activities as if it's business as usual. I'll follow you. Discreetly."

It occurred to her that the way he gave in was too easy. She lifted a brow. The risks to this approach were all too apparent. "If I don't stay in the safe house and go about my life, then it's more likely he'll come for me again."

"That particular downside is true. Easier to lure him out if you're in front of him, easy to see, rather than holed up at my place."

"I guess so. It's not like I'll be unprotected. Anything to catch him."

"You're very brave."

She didn't feel brave. More like terrified.

Bo turned down a long road bracketed by woods and a house appeared in the distance. A cabin on a large piece of land.

"I thought it was better to be in a highly populated area for security reasons," she said.

"In general, it is. But I like my privacy." Bo pulled up in front of the house that sat at the end of the long road on the outskirts of town and threw the gear of the Tacoma in Park.

"Trading privacy for security isn't a luxury I've had." Striking the right balance had been the key.

She looked around at the dense woods surrounding his cabin.

Ironside Protection Services had an excellent reputation that had only grown since she'd been in Bitterroot Falls, but staying in the middle of nowhere—a remote, isolated location—defied everything she had learned over the years that had helped her stay safe.

She'd insisted on Bo protecting her based on their limited interaction—which had previously been positive, almost warm—and her instinct. That preternatural ability to know the best way to keep breathing that came to her as a little voice inside. It had never led her astray. But maybe she had confused that sixth sense with something else.

Awareness.

Attraction.

Nora didn't want to go there. Entertaining such thoughts was a different kind of torture. She led a minimalist life. She kept only the bare essentials that she could leave behind at a moment's notice if she had to. A boyfriend, having anyone she cared about deeply, would've been a sticky thread tying her to a place. The ties that bind would tempt her to stay and only get her killed.

It was instinct. That's what made me choose Bo. Nothing more.

The little voice inside snickered and whispered, *Keep lying to yourself if it makes you feel better.*

Wringing her hands, she made the voice quiet down.

"There are other considerations," he said, as if picking up on her concerns. "With lots of neighbors, it's easier for someone to get close to your house and blend in. Come up with a plausible excuse to be in the vicinity. Out here, there's no hiding. No excuses. Either you're here because I expected you or you're a threat."

That was the most he'd spoken on the entire drive.

She glanced around at the snow-covered trees and icicles that hung from branches, glistening in the sunlight. "Isn't it easy for someone to hide in the woods at night and keep watch, the way he did at my place?"

"I have motion-activated sensors and cameras in the trees in case anyone approaches from the woods instead of the road."

"Never thought of that." His level of preparation and vigilance eased her qualms. "It's smart."

"It's my job."

I have a bodyguard. Real protection for once.

Bo grabbed her bag from the backseat and hopped out of the truck. She slid down from the pickup.

Puffy white clouds rolled across the azure sky against the backdrop of the snowcapped mountains. The location, nestled in the countryside, boasted an idyllic charm that was both captivating and peaceful. Serene. But amidst the breathtaking beauty, there was an undeniable foreboding in the air.

Nora turned to the house. Even though he was out in the middle of the woods, with no neighbors around, he'd put up colored string lights around the eaves as well as two evergreens flanking the house. He was a Christmas guy.

Along the roof, she noticed a railing. "Do you have a deck up there?"

"Yeah, it's great to hang out up there in the summer. Kick back with a glass of lemonade and take in the views."

"Sounds nice."

At the door, he turned to her. "Come here. I want you to pick a six-digit code that you'll remember. Think of it as your key to get into the house. Don't choose anything personal to you like a birth date. When you see a green light flash, put it in. Ready?"

She thought about it for a minute. For her to remember it, the number had to be based on something personal, yet unobtainable through public searches. She settled on the date she became Nora Santana. The only other person who'd know it was Charlie Sharp. "I'm ready."

He hit a couple of buttons and then held one down until she saw the little green light. "Go ahead."

She entered the six-digit date on the sleek, black keypad but backward. The smart lock beeped.

"One more thing." He took out his phone, brought up an app and typed something in. The entire keypad glowed white. "Press your thumb there and hold for three seconds."

Nora did so where he indicated. Another beep followed.

"Now you have multiple ways to get into the house. You can use the code or your thumbprint." He twisted the knob, went inside and held the door open for her.

Bracing herself for more holiday decorations, she followed him into the house.

The cabin was small but cozy with an open floor plan and modern furnishings. Simple, yet sophisticated, the rustic, chic abode was a warm and welcoming retreat.

Thankfully he hadn't gone bananas with the decorations, from what she could see. Aside from a massive Christmas tree—tall enough to reach the ten-foot-high ceiling in the corner—covered in white string lights and ornaments, complete with a star and fluffy skirt, there was only a garland hanging across the fireplace mantel.

She took off her down parka, and when he did the same, she noticed the gun holstered on his hip that hadn't been there during the meeting. He took their coats and hung them on the hook near the door, along with his blazer, cowboy hat and sunglasses. Next, his shoes came off.

Not a fan of tracking dirt or snow inside a house either, she pulled hers off as well. She kept her purse tucked against her waist, clutching the shoulder strap. An old habit of having her phone and gun close at hand, especially in an unfamiliar place.

He looked at her like he was gauging her reaction to his home.

To her new safe house.

Her heartbeat ratcheted up at having his full attention, which was more than a little overwhelming.

Forcing herself to relax, she stared back into his eyes. Deep brown and fathomless. His expression was still inscrutable, making her grit her teeth.

The perfectly straight edges of his low buzz cut, his perfectly pressed white shirt and his perfectly symmetrical face with high cheekbones and sharp angles made him a striking figure that drew admiring glances wherever he went. On numerous occasions, she'd seen him strutting around town and was guilty of being an awestruck gawker, too.

A rush of heat bloomed in her cheeks, flared in her neck and slid down her spine like liquid honey. She bit her bottom lip.

"Not much to see," he said, gesturing to the house. "Feel free to look around." His voice was soft and comforting, his demeanor now one of grim acceptance.

Then he added an encouraging nod that left her feeling closer to settled. It shouldn't have been a thing of any significance. But it was.

She strode around and he trailed behind her closely. Each space was well-defined. An area rug in the living room and dining room solidified the appearance of faux separation. There was a four-person leather sofa, a coffee table and a large TV mounted on the wall next to the wood fireplace.

In the kitchen sat a square table with chairs rather than an island, and she imagined him eating most of his meals there. The countertops were a simple quartz. All the walls were painted a neutral color.

To her surprise, the place was spotless. Nothing out of place. No dust. Not even a dish in the sink. She prided herself on being tidy, but this was next level.

Turning to the floor to ceiling windows along the wall of the living room, she took in the view of the woods and mountains. Stunning.

"I guess with no neighbors, you don't have to worry about anyone peering in. Is that why you don't have any curtains?" Window coverings seemed a necessity for her situation even if he had motion activated cameras hidden in the trees.

"I designed and oversaw the build of the cabin. I installed bullet-resistant glass with a privacy film. During the day, we can see out, but no one can see in. I didn't want anything to obstruct that view."

The view was priceless and she could see why he'd chosen this plot of land. "What about at night?"

"When the light inside the house exceeds the light outside, the privacy film is nullified, and a potential onlooker would be able to see in. Especially at night. To fix that problem, I had boxes hidden in the ceiling of the perimeter of the house with blinds in them. I prefer the look with them concealed." He pointed to the thin outline of them in the ceiling. "When the balance of light between indoors and outdoors shifts, I have them automated to roll down, but they can also be activated manually," he said, gesturing to a panel mounted on the wall.

"How did you think to do all of that?"

"I was a combat engineer. So were Tak and Eli, the other guys at IPS. Chance recruited us from our last duty station, the 819th RED HORSE Squadron out at Malmstrom Air Force Base."

The Air Force. That made sense. Explained his military bearing, the straight posture and his neatness. "RED HORSE?"

"Sorry. Rapid Engineer Deployable, Heavy Operational Repair Squadron, Engineer. Somewhat redundant I know. The unit is always wartime ready. They rapidly mobilized people, equipment, and provided heavy repair capability, construction support and combat engineering anywhere in the world. Bottom line, we facilitated the mobility of friendly forces while impeding that of the enemy."

"That's impressive. Did you see a lot of combat?"

"More than I wanted. My last two deployments were with Special Forces. Those were rough."

"How long were you in?"

"Fifteen years. I joined straight out of high school."

He appeared far younger than he really was. She guessed thirty-three. Maybe thirty-two.

"Isn't it twenty years to retirement?" she asked, wondering why he would leave early.

"Yeah. I thought I'd be a lifer, but then I met Chance Reyes and he changed my mind. The clever guy knew exactly what he was doing. Very persuasive. He'd just opened the IPS office. The owner, Rip Lockwood, another guy from Laramie actually—"

"*The* Rip Lockwood. Infamous president of the outlaw motorcycle gang The Iron Warriors?"

"I don't know about infamous or outlaw, but yes. He started his company by gainfully employing the men in his motorcycle club and branched out from there."

Iron Warriors.

Ironside Protection.

The connection was obvious in hindsight.

"I met him once," Bo said. "He was a marine. Special Forces. Sharp. No-nonsense. I liked him. Rip had offered Chance a sweet bonus for recruitment with double the money if he got vets to join since Lockwood is a veteran himself. Chance scooped us out somehow, specifically eyeing people from RED HORSE. He was upfront and told us that he'd cut us in on a generous percentage of his bonus as a new hire incentive. Chance got the three us in one fell swoop, making IPS history to be the fastest to fully staff an office with all vets."

From her brief interaction with Chance Reyes, she'd gotten the impression he was a slick, smooth talker. Then she'd learned he was also a lawyer and it all made sense, but he struck her as a good guy. "Any regrets?"

"Nope. Not a single one. I didn't want to PCS and leave Montana for another duty station. Deploying all the time was hard. Tiring. IPS is more than a job. It's a career I'm passionate about, good at and it's given me a family that I wouldn't have otherwise." He lowered his gaze like he wished he hadn't told her so much.

She should've backed off, left it alone, but she moved closer to him. "Why not? Why don't you have any other family?"

"I grew up in foster care."

Questions raced through her mind. He'd already opened up more than he appeared comfortable with. She didn't want to push him.

Nora put her hand on his arm. Rock-hard muscle flexed along her palm beneath his shirt, and she couldn't help but curl her fingers around his sculpted bicep. "I'm sorry. I can't imagine growing up without any roots, but I do understand what it's like to go through life alone with no one to rely on, to support you, to share things with. Good or bad." A familiar ache pulsed in time with her heartbeat.

He glanced down at her hand and his expression hardened.

She lowered her palm as he moved away from her.

"You should see the rest of the house." He strode through the living room to an open door.

She peeked inside. It was a bathroom. "Only the one?"

He nodded.

"At least it's large," she said with a smile. It was huge. Two sinks with plenty of counter space. Soaking tub. Toilet tucked away in a water closet. A shower large enough to fit four people with dual rain heads, handheld wands, body jets and a built-in bench. She glanced up at the ceiling. "Are those built in speakers?"

"Yes. I'm more of a shower person."

"You like to relax in there, not just get clean?"

An uneasy nod, like she'd peeled back yet another layer he didn't want exposed. "The shower also doubles as a steam room."

"Wow," she said. "You really put a lot of thought into every detail." The house had been carefully crafted to fit his lifestyle.

He steered her to the room on the left. "This was the guest room."

Which he had turned into an office. Or rather a command center. There were three large screens on the long desk, in addition to a computer and lots of gadgets.

It shouldn't have been surprising since providing protection services was what he did for a living, but it was.

He sat behind the desk and typed on the keyboard, waking the monitors. "I don't keep the system activated unless I have a reason." A series of codes flew across the screen in time with the clacking of his typing. Tiny screens popped up on the three large monitors. Each showed a different part of the property. Front of the house. Left and right sides. Rear. The road leading up to the house. Various shots of the empty woods, where he had cameras mounted. Thorough coverage of the place. Bo handed her a tablet. "With that, you can see everything I can see from in here. Just power it on. You'll see a green button to 'monitor system' and tap it. That simple."

"Thanks."

She tucked the tablet under her arm as he spun out of the chair. Bo was back in the hallway beside her.

Moving to the room on the right, he shoved the door open wider. "This is the primary."

Her gaze fell to the king-size bed and dark walnut furniture that matched the hardwood floors.

It was also the only other room.

"Where am I supposed to sleep?" she asked.

"In here." He gestured to the bed.

Her lips parted on a sigh and she stared up at him wide-eyed.

"I'm going to put on fresh sheets," he said quickly. "I promise it'll be comfy."

Fresh sheets? She wasn't concerned about the bedding. "I'm supposed to sleep in here…with you?"

Shaking his head, he averted his gaze. "Oh, no, no. Of course not. I'll be out on the sofa."

"Is it a pullout?" Didn't look like one to her, but they were making them sleek these days.

"No, but it's long enough to fit me. Comfortable. Eli slept on it a few times after having too many beers when we've watched a game."

"I can't impose and have you sleeping on the sofa. I didn't realize—"

"Nora, stop," Bo cut her off, meeting her gaze, his voice deep and commanding.

The authority ringing in his tone shouldn't have been so appealing since she hated others having any power over her. Really, she did. But she couldn't ignore the tingles that danced over her skin at the way he'd spoken her name.

She raised her chin, looking back at him. "Okay. I just didn't want to put you out."

He watched her warily. "You're the client. It's not an imposition. This is my job."

So he kept reminding her.

A soft beeping sounded throughout the house, almost like a chime, repeating over and over.

"What is that?" she asked. "The alarm?"

"That sound means someone is coming down the road," he said, ducking back into the office. "It'll beep for ten seconds." Almost on cue the noise stopped. "If someone was getting close to the house by approaching from the woods, then the alarm would go off. It's a different sound. Much louder." He scanned the monitors, and she looked alongside him. A pickup truck was headed down the driveway. A silver Dodge Ram. "It's okay. A friend."

She followed him through the house. By the time they reached the living room, she heard the vehicle pulling up to the house. A car door slammed, heavy footfalls resounded up the stairs and then a hard pounding on the door made her flinch.

Bo was already at the front of the house. He glanced through the peephole—she supposed out of habit—and opened the door. Logan Powell stood on the other side.

"Come on in," Bo said.

Why was the detective here?

Logan stepped inside, but stayed on the wide doormat, apparently familiar with Bo's unspoken no shoes policy. "Hey. Chance asked me to get the police file on the Yuletide Killer from the Cold Harbor PD. They were quick to respond. I sent it to him along with the hotel security footage of the perp breaking into Nora's car. Unfortunately, we couldn't make a positive ID. I believe Chance is forwarding everything to the entire team."

"You didn't come all the way out here to tell us that," Bo said. A statement, not a question.

"No, I didn't." The detective removed his Stetson and raked a hand through his blond hair, his expression turning grim. "The ring that was in the box left for you… We believe we know who it belonged to. This morning, your neighbor, Mrs. Denise Moore, was found dead."

Nora rocked back on her heels, the words hitting her like a physical blow. "Murdered?"

"I'm afraid so."

"She was…" Her voice failed her a moment. "She was my friend." Mrs. Moore and her coworkers were the closest she had to friends. They cared about her and she cared about them.

Bo's eyes had gone steely hard. A muscle ticked in his cheek. "How was she killed?"

"I've never seen so much blood at a crime scene before,"

Logan said. His jaw clenched. He looked down at the hat in his hands. "He did unspeakable things to her. Killed her slowly. A neighbor reported blood in her driveway and that she didn't answer her door after he and his wife knocked loudly. The guy went around to the side of the house and peeked through a window. Saw the scene. Retched in the yard. Called 911."

Her chest tightened. She could barely breathe.

"Poor Mrs. Moore. She was so sweet and warm. Her son and grandkids are expecting her. She was supposed to leave to visit them tomorrow." A sob lodged in her throat, choking her. "He warned me. That monster told me that if I didn't play Santa Says, that there would be a new game." Sharks and Minnows. "A painful one. A game that will get very, very bloody."

Reality barreled through her hopeful facade, smashing it into bits. Terror and grief filled her heart. She was trapped in a horror movie. The killer would never stop. Not until she was dead. Tears filled her eyes, blurring her vision

Bo wrapped his arms around her, pulling her into a tight hug against his solid frame, and Nora realized she was shaking.

Resting her head on his chest, she breathed in through her nose and out through her mouth to loosen the knot in her throat and quell the rising tide of nausea that was swelling into a tsunami. "He told me I'd regret not playing his game." *He was right.* "And now she's dead." A sob slipped from her lips. "Mrs. Moore is dead because of me."

Chapter Four

Bo toggled from the cold case report back to the hotel security footage on his laptop and hit Play for the tenth time. A hood covered the back of the perp's head. The guy was around six feet tall with boots on—average build—and he kept his face turned away from the security cameras. He was in and out of Nora's car in less than sixty seconds.

A noise snagged Bo's attention. It came from inside the house. He pulled out the one earbud he'd been using to listen to jazz while he worked—the music helped him focus. He got up from his chair at the kitchen table and stepped into the hallway. The door to the primary bedroom was closed. He listened and heard nothing.

He would've sworn Nora was moving around, but no sound came from the bedroom. She was still resting.

Exhaling with relief, he sat back down at the handmade oak table in the kitchen.

For most of the day, she had been inconsolable, believing she was responsible for her neighbor's murder. The shock and guilt consumed Nora, and she seemed convinced she could have somehow prevented the tragedy. Bo had been at a loss about how to ease her conscience and make her feel any better. Hugging her tightly, holding her hand, offering words of reassurance—none of it did any good. Despite his best efforts, her tears kept flowing, along with her self-recrimination. Exhausted, she had showered and retreated to the bedroom to lie down.

Picking up his cell phone, he checked the state-of-the-art security app that he had downloaded. Prior to having Nora stay with him, he'd never had a need to have it on his phone. As he swiped through the interface, he noticed that all the lights on the app glowed a reassuring shade of green. The security system was functioning flawlessly and there were no signs of any movement near the house, giving him peace of mind.

However, he wasn't at ease for long. With a deep breath, he turned back to the cold case that had plagued his thoughts since he opened the e-mail from Chance. Carefully, he read through the police report once again, determined to uncover any missed clues that could bring closure to Nora's decade-long nightmare.

He stared at a picture of the note card that had been left at the crime scene. It was similar to the one sent to Nora, with the same hand-drawn images lining the border—except there was blood splattered on it and a single word typed in the center in all caps.

NAUGHTY.

The report detailed the exhaustive investigation carried out by the detectives. They had questioned every person connected to the case. Family members, friends, high school staff and even neighbors of Nora's and the three murdered teenage girls had been subjected to intense scrutiny.

No stone had been left unturned, or so it seemed. The detectives interrogated anyone who might have had a connection to the victims. Despite their tireless efforts, however, the investigation had yielded no concrete leads, no suspects, no motives beyond the sick thrill of a killer.

The murderer had gotten away scot-free with a heinous crime. Why take the risk of stalking Nora? Was he obsessed with her? Or was it because she was the only one who got away, and he refused to let her go? Or was there some other reason?

Bo scrolled through the file and found the numbers to two detectives that had been assigned to the case. One, Stacey Gagliardi, had more thorough reports and had questioned Nora's stepfather, Frank Howard, on her own several times.

On a hunch, he dialed the number for Detective Gagliardi, hoping it was still good.

It rang and rang and rang. Sighing, he prepared to leave a message that would probably never be returned.

"Hello," a woman finally answered when he thought it would go to voice mail.

"Is this Detective Gagliardi?"

"It is. Who's asking?"

"My name is Bo Lennox. I'm a private investigator with Ironside Protection Services in Bitterroot Falls. We've been hired to protect Noriyah Howard. We have reason to believe that the Yuletide Killer has found her and is stalking her again, with the intent of finishing what he started years ago."

The detective swore. "I saw her on the news a couple of months back. She was a victim of a mass shooting. Goes by the name Nora Santana now, right?"

"Yes, ma'am. That's correct."

"I wondered if he would come for her. Or if it was finally over. It had been so long, I had hoped that she would be okay, but then I heard the Bitterroot Falls PD had requested a copy of the file. I've been reexamining the case in my head all day. What can I do for you?"

"Detective Logan Powell made the request and shared the file with IPS. I've been reviewing it and had a few questions."

"I'm not sure how much help I can be after all this time," she said, sounding weary, "but go ahead, fire away."

Bo looked down at the notes he had made and started in no particular order. "You interviewed everyone close to the girls who were murdered as well as Nora, except for her biological father. Why is that?"

"The father, Jamal Banks, was living in Canada at the time—had been for several years prior—and he had no active relationship with Noriyah or her mother. I knew him. He used to be a corrections officer at the state prison. He's a Mountie now, like Dudley Do-Right. We had no reason to look into him."

"Nora mentioned having a best friend around that time. Savannah Watts. Do you know why the Watts girl wasn't at the slumber party the night of the murder?"

"If memory serves correctly, she wasn't invited. I believe the girl who was having the party, Jessica Graham, didn't get along with Savannah. But even if Savannah had been invited, she wouldn't have gone because she had the flu. The only reason Noriyah ended up going was because her bestie was sick. We spoke to Savannah the day after the murders, and I remember she didn't look good. The father took Savannah's temperature while we were there. I noticed it. Discreetly, of course. She was running a 101 fever. The illness was legitimate."

"Even though she wasn't invited to the party, did you look into Savannah's parents?"

"Sure did. The mother had been a nurse, a real pillar of the community until she got pancreatic cancer. She died before the murders. The father, Terry, used to be a cop. An accident ended his career, left him disabled. He needs a cane to walk now. Terry was home taking care of Savannah that night and her older brother Dylan was out at a party."

Bo referred back to his list of questions on the screen. "Jessica's parents were out of town that night. Any reason to suspect them? Did they make a habit out of leaving her alone?" The murders had taken place in the Graham house, yet there wasn't much in the case file on the parents.

"They left to attend a wedding. Spent two nights in Missoula. There was one thing that wasn't in my report. The father had a life insurance policy on his wife and Jessica."

"For how much?"

"A hundred thousand each."

Not enough to get rich but plenty to raise eyebrows. "Why did you leave it out of your report?"

"At the time, Jessica's father, Keith Graham, was mayor. My captain deemed the wedding a tight alibi and didn't want the existence of the insurance policy to unduly taint the case. When the perp went after Noriyah and tried to abduct her, my boss considered it proof that the mayor was not behind it. I disagreed but was ordered to drop Graham as a suspect."

Bo made several notes on the document he had opened on his laptop. The life insurance policy could be seen as questionable or practical depending on perspective. What troubled him more was the captain's insistence to eliminate Keith Graham prematurely as a potential suspect.

"It looks like you questioned Nora's stepfather several times," Bo said. "More than anyone else." The detective had put him under the microscope of suspicion for months. "Why is that?"

"For one, Frank's a former cop. He had retired a couple of years before the murders. You know who makes the best criminal? A cop. Hate to say it, but it's true. We know what our own are going to look for, how to cover our tracks, make evidence disappear. Second, I didn't trust his alibi that night of the triple homicide, when only his stepdaughter survived, that he was with his other children."

Bo glanced at the report. Son, Spencer, and daughter, Rosalinda, ages twenty-one and eleven at the time. They'd be thirty-one and twenty-one respectively today.

"Rosa said she was asleep. The son claimed to be in his room watching movies and had seen his dad in the house periodically. The thing is—Spencer and Dylan were close friends, even though the Watts boy was a little older. Thick as thieves. The same as Savannah and Noriyah. So why wasn't Spencer at the party with Dylan? When I asked him, Spencer lied. Right to my face."

Why lie? What was he hiding? "What about Nora's mom?"

"The mother, Luisa, was deceased by then. Killed in a car accident. Shortly after Spencer gave us an alibi for his father, Frank greased the wheels to get the kid hired as a cop. Fast-tracked ahead of a long waiting list of more qualified individuals, and off Spencer went to the police academy. Almost like Frank didn't want us asking him any more questions."

"Spencer's a cop, too? Seems like half the town is."

"In Cold Harbor, you're a cop, corrections officer at the state prison, coal miner or work in the service industry. The first three pay better than the last. I'm not saying that Frank helped Spencer in exchange for covering for him. But the timing was suspicious. You know what I mean? Not only that but Frank was hiding something during that investigation. So was Spencer. I'm one hundred percent positive about that. What it was that either was hiding, I may never know."

"What did your partner think?"

Gagliardi sighed. "Karl thought the only thing Frank was guilty of was being an alcoholic."

That might have been true, but cops also had a tendency to defend other cops, especially in small towns like Cold Harbor or Bitterroot Falls.

"After his wife, Luisa, died," Gagliardi continued, "Frank started hitting the bottle hard. He'd show up blitzed, reeking of booze. He hung on to his badge for two more years and then he was given a choice. Retire or be fired."

"What were the circumstances surrounding the car accident that killed Luisa?" Bo asked.

"Fourteen years ago, the Howards and Watts were together at dinner. Couples' night out. The two families were close. They'd all been drinking. Luisa was behind the wheel because she'd only had a glass of wine. Crashed the car. She was killed on impact. That was also the accident that ended Terry's career when he severely injured his leg."

"Do you know if Frank is still drinking or if he ever got help?"

"Looks like he's cleaned up his act. Heard he's been sober for a while now. Ever since Spencer got married and had a baby. I guess becoming a grandparent changed him for the better."

Bo glanced at his notes. "Did you ever have any theories about the killer's motive?"

"No. We never found any other than that creepy note with one word on it, *naughty*. Parents were afraid to leave their teens home alone after that. My partner, Karl, floated the idea that it was a nut job on a killing spree. The captain went with it. Once Noriyah moved to Wyoming and we had no other leads, we closed the case. In the end, we lacked the evidence to identify a prime suspect and to make an arrest." She huffed. "I really don't know what more I can tell you."

"Thank you for your time, Detective. I appreciate it."

"If you need anything else, don't hesitate to reach out."

"Will do. Happy holidays." Bo hung up and absorbed the details of the case and the information Detective Gagliardi shared with him.

Compiling his notes into a report for the team would help him process everything. For now, he couldn't help but feel a mix of frustration and determination. The absence of any solid leads only fueled his resolve to solve the perplexing case. Unearthing the truth behind the night that a monster claimed the lives of three teenage girls might be the only way to get justice.

Closing the report, he leaned back against his chair, the wood groaning beneath him. His mind buzzed with a sense of purpose. He knew that the answers he sought were hidden somewhere within the depths of the cold case, and he was determined to uncover them.

The bedroom door creaked open. Nora padded barefoot into the kitchen. She straightened the sweats and oversize T-shirt she'd put on. With her curly hair tousled and wild, she looked groggy. Sexy.

Yawning, she stretched as she came into the kitchen and he could tell she wasn't wearing a bra beneath the shirt. Watching her, he got the impression of a feline. Sinuous and elegant. There was nothing blatant or deliberate about her movement. Yet, she had a sensual allure he found captivating.

"You slept," he said, giving her a tentative smile. "I hope I didn't wake you. I tried to be quiet."

"I didn't hear a peep." She smiled back and set her cell phone on the table. "Thank you. For taking my case. I was able to sleep a little because I knew you were out here protecting me."

Warmth tickled his chest. "Are you hungry?"

"Did you just hear my stomach growl?"

"No, but you didn't eat anything all day. How does pizza sound to you?"

"Great."

"I always order from Giorgio's." He picked up his phone and hit the number to call them.

"You must eat a lot of pizza if you have them on speed dial."

He stiffened at how she had picked up on that small detail. There wouldn't be much he'd be able to get past her. That thought made him squirm just a bit.

"Giorgio's, how can I help you?" the hostess asked.

"What do you want?" he whispered to Nora.

"Anything is fine with me," she said, and he frowned, not believing her. "Really. I'll eat anything."

"Order for delivery." He gave the hostess his phone number, and they verified his address.

"What can I get for you?" the woman on the other end asked.

"One large mushroom and spinach with two side salads."

"Okay. That'll be one hour."

"Let the driver know there's a ten-dollar tip for him if he can deliver it in less than thirty minutes."

"I will."

He hung up.

"Big spender," Nora said.

"The delivery driver is always the same guy. Jeremy.

He's a college kid who really relies on tips. I like to do what I can to help him."

"It's nice of you to do that. Little things can make a big difference."

She reached over and covered his hand with both of hers. Her palms were warm, her hands small, but also so capable. This woman had faced danger and death multiple times and still chose to fight. Even when she ran, she made sure she protected herself, taking self-defense classes, changing her name, pulling away from those she loved most. A huge sacrifice. That took strength and courage.

So did walking into his office, looking him straight in the eye, and pushing him to personally handle her case.

They didn't say anything for a long moment as the heat from her skin seeped into him. It felt good. Nice. Bo couldn't remember the last time he'd been touched like this. Her affection, no, her kindness singed him with heat.

He wanted to take the warmth and tenderness she offered.

But he kept crossing the line with her and needed to get it together. Tearing his gaze from hers, he pulled his hands into his lap.

"At the IPS office, no one explained how this is supposed to work with the expenses, like the pizza," she said. "We didn't discuss fees. I didn't even sign a contract."

"Don't worry about anything. I'll keep track of all expenses and IPS will reimburse me. As for you, you won't owe us a dime. Chance decided this will be pro bono."

A look of perplexed surprise crossed her face. "I don't understand. Why?"

"Chance works very hard to bring in wealthy clients, so that when we have a special situation, such as yours, we can afford to do it pro bono."

"I can afford to pay. Maybe not your standard fee, not that I'm entirely sure what it is, but I don't need charity. Someone else with more limited resources than I have might need your services. Surely you can't take on every deserving case free of charge."

She was a good person with a big heart.

He'd already suspected as much about her. "Each situation is unique. Chance makes the call on how we handle it, or if we do at all. But not every case is as dire as yours."

"You mean most of your clientele don't have a serial killer stalking them?" Her tone was light, but her eyes were somber.

"Honestly, you're the first. I can't imagine anyone more deserving of our services free of charge than you."

She pursed her lips. "Can I ask you something?"

"Of course."

A curious glint flickered in her eyes, making him think of a lioness prowling the grasslands.

"If what you told me is true," she said, her voice soft, her gaze piercing, "that you can't imagine anyone being more deserving of IPS services, then why didn't you want to help me? I practically had to twist your arm into it."

A taut silence fell between them.

For several strained beats of his heart, he sat there, staring at her, with no clue how to answer. He decided to tell her the truth.

Chapter Five

Bracing herself for his answer, Nora stared at Bo.

"I didn't think I'd be the best fit for your situation," he said.

The response told her nothing, and she suspected that it had been his plan. "Why not?" she asked, digging deeper.

His lips twitched and he clenched his jaw. "It's nothing bad about you. I, um, I'd prefer not to say. A personal reason. Is that okay?"

She nodded slowly. "It is. Living the way that I have, hiding, not getting close to people, has made me very good with boundaries," she said, dropping it. He looked relieved. "I just hope this assignment won't get you into trouble with your girlfriend." She cringed inside that she had been too obvious with her question. Was he single? Or did he keep putting up a wall between them because he was involved with someone?

Normally, she was the one to shy away from questions and lingering glances and any touch that made her feel, but whenever she was near him, there was a magnetic pull tugging her toward him. The idea of getting close to anyone frightened her, but the thrill of being in his proximity was stronger.

"No trouble to worry about," he said. "I had a girlfriend back when I was still in the Air Force, but after I got out, she left because of her change of duty station, and I didn't want a long-distance relationship. It came to a natural end."

"No one in your life since?" she asked, trying to filter the uncertainty from her voice.

"The job keeps me busy and in a small town, I need to be careful. If I date too many women, I'd quickly develop a reputation as a lady's man, like Chance before he settled down with Winter. It's simply easier not to date than to fish in a tiny pond," he said, lifting a shoulder in a shrug.

She bit her bottom lip. His gaze dropped to her mouth, and she wondered what his full lips would feel like pressed to hers. Not that she'd kissed many guys—she could count them on one hand and have fingers left over—but she was curious about *this* man.

Keeping her gaze locked on his, she propped her elbow on the table and leaned closer. "How long have you worked at Ironside Protection Services?"

The only light in the room came from the white twinkling lights wrapped around the Christmas tree, creating an intimate bubble in the dimly lit space between them.

"Three years."

Three years since his last relationship, give or take.

"What about you? No one special in your life?"

"There's no one. I never know when I might have to pick up and leave. Makes a relationship a complication I can't afford to have."

"People tend to describe relationships as complicated. This is the first time I've ever heard anyone refer to it as a complication."

Nora lowered her head and took a breath. "After my roommate, Jane, was murdered, I always worried that if

I let anyone get close, I'd only be putting them in danger. So, I never have." She looked around the room. "I didn't realize how late it had gotten."

The sun must have set hours ago, activating the automatic shades. Aside from the lit Christmas tree, the rest of the house was dark.

"Siri, turn on living room lights at sixty percent," he said. Soft amber lighting illuminated the space.

"Voice controlled smart lights. Nice. Can you do the same with the locks, thermostat and music?"

"Siri, play my work playlist—shuffled."

The smooth sound of jazz flowed from the speakers. "Coltrane?" she asked.

"Good ear," he said with a nod. "This is from his *My Favorite Things* album. You like jazz?"

"My stepdad loves it." The smile on her face faded. "At least he used to listen to it all the time. Now, I wouldn't know."

"Were you close to him?" he asked.

"Yeah, I was. Closer to him than my biological father. I called him Pa. My mom thought it was a nice compromise."

"Was a compromise necessary?"

She shrugged. "Mom used to say that my dad was a good guy. The memories I have of him are hazy. He stopped coming by to see me after he moved to Bull River, up in Canada. Mom said the divorce was hard for both of them, but he had difficulty watching her build a new family with Pa."

"How old were you when he relocated?"

"Not really sure. My sister, Rosa, was a toddler around that time. I guess I was about seven or eight." A rhythmic beeping sounded, the alert system warning a vehicle was headed toward his house.

"The pizza must be here."

"Does the alert go off as soon as someone turns down the road?"

"The wireless sensor has a quarter-mile transmission range, but I programmed it to go off once a car gets one hundred feet down the private road. The buffer gives someone a chance to make a U-turn in case they've taken a wrong turn before triggering the system."

Grabbing his phone with one hand, he got up from the table and rested his other hand on the hilt of the Glock holstered on his hip.

"I'm starving," she said. "Where are the plates?"

He started toward the front door. "Cabinet above the dishwasher."

A car door in the driveway closed.

"Bo," she said, drawing his attention. He stopped, looking back at her. "Thank you. For saying yes. For letting me stay here. It's nice not to be on the run again, alone in a hotel room, with only my thoughts to keep me company."

"YOU NEED HELP. We'll do everything in our power to protect you." Bo meant every word. Not only did Nora have him to rely on, but she also had the full force of IPS behind her. Although Chance was in Colorado, working on different IPS business for Rip Lockwood, he was only a phone call away. Autumn was busy analyzing the note cards that had been left for Nora and building out a profile of the killer. For years, Autumn had worked as a consulting forensic psychologist for the FBI before she burned out and sought a professional change in a location closer to her sisters. The other two guys, Eli and Tak, were going to begin updating the security system for a local business tomorrow, but if Bo needed them for an emergency, he could count on them to drop everything and be there.

"I appreciate it," Nora said.

Bo went up to the peephole and looked through it. Jeremy rounded the rear of his car and bound up the steps, carrying the food.

Taking his wallet from his back pocket, Bo fished out enough cash and opened the door.

Jeremy greeted him with a wide smile. "Evening. I made it here in twenty-four minutes."

"I hope you didn't have to speed to do it."

"Nope, I just made you my first stop."

Bo glanced over his shoulder while the kid tugged open the Velcro flap of the insulated bag. The driver's side door of his vehicle hung open. "Did you close one of the car doors? I thought I heard one shut."

Jeremy handed him the food and took the money. "Oh, that was probably the delivery guy."

Prickles crept up Bo's spine. "What delivery guy?" he asked, everything inside him tightening as he went on immediate alert. He looked around. Saw no one else.

The rhythmic beeps chimed. Bo whipped his phone out from his pocket.

"He was just here," Jeremy said. "A van was sitting on the main street like the driver was lost, but then he turned down your road right behind me."

Nora came up beside Bo.

He handed her the food. "Get back," he said, urging her away from the door. He brought up the security app, managing to catch a glimpse of the van leaving before it disappeared from sight.

"I assumed he was a delivery guy," Jeremy said, "because he hopped out with a package, dropped it off, and left before I even got out of the car." The young man bent down and picked up something nestled in the outer corner of the doorway. The kid handed him a red and gold box with a bow on top. "Here you go."

"Did you get a look at him?" Bo asked. "Did you see his face?"

"No. He had on a ball cap and hood. His head was down. I didn't think anything of it. Figured he was cold and in a rush. Why?"

Bo dropped the box on the floor and looked at Nora. "Get your gun and keep the door locked until I get back. Don't open it for anyone." He slammed the front door shut and hit a button on the keypad, locking it.

"Is something wrong?" Jeremy asked.

Without responding, Bo drew his gun, ran to his truck and fired it up. He sped down the private road, his heart slamming against his rib cage. Reaching the main street, he scanned the intersection in the hope of seeing which direction the van had gone.

No sign of the vehicle. He could've left either way. Both routes would eventually lead to the state highway.

Slamming his hand on the steering wheel, Bo swore. That monster had found her.

After they left IPS earlier, on the ride to his house, Bo had checked his mirrors to see if they were being followed, but truth be told, he hadn't been as vigilant as perhaps he should've. Had he been so distracted by her proximity in his truck that he'd missed a tail?

The killer had sat on the main road and waited for an opportunity to get close. To leave another package for her. *Nora.*

Whatever was inside that box, he didn't want her to be alone with the contents.

Bo threw the truck in Drive, made a U-turn and rushed

back toward the house. Jeremy drove past, giving his horn a little honk and waved.

At the house, Bo screeched to a stop, dashed up the steps and inside to find Nora sitting still as stone at the table.

The red and gold box was open in front of her.

His mind raced with terrible possibilities of what might be in the box. He crossed the room, and the smell hit him first. The same cologne—smoky, spicy, a hint of sweetness. Reminded him of a campfire.

Tension crackled along his nerve endings like static on a dry day as he stepped up to the table. He looked over Nora's shoulder, down at the contents.

Another lump of coal. More sugar plums.

And another typed message on the same kind of card.

Denise Moore screamed and begged before she died.
Because you didn't play by the rules.
No police. No private investigators.
Go home. Alone. Or else.

Bo put the lid on the box, covering it. The note wasn't his most pressing concern. It was Nora. Sensing her vulnerability after what happened to her neighbor, he moved around the chair and crouched beside her. He gently took her trembling hands and held them. "Hey, look at me," he said, and her gaze lifted from the table to meet his. "You're not going back home and you're not going to be alone. Calling the police, going to IPS, was the right decision."

Her eyes turned glassy as she shook her head. "I got her killed."

"You are not responsible for what happened to your neighbor. You didn't take Mrs. Moore's life. That sick monster did. Don't let him saddle you with that kind of guilt because that's exactly what he wants. If you do, you'll react emotionally to this, and then you're as good as dead," he said, desperately needing her to believe him.

"It doesn't matter what I do. Where I go. He keeps finding me. Maybe I've been living on borrowed time and—"

"Nora," he managed to grind out and she stopped talking. "Santa Says, Sharks and Minnows—that's all a diversion. *This* is the real game. Getting you to give up. Getting you to make a mistake. Everything that you do matters. You have to keep fighting. You can't let him win."

She let out a shaky breath. "I want to see him behind bars or dead. But..." She tipped her head back and closed her eyes. "I don't want anyone else to get hurt because of me."

"You can't play his game. Do you understand?"

Sniffling, she nodded. "I refuse to let him win."

He was relieved to hear her say the words, but something in her voice didn't fully convince him.

The twisted animal stalking her had figured out Nora's weakness—her empathy. Her big heart and the way she cared about others, even for a neighbor. Like any weak spot, the killer was using it against her by applying pressure.

That perverse exploitation and the way she struggled not to cave to it reached out and grabbed hold of Bo. It gripped him where he was most vulnerable, making him long to comfort and protect her.

He put a palm on her cheek and caressed her face, and she looked down at him. He saw fear in her eyes, but determination, too. A resolve that had kept her alive thus far.

"I know that you've done this on your own for so long that it might be hard for you to trust IPS," he said. "To trust me. But you hired us, asked me to get personally invested, and now I am. You're not in this alone. Not anymore."

Tears tracked down her cheeks and she wrapped her arms around his neck. On a reflex, he pulled her into a hug. Awareness infiltrated his veins as the smell of her hit him. Sugar cookies and sunshine—if sunshine had a scent that was what it'd be, light and warm and ethereal. The smell triggered a response deep inside him, one that he struggled to dismiss and, at the same time, ached to explore. He wanted a piece of that big heart of hers. Holding her close, with her face pressed to his throat, he wondered what it would be like. To have someone so brave and capable in his corner. Caring for him.

Maybe once the chaos subsided and they stopped the killer terrorizing her—and he wasn't her bodyguard anymore—he would ask her out on a proper date.

Maybe.

For now, his full focus had to be on protecting her. No room for anything else.

"Nora." Her name left his lips in a whisper. The killer wanted her isolated and afraid. Bo wasn't going to allow misplaced guilt to drive her to make a mistake that she'd regret. "Let me help you," he said.

"I will." She tightened her arms around him. "It's just that nothing ever works. Not for long. He just keeps coming after me."

Her breath brushed his cheek, warmth tickling his chilled face, and a shiver teased over every male nerve ending in his body.

The dampness from her tears soaked into the collar of his shirt and Bo held her tighter. He rubbed her back and gently squeezed her shoulder, doing his best to comfort her, to ease her trembling.

But she continued to shake and sob. He planted kisses on top of her head. "Shh. I'll get you through this." He kissed her brow and the corner of her eye, tasting her salty tears as he petted her hair. Trailed his lips lower, across her cheek.

Awareness buzzed through him. The need to console her slid toward something deeper, something more primitive. He eased back before he crossed a line, and they were nose to nose. His gaze fell to her mouth. Her rosy lips parted on a sigh, her breath hitching on a sob.

Her glassy eyes met his and then she looked down at his mouth.

Was she thinking the same thing as him?

If so, it made the thought doubly bad.

Clearing his throat, Bo started to stand, but Nora gripped his shirt collar, pulled him back down and pressed her lips to his.

Surprise jolted through him, pinning him to the spot, and he hesitated until her tongue penetrated the seam of his mouth. Electricity flared between them, and he kissed her back. Curling his fingers in her hair, he absorbed the feel of her soft curves moving against him. The heat of her mouth, the slip and slide of her tongue tangling with his, the warmth from her body seeping into him, seared him down to the bone.

Her hands roamed over him with a hunger that matched his. She tasted rich and sweet, fueling the desire burning in his veins. Lean muscle flexed beneath his palm, wicked curves molding to his hands as he explored her body.

Clinging to her, he lost himself in the moment. In her. In the way she sighed and how she excited him, rousing parts of him that had been dormant for far too long. He needed this kiss like a drowning man needed oxygen.

Her fingernails scraped against his scalp. "Bo."

The sound of his name pierced the bubble and it burst, bringing him back to his senses. What was he doing?

With a shuddering breath, he pulled back, dropping his hands to his sides. "I'm sorry. I don't know what I was thinking." That was the problem. He hadn't been thinking at all. Too caught up in the moment, feeling. "I shouldn't have done that."

She was upset. Distraught. Needed comfort.

Not to be pawed at and kissed and taken advantage of.

He should have consoled her. But only with his words. Nothing more.

Still, he wanted to kiss her again, with no holds barred.

She blinked up at him. Tears clung to her lashes, but she'd stopped crying. "Don't be sorry. I'm the one who kissed you."

True, but the problem was he had kissed her back.

"It wasn't professional," he said, stepping away from her. "It won't happen again."

But she eased closer, testing his restraint. "It's your job to help me, isn't it?"

"Yes, but…" Giving into his baser instincts wasn't what he wanted. His gaze dropped to her mouth again, and all sorts of dirty ideas sprang to mind. Ideas that would get him fired and get her hurt.

Hell. She was sexy and sensual and so soft. From the day he'd met her, he'd wanted her. And that made him the ultimate jerk because, at the time, she'd been shot and scared. Just as vulnerable then as she was right now.

He was the worst.

"A minute ago, I didn't need *professional* from you," she said. "I needed something more personal. A connection. To not *feel* alone." She swallowed as though it was hard for her to admit it. "You gave me that. To get through this, I might need more than a bodyguard. Maybe I need a friend, too." Taking another step, erasing any space between them, she rested her head on his chest and leaned into him.

Steeling himself against the tempting feel of her body, he wrapped his arms around her, loosely, and steered his thoughts toward the job. The mission and nothing else. "We're going to find him," he said, thinking of the monster who had the audacity to leave that box on his doorstep, "and make him pay for what he's done."

No matter how long it took. Of that fact, he was one hundred percent certain.

How they would accomplish it, he had no idea. But he had to figure it out quickly. Something in his gut told him that from here on out, things were only going to escalate.

Chapter Six

The next day, three house tours had gone smoothly aside from the fact she didn't make a sale. The morning and lunch had been thankfully uneventful. Bo's diligence as a bodyguard should have put Nora at ease, but she was still on edge. Jumpy. Nerves raw.

She reminded herself it was to be expected. Somehow, she had managed not to think of Mrs. Moore or the threatening notes every single minute. Having Bo at her side helped. He was like a guardian angel, ready to shield her from any harm that might come their way. His protective instincts were sharp, and his unwavering commitment to keeping her safe gave her the confidence to face anything.

But in the back of her mind, it was like she was waiting for the guillotine to drop. Waiting for the killer to exact a new punishment for her defiance. Waiting for his next attempt on her life.

Emotions seesawed through her as Bo turned into the parking lot of the Methodist church that was situated between Bitterroot Falls and Cutthroat Creek. He drove around back and parked close to the auxiliary building where they ran the food pantry and soup kitchen.

She turned to him, wondering how they were going to

handle things inside. "It was easy enough to pass you off as my assistant earlier while I was showing the houses, but that won't fly here." She nodded at the church's auxiliary building.

The pantry was open for three hours, three days a week, and once a month they served a hot meal. She donated her time whenever she was available.

A line had already started forming. The days when the church provided hot meals were the most popular. Not everyone who came was unhoused. Many were veterans or elderly, but all were in need, having a hard time making ends meet with the high cost of groceries.

"They know me and the real estate agency here," she said. "It's a small company. No one has an assistant." She certainly didn't want word of one to get back to her colleagues, stirring up professional trouble she didn't need. "Everyone will notice you hovering and you're not dressed like someone in need of a free meal. What should I tell people when they ask who you are?"

"Who do you want me to be?" he asked, his gaze searching her face.

A dangerous question that had her mind careening back to the hug he'd given her last night. To all the hugs since she'd learned of Mrs. Moore's murder. To the kiss they'd shared that had left her melting and aching for more.

She could take care of herself, but it was nice not to have to. Each time, his strong arms wrapped around her, it felt so good. Warm and comforting. It was an unexpected, pleasant change to have someone she could lean on.

Before one of Bo's embraces, she never would've thought a simple hug held the power to make a situation better. A little brighter. His strong yet gentle touch was a source of solace for her in the midst of this nightmare.

And kissing him transported her away from reality, made her want to forget the reason he was actually with her.

Because a relentless killer found me again.

Nora shrugged in response to his question. "I can't say you're a friend from out of town visiting me." Half the women in Bitterroot Falls had already noticed him strutting around. The other half found out who he was seven weeks ago. "The mass shooting made Ironside Protection Services a household name after you helped apprehend the sniper." The entire IPS team had been featured on the front page of the *Bitterroot Beacon*.

"Then there's two ways we can approach it. Option A, you could introduce me as your bodyguard. Explain that you've been harassed, threatened, and have a legitimate fear for your life."

Her stomach did a somersault at the suggestion and nausea swamped her. "I don't want to admit I have a bodyguard. There'd be too many questions. About me. My past. The looks of pity I'd draw." She shook her head as her chest tightened. Being in the spotlight was the last thing she wanted after years of learning how to navigate the shadows. "What's option B?"

"We tell them I'm your boyfriend," he said, and the knot in her chest loosened. "We say I've taken off a few days from work and I want to spend as much time with you as I can. But that would require us to act familiar with each other. Close. I'd have to touch you. Nothing to cross the line, just hold your hand or put an arm around you. Something like that."

A shiver trickled down her spine at the idea of him being her boyfriend. Faux boyfriend anyway. At having people believe it. But would they?

Licking her lips, she swallowed and looked away from him, suddenly worried about what he might see on her face.

She was always alone. Never dated. She hesitated at what to do.

"I think telling the truth is the way to go," he said, lightly. "It'll be awkward at first, but once folks get over their initial surprise, they'll be more apt to pay attention to anything suspicious, which is a good thing."

If they knew, they'd treat her differently. That would not be good for her. Half the day had been normal, or as close to it as possible. She wanted the remainder of the day to be the same. Was that too much to ask for? A bit of normalcy instead of nonstop turmoil?

The story was better than the truth and worth a try. "I don't want to tell them. Please."

"Well then, boyfriend it is."

Ignoring the sudden flare of heat in her cheeks, she nodded, suppressing a smile. "How long have we been dating in case they ask?"

"Keep it vague. Say it's new."

"Okay."

She tucked her purse under the passenger's seat. Sometimes drug addicts popped up for a hot meal and the director of the program, Susan Whitehall, advised them that it was best to leave any valuables locked in their vehicle.

They climbed out of his Tacoma. Bo came around to her side, took her hand in his, interlacing their fingers as they headed for the auxiliary building.

Big and brooding with a patient nature that calmed her and made her feel safe, Bo was the only one at IPS who she was willing to trust with her life. Having him pretend to be her boyfriend was a consolation prize for the fact that she needed protection.

"Do you think everyone has heard about Mrs. Moore?" she asked him. "I didn't see anything on the news about her this morning."

"Logan texted me that he was able to keep it quiet. Reporters haven't caught on yet. They will soon enough. But since the neighbors called it in, there's no way to know who they might've told. Just be prepared in case it comes up."

She nodded, bracing herself for anything.

Skirting the line, they went up to the door that had a sign stating the hours, and she knocked.

Susan glanced out through the glass panel at the top of the door and spotted her.

Nora smiled and waved.

The door swung open. Susan stepped out. "I was starting to get worried you wouldn't make it." The sixty-two-year-old woman gave her a one-armed hug and then gestured for them to enter. She turned to those standing in line. "Ten more minutes and we'll be ready for you all." Susan shut the door and faced the two of them. Her salt-and-pepper streaked hair was up in a bun. Reading glasses with a tortoiseshell frame hung from a braided leather strap around her neck. "I can always count on you, Nora, to keep the line moving. I don't know what I would've done without you. November and December are our busiest hot meal days." Susan looked at her companion. "Who do we have here?"

"This is Bo Lennox, my boyfriend," Nora said, without the last word sticking to the roof of her mouth.

Susan's face brightened with a wide smile. "Welcome, Bo. I recognize the surname as well as the face. You work over at that Ironside agency, don't you?"

"Yes, ma'am, Ironside Protection Services."

"If you call me ma'am, you'll make me feel my age. I'm Susan. We're a little short-staffed today. I could use you over in toiletries," she said, pointing to one end of the room. "Nora, you can work the food line as usual." Susan nodded to the opposite side, tables and chairs filled in the long space between.

"Today is my day off." Bo put his hand on Nora's lower back. "I was hoping to spend the day with her. Would you mind if we worked together?"

Susan smiled again, radiating warmth. "How sweet. I wish I had a handsome young man who couldn't keep his hands off me and wanted to spend the day at my side." She laughed, and they chuckled. "I can ask Roger to switch to toiletries, but he can be stubborn."

"Introduce me to him," Bo said, "and I'll take care of it."

Raising her eyebrows, Susan smirked. "You're welcome to try." She led the way over to the food line where everyone was setting up and introduced Bo to the group, saving Nora from doing it. "Roger, can you spare a minute?" Susan motioned for him to follow her off to the side.

Bo kissed Nora's cheek. "I don't think this will take long," he whispered.

"You don't know Roger," she responded in a low voice.

He winked and went to join Susan and Roger.

Nora watched him walk away and shake Roger's hand.

"I need to get shot," a woman said, and Nora jerked her gaze away from Bo's back—*and his very nice backside*—to see Kimberly setting down a pan of vegetables beside her.

"I'm sorry. What did you say?" Nora must've misheard her.

"You told me that a hot guy from IPS interviewed you after you were shot by the sniper. Remember? That's him, isn't it? You told me he gave you a ride home and everything." Kimberly waggled her eyebrows.

"There was no *everything* to the ride home. He was

a perfect gentleman, and I didn't say he was hot." Even though he was hot enough to set every cell in her body ablaze.

Bo looked back at her and, to her surprise, gave her a discreet thumbs up. She smiled at him, her cheeks heating.

"You blushed when you spoke about him the way you're doing right now. Besides, all the guys at Ironside are yummy, aren't they?" Kimberly laughed and nudged Nora's arm with her elbow.

Everyone at IPS was smart, capable and undeniably attractive—including Autumn—but only Bo made her pulse quicken and her thighs tingle and her thoughts stray. Looking at him now, one word ran through her head on repeat. *Wow*.

"Good for you, finally getting a boyfriend and a handsome one to boot. You only had to take a bullet to do it."

"Is Carl here today?" Nora asked, mentioning Kimberly's husband.

The busty blonde-haired woman flattened her mouth in a tight line. "Yeah, he's over in toiletries." She waved a hand toward the far side of the room.

Grinning, Bo came back over. "It's done."

"How?" She lowered her voice. "He's the most resistant man."

"I disarmed him by starting off with the worst thing that might pop into his head. I told him he wasn't going to like what I had to say and even though he didn't know me, he was going to think I was a jerk. Then I simply asked him for a favor, explained the situation, apologized for the inconvenience and said that I'd be grateful."

"And that really worked?"

"Sort of. Roger likes you. Said how nice you are five times. I did have to promise to treat you right." He put his arm around her waist and kissed her cheek again.

Her face heated and she couldn't stop a smile from surfacing.

"She is the nicest," Kimberly said, reminding Nora of how close the woman was still standing. "Always volunteers to stay late for cleanup."

"It's a part of the job." Nora grabbed aprons, hairnets and gloves and handed Bo the things he needed to work the food line. "We all have to pitch in, even for the parts we might not enjoy."

Kimberly frowned. "Tell that to the ones who never help clean."

The comment was valid but pointing fingers never solved anything.

"I'm happy to pitch in and clean up," Bo said, "if I get to do it with my lovely girlfriend."

Another wave of heat suffused Nora's cheeks.

"Aww. I wish Carl said sweet stuff like that to me."

Susan clapped her hands, getting everyone's attention. "This is our last day to serve a hot meal for the rest of the year. Don't forget to smile and wish everyone a happy holiday. In two minutes, I'll start the music and let everyone in."

Nora couldn't help thinking about Mrs. Moore and how the sweet older woman wouldn't get to spend Christmas with her son and grandkids. Guilt didn't inundate her this time. Something Bo had told her last night clicked in her head.

Instead of allowing herself to feel guilty, she'd cling to her anger and her resolve and do the one thing the killer didn't want her to do. Survive.

Christmas carols played over the speakers and hungry people flowed inside, making her nerves flutter.

Yet, that little voice inside told her that as long as Bo was by her side, she'd be all right.

Chapter Seven

Bo smiled until his cheeks ached. "Happy holidays," he said with each serving of roast turkey he put on a plate. This was the third pan of meat that had been brought out from the kitchen.

Prior to today, he had no idea that there were so many people in need in the town and surrounding area. This wasn't a large city with unsheltered individuals living on the streets. But families and veterans and even college students who couldn't afford food filed into the building, thankful for the meal.

The food service was nearly finished and so far, so good. Keeping his head on a swivel, he scanned the room, memorizing faces, watching the crowd, scrutinizing any male around six feet tall with an average build. The killer could hide in plain sight here and they'd never know.

Bo had played back the video feed coverage from the front of his house when the pizza had been delivered. The man had anticipated a camera above the door and wore a scarf pulled up over his face and a nondescript ball cap with a hood, and he'd kept his head tilted down.

The killer had been on his doorstep, within his grasp, and yet, Bo wasn't any closer to identifying him.

No one had shown any aggression toward Nora at the church. Though there'd been some attention that Bo had considered unwanted. One man kept looking at her like he was undressing her with his eyes and another asked her for extra bread rolls whenever there was a small break in the line.

"When are they going to let people have seconds if they're interested?" Bo asked her, though it was impossible to whisper amid the din of music and voices. Every table was full and engaged in lively conversations.

"Any minute now since things have slowed down. Less than a handful of new people have shown up during the past three songs."

He searched the crowd. "Where's that guy?"

"Which guy?" she asked, though he was certain she should know who he was talking about.

"The one who keeps asking for more rolls. He's too chatty. Complimenting you every time he comes over." Bo suspected he was on drugs. He had the classic signs of a methamphetamine user: shifty red eyes with dilated pupils, thinning hair, gaunt, decayed teeth and scabs on his face. He moved and spoke fast. Another guy with good, thick-soled work boots kept his distance at the far side of the room near toiletries and also gave Bo a bad vibe. At the moment, he couldn't spot either of them.

"He's only trying to get on my good side," Nora said, "so I give him extra bread. It doesn't mean anything."

"Everything means something."

The meth head emerged from the bathroom, and Bo watched the guy sit back down at a table near the food service line.

Bo's phone buzzed. Not a missed call or a text message. The vibration was constant, making his pulse spike.

He dished out the serving of turkey he was holding onto the plate in front of him, set the tongs down and took out his cell phone.

"What is it?" She glanced at him as she spooned vegetables onto the person's plate and then added a bread roll. "Happy holidays," she said to the woman.

Bo looked down at the alert on his phone and tapped it. The steady vibration from his phone automatically stopped when the app opened, and he read the system message. "Someone's in the woods, approaching the house."

"Could it be an animal?"

"It's possible, but doubtful," he said, and alarm widened her eyes. The sensors had a fifty-foot-wide motion range and sometimes deer set them off, but he'd placed them well to reduce the probability. The real concern was the pattern of movement. "The first sensors triggered were near a road where someone would park and then enter the woods on foot. I can't see who or what it is. The cameras are positioned closer to the house. Right now, I only know there's movement."

Movement that had to be investigated.

"Do you need to leave?" she asked, as if picking up on what he was thinking. "Go out there and see who it is? If it's him?"

Bo didn't want to miss another opportunity to catch this guy, but he also couldn't leave Nora unprotected.

"No. I won't go, but I need to call the team. See if Tak and Eli can head out there." "Jingle Bells" boomed from the speakers. Kids ran around the space, playing and laughing. Mealtime chatter had grown even louder. "I'll step outside and give them a call."

It would also give him a chance to check for anyone suspiciously loitering outside the building. Movement at his house wasn't cause for him to lower his guard here at the church. This event was the perfect excuse for people to mill around with no questions asked.

"Okay," Nora said. "But if one of the guys can't investigate it, I understand if you need to leave. Everyone will be here for hours. We'll be serving food until seven and then we still have to clean up. I'll be fine if you need to go."

Bo wasn't willing to take that chance. "I'll be back in a few minutes." He leaned in and pressed a quick kiss on her forehead, his lips brushing against her warm skin. Only for the sake of maintaining appearances that they were a couple—at least that's what he told himself. But Bo found it hard to deny the faint flicker in his chest, the gentle spark that ignited between them every time he touched her.

Choosing option B had been a risky move because there was a glimmer of something real beneath the pretense. For him, anyway. He wondered whether it was the same for her.

If that kiss last night was any indication that she was interested in him and hadn't simply been in need of affection, the comfort of any bodyguard, then he had his answer.

Dismissing the rogue thought, he made a beeline for the door and brought up his list of favorites on his phone. He hit Tak's name first.

"We have enough food left," Susan said, "to invite those still hungry to come up for a second helping. We ask that you allow expectant mothers and children to go to the front."

People got up and started forming a line again.

A commotion at the other end of the room had Susan rushing to the far side, where toiletries were handed out.

The guy Bo had mentioned jumped up out of his seat and

hustled over to her. "Can I just take four rolls? I'll leave the meat for the others. Please, pretty lady. Those keep and I can munch on them for a couple of days."

Sighing, Nora looked at the kids moving through the line toward her and then down at the aluminum pan. There were only six rolls left. "Go ahead and take the rest."

"You're an angel." Beaming, the guy scooped up the remainder of the bread. "Thank you so much."

She turned to Kimberly. "Cover the turkey and veggies. I'm going to run to the kitchen to grab some more bread rolls. Tell whoever wants any more to hang here until I get them. It'll only take a sec."

Kimberly nodded. "Sure thing."

Nora grabbed the pan and hurried off through the double doors into the kitchen. Glancing around, she spotted the bags of bread lined up on a long, stainless-steel table in the rear of the room. She headed to the back part of the kitchen, set the pan down and started opening the rolls.

Dumping the last bag of bread that would fit in the pan, she sensed a presence right before she heard the footsteps drawing close, the soft thud of thick rubber soles on the linoleum floor.

She turned and took a step back, a gasp stuck in her throat. Alarm crawled up her spine.

A man glared down at her. His eyes were barely visible, his features distorted through a nylon stocking covering his face.

Her pulse skyrocketed when she tried to run. But he was already too close and lunged at her.

He threw her into the stainless steel table, dazing her. A tremendous weight slammed onto her, his chest bearing down on her back. His arm coiled around her throat, putting her in a chokehold, cutting off her windpipe.

Panic raced over her like a thousand fire ants, stinging her skin.

"Get rid of him," he growled in her ear.

Without thinking, she clawed at his forearm, trying to dig her nails into his flesh, but the padding of his coat was too thick to do any damage. Her reflexes were slow and sticky as glue.

"Get rid of him and go home alone. Understand?"

Her vision blurred, her head starting to swim as she battled for oxygen. Dark spots flashed in her eyes. She flailed, hitting his arm, scratching his face, trying to get free, but felt like she was sinking, going under.

Six seconds. That's all she had. Maybe eight and she would lose consciousness. She had to do something.

"If you don't," he said, his breath foul, "more will die. More minnows will bleed."

The last words sliced through the paralyzing haze clouding her mind. Panic receded, like the tide ebbing, and all her training flowed back into her. She put her foot up on the table and used it as leverage, pushing away from it as he repeated the same warning.

"Get rid of—" The force cut him off, and he reared back from the table, dragging her with him.

The move created a pocket of space between her chin and his elbow. Wedging her fingers into the gap, she tucked her head, relieving the pressure on her throat. She could breathe.

Muscle memory kicked in, spurring her into action.

With a sudden burst of adrenaline, she dropped one hand from his arm, twisted her torso and thrust her elbow back hard into his belly.

A shocked grunt whooshed from his lips, and he released his grip on her.

She raised her forearm, keeping her elbow bent parallel to her chest, and rotated her entire body, generating as much momentum as possible as she spun on her heel and struck his head with her arm.

He wobbled backward, knocked off balance.

A deep ache flared in her bad shoulder, but she ignored the pain and sucked in a breath. Seizing the opportunity, she rammed the hard, meaty part of her palm up into his nose. A sickening crunch of bone and snap of cartilage filled the air, and he cried out in pain. She drove her boot heel into his groin, shoving him away from her.

The man doubled over in agony and reached out for the counter, steadying himself. Swearing and calling her foul names, he grabbed something. Metal glinted in his hand. A knife.

A surge of dread spiraled through her, spilling into her mouth bitter as bile. She backed away. Spun for the double doors and ran. For help. For safety.

Fueled by desperation, she cried out.

The man's vulgar insults and profanities barely registered in her ears over the pounding of her heart and her own shrill voice.

Screaming, she shoved through the doors and out of the kitchen and barreled into a wall of solid muscle.

"Nora!" Bo's arms closed around her. "Are you all right?" His frenzied hands raked over her. "What happened? Are you hurt?"

She shook her head. Nausea robbed her of the words. She fought to find her voice and snuff out the panic and fear flaring through her as hot and uncontrollable as wildfire.

"It's him," she panted. Everything hit her in a wave, bowling her over, and she crumpled to her knees. "He attacked me. In the kitchen."

Others rushed to her side. Bo leaned Nora against Kimberly, who held her, and he took off, disappearing through the double doors.

Shaking, Nora squeezed her eyes shut, taking deep breaths, trying not to throw up.

"You're going to be okay," Kimberly said as Nora faintly heard someone on the phone with 911. "Oh, my God. You're bleeding." Kimberly held up her bloody sleeve. "Were you cut, honey?" The blonde inspected her arm.

"No." The word squeaked out of Nora. She tried to remember exactly what happened, and it was like pressing down on an open wound. The man had gotten a knife, but he hadn't cut her. "I don't think so." She'd thrown a palm-heel strike to his face. "I think it's his blood." From when she broke his nose.

She couldn't stop shaking.

Safe. She was safe.

A small crowd had gathered around her. She would be all right.

Seconds passed—maybe minutes—before Bo reappeared, pushing through the kitchen doors. He cut through the bodies, parting the crowd, and rushed to her, sinking to his knees beside her.

He pulled her into his arms and held her close. "He got away. Through the back door. Ran to his car. I got a make and model, but only a partial license plate." Rocking her gently, he kissed her forehead and stroked her hair. "Shh. We'll get him. Don't cry. I've got you." More kisses. "Please, don't cry."

That's when it hit her: she was sobbing.

She struggled to get a grip, to regain control. She sank into his embrace and strained to draw on his strength, but all she could do was clutch Bo tighter as tears continued to fall.

Chapter Eight

Staring at Nora as a doctor treated her in the Cutthroat Creek Community Hospital emergency room, Bo stood in terrified shock. His heart had been lodged in his throat since she was attacked at the church.

Bo slipped up, and it stung. But what he felt meant nothing. Nora was terrified and in pain. Only she mattered.

"You're not seriously injured. But I don't like the bruising on your throat," the ER doctor said as he examined her neck. He traced the line of her old scar with a gloved finger. "This isn't the first time that you've been attacked."

"No," she said, her voice raspy. "It's not."

But it was the first time that monster had gotten close enough to touch her since she'd hired IPS, and he was supposed to be protecting her.

He'd left her alone for a short time. *Ten minutes. Less. Surrounded by people.*

People who didn't know they needed to look out for her. Who were unaware that she was in danger.

Because they'd chosen to go with option B—a lie.

A lie he'd gotten wrapped up in, playing the part of her boyfriend when his sole focus should've been on his role as bodyguard.

A lie that endangered her.

The mistake was his and the blame for the harrowing ordeal she'd barely survived rested squarely on his shoulders. He allowed her to carry on as if nothing was wrong, business as usual, hoping to lure the killer out. And it had worked. They had baited the devil himself.

Bo never should have left her side. Not for a single minute. He swore beneath his breath.

"Will I have to be admitted?" Nora asked. "Or am I okay to leave?"

"Your throat is going to be sore for a few days. Ice the bruises. I'll get your discharge paperwork started and write a prescription for painkillers."

"You can skip the prescription," she said. "I won't take anything that'll make me drowsy."

Of course not. She needed to be alert and ready for anything, especially with Bo as her bodyguard. He clenched his jaw.

"If you say so, but you should take an over-the-counter anti-inflammatory." The doctor jotted something down on a clipboard. "We'll get you out of here in a little bit."

At the sound of footsteps, Bo looked over to his right and spotted Logan at the nurse's station along with Tak and a female officer in uniform, who was most likely there to collect any forensic evidence.

The nurse pointed to the bay Nora was in. Their gazes found him, and Logan motioned for Bo to come over.

Bo gave a single nod to him and looked at Nora. "Logan and Tak are here. I need to talk to them while an officer collects any possible physical evidence. She'll inspect under your fingernails and most likely clip them. Maybe you scratched him and have his DNA."

"You're leaving me again?" she asked, her eyes wide, her voice hoarse.

His heart sank.

The doctor glanced between them. "I'll give you two a moment," he said, then stepped out of the bay.

"No. I'm not going anywhere." Bo found himself needing to soothe her, to alleviate the anxiety he'd caused with his negligence. "I'm sorry I left you. For what happened." *On my watch*. He eased closer and took her hand. "I'll be at the nurse's station, just a hundred feet away, where I can keep an eye on anyone coming in and out of this cubicle." He wouldn't so much as go to the bathroom or grab a cup of coffee. Not unless Tak or Logan was within arm's reach of her. "I promise," he said, giving her hand a reassuring squeeze.

She hesitated and then nodded.

As he stepped out, the female officer entered the bay, carrying an evidence kit.

"Hello, Ms. Santana. I'm Officer Midthunder. I'll collect any possible DNA from the perpetrator."

"His blood is on her sleeve," Bo said, wanting to make sure it wasn't missed.

"Thank you. I'll go over everything with Ms. Santana," Officer Midthunder said and pulled the curtain closed.

Bo headed to the nurse's station.

"How is she doing?" Tak asked as Bo approached them.

"No serious injuries." Bo stood in between them with his back to the desk so that he could see the curtained cubicle Nora was in. "But the doctor doesn't like the bruises on her throat." Neither did Bo. He gritted his teeth at the pain she was in.

"I'm sorry to hear about what happened," Logan said. "I put out an APB on the car."

A black Subaru Outback. There were so many of those in the area that it might as well have been one of the unofficial state vehicles, second only to a Ford F-150. "But since you only have a partial plate, the odds are low that you'll find it. Right?"

Logan sighed. "A partial is better than nothing. Unfortunately, we didn't get anything helpful on CCTV. Not much coverage around the church."

Bo swore, his frustration wrestling with his anger. The only thing that was stronger was the guilt welling behind his sternum. This guy put his hands on Nora—hurt her, nearly choked her to death—and somehow managed to slip through Bo's fingers again.

"I questioned the folks who were still at the church," Logan said, taking out his notepad. "Turns out a tweaker saw the most." He thumbed through the notes. "Ricky Rooney is his name. Rooney knew Nora was going to the kitchen to refill the pan with bread rolls and watched her, hoping to snag some more before he left. Rooney saw a guy lurking in a corner. White man with a goatee, average height, average build. Dark eyes. Black hair. Broncos ball cap. Rooney claims the man crept toward the kitchen in a hurried manner. That he looked 'sus.' The man shoved his cap in his pocket as he took something else out. Whatever it was, Rooney stated the man pulled it over his head when he slipped into the kitchen."

Bo clenched his hands into fists. "The guy with the good work boots." The ache in his chest began to give way to a burning fury. "I spotted him, but he kept his distance. Stayed at the far side of the room with his head down. I thought he might've left when I stepped outside to call Tak because I didn't see him hanging around anymore," he said, his gut burning. "Why didn't Rooney tell someone about this guy after he saw him following Nora into the kitchen?"

Logan shrugged. "Rooney is an addict. Drawing attention to trouble isn't second nature to a guy like him. In fact, his survival instincts probably told him to look the other way. We're fortunate he gave us a statement at all. He said that Nora was so nice to him—the only one to let him have so many bread rolls—that he felt bad for her. I did find the ball cap at the scene, and I'll have it processed at the lab."

"Has Rooney ever seen the man with the goatee before? Maybe at the church?" Tak asked. "Is he a regular?"

"Nope." Logan shook his head. "Never seen him before. Rooney said the guy didn't eat. Only got toiletries and kept to himself."

Bo lowered his head, wishing he had handled things differently. "I knew the guy with the goatee was trouble." Precisely what kind, he hadn't been sure.

The guy who had dropped off the package at his house wore a plain black ball cap and moved differently. There was a slickness to him. Better stealth. Whether or not he had facial hair, Bo couldn't say because of the scarf over his face. Mr. Goatee with the work boots struck him as a criminal. A petty thief. Someone who snatched purses, stole cars, broke into someone's house while they were on vacation.

Not a cold-blooded killer with the patience to stalk someone for a decade.

How could Bo have gotten it so wrong? Why didn't he haul the guy outside and interrogate him, even if it was only based on a vibe? He could have dealt with any questions from the church staff and complaints from the guy later.

"I should've taken an aggressive, not-so-subtle approach

with him," Bo said. "Then Nora wouldn't have been attacked."

"Beating yourself up over it isn't going to help Nora," Tak said. "Besides, now we have something to go on. If we have his blood, we've got his DNA. Plus a make and model of his vehicle. That puts us a lot closer to catching him than we were before."

"He's right." Logan nodded in agreement. "If you had scared him off before he had a chance to act, we'd never know who we were looking for. As unfortunate as the circumstances are, this helps."

The two men were his friends, his family. They were going to support him in this. Bo wished Eli was here. They were close as well, but E didn't care if he hurt someone's feelings. Not if they had messed up and needed a dose of harsh truth to get their act together.

"I need to get her statement," Logan said. "Officer Midthunder should be wrapping up."

Bo led the way toward the curtained cubicle.

A nurse he recognized entered the corridor. Kimi. She was the younger sister of Jacy, a combat engineer they'd served with who had died on a deployment. Jacy and Tak had been best friends.

"Hey, Kimi," Bo said when she stopped in front of them.

"What are you guys doing here?" Kimi glanced at the group. "Is everyone okay?" Her gaze landed on Tak, but he didn't respond.

"We're fine," Bo said, and a look of relief washed over Kimi's face. "It's a long story, but an IPS client was attacked. She's going to be okay. The doctor says she can be discharged soon."

"Glad to hear she's all right." Kimi folded her arms, her

expression turning uneasy as her gaze shifted. "Takoda, do you have a minute to talk in private?"

Tak shook his head. "I'm working," he muttered and gestured to Bo that they should move on.

The tension was palpable. Bo had never seen Tak be cold to anyone, much less Kimi, but Bo had his own problems to deal with.

"Bad timing. We're really busy," Bo said. "We'll catch up soon." He gave Kimi a quick hug and proceeded to Nora's cubicle. "Knock, knock. Is it okay for Logan to get your statement now?"

Officer Midthunder pulled back the curtain. "We're all done in here." The cop closed the kit and removed her latex gloves. "Ms. Santana got the guy good. His blood and skin were under her nails. Based on what she described during the altercation, I think she might have broken his nose."

"Not 'might,'" Nora said. "I did."

Tak smiled at her. "Good for you."

Officer Midthunder grabbed her kit. "I'll get out of your way so you can get your statement, Detective," she said and left.

"Nora, you never should've been in that position—where you had to defend yourself," Bo said, looking at her. "I should have been inside the building next to you the entire time." He took a breath, steadying himself for the next thing he had to say. "If you don't want me on your case anymore and would prefer to be reassigned to someone else at Ironside, no one would blame you." Tak and Eli had tactical training. The same as him. Any one of them would be a suitable replacement.

To his surprise, he now hated the idea. Deep down, he no longer wanted anyone to replace him.

Bo wanted to be the one to protect Nora. Which was ludicrous. But it was also as real as his feelings for her. He didn't want to leave her or let her down.

He only wanted to make good on his promises to her.

Nora narrowed her eyes at him, giving him a dirty look. "You didn't want to be my bodyguard from the beginning. If you want to use what happened at the church as an excuse to have someone else assigned to me, then just say so. But don't turn it around on me because I have not lost faith in you," she said, and he was humbled by her confidence in him. "It's not too late for me run again if you want to wash your hands of me."

Bo met her fiery gaze evenly and gave her a steady nod. "No. I want you, Nora." The words effortlessly slipped out of his mouth, and her face softened. Then he realized what he'd said. "To stay with me. As my assignment." He shook his head. "I mean client." Nothing sounded right.

A tentative smile tugged at the corners of her mouth.

Tak put a hand on Bo's shoulder. "I think we've settled that and don't need to say anything else on the matter."

Bo was grateful to his friend, the man who was as close to him as a brother, for the change in the subject as well as for the way Nora was looking at him now. With a soft smile and a gleam in her eyes.

Logan pulled out a pen. "Walk me through what happened, Nora."

She sat straighter, looking poised, almost as if nothing had happened at all. But the path of recent tears stained her cheeks, her left hand trembled ever so slightly and there was no ignoring the nasty bruises on her neck. She wasn't as composed as she appeared, but she was doing a good job faking it. Bo respected the hell out of her effort after what she'd endured.

"We were on the line, serving food, when Bo got an

alert on his phone that there was movement on his property," she said. "It was noisy inside with the music playing and everyone talking, so Bo went outside to call someone on his team to go to his place and check it out. We ran out of bread rolls and one guy really wanted more. I would've asked Susan to grab them, but something happened on the opposite side of the room—some kind of commotion that she needed to attend to. So I went to the kitchen to get them. I've done it before. Plenty of times. It usually only takes a couple of minutes."

One vulnerable minute, sixty seconds, was all that animal had needed to get to her.

Nora took a deep breath like she was forcing herself to continue and Bo wanted her to get through it as quickly as possible.

"He snuck up on me. By the time I realized he was there, it was too late."

"Did you get a look at him?" Logan asked.

"Briefly. Dark hair. Dark eyes. Facial hair."

Logan nodded. "Do you think a forensic sketch artist could help you recreate what he looks like?"

"No. He wore panty hose over his head. It distorted his face. His features were all mushed against the nylon."

"About how much did he weigh?"

She shrugged. "Maybe a little less than Bo."

"Two hundred." Bo had sized the guy up and estimated he weighed about ten to fifteen pounds less than he did.

Logan wrote it down. "He surprised you. Then what happened?"

"He grabbed me around the throat. Got me in a rear chokehold. But I fought him off."

"I'm sure the incident must've been terrifying," Logan said, sympathy heavy in his tone. "If he caught you by surprise and overpowered you, sounds like you got lucky to fend him off."

"I got lucky when I was sixteen and a couple of guys stopped him from getting me into a van. I got lucky when my roommate came back to the dorm early and he killed her instead of me. This time, it wasn't luck. I've trained for years in self-defense and martial arts so that when he attacked me again, I would be prepared." Her fingers curled around the sheet covering the lower half of her body and she looked down. "But I was petrified. At first, I froze. My mind blanked." She put a hand on her throat that was red and bruised and would be purple tomorrow. "I responded instinctively until my training finally came back to me. Muscle memory kicked in and I kicked his butt."

Bo wrapped an arm around her and rubbed her shoulder. "That was brave of you. To fight through the fear. Not everyone can."

She flicked a glance at him and offered a small smile, but it didn't last. "When he grabbed a knife, I saw a chance to get out of there and took it. I ran."

"Did he say anything to you?" Bo asked.

"Actually, he did. He warned me to get rid of you. Get rid of you and go home alone. Or more will die. More minnows will bleed."

"He referred to me, specifically? Not IPS like he did in the note card last night?"

"Yes. *Get rid of him.* That's what he demanded."

"Back up." Logan put a hand on his hip. "What note card last night?"

Bo quickly explained about the box that had been delivered. He'd updated the team, ensuring Autumn received pictures of everything, but he should've looped Logan in as well.

"Anything else you've forgotten to tell me?" Logan asked.

Bo shook his head and looked at Nora. "Did he use a voice modulator? You told us that every time you've had any interaction with him, even over the phone, he used a digital voice modifier."

She thought for a moment. "No," she said. "But he kept his voice low, kind of raspy. It made me think of a geriatric smoker, like he was trying to force it to sound different from his normal voice. I don't know. Maybe I'm reading too much into it."

"Did you smell anything?" Bo asked. "The same cologne from the note cards?"

She shook her head. "He reeked of cigarettes. The smell was on his clothes and his breath when he warned me. Then he dragged me backward. I went on autopilot, I guess. Fought back, got away from him and ran from the kitchen."

Once Bo walked back inside the building and he saw Nora missing from the food line, it was as if the devil had crawled out of hell and ripped his heart out of his chest. He asked Kimberly where she went and rushed to the kitchen.

"At that point, I came back inside," Bo said. "I realized what happened and ran after the guy through the back door of the kitchen. But he got away."

"Was anyone able to check out the sensors at your house?" Nora asked.

Excellent question. "Did you find out who was at my place?" he asked Tak.

His buddy shook his head. "No. I walked through the quadrant you identified from the triggered sensors. There were fresh tracks. Human. And white-tailed deer, too. Looked like someone was hunting. Whoever it was made a kill and dragged the animal back to his vehicle. A couple of shots hit some trees. Took out one sensor. Could've been an accident."

Everything about this situation rubbed Bo wrong. "Maybe."

"It's pretty late in the season for hunting," Logan said. "Unless you're using a muzzleloader. Did you see any evidence that he was?"

Tak shrugged. "Can't say for sure. The hunter dug out the ammo that hit the tree and knocked out the sensor. But I replaced it with a camera for you and made sure it was working properly on your security system."

Both Tak and Eli had access to his place in case of an emergency, and he had access to theirs. "Appreciate it."

"What's a muzzleloader?" Nora looked between them. "And what difference does it make?"

"A muzzleloader is any firearm where the user has to load the projectile and the propellant charge into the muzzle end of the gun," Bo explained. "During the general season, which ended in November, regular rifle hunters have a huge advantage over muzzleloaders—just like archery— so they have their own season. Which is now."

"Do you usually get a lot of hunters out there?" Logan asked.

"When I bought the place, the previous owner told me it was a great hunting spot and he allowed others to use the land. I painted a purple stripe on trees along the perimeter of the property line to let folks know they're trespassing, but on occasion, a hunter will follow prey past the line. In an effort to be a friendly neighbor, I always let it slide. It wasn't a big deal." Then again, he'd never used his place as a safe house before either. Now any trespassing was a serious issue. "That's why I don't normally keep my security system active."

"Well, muzzleloader season will be over soon." Logan glanced at his phone. "In fact, today is the last day. Starting tomorrow, anyone hunting, even with a license or a muzzleloader, is breaking the law. That's in addition to trespassing. Any activity on your land should stop."

Tak slid a furtive glance at him. The question in his eyes was evident.

What if the activity in the woods didn't stop?

Then that meant it wasn't a coincidence and Bo's problem was about to get a whole lot more complicated.

Tak nodded as if reading his mind. "You need me, I'm there. E, too."

With a phone call, Tak could be on the west side of his property in ten minutes. Eli to the north in fifteen. "Yeah, I know. Thanks."

The monster stalking Nora wasn't just dealing with Bo. The entire IPS team would be there for her.

Chapter Nine

Sated, but not filled to excess, Nora set her chopsticks down on her plate. She'd showered and changed into a T-shirt and sweats as soon as they got back to the safe house.

"Did it hit the spot?" Bo asked her, packing up the left-overs.

"Dinner was good." Eating late was something she generally avoided, but it was either that or not eat, yet again. She skipped dinner last night after the red and gold box had been delivered. Tonight, between the incident at the church and the trip to the hospital and the police report, they didn't get back to Bo's house until nine. "I've never eaten at the Golden Dragon." She grabbed both their plates and took them to the sink. "When I'm in the mood for Asian food, I always go to the Ramen House for some reason."

"It's because you're loyal." He came up alongside her, taking the dishes from her hands.

"Oh, you think so?"

"Yep. I bet you know the name of the owner, who probably gives you a discount and allows you to leave your business cards for patrons to take because you're so loyal."

Mr. and Mrs. Yee were a sweet couple. They always gave her a free order of soup instead of a discount and did let her leave her business cards.

Grimacing, she shook her head. "Am I really that easy to read?"

"Not at all." He started washing the plates. "I just pay attention to the things you say, the way you speak about people. Take me for example. After what happened to you this evening at the church, you should've kicked me to the curb and insisted on a new bodyguard," he said, almost sounding annoyed with her for not having done so.

Pursing her lips, she grabbed a dish towel and dried the first plate. "That wasn't your fault." She set the dish on the rack.

"Like hell it wasn't." He handed her the second one.

As she took it, their fingers grazed. Electric heat zipped through her. Their gazes met and held. And held. And held. Her breath caught in her throat and she tried to ignore the spike of heat that was spiraling through her body.

He looked away and lowered his hand.

She dried the dish, set it down and turned toward him. "You didn't leave me. You stepped outside to make an urgent phone call. It was hard enough to hear yourself think in there with the music and everyone talking and the kids running around." She expected no less. It was the holidays after all. Even though she dreaded this time of year, the staff who organized the food pantry didn't want folks in need to dread it. They wanted hungry people to enjoy a hot meal and not to worry about where the next one was going to come from for an hour. She helped give them that. "We needed you to be discreet. Remember? You, yelling on the phone, not able to hear the person on the other end, would have defeated that goal."

"For all the good it did."

She put a hand on his chest and it was like touching a

flame. She soaked in the heat of him, wanting to steal some of it, wanting him to warm every cell in her body.

"The truth is that I shouldn't have gone to the kitchen alone." She'd done it a hundred times. Didn't think twice about it. But today was different and she should've acted accordingly. "I could've asked Kimberly to grab extra rolls. Or I could've waited until Susan was free again. You expected me to stay on the line, surrounded by people, and I didn't. I made a mistake." And paid the price. "You know what they say about hindsight being twenty-twenty."

He caressed her face. "Nora—"

"Bo," she cut him off with that firm tone he liked to use on her. It worked, too, though his gaze was fixed on her neck. On her bruises. "I'm not giving up on you and you're not getting rid of me that easily." Moving her hand from his chest, she tugged on her collar, wishing she was wearing something with a higher one, then playfully punched his arm. "Got it?"

"Yes, ma'am."

"I don't want to think about it more." When he called her ma'am, it reminded her that she was the client, which meant she was in charge. Sort of. "Right now, your job is to distract me."

He sighed. "Do you want to play cards?"

"Sure. Gin rummy?"

Nodding, he led the way into the living room where he had already built a fire. He grabbed a deck of cards from inside a side table. "Siri, play Christmas music."

"Deck the Halls" started.

She groaned and sat beside him.

"Not a fan of the artist or genre?" he asked, shuffling the cards.

"The entire season. The Yuletide Killer ruined it for me."

"Siri, stop." He frowned. "I should've anticipated that. It makes sense, considering. I'm sorry."

"You're not a mind reader. No need to apologize."

"What kind of music do you listen to? And don't tell me 'anything.'"

She smiled. That was going to be her answer. Surviving meant getting along with others. Not standing out or making waves. Blend in to stay alive. "Country and alternative rock."

"Alternative rock can vary quite a bit. Name three of your favorite bands."

"U2, Imagine Dragons and Muse."

"A woman after my own heart. Siri, play Alternative Soul playlist."

An artist she didn't recognize came on, but she liked it. "Who is this?"

"AWOLNATION. If anything pops up that you don't care for, just let me know." He offered her the cards. "Hey, I was wondering, after your biological father moved to Canada, you never saw him again?"

Shaking her head, she cut and handed the cards back. "He agreed to sign the paperwork for Pa to adopt me and I heard he later remarried. Had another kid. Moved on like my mom did, I guess."

"You were never curious about him?"

"He bailed on me. Frank essentially raised me. I'm the woman I am today because of him and my mom, right?" And also because of that sick man who killed her friends. He forced her to become strong, to learn how to fight to survive. "Since my dad chose to leave me, I guess there was always something… Not missing, but this other side to things, I suppose. It's hard to explain. I'm grateful to Frank, for stepping in and being a dependable father figure for me."

. "You were fortunate to have that."

Not everyone did. Like Bo. "I've been meaning to ask you something."

"What's that?" he asked, passing out the cards.

"Is 'Bo' short for something?"

He stopped dealing. For the longest moment, he said nothing, holding the cards, and when his gaze finally lifted to hers, his expression was shuttered. "Yes. It's short for Boaz."

Boaz. Strong. Unique. Like him. "That's from the bible, isn't it?"

"The name is in the bible, but I don't know if that's the reason it was given to me. Maybe it was a family name and there's no religious meaning to it." His broad shoulders shrugged like it meant nothing.

But she could tell that it meant quite a lot.

Nora put her hand on his forearm. "We don't have to talk about it. I only ask because I want to get to know you better."

"I wish I knew more so that I could tell you. About my childhood. My family. My mother."

"How old were you when you were put into foster care?"

"Six."

So very young. "Do you remember her, your mother?"

"Bits and pieces. I remember her bathing me. Singing to me. Making me laugh. I never had a lot of toys. But there were a ton of books. And crayons. She read to me a lot and always asked me to draw her a picture."

Running her hand over his arm, she pressed her cheek to his shoulder. Subtle traces of soap clung to his skin, citrus and cedar, mingled with the warm scent of a man.

"With a library card, books are free," she said, "unlike toys. Sounds like she loved you. A lot."

"Yeah. Maybe," he said, his voice dismissive. "I like to think so." His swallow was audible. "But then a little voice reminds me that she didn't love me enough. I wasn't enough to get her to stay clean and sober. I wasn't worth fighting for. Worth living for."

Nora wanted to ask more about his mother and the situation. Instead, she held her tongue and let him continue when he was ready. She kissed his shoulder and stroked his hair. Several minutes passed in silence with her touching him.

What he shared was heavy. What if he thought she wasn't strong enough to hear it, to carry his truth?

"Your dad?" she asked. Two words, telling him she wanted to know more if he was willing to share it with her.

"According to my file, my mom was a single parent with no other living relatives. She struggled to stay away from alcohol and drugs. It's the reason I'm not a big drinker. Two beers. That's my max."

She hadn't seen any alcohol in the house and not even beer in the fridge. "Did a social worker get involved somehow when you were little?"

"Yes. Someone reported an illegal daycare operating from an apartment in our building."

"Where was this?" She had no idea where he grew up.

"Back in Denver. Social services looked into the situation and investigated the parents of all the children. The case worker, Tania Burgess, gave my mom opportunities to make changes." He shrugged. "Ms. Burgess finally deemed my mom unfit to provide a safe and nurturing environment. I went into the foster care system. I was constantly transitioning, bouncing from home to home. Some of the families I was placed with were kindhearted people. Unfortunately, not all foster parents had the same dedication.

For some, fostering was merely a means to collect a check. I was trapped until I aged out of the system when I turned eighteen. By then, my mother was dead. Leaving me alone with so many unanswered questions."

The gravity of that hit her right in the chest, making her hurt for him. She'd been robbed of so much of her life because she had to run, hide and avoid any emotional entanglements, knowing she might have to disappear at any moment.

He'd been robbed, too. Of his past. Of his history. Of knowing where he came from. But at least he'd found a place where he belonged.

She stole a glance at his face.

His eyes were cast down at the table. He sat on the sofa's edge now, his knees spread wide, leaning forward, with his elbows resting on his thighs.

Nora ached to touch him, more than his forearm or his hair. To comfort him, the way he had for her. "Addiction can be hard." Putting a hand on his back, she spread her fingers wide and rubbed him gently. Curled her other hand around his arm. Pressed her cheek to his shoulder. "The way it destroys a person, their life, the lives of those closest. Especially if they don't have a support system, which it sounds like your mom didn't have," she said softly. "Her struggle had nothing to do with you. It didn't mean she didn't love you. Didn't mean you weren't worthy. The baths, the books, the singing and the laughter—those good memories meant she tried because she cherished you."

He didn't pull away from her. Didn't react. Not for several heartbeats, until he covered her hand—which gripped his arm—with his own and tilted his head so their foreheads touched.

"Have you ever thought about doing one of those genealogical tests, to track down other relatives?" she asked, wondering if she was a horrible person for pushing this.

"No. I don't trust the companies. There are too many lawsuits against them for not properly disclosing what they do with your data. And what happens to your DNA when one of those companies goes out of business? Even if your genetic data isn't sold, it can always be stolen by hackers. I'm too paranoid."

Keeping up the caress on his back, she angled toward him and brushed her lips on his brow. Slowly, she felt his muscles relax beneath her touch. "What about contacting the social worker who handled your case? Maybe she remembers something that wasn't in the file you read."

"That was so long ago. I doubt she'd remember me or my mom out of thousands of cases. We're talking twenty-seven years since then."

Longer than she'd been alive, but the timeline nailed down his age to thirty-three as she'd guessed. "I wish you got closure or at least some answers."

"I have these vague, disjointed, happy memories of my mother. But they're all tied up with sadness. And loss. Like…" His voice trailed off.

She ran her fingers over his hair and guided his head to her shoulder. Lying back against the sofa, putting her head on the arm, she eased him down with her and wrapped her arms around him.

To her surprise, he let her.

"Like what?" she asked softly.

"Like there's a hole in me," he said, his voice a hoarse whisper that broke her heart. "One that my mom left behind."

Nora stroked his hair, not saying a word. She didn't want to pity him, something she hated when directed at her. She didn't offer meaningless platitudes or hollow promises. She just held him, touching him, letting him breathe. Hoping he knew she wouldn't judge him.

"I tried to fill it with the Air Force. I joined as soon as I turned eighteen."

"Did it help?"

"Yeah." He sighed. "For a while anyway. Then I tried to fill it with relationships."

She waited and waited. "But?" she prodded when he remained quiet.

"I never connected with anyone. No one came into my life that I felt the need to hold on to. That I couldn't live without."

This man was *not* a big sharer. A tiny part of her wanted to believe that he was only this way with her, telling her so much because maybe they had a connection. But she didn't dare allow herself to believe such a thing.

Not yet.

These were abnormal conditions. They'd been thrown together. She was his assignment. He was her bodyguard. Forced proximity in a safe house that was his home, with high stress mixed in. A life and death situation that made them both vulnerable.

Bo was the first man she felt like she could risk getting close to and yet, at the same time, forming an emotional bond with this man under these circumstances wasn't smart.

Was any of it real? If they were dating, like two normal people, would they have this closeness?

He was quiet for so long that she wondered if he was going to say more.

"Then I got out," Bo said, "and the guys at IPS and the Strattons and Logan, even Declan, they became my family."

Strattons? "Autumn has siblings?"

"Two sisters. Winter is with Chance and Summer is engaged to Logan. They're having an official engagement party next week."

All three sisters named after the seasons. For some reason, it made Nora smile. "Who's Declan?" No one else had mentioned him.

"Declan Hart is Winter's coworker. They're both DOJ Division of Criminal Investigation agents. He worked with Logan and Summer on a murder investigation of someone close to them. After that, those two fell in love and moved here. Her sisters followed. Somewhere along the way, Declan was included in our get-togethers. Now he's a part of our pseudofamily."

"Sounds nice. To find a family even if you can't be with the one you were born into." She didn't move, keeping her arm around him and stroking his hair. It felt good to hold him. To feel the weight of his body pressing down on her. Steady. Solid. So warm. His muscles relaxed even more as he nuzzled his face into the curve of her neck. "Does having them fill the hole?"

"In a way."

But not really.

"I'm still missing something in my life," he said.

Nora didn't know how to respond. She was missing so much in hers—stability, friends, family, love—that her life resembled Swiss cheese. "I can relate. The murders in Cold Harbor—hearing my friends murdered—when he almost got me into that van, being attacked in my college dorm… Every incident was a brutal blow, breaking something inside of me. Leaving pieces that I can't glue back together," she whispered, and Bo nuzzled closer, tightening an arm around her. "Sometimes I feel more like a ghost than a person. No connections. No bonds." No anchors. Constantly drifting. No roots. No place to call home. "Whenever I've left a place, I doubt people noticed I was gone or even missed me. Not that I blame them. I'm the one who always keeps myself at a distance, too terrified to get close to anyone. To care so deeply I wouldn't be able to leave if I had to."

"The way you were prepared to run at the office."

She nodded. "It's been really hard. Really lonely."

"I'm sorry I dumped all of that on you with everything you're going through."

"I'm not," she murmured into his ear. "Please, don't be."

"It sounds selfish."

"No, it doesn't. People don't share things with ghosts. It felt human. Personal." Exactly what she needed.

"The guys don't know any of that. It's not stuff I talk about."

Holding each other close, she smiled and kissed the top of his head, her hand caressing his cheek. The rough texture of his five o'clock shadow, more like eleven now, tickled her fingers and made her sigh. "Thank you for telling me. Trusting me." She'd poured her guts out to him since they first met and she was glad he opened up to her.

When he came to the hospital with follow-up questions after she'd been shot, she'd confided in him that she didn't have a ride home. No one in her life to turn to. On the drive to her house, he'd been so easy to talk to that she'd blabbered nonstop. He had escorted her to the front door and hesitated. There was a moment—a shared look, a charged tension building. The kind that told her a guy was interested. And she'd thought—*no*, she'd hoped—he'd ask her out on a date.

But then he didn't, and she told herself that it was for the best.

Rules kept her alive. Turning down dates and offers to grab coffee or see movies were done to prevent emotional ties. No sticky threads binding her to a place. Not when she might have to leave if she sensed danger.

She wanted this to be different. For all the long glances with him—the little touches and kisses they'd shared that seemed to soothe and set off sparks for them both—to mean something.

But how could she trust her feelings as long as he was forced to have her there and she was a professional obligation?

His fingers slipped into her hair and played in her curls and his lips brushed her throat in a kiss. Gently. Tenderly.

Excitement rippled over her skin. Questions and doubts evaporated. There was something real between them. Even if it was only chemistry or attraction.

He eased her worries, listened and made her feel safe when no one else ever had. And she wanted to do the same for him. For however long their circumstances lasted.

"I'm so sorry he hurt you," he whispered, and the remorse in his voice gripped her heart. "What can I do? Anything to make it better?"

"Just hold me, Bo. Let me stay with you like this tonight." *Warm and safe in your arms.*

"I'm not too heavy on you?"

"No." Just the right amount of heavy. The right amount of strength. The right amount of sweet.

Being with him just felt right.

Leaning in, she pressed her lips to his brow, wishing she were kissing his mouth instead. An ache trickled through her entire body, pooling in her belly and coiling even lower.

She wanted to get closer to him, feel his skin on hers, to touch him everywhere, to be touched in return.

A vague awareness of sexual frustration, something she'd never experienced and had only heard about, set in like an itch in the back of her mind. She yearned for the raw intimacy that could only be found in the arms of another.

Maybe one day.

Maybe with him.

Not because she was curious. Not because he was convenient. There was something about Bo that made her want to lose herself completely in his heat and his touch. She pressed her cheek to his head and ran her fingers over his spine.

He wrapped an arm around her waist and nuzzled against her. "I've got you, Nora," he said, and the words sounded like a vow.

Perhaps they had each other and that was how she'd get through this nightmare. With him.

Regardless, she was going to cling to his promise in her heart.

Chapter Ten

The smell of sugar cookies and sunshine curled around him. Then Bo woke with a start, his heart skipping a beat.

Nora was gone from the sofa, no longer beneath him. Her scent had also faded. His hand went to his hip. His weapon wasn't there either.

The shades were drawn. It was dark outside. The only light in the room was from the Christmas tree that was still on.

His mind raced. He tried to remember what had happened. He jackknifed up and a blanket slid down, falling to the floor.

"Nora!" his voice was hoarse and heavy.

"I'm here," she said behind him.

He whirled on the sofa to see her sitting at the table, sipping from a mug.

"Do you want coffee?" she asked. "I just brewed a pot."

Bo looked around the dimly lit space. There was a pillow on the sofa. She must've propped it under his head. The coffee table was clear. "Where's my gun?"

"On the side table. You shifted in the night and your weapon dug into my side, so I took it off you and set it there. Is that okay?"

That was not like him at all. He always secured his gun before he fell asleep. Even more disturbing was that she had gotten up, removed his gun and placed a pillow under his head, all without him waking. "Yeah. It's okay."

They had been snuggled up together, cozy in front of the fire. She was soft and warm and smelled good. He'd been incredibly turned on, wanting to touch her and taste her, the memory of kissing her seared into his brain. But more than anything he needed to simply be close to her while not making another mistake.

She had wanted the same and he'd taken the comfort, a night of closeness and connection.

Goodness, he'd never opened up like that before, letting his guts spill out all over the place. Ugly. Messy. Showing pieces of himself that he wasn't proud to share. The things he'd told her... And after everything he'd said, she wanted to hold him.

To *sleep* with him.

Not have sex, or make love, but they had been far more intimate last night than he had ever been with any of his previous lovers, and they didn't even kiss on the sofa.

Bo didn't sleep with women. Sure, he dated, but he never invited anyone to stay the night. With his work schedule of early mornings, late evenings and short-notice deployments, that arrangement suited him. He was blunt and direct from the beginning, careful to never mislead anyone. A few women had pushed for more, but they had accepted what he was prepared to give until they were ready to move on. No broken hearts. No hurt feelings. Though his last girlfriend had cried when he told her he had no interest in continuing a long-distance relationship but that he wished her every happiness.

He had only been assigned to protect Nora for less than

forty-eight hours and they'd slept together. More significantly, he'd wanted to and enjoyed it. Granted, they had been on the sofa, fully clothed, with her nestled beneath him and his head pillowed between her breasts. Still, they'd shared personal things, stuff he'd never confided to another soul.

To be honest, he hadn't given anyone else a chance.

Bo waited to be filled with shame for baring his soul to her, but he wasn't. He didn't feel regret and was not the least bit unsettled. He took it as a testament to how comfortable he already was with her. How much he trusted her.

Every time he'd been near Nora—this knockout, who was smart and mysterious—that magnetic thing between them pulled him to her. He didn't understand. It might as well have been a jigsaw puzzle that he had to figure out while blindfolded. A hundred different confusing pieces that could not possibly fit and in trying to, he risked getting his heart broken. But then last night, they talked—truly shared, touched each other deeply—and every single piece snapped together.

She had a vulnerability, a fragility about her that he recognized within himself. The loneliness. That black hole. It sucked him in, spoke to something deep inside him, drawing him to her. He realized now that it wasn't just her beauty or the fact that he was attracted to her. They both had similar wounds, and when he was around her, she soothed him, eased the gnawing ache.

Their current circumstances complicated everything. She was a client. An assignment. He could not live with himself if he failed her.

Nora was special. One of a kind.

Once this job was done and she was safe, he wanted to follow this connection and see where it could lead.

"What time is it?" he asked, stretching his arms.

She got up from the table and went to the kitchen cabinet. "Seven thirty."

"Goodness." He yawned. "I can't believe I slept so long." Or so well.

Grabbing the coffeepot, she filled a mug. "I guess you must've needed it."

Maybe he had. The night before, he hadn't slept much, if at all, worrying about the package that had been delivered and about how it had upset Nora. Bo'd been exhausted and had fallen asleep easily pressed against her.

"How about you?" he asked. "Were you able to get any rest with me on top of you like a chopped down log?"

Her lips curved as she handed him the mug. "I got solid sleep until a little after six. I tried to be quiet because I didn't want to wake you."

"Thanks." He gestured to the coffee and took a sip. Burned his tongue. "Hot."

"I should've warned you. Sorry."

He shrugged. "What is on the agenda for today?"

"A bunch of house showings, starting at nine." She picked up her phone and scrolled. "I logged into the system once I had my first cup of coffee to double-check everything on the schedule. Two more appointments were added last night. We have six right now, but that could change."

Bo frowned.

"What's wrong?" she asked.

"I don't like changes."

"Well, I have this picky family today and they're probably going to add new houses to the list or refuse to see ones I've selected for them. We need to be flexible with changes."

"Not that kind." Bo rubbed his jaw, his day-old stubble itched. He needed to shave.

She arched her brows. "Then what's the problem?"

"The two last-minute appointments." He blew on his coffee and sipped it. "Do you recognize the names? Have you shown them houses before?"

"No, they're both new."

New meant unvetted. "I don't like it." She got attacked, the assailant got away and now she had new clients who could really be anyone. Unexpected changes plus this co-incidence were cause for concern. At minimum, extra pre-cautions.

"Fairly common in real estate."

Maybe. "Even in mid-December? Doesn't business usu-ally slow down by now?"

"Usually, yes, but like I said, I have this family who are relocating to the area and the teens are quite vocal about what they do and don't like. Also, I have two owners who are eager to sell. I'm grateful to have anyone willing to come out and see their houses. And one person is looking for an agent to show them two places."

"Do you have the addresses?"

"Yep. For the houses people have specifically requested to see." She came around the sofa and sat next to him. "Bearing in mind that the—"

"Fussy family of four is prone to making changes."

Grinning, Nora nodded. "Exactly." She held up her phone, showing him the real estate company app.

He could have taken it from her hand to look at it, but he leaned in to see the screen, his shoulder brushing hers.

She put her hand on his thigh.

Bo tensed, not wanting a resurgence in the excitement the lower part of his body had shown when she touched him last night. Lying on his side, he'd been able to hide his arousal, but he'd woken up still thinking of her, hungry for her instead of breakfast.

He sat beside her in the dim light of the Christmas tree. The room was warm and quiet and had him craving more of this intimacy. He scrolled through the addresses, inhaling her scent and letting it calm him. This morning, she was all natural. Gone was the smell of sugar cookies, but the scent of sunshine was pure Nora.

He glanced over at the app. "Which two names are new?" he asked, and she pointed them out.

The ten a.m. and five p.m. appointments, sandwiched in between the family.

She slid her palm along his thigh, and his brain scrambled like eggs in a hot pan.

Covering her hand with his, he stopped the sensual caress of his leg. "You're killing me, here."

"Oh." She let out a small chuckle. "I thought you'd like it. Should I stop?"

No, don't stop. "I do love it, Nora. A little too much. Makes it hard to focus on work because all I can think about is you and…"

She smiled, her gaze searching his face. "And?"

"How much I want to touch you. Hold you. Kiss you. But doing any of that will distract me from doing my job."

The smile on her face abruptly disappeared. "Wasn't last night nice? Don't you want to do that again?"

Drawing in a deep breath, Bo wrestled between complete honesty and what he thought he should say. "Yes." The truth won.

"Don't you want *more than* just that?"

Hell, yes. "I want you, but I need to do my job. To keep you safe."

"Do both. It doesn't have to be one or the other."

Sighing, he lowered his head. He'd give anything for both. To have her and protect her. This was his fear from the beginning—failing at one because he endeavored for the other. "If only it were that simple."

"It can be as simple as we choose to make it." She caressed his cheek and tilted his face back up to hers. "I have a proposal. While we're out there, it's business as usual, and we both focus on our jobs. But later, when we're back here, locked away in the safe house, we give ourselves permission to set the professional aside and get personal." She leaned in, and he thought she might kiss him, but she stopped a hair's breadth away, putting her forehead to his. "Spending time with you last night in that way helped me push away the ugliness and fear and forget," she whispered, her breath brushing his lips. "You gave me exactly what I didn't know I needed. Even if it was only for a few hours."

"You needed me crying on your shoulder?"

She stroked his cheek, her fingertips tickling his skin, and stared into his eyes. "Maybe. Focusing on you made me feel useful. Instead of helpless and afraid."

"You're strong and capable. You didn't need me to rescue you yesterday." She did that all by herself.

"But I did. Fighting. Surviving. That's not enough. It's not living. You rescued me from the darkness that haunts me every night." Her lips parted on a sigh, and he longed to kiss her. "Besides, you did say you would do anything to make me feel better."

Nora was a persuasive woman. She knew precisely how to push his buttons. Not that he needed much convincing.

"Okay." He swiped her curls off her face and behind her ear and ran his hand down her arm. "We'll give it a try," he said. Pulling back, she beamed at him, and it was like a sucker-punch to the solar plexus. He could barely breathe. She was so beautiful. The only mission he wanted was to make her smile like that every single day. "But right now, I have to be in work mode. I'm going to see what I can find out about the two new individuals before the appointments."

Straightening, she pulled her hands into her lap. "Understood. I'll stay out of your way." She rose from the sofa. "How about I make us breakfast while you do your bodyguard thing?"

"Sounds good. I could eat." He was starving, but he wanted more than food. Staring at her, he wasn't sure if he did a good job of hiding the hunger from his eyes.

"If you keep looking at me like that, it'll be hard for either of us to work."

Guess he got his answer. Averting his eyes, he nodded. "You're right."

"I'm going to shower," she said, her voice husky.

His thoughts tumbled straight to the gutter.

Get a grip, Lennox.

Refusing to watch her walk away, no matter how tempting her body was, he stared at the two new names on the list.

They couldn't afford any more surprises.

Chapter Eleven

To Nora's relief, her first appointment at nine turned out to be legitimate. A couple of empty nesters looking to down-size from their house and buy a new condo overlooking Bit-terroot Lake while the developer offered a holiday discount.

After two other appointments that had already been in the books, they spent the rest of the day with the Grice family.

"What do you think?" Nora asked as they all finished touring the fifth house of the day and gathered in the liv-ing room.

Mr. Grice stroked his jaw as his wife shrugged. Not good signs.

Bo went over to the corner near the front door and flicked on the light. The sun was already setting and it was starting to get dark in the house. He gave Nora a fur-tive glance and tapped at his wrist, indicating the time, even though he wasn't wearing a watch.

Nora nodded, well aware this was taking far too long, as usual. She strolled closer to him to get another whiff of him. He smelled sexy. That aftershave he wore boosted his appeal to irresistible—masculine, earthy mixed with a hint of musk, but subtle. The scent was addictive, making it hard to stay focused on her difficult clients.

"Well, I think this isn't going to work," the sixteen-year-old daughter said, stomping into the empty living room, the sound of her boots echoing off the walls. "It's not fair if he gets a bigger bedroom than me."

The burly father crossed his arms. "Your brother is older," he said with a firm tone.

"By thirteen months! That doesn't make it fair. Besides, I'm the one who always makes honor roll. I have a 4.0 GPA."

"And your brother plays football." The mother studied the living room, and Nora hoped the woman was imagining her furniture filling out the space. "While getting good grades, even if it's not a 4.0."

The girl huffed. "Our rooms should be the same size."

In a perfect house they would be. Nora swallowed the words dancing on the tip of her tongue. She was beginning to wonder if this family was ever going to pull the trigger and buy something.

"There's only one extra bathroom and I don't want to share with her." The brother hiked his thumb back at his younger sister. Always wearing his varsity jacket, he had made it known multiple times he was going to hate living in a state that didn't have its own NFL team. "She's going to hog up all the counter space with her endless sea of products."

Bo rolled his eyes as a grumble rattled in his chest, and Nora was grateful that no one else was close enough to him to hear it. She hoped not anyway.

She shared his frustration. Someone in the family had an issue with every house—usually more than one person.

If Nora didn't find a way to wrap this up soon, they were going to be late for their next appointment. She plastered on a patient smile. "I really do think one of the new builds would suit your needs better. Aside from the primary bedroom, the others tend to be about the same size, and in these older homes you're going to get fewer bathrooms. I'd be happy to line up something for you to see tomorrow."

Sighing, the mother waltzed around, staring at the ceiling. "But look at this crown molding. It's gorgeous. We just won't find this level of detail in a newer house. I want our home to have character."

The real estate buzzword Nora dreaded—*character*. Clients looking for the character of an older home invariably also wanted the amenities of a newer one: updated appliances and plumbing, bigger bedrooms, extra bathrooms, fewer repairs.

Holding her fake smile in place, Nora nodded. "The molding is divine, but no house is going to have everything. I think we need to find the right compromise between charm and functionality," she said, keeping her tone light. No client wanted a lecture.

"Can you show us a house like this one?" the father asked. "But with an extra bathroom and one that needs fewer updates. Not finished, mind you, because I still want to put my stamp on it."

Of course, he did. Would a rubber stamp work? She could pick one up from the arts and crafts shop and Mr. Grice could stamp away until his heart was content.

"And I need a bigger bedroom," the Grice princess added.

"Certainly," Nora said, wishing she had a magic wand to make their impossible request a reality. "I'll see what I can find, but as I've told you, inventory is limited right now. Unless you're willing to wait indefinitely, I strongly suggest you reconsider looking at a new construction home. You could move in before the kids start school in January. No updates to worry about. All the bedrooms will be good in size. Your teens won't have to share a bathroom. Large windows with plenty of natural lighting. And, Mrs. Grice, you can always add little touches to the house to give it personality and Mr. Grice, I'm sure we can find a project for you so you can make it your own."

"Please, Mom," the daughter begged, pressing her palms together and making a pouty face.

"Makes the most sense." The son shoved his hands in his pockets. "We all get what we want that way. Let's at least look at it."

The woman's mouth twitched. "I don't know. I really have my heart set on a house with character. Not some cookie-cutter new build."

Bo put a palm on the small of Nora's back and patted, signaling her to hurry things along. Her cheeks heated, and for a second, she found it hard to think about anything but the feel of his hand on her, wishing it would slide a little lower and that they had on fewer clothes while he touched her.

Glancing over her shoulder at him, she bit back a smile and mouthed, *Okay.* Then she turned back to the family. "I'll send you a link so you can take a look at the photos of a couple of additional homes that I have in mind. Builders are offering good deals at this time of year. You could shave off thousands from the list price of a new build." She moved toward the door. Thankfully they followed. "If you want to see them, just give me a call or you can go through the office to set up an appointment."

They thanked her, mumbled good-byes and left as they continued to debate the pros and cons of the houses they'd seen.

"Why do folks bring their kids along?" Bo asked. "It only seems to make the process harder."

Grabbing her coat from the hook, she shrugged. "At least the teenagers think new construction makes sense." Made them the more reasonable ones to her. Too bad they weren't the ones with the money. "I think it's nice how the parents take their kids' opinions into consideration." While it was unusual for her to manage the entire family, the Grice couple had pulled their teens from school early before the Christmas break since they would be attending a new high school in Montana at the start of the year. "My mom and Pa never would have, but I think it's kind of sweet." Albeit a tad frustrating.

Bo scowled. "And I think it's a big headache listening to four opinionated voices when only two are going to pay the mortgage."

Chuckling, she unzipped her purse, moved some things around and frowned.

"What's wrong?" he asked, concern in his voice.

"I can't find my phone. I was going to text the next appointment and let Dr. Hiller know we're running behind a few minutes."

Bo lifted his hand. He was holding her phone. "You left it on the counter in the kitchen."

"Oh, I didn't realize." She took it from him and headed out the door.

He was right behind her. "You set it down when you started showing them the appliances. From an operational security perspective, it's best to leave it in your purse and carry your handbag with you."

Bo even made the phrase *operational security* sound sexy.

"I do keep my purse close." With her loaded gun tucked inside. "But if my cell phone is stuck in my bag, sometimes it's hard to hear a text when I'm busy trying to sell or during an open house when a home is filled with people."

She locked up the place and they got into the truck.

Bo pulled off for her next showing. She sent a text to her potential new client, hating to make a bad first impression by being late. The Grice family consistently ran over their allotted time with their hemming and hawing. Nora just didn't have the heart to hurry them along when they could be purchasing their forever house.

"You have far more patience than I do," he said.

"That's not true." The first time he questioned her at the hospital after the mass shooting, she'd stonewalled him. Too terrified any cooperation would lead to her exposure. Turned out, her concern was misplaced and should've been solely directed at the press. "You've always been nothing but patient and kind with me." Being shot had been horrific and she had appreciated his compassion at a difficult time.

"Well, you're special." Glancing at her, he smiled, and her heart rolled over in her chest.

He pulled in front of the site of her next appointment. A ranch-style home that had a long, low profile with a low-pitched roof and wide eaves. The place featured stone and wood and had large windows to take advantage of the mountain views. The owners were only selling because of a recent divorce and hoped to start the new year with a fresh start.

"Looks like we beat Dr. Hiller," Bo said.

No other cars were parked at the house. "That's a relief. I'm glad I didn't have to make him wait." She climbed out of the truck. Her dress had hitched up a bit on the ride over, and she tugged it back down over her knees. "What did you find out about my potential new client?"

Bo came around to her side and took her arm, helping her walk over a patch of ice. "He's a dentist over in Cutthroat Creek. Fifty-nine years old. Balding. Blue eyes. Wears glasses. If someone other than a man meeting that description shows up to see this listing, I want you to make an excuse to go to the truck, get inside, take out your gun and drive straight to the police station." He handed her his keys. "Got it?"

"Yeah, sure, but Dr. Allan Hiller is a real person."

"Doesn't matter. Easy enough to look someone up on the internet and use their name to book an appointment. Especially since the guy who's after you knows you hired IPS."

Swallowing hard, she put his fob in her pocket as they headed up the driveway. "The place should be good to go, but I should do a quick walk through and I need to open all the curtains. It's a hassle to close them after every showing only to open them again, but the owners are worried about someone breaking in and stealing the copper pipes if thieves realize no one is living in the house."

"The owners already moved out?"

"Yeah. They're going through a divorce and with the holidays, they thought it would be easier this way. It's sad. They're such a nice couple."

"Not every relationship is forever."

She entered the code for the lockbox and grabbed the key. "What's your longest?"

"A year, but it never got serious."

How could you be with someone for a year without it getting serious? But she decided against asking the question. At least right now.

He put a hand on her back. "How about you?"

"I don't date. No attachments, remember?" Her hand trembled as she tried to get the key in the lock.

"Not ever? Not even in high school before everything happened?"

Before three of her friends were slaughtered while she was forced to listen to their screams.

"Uh, no. I was a late bloomer." *Dang it.* She couldn't get the key in. "No boyfriends."

"At all?" The surprise in his voice grated on her nerves.

"Nope." The keys slipped from her hand and clattered to the ground.

Bo bent down, picking up the keys for her. "I didn't realize you were so cold," he said.

That wasn't the reason she was shaking. Her throat tightened and a different kind of heat crept up her chest. She was ashamed that what rattled her wasn't the memory of her friends dying. The awkwardness stemmed from Bo finding out that she'd never had a real boyfriend. From him eventually connecting the dots to the fact she had never been intimate with a man.

He slipped one of the keys into the first lock, made quick work of the dead bolt and then handed her the keys.

"Thanks." She pushed the door open and switched on the light.

Her breath hitched and then she screamed, dropping the keys on the hardwood floor.

Chapter Twelve

"Oh, God!" Nora rushed into the living room before Bo could grab hold of her. "No, no, no. Amanda," she sobbed.

A redhead lay spread-eagle on the floor, shirt ripped open and covered in blood.

"Stop, Nora!" He managed to snatch her arm and haul her back before she stepped in the blood that had pooled and congealed on the floor around the body. Spinning her around, he brought her in against his chest and held her, keeping her face turned away.

"Is she dead?" she said, her voice so low it was barely audible.

There was no doubt in his mind that the woman was dead and had been for several hours. "I need you to go outside and call 911."

"Amanda. Is she dead?" Nora asked again.

"Yes," he said, softening his tone. He stroked her hair, trying to be as gentle as possible. "She's dead."

Nora cried harder, and he tightened his arms around her.

On the bright white wall, written in blood, were two words: *ANOTHER MINNOW.*

Bo's gaze dropped back to the body. "How do you know her?"

"She…" Her voice broke on a sob. "I work with her. Amanda. She's a real estate agent."

Two women dead in two days—both people Nora knew well. A neighbor and now a coworker.

Bo kissed the top of her head. "Listen to me," he said firmly. "Step away over there and call the police. Tell them to notify Detective Powell."

She didn't move.

"Nora." He sharpened his voice. "I need you to do it now."

She glanced up, her watery, shocked gaze meeting his. Giving him a solemn nod, she backed away toward the door and stayed where he could see her.

Bo pulled latex gloves from his pocket. When he was working on a job, he always carried a pair, along with his weapon and some zip ties. No telling if they might come in handy. He dragged on the gloves. Only as a precaution since he had no intention of touching anything. He crouched for a better look at the dead body without getting too close.

She'd been stabbed several times. From what he could see, at least ten wounds. The medical examiner might find more under the blood. There was so much of it on the walls, the floor and covering the woman's torso. Her skin was gray.

Bruises covered her throat. Although her limbs were spread apart, her ankles and wrists had duct tape around them. Like the killer had cut her loose once she was dead and repositioned the body. A strip of black tape also covered her mouth. He didn't want the neighbors to hear her scream.

Bo turned his attention to Nora, who was staring down at the horrific scene, her eyes glazed, her expression shaken.

The phone was in her hand, hanging at her side. She was in no condition to call the police.

A woman came up the walkway and gasped. "Oh, dear heaven."

Holding up a palm, Bo went to the doorway to keep the woman from running into the house. "Please, step back, ma'am. You have to stay outside." Gaping at him, the gray-haired woman nodded as he dialed 911.

The emergency services operator answered.

"This is Bo Lennox with Ironside Protection Services. I need to report a homicide." He passed along the address and responded to all the operator's questions. "I have reason to believe this is related to an ongoing investigation and request that Detective Logan Powell be notified as soon as possible."

The older woman had caught the attention of a neighbor, who flagged down another person. The houses were clustered close together and this was prime time for folks to get home from work. In a matter of minutes, a crowd was gathering outside.

Bo went to Nora, tugging off his gloves before putting an arm around her. Guiding her out of the house, he stood guard against inquisitive onlookers who had begun to converge. He pulled the door nearly shut, only leaving a crack. Holding Nora, he shielded her face, putting her cheek to his chest.

Then he fired off a quick text to the IPS group chat with the address and added four words.

Second victim. Here now.

Whoever was available would come, but he needed to make sure one person hightailed over there. He dialed Logan's cell. "Has dispatch notified you yet?" he asked once his friend picked up.

"Notified me about what?"

Clenching his jaw, Bo had his answer and didn't like it. "I'm going to text you an address. I need you here right now."

"I'm already in my truck. Just tell me the address," Logan said, and Bo gave it to him. "What's up? Has something happened?"

"There's a body," he said low, hyperaware of the people standing within earshot, hoping to get any morsel of information they could use for gossip. "Nora and I found her." Precisely the way the Yuletide Killer had planned.

Logan sucked in a harsh breath and swore. "I'm on my way. Not far from you."

Turning to the growing crowd outside the house, Bo waved people back. "Please stand on the sidewalk. The police will be here soon. The easier we make it for them to get inside, the better."

Slowly, they listened to him, to his surprise.

"Bo, do you know who the victim is?" Logan asked on the other end of the phone.

"One of Nora's coworkers. A real estate agent. Amanda. I don't know her last name."

"Collins," Nora said, her voice shaky, racked with sobs.

"Amanda Collins. I already called it in to 911 and requested that they inform you. The police should be here any minute."

"I'll notify dispatch that I'm en route, two minutes away, but in case a patrol officer beats me there, I don't want anyone to disturb the crime scene until I arrive. How is Nora holding up? First her neighbor, then an attack on her and now this?"

"About what you'd expect," he said. She was trembling against him, softly weeping, teeth chattering. "She's in shock."

"See you soon." Logan disconnected.

Bo slipped his phone into his pocket and focused on Nora, drawing her closer. All he could do was hold her while she completely broke down.

"How many more?" Her hands grasped at his coat. She looked up at him, her cheeks wet, tears streaming down her face. "How many more lives is he going to take?"

At a loss for a response, Bo shook his head. He had no idea. Nora had gone to great lengths not to get close to anyone and yet, somehow, this monster had managed to hone in on the few individuals in Nora's orbit.

More will die, Nora's attacker had said. *More minnows will bleed.*

"Were you close with Amanda? I realize you weren't hanging out at her house and having spa days together, but I mean relatively speaking."

"Not really. She was always chatty with me in the office and talked about everything. Listings. Church. Her love life or lack thereof. A couple of weeks ago, we had an office holiday party, which was just dinner at a restaurant. Joe, the lead agent, started making it mandatory because I would never go."

"Which restaurant?"

"The Wolverine Lodge. It was the office manager, Tad, and the three of us agents. After dinner, she asked me to stay a little longer. Have a drink with her. She really pushed me and I caved."

Nora wept harder, covering her mouth with her hand as if to mute the sounds coming from her. He tucked her head under his chin and held her.

They must've misjudged the situation from the beginning and got it all wrong. This perverse man must have been watching Nora for weeks. Waiting. Preparing. Anticipating that she would refuse to play his game. Planning who he would kill to punish her. To make her suffer.

All this time the danger hadn't only been to Nora. Now her neighbor and coworker were both dead. Collateral damage. And the killer's identity was still a mystery to them.

This monster had brutally murdered two women and wanted to do the same to Nora. They had to find him.

Bo stroked her hair and kissed her forehead.

Nora stared up at him, her eyes turning hard despite the tears still flowing. "We have to stop him," she whispered. "Before he kills anyone else."

"I know." They were playing defense with a bloodthirsty devil when they needed to be on the offense. "Maybe the only way to do that is to take the fight to him."

She blinked at him. "But how?"

"I think we have to go back to where it all started."

"Home?" she asked, pulling back with a shudder. "Go back to Cold Harbor?"

He nodded. "Yes."

A silver Dodge Ram with red and blue flashing lights on the dash screeched to a halt and a patrol cruiser stopped behind him. Logan got out, followed by two officers. They proceeded to get the crowd under better control. The uniformed cops instructed the curious neighbors, some who were on the phone and most likely spreading word, to back away from the property and into the street or to return to their homes.

Bo hoped he could get Nora out of there before any reporters showed up. He didn't want her to have to face the media or intrusive questions or to have her face splashed all over the news again. She'd already been through enough.

She put her forehead on his chest. "I need this nightmare to end."

"I know," he said gently, stroking her hair. "We're going to make that happen. Find him. Put an end to this." One way or another.

"He stabbed her. So many times." A sob stuck in her throat. "Why? Just to hurt her?" She was crying again, and he wanted to ease her hurt. "To make her suffer?"

"I wish I knew." He wondered if the crime scene at Mrs. Moore's had been similar.

"And her throat, Bo." She took a shaky breath as she wept. "Did he strangle her, too?"

He held her and rubbed her back, to comfort and warm her. "I believe so. Yes."

As Logan made his way to them, Bo spotted Autumn parking her vehicle.

"I'm going to need to ask you some questions before you leave," Logan said to him.

"I figured." Bo nodded. "Give me a minute."

Logan pulled on gloves and glanced over his shoulder at the crowd. "Hey, let Dr. Stratton through," he said to the officers while gesturing to Autumn. "She's with IPS." Then he disappeared inside the house.

Taking one of Nora's hands, he held it. "I'm sure someone has notified the news station by now. They could be here at any minute, and I don't want you around when the reporters descend."

Autumn hurried over and gave Nora's arm a sympathetic pat. "I got here as fast as I could. Eli is on the way, too. Tak is busy with a client."

"Can you take her to your car?" Bo asked. "Lock the

doors. Get her warm. I think she's still in shock. When E gets here, take her to my place." Since Autumn didn't have tactical training, he wanted her to wait for backup. His house was secure, but anything could happen on the ride over with this savage murderer on the loose. "I don't want her here and I'm not sure how long it'll take with Logan." Bo needed to tell Logan everything he knew and get questions of his own answered before he could be with Nora.

"Yeah, sure," Autumn said.

Nora didn't protest. She looked like she was going to be sick.

Autumn and Eli would take good care of her until he got to the house. He was thankful Nora would have the emotional support of a skilled psychologist to confide in if she needed to talk. The past two days had been riddled with fear and trauma for her.

He glanced at his teammate. With Autumn's puffy coat, Bo couldn't tell if she had her weapon on her. "Are you carrying?"

"We have a murderer stalking a client." She glared at him. "Of course."

It should've gone without saying, but he had to be certain. "Sorry."

"I've looked at the case," she said, "and done a little digging. I have some thoughts. When there's time, we should discuss it."

"Yeah. I want to hear what you've found." Autumn had been instrumental in helping them find the sniper from the mass shooting. Though she moved here to slow down after burning out in Los Angeles, cases kept finding her and she couldn't resist diving into them. It was a good thing, too, because her talent would be wasted if she was sitting on the sidelines. "Let me get through this first."

An ambulance turned down the street, lights flashing, siren off. It was protocol for them to be here.

The crowd had swelled to at least a dozen. More than one person held their phone up—taking video footage or pictures or waiting for the dead body to be removed.

"I'll walk you to the car. Nora, keep your head down. Autumn and I will do our best to block the crowd's view of your face as we go."

He glanced at Autumn, and she nodded that she was ready.

He kept his arm around Nora and she angled her cheek toward his chest and shielded the rest of her face using her hand. With Autumn blocking the view of her from the other side, he hoped it was enough to prevent her name and face from making the news.

As they headed across the snow-covered lawn, Eli arrived, pulling in beside Autumn's vehicle. *Perfect timing.*

"Let's get her into Eli's truck," Autumn suggested and opened the passenger's side door.

Bo took his key fob from Nora's coat pocket and helped her climb inside the cab of the truck. He stepped up on the running board. "Hey, E. Take her to my place. Autumn is going to follow. I've got to talk to Logan."

"Yeah, no problem."

From the corner of his eye, Bo noticed Sierra Shively from Forensics getting out of her vehicle and marching up to the house.

He cupped Nora's cheek. "I'm going to check in with you," he whispered. No need to make sure she was safe because he was confident that E and Autumn wouldn't let anything happen to her, but he didn't want her to feel like he'd simply left her after yesterday's incident at the church.

"Will you be gone long?" she asked.

"Only as long as necessary. Okay?"

Her throat worked as she swallowed and nodded.

He swiped his fingers over her cheeks to dry them from her tears and kissed her forehead. It wasn't until afterward that he realized touching her had become a reflex somewhere along the way. He wondered what Eli would think of how close he'd gotten to Nora. What his friend would have to say about it. He also realized that he didn't care. She needed him and he intended to be there for her in every way possible. Bo would simply have to deal with a lecture later.

"Thanks," he said to Eli, who was looking at him with narrowed eyes, his gaze bouncing between him and Nora.

E gave a slow nod.

Bo climbed down and shut the door.

Autumn was already in her SUV, prepared to leave.

He lifted his hand in a quick wave and watched their vehicles take off, navigating the congested street.

The two uniformed officers at the scene knew him and let him pass without a problem. IPS had developed a good reputation. They worked hard to cultivate a positive relationship with the authorities and it helped that Detective Powell was already there.

Putting on his gloves, he stalked back to the house and went inside.

Shively was taking photos of the dead body, her mouth set in a grim line while she worked.

"Did Nora leave?" Logan asked when Bo joined him in the living room.

"Yeah." Bo's temple throbbed. He should take something to fight back the headache beginning to pound in his skull, but he wanted to get through this. "Autumn and

Eli are taking her to my house. They'll stay with her until I can get there."

"I asked Winter for a favor—to run the DNA evidence we got off Nora yesterday through the DCI lab. Faster than ours. We should know something by tomorrow." Logan stared down at Amanda Collins with a stony expression and pointed to the upper part of her body. "She was strangled and stabbed. Same as Mrs. Moore."

"Same level of…" He searched for the right word. "Gore?"

"The scene was worse with her elderly neighbor. The woman's ring finger was severed. I didn't want to mention the gruesome detail in front of Nora." Logan shook his head, the hardened look on his face remaining unchanged except for his jaw tightening. "Not that what this scumbag did to Amanda is any less heinous."

Something about the way he said her name struck Bo. "Did you know her well?"

Logan gave a brief, curt nod, still studying the body with angry focus. "I knew her. But not very well. We weren't friends."

"Any idea how long she's been dead?" Bo asked.

"The ME will give us a time of death."

"Come on, Logan. I can tell it's been hours. Give me a rough estimate of how long."

The detective sighed on a shrug. "Around twenty-four hours would be my *rough* guess."

"Definitely sometime last night," Shively agreed. She lowered the camera and turned to them. "I bet no one has heard from her or seen her today. That's my two cents for what it's worth."

Bo nodded. "It all counts."

"There you go. Two unofficial opinions," Logan said. "You're welcome to come with me to the morgue and get a better estimate firsthand from the ME until the autopsy is done or I can let you know."

"Thanks. I'll tag along." The sooner they had more information, the better. He would give Nora a call in a few minutes to check in. Make sure she got to the house all right and update her on his plan to go to the morgue.

"No telling how long he had her before he killed her." Logan indicated a stack of clothes neatly folded off to the side of the body. There were jagged cuts throughout the material like it had been slashed. "He cut off her coat and blazer."

"Did he do the same with Mrs. Moore?" Bo asked.

"Yeah," Logan said. "Folded them, too. This guy was just as thorough at the Moore place. He left the kitchen spotless. A boning knife cleaned and put in the dish drainer. No prints. He wiped the entire kitchen with bleach. The same type of knife is in the kitchen here. The only utensil in the house."

"Bleach, too?"

"The smell of it is potent in there, but I haven't seen any bleach or spray bottles on my preliminary check. I doubt I'll find any when I go back through."

"You're thinking he brought it with him?" Bo asked.

Another nod from Logan. "This was planned." He looked up at Bo. "Walk me through what happened with you and Nora."

"This morning, Nora checked her schedule, with an app the office uses. She had two new clients slated to view houses. One at ten and this one at five. I had a bad feeling about the last-minute additions after the attack on her at the church. Did my due diligence—looked up the names to see what I could find."

Logan took out his notebook and a pen. "Who was scheduled to meet her here?"

"A dentist from Cutthroat Creek. Dr. Allan Hiller. His office is closed today and I didn't have time to get his personal number to verify him because she had appointments starting first thing this morning." Then he remembered something. "Nora texted the number listed to say that we were running late. No response."

"Do you have the number?"

"Yeah." Bo took out his phone and gave it to him.

"The scumbag probably looked for an easily verifiable identity online. Someone local. Picked the dentist. Left a number to a burner phone for the appointment. But I'll check it out," Logan said. "Go on."

"As I was saying, we were running late. Maybe fifteen minutes. When we arrived, I noticed that there were no other cars parked outside," Bo said, thinking. "Which makes me wonder where Amanda's vehicle is. Do you think he nabbed her somewhere else and transported her here?"

"It's possible. I'll check with the real estate company to see if she had any late-day clients or missed any appointments. When Summer and I were looking to buy a house, we worked with Amanda. Very friendly. Far too trusting. She offered to drive us around in her car. I couldn't have her chauffeuring me around, so I drove the three of us. She might've gotten into the killer's car willingly, believing she was with a legitimate client. It would explain why there was no forced entry into the house."

"And the perp put the key back in the lockbox to make it appear as if everything was fine."

"So, you got here, and Nora got the key out of the box?"

Pinching the bridge of his nose, Bo nodded. The throbbing in his head was spreading. He needed to stop at the drugstore on his way home and pick up something for a tension headache. "Yeah, but her hands were shaking. She dropped the keys and I was the one who unlocked and opened the door."

"Any idea why she was shaking? Was she nervous about something? Did anything seem off before you got inside the house?"

Bo shrugged. "I think she was just cold." He thought back on it. "We were talking about, um, well, personal stuff." Her not having a boyfriend. Ever. Did that mean she'd never been intimate with anyone? "Nothing seemed odd or out of place outside. We went into the house. She turned on the lights and that's when we saw the body. The client was a no-show of course." A fake. "The whole thing was a setup. This grisly scene that he left for Nora."

"Was she friends with Amanda?"

"No. They were friendly, but they didn't socialize regularly. There was a company party. A couple of weeks ago at the Wolverine Lodge. It was the first time they hung out. Stayed after dinner at a restaurant and had drinks. Just the two of them. When she told me that, I realized he must've been watching her for weeks. We'll get the surveillance tapes from the restaurant. See if we spot anyone following Nora—watching her. It's the only way he could've figured out who she knows…who she might care about."

"Which deaths would hurt or rattle her the most," Logan said.

"I don't think he wants to simply kill Nora. Torturing her first is a part of this for him." Every detail of this twisted soul's plan was meticulously crafted. He wanted to ensure each moment of agony she experienced would be etched into her memory forever.

Was it simply for sick satisfaction?

Was it insurance that he would hurt her in the event she got away again?

Or was it to wear her down, to finally break her, so that she would give up on running altogether?

Bo looked back at Amanda's body. Bruised. Bloodied. Butchered. This could've been Nora.

It might still be Nora's fate if they didn't do something.

Whatever the cruel devil's goal, Bo was determined to make sure he didn't succeed.

Chapter Thirteen

Nora answered the call on the first ring. "Hello."

"Are you all right?" Bo asked.

The sound of his voice on the other end of the phone calmed her nerves, the muscles in her tight shoulders loosening. She knew the update wouldn't be good since the last time they spoke—which was hours ago—he was on his way to the morgue, but talking to him eased her worries a bit.

"Yes. I'm fine. Still with Autumn and Eli. They're looking out for me. By the way, you're on speaker," Nora said, with her cell phone on the table so that Autumn and Eli, who were both in the kitchen with her, could hear. "What did you learn at the morgue?"

Bo didn't immediately answer, like he was deciding how much to tell her.

"You don't need to filter anything for my sake," Nora said. "I can handle it."

"The cause of death was asphyxiation. He stabbed Amanda to torture her. Then he strangled her. The rest of the stab wounds were done postmortem. Twelve cuts in all. It was the same with Mrs. Moore. I went back over the Cold Harbor police report. The girls weren't strangled, but they were each stabbed twelve times."

A shudder ran through Nora as the memory of her friends' screams echoed in her mind.

"I wonder if the number twelve is related to the twelve days of Christmas," Autumn said, "or has some other significance." The woman's gaze fell to her.

Nora shrugged. "I have no idea. At the time, the detectives thought it was an aspect of a ritual kill. I don't think they examined the specific number beyond that."

"I don't want you to focus on that right now," Bo said. "Rehashing everything. Tonight has been hard enough on you already."

"If only I had known that he might go after Amanda." Nora wiped at her eyes. "Maybe I could've warned her. We could've protected her somehow."

"Nora, you might've chosen not to have any friends to protect yourself," Bo said, "but you're friendly with lots of people. We can't protect half the town."

Her shoulders sagged under the weight of that realization. Autumn put a hand on her arm.

"ETA, man," Eli said.

"I should be there in thirty minutes. I need to stop at the drugstore on my way. Nora, I'll get there as soon as I can."

"I'll be waiting."

Bo ended the call.

Autumn slid the broth that Nora had been nursing closer.

Picking up the mug, Nora held the cup of warm liquid between both her hands and took another sip. Even though she'd told Autumn that she didn't want anything to eat or drink, Nora was glad to have listened to the doctor. Even if Autumn wasn't a medical doctor.

The broth settled Nora's stomach and warmed her up, getting rid of the tremors.

Autumn poured a cup of freshly brewed coffee for herself and sat at the kitchen table beside her with a sympathetic expression.

A delicious aroma permeated the kitchen. Eli was busy baking. Shortbread cookies. It took him twenty minutes to throw the simple ingredients together and pack the dough into a pan. With his arms crossed over his chest, he stood near the oven, waiting to take them out.

The smell of yummy goodness was almost strong enough to lighten her mood and steer her mind from something other than death, but then the image of Amanda's body flashed in her head again. She couldn't help but wonder if that was how the police had found Mrs. Moore. Brutalized and bloody.

All because Nora refused to obey a monster's orders.

"You can't blame yourself for these deaths," Autumn said, as if reading her mind. Once again trying to make Nora feel better by absolving her of any culpability. "The killer has engineered this sadistic game. All in an effort to manipulate you into doing what he wants. Shouldering any guilt, no matter how small, only empowers him over you. Don't do it."

Nora sipped the broth. "Easier said than done, Doc."

"None of what you've been through has been easy," Autumn said. "Coming out on the other side won't be either, but you've already suffered losses no person should have to endure. Your innocence. Your adolescence. Family and friends. Your freedom to grow and explore without fear. And despite it all, you're still a fighter. You can do this."

"I keep asking myself—how many more people have to die in order for me to live?" Nora set the mug down. "If he just takes me, then no one else will get hurt and this will end."

A timer Eli had set started beeping. He shut it off. "This

won't end until we catch this guy and make him pay in a court of law for everything he's done," he said, slipping on oven mitts. "Or we kill him. Either way works for me." The gritty tone as the big, muscular guy took cookies out of the oven formed an incongruous image. "Anything else is unacceptable." He placed the pan on top of the stove.

Autumn put a hand on her shoulder. "Eli is right. All of those victims—your friends, Mrs. Moore, Amanda Collins and you—deserve justice."

"I know this isn't my fault," Nora muttered, more to herself than to the others in the room.

"This is most certainly not your fault," Autumn said, making Nora blink up at her.

"I just…" Nora dropped her head into her hands, hating that she felt this way. "I just don't want any more deaths on my conscience."

Eli sliced the cookies with a knife. "Let IPS and the cops carry that burden. We have to do our jobs, which includes protecting you." He used a spatula to scoop some from the pan and put them on a plate. "Every day that killer is on the loose—every life he takes—it's on us. Not you."

"You've survived this killer's best efforts," Autumn said, "but he's taken so much from you already. Don't let him take anything else. Especially not your peace of mind during quiet moments when you can catch your breath. I want you to practice the three *R*s. Recharge. Recognize. Remember. You have to recharge your body and spirit. No one can run on fumes. Recognize the good things that happen and hold on to them. It's human nature to let the darkness overshadow the light in difficult times. I want you to battle against that inclination. Most importantly, you have to *remember* what you're fighting for. What do you want your life to look like when this is over?"

Nora stiffened. No one had ever asked her that before. She'd spent so long living like a ghost that she didn't have a clue what having a *real* life would look like. How it would feel. To be free instead of a prisoner to a madman's obsession.

She glanced up and they were both staring at her.

"Have a cookie," Eli ordered, popping the bubble of tension. He set the plate down on the table in front of her. "That's my mom's recipe. The secret is a tablespoon of milk. Makes them super soft unlike traditional shortbread. One of those will melt in your mouth. Guaranteed to banish the blues. Try one."

Her throat closed from the kindness they were showing her. If this was how they rallied around a pro bono client, someone they barely knew, she could only imagine what they would do for a friend or family. Bo was lucky to have them in his life to look out for him.

Nora glanced down at the cookies, tempted to take a nibble, but she wasn't ready to feel better. Not quite yet. She still couldn't believe Amanda was gone. Sweet, funny Amanda who had done nothing wrong. Who would never again get to sip broth and eat homemade cookies because she was dead.

Murdered.

"Thank you for going to the trouble to make the cookies." Nora was grateful for the distraction that kept her from overthinking or worse—crying. "I'll eat them. I promise. In a little bit. Okay?"

"Sure, no rush." With a compassionate look on his face, Eli nodded. "But they are sublime when warm." He picked one up and munched on it, making a face like he was in heaven.

Autumn followed suit. "Oh, my goodness, Eli. These

are fantastic." The enthusiasm on her face and in her voice was genuine.

"See?" Eli said to Nora. "I told you."

She offered them a grin. A fake one. She was in no way happy, but she wanted to show her appreciation for their efforts. To repay them somehow, even if it was only a forced smile.

The alert sounded, signaling someone was coming down the road.

Eli headed for the office. A moment later he called out from down the hall, "It's just Bo."

"Are you okay?" Autumn asked. "Feeling any better?"

Nora wasn't okay, but she would be. "You and Eli helped a lot." Autumn's perspective as a psychologist and Eli's baking. "The sooner we catch him, the sooner I can move on from this." For far too long, she had been this killer's prey.

She was sick of running and ached to take the fight to his doorstep.

The truck door slammed shut.

Her heartbeat picked up, something inside her already lightening in anticipation of seeing Bo.

As the dead bolt unlocked, there was a soft mechanical whir, and then the front door swung open.

Bo stepped inside and removed his coat. Nora's heart stuttered and she was out of her seat and wrapping her arms around him before he could take off his boots.

Giving her a hug, he tucked her head under his chin, and she immediately felt better with him there. She took in his scent—that enticing male smell along with his aftershave—and relaxed against him.

He eased back, propped a knuckle under her chin and tipped her face up to his. "Hey."

"Hey."

His brow furrowed. "You told me they were taking good care of you," he said, the question clear though unspoken.

"They have been. They're both amazing. Eli even baked cookies," she said, and his gaze flicked up to someone behind her, his expression turning unreadable. "I'm just glad you're back."

Autumn and Eli moved to the door and put on their shoes.

"Your phone calls made a difference," Autumn said. "Every time you checked in, she relaxed a little more."

Was she that obvious? Nora stepped away from Bo.

"It's late. Tomorrow, I can tell you what I've learned." Autumn slipped into her coat. "And we can go over my theories."

Bo nodded. "First thing in the morning. We can meet at IPS. The whole team. We can have Chance sit in on the meeting by phone. There's something I wanted to discuss, too."

"I need to talk to you," Eli said to Bo. "Privately." His entire demeanor changed from considerate baker to ticked-off guy with a chip on his shoulder.

Bo sighed. "It can wait until tomorrow."

"No, it can't." Eli folded his arms. "You don't even know what it's about."

"I've got a good idea and I'm not in the mood to hear it. Not tonight."

Autumn eyed them. "Is this a personal or professional matter?" the doctor asked.

Both men responded at the same time.

"Personal," Bo said.

"Professional." Eli narrowed his eyes at Bo.

Autumn rubbed her forehead, clearly fatigued. "It's almost midnight, Eli." Taking a breath, she rested a hand on

Eli's shoulder. "We should both go. This discussion, whatever it's about, can wait until tomorrow. It's been a long day. Nora needs to rest. We all do."

Eli's jaw clenched and he hesitated a minute, but the man relented with a nod. "Fine. But we talk before the meeting."

"I'm fine with that," Bo said.

The tension between them was still thick.

Nora turned to Eli. "Thanks again for the cookies."

"You made me a promise. I hope you'll keep it."

She smiled. "I will."

A muscle twitched in Bo's cheek as his gaze slid from her to Eli.

Autumn gave Nora a one-armed hug. "Please get some sleep. Good night." The doctor left.

Eli snatched his coat from the hook. "Tomorrow," he reiterated, then stalked out into the cold.

Bo locked the door and slipped off his boots. Facing Nora, he took her hand and put her palm on his cheek. The faint scrape of his stubble anchored her. This was real. He was warm and solid and she could count on him to stick with her through this nightmare.

But what about when it was over?

What was she fighting for?

"What promise did you make Eli?" he asked, his tone gentle.

"Nothing special. Just that I would eat the cookies he made."

A grunt came from him. "That's his thing. Baking. It's how he takes care of people, processes things, relaxes, makes decisions. By baking treats. Not cooking, mind you," he said, and she smiled. "The guy subsists on pizza and spaghetti. Though, he does make a mean meatball." His voice still held a note of irritation.

She didn't know what was going on between him and his friend, but she didn't want to talk about Eli. "What's your thing? Listening to music?"

"I guess." Shrugging, he went into the kitchen and washed his hands. "Never really thought about it. But listening to music is not as useful as baking."

"Depends on what you're doing while you're listening, I suppose."

"Do you want some milk to go with the cookies?" he asked, and she nodded. "Warm or cold?"

"Warm. I'll do it." She went to the cabinet that had the pots and pulled one out. "You want yours warm, right?"

"I do."

She grabbed milk from the fridge and poured enough for two in the pot and turned on the stove. "Play something for us."

After he put on sultry, smooth music, he built a fire. They met on the sofa. Nora handed him a mug and set the plate between them on the coffee table.

When she finally tried a cookie, her palate was completely unprepared for the divine mixture. A moan slipped from her. "This is incredible."

"Yeah. He's a great baker."

They enjoyed the cookies, listening to the music and drinking their milk.

She glanced over at Bo and recognized the moment for what it was—a good thing. He was a good guy. She wanted her future to have more of this. Quiet, tender moments. With him. In this town that she'd grown to care about. Surrounded by friends she had over for dinner and met for drinks. Forging a family to love.

But before she could have any real future, she had to face the past that was hunting her.

"I've thought about your suggestion of us going to Cold Harbor."

"And?" he asked, wiping crumbs from his hands.

A part of her wanted to see her stepbrother, half sister and new niece. To visit her old friend Savannah. To catch up on all the things that she missed. Even though she had little to share in regard to her own life. "This might sound silly, but what if I make it worse by going back home?" What if doing so antagonized this monster more? Put her family in harm's way?

Bo's knee brushed hers. "It doesn't sound silly. That's why we're going to discuss it first with the team. Weigh the risks versus the reward. See how we cover all the bases." Bo leaned toward her until his face was inches away. "I'm going to protect you until the threat is eliminated, no matter what we have to do to make that happen."

"What about the people I care about there? You can't promise to protect them, too."

His gaze fell. "You're right. Going to Cold Harbor might be the only way to end this, but we won't do anything you're not comfortable with." Looking at her, he came closer still—until his face was all she could see—and cupped her cheek. "You're the client. The choice will be yours."

My decision.

My choice.

Her fear subsided as his words sank in, taking root. Bo was not a careless man. At the church, if she had stayed on the food line, like he had expected, nothing would've happened to her. She trusted him to plan for contingencies. To take her concerns into consideration and keep her from danger.

She missed having this safe space, knowing there was

someone she could count on who would be there when she needed them most. Even if this was only a professional obligation for him.

With him sitting so close, his face taking up her full focus, she allowed herself to drink in the sight of him. Such masculine beauty. Nora took in short, shallow breaths, the proximity of him sucking up all the air around her.

His eyes heated, but he didn't move a muscle other than his thumb stroking her cheek. He held her gaze steadily, unwaveringly, like he was waiting for something.

If she leaned her head forward the smallest bit, their lips would touch, but she shuttered her eyes and stayed still.

What do you want your life to look like?

She wanted warmth and connection. Friendship and family. To no longer be trapped and alone. To be safe to finally let herself fall for someone.

Someone like Bo.

But what if she had already fallen?

"Nora," he whispered. "Look at me."

Her gaze lifted to his and she thought she saw the same thing in his eyes that filled every pore in her body. Desire. Need. Longing for something deeper.

Her fingers ached to touch him, and her hand lifted as if beyond her control. She skimmed her fingertips across his cheek and electric heat vibrated through her.

You don't have to be alone. Not tonight.

Then she kissed him, or maybe he kissed her. She wasn't sure.

All she knew for certain was that Bo was touching her and kissing her like he was starving and she was what he craved.

His mouth was hot and possessive. Deepening the slow kiss, he sought her tongue with his own. Sliding her arms around his neck, she drew him closer and everything heated. She pulled him down onto the sofa and when he pressed his solid, heavy body against her, she moaned in his mouth.

This was better than cookies. Better than anything she'd experienced.

She didn't know her heart could be full of grief and exhilaration, both filling the space at the same moment.

The brutal murders, the senseless loss of life—none of the sorrow left her. The weight still pressed down on her shoulders. But the thrilling rush of this beautiful man touching her, making her ache with need, buoyed her.

She loved the way he tasted, the way he caressed her. Each stroke firm and confident. She loved the way his tongue slid over hers, the way his fingers coiled in her hair.

"You always smell so good," he muttered against her throat.

She kissed him again, lighting up from the compliment. Wrapping her legs around his hips, she yearned for more.

Everything he was doing was perfect. The intensity of his kiss. The searing heat of his hands diving under her sweater. The expert stroke of his fingers making her tingle all over.

But it wasn't enough. Not nearly enough.

Chapter Fourteen

Careful. Go slowly.

He repeated the warning in his mind, but her scent filled his head and her curves filled his palms, kicking his entire body into overdrive. Pent-up desire turned to pulsing need. Yet somehow, he managed to keep a tight hold on the reins of his touch, his kisses slow and gentle, so gentle that it produced an overwhelming ache. Not just a physical ache, but an emotional one, buried so deep inside him that he hadn't even known it existed until this very moment.

The strain from the effort of holding back sent a quiver arrowing straight through him.

He cupped her breasts over her sweater and the shiver that ran through her was impossible to miss. She rocked her pelvis, slow and steady, undulating against him, driving him out of his mind. His jeans tightened painfully in the crotch. He had to do something about the need pounding through him before he combusted.

But the warning sliced through the hormone-fueled fog of his brain again.

Careful. Go slowly.

Bo pulled back. "Nora, what do you want?" he asked, nearly breathless from the hunger tearing at him.

"More."

More. Whispered in that sweet, sultry voice, the word was like an engraved invitation to everything he craved. But he didn't want to mess this up. He needed them both to be clear for her sake.

"More what?" he rasped, his heart thundering in his chest.

"Of this. Kissing. Touching. Everything. But with fewer clothes."

"Fewer?"

"No clothes," she said, then nipped his bottom lip.

He longed to strip off every stitch of clothing from her, but he had more questions. Important ones. Caressing her cheek, he stared into her eyes. "Have you ever been with anyone?"

She stilled and blinked at him. Then shook her head.

"I'd be your first?" he asked hoarsely, needing her to confirm it.

A slow nod. "Is that okay?"

It was and it wasn't. She never had a boyfriend, never allowed herself to get close to anyone, never gave herself a chance to see what she wanted in a lover, in a partner.

An impulsive decision tonight could easily become a painful regret in the morning for her. And he couldn't take advantage of a young client in a stressful situation while she was stuck in his safe house, reliant on him to protect her.

Bo wanted her more than he'd ever wanted any woman, and there had been many. He'd even stopped at the drugstore and while he bought painkillers, he also got condoms since he didn't have any. Always be prepared.

But what he wanted more than her body was her happiness.

Doing this now—rushed, on a whim with no time for her think—was wrong.

She stared at him, waiting for a response. "Please. Don't say no."

He'd made a decision and then she went and said something like that, making him second-guess everything.

No, he chided himself. Even though his body screamed for release, he couldn't do it. "Nora, I—"

A high-pitched frenetic beeping blared in the house, the sound distinct.

The alarm.

Not just the heads-up that a car was headed down the road.

He was off the couch and on his feet. "Someone in the woods tripped the system."

"You mean someone is coming toward the house," she said in a dazed way, sitting up.

"Yeah." He hustled to the office, grabbed the mouse, and the computer monitors sparked to life. With a few clicks, he brought the security system up on the screens and took a look at which sensors had been triggered. Exact same quadrant as yesterday. He followed the flow of activity as one motion-activated detector after another lit up on the screen.

Something or someone was moving in a steady, straight line toward the house, setting off sensors along the way. But it was no animal and no hunter. He was certain of it.

Bo whipped out his phone and sent a text to the IPS group chain.

Activity in the same quadrant. Need backup.

Then he silenced the security system shrieking in the house while keeping it armed so he could track the activity and dialed Tak.

His friend answered on the second ring. "I saw your message. I'll be there in ten minutes. Don't worry about calling E, I'll do it on the way."

"Thanks. I'm going to give you authorization to access my security system remotely, so you can track what I'm seeing. I'll text you a passcode." Bo hung up and got into the system on his phone.

He didn't know if Autumn would get the message about needing backup or if she was already asleep, but he didn't expect her to race out to his place when she lived on the other side of town even if she had seen it. Autumn was a valuable team member, but without tactical training he couldn't use her out here for this.

It was good to have the two other former combat engineers living so close. After they all started working at Ironside Protection Services, they decided to buy properties near each other. Since they were friends beforehand, the best-case scenario was it would be easier to hang out. Worst-case, they could quickly respond if there was an emergency. Their rapid-deployment, wartime-ready nature was ingrained in them.

Always be prepared.

They were each more than capable on their own. But together, they were a formidable force to be reckoned with.

"Is it a person or an animal?" Nora asked as she came up behind him.

"Not sure yet." Bo finished authorizing access for Tak and Eli and texted the code they'd need to get in. Then he hit a couple of different buttons on the keyboard, pulling up the new camera that Tak had installed when he replaced the sensor that had been shot.

Nothing. The screen was pitch black, but the camera was active. What the hell?

Without a doubt, Tak had ensured the camera was functioning properly.

"Why can't we see anything?" Nora asked.

"Good question," he said. "Something's wrong with the lens."

He rewound the footage, going back to a few minutes before the motion activated sensor had been triggered and hit Play on the camera feed.

A clear view of the woods popped up on the screen. Seconds later, a man wearing a ski mask over his face, dressed in all black, entered the periphery of the camera's field of view. He lifted his hand, holding what looked like an air rifle.

Then the screen went black.

"What happened to it?" Nora asked. "Did he shoot it out?"

"No, he didn't destroy the camera. He used something to block out the lens. A paintball would be my guess," Bo said, thinking aloud.

"Why use paint when he could use a bullet?"

"Bullets are loud. Unless you're using a sound suppressor." Which meant this guy wasn't using a silencer. A small comfort in that detail, but not much.

Bo needed to go out there, find him and deal with him personally. Put an end to this nightmare for Nora once and for all.

He refused to simply sit back and allow that brutal monster to slip through his fingers for a third time. *I'm coming for you.*

He jumped out of his chair and hurried toward the front door. "Get your gun."

Nora was right on his heels. "Are we going to see if it's him?"

We? "I don't want you out there. You have to stay in here where you'll be safe."

"Are you leaving me to go out there by yourself?" she asked, fear changing the pitch of her voice. "You shouldn't take him on alone."

A sudden prickling sensation crawled up the back of his neck and made him freeze dead in his tracks. It had nothing to do with his intention to go out in the woods alone. The memory of Nora screaming, bursting through the kitchen doors with blood on her, replayed in his head. How she'd been overcome with terror and fell to her knees in tears, her body racked with sobs.

The blind rage, the fear, the impotence he'd felt in that moment flooded him once more.

The last time that sensor had been activated, he'd left her side to deal with it and that monster had attacked her.

Now, Bo stood there, contemplating doing it again, over activity in the same quadrant of his property.

Coincidences made his inner alarm bell ping because he didn't believe in them.

Maybe this sadistic killer who loved playing games was trying to bait Bo into leaving the house. With the intent of isolating Nora.

But to what end?

His home was secure. The windows were bulletproof. The doors were reinforced with steel and the locks couldn't be picked. They had to be hacked. Which would take time.

Still, the thought of separating from her had his gut tightening with dread.

"No," he said, shaking his head. "I'm not. I'm staying with you."

Relief cascaded over her face, but worry was still heavy in her eyes.

He shoved on his boots and had her do the same. "Get your gun," he ordered as he marched back to office.

They needed to be ready for anything. He opened a drawer, took out extra loaded magazines and shoved them into his pocket.

He sat down in his chair and turned back to his screen.

Sensors had been activated all the way up to his cabin. He checked the four security cameras around the perimeter of the house. Three of them had been blacked out. He toggled over to the feed of the fourth.

Just as the field of view came up on the screen, a paintball hit the camera, covering the lens.

Where are you?

More importantly, what was that devil doing?

If that guy tried cutting power to his house, Bo was prepared. He had a covered generator up on the rooftop deck, making it less visible and harder to sabotage.

Power would be diverted within less than a minute to the house, with only a temporary delay in the security system, but the reboot would take longer. Up to ten minutes. But, with the cameras blacked out, Bo was already blind to what was going on outside.

Sensors in the woods lit back up.

Was the guy on a fishing expedition? Tampering with his cameras and sensors? Testing Bo's security procedures? Or was he still trying to lure Bo from the house, away from Nora?

"Do you smell that?" she asked.

Bo sniffed the air, then went rigid. He did smell it. He looked at the doorway.

Smoke drifted in the hallway. Willowy white streams rolled through the air. The smoke detector screeched, the piercing sound grating on his ears.

"Oh, my God," Nora said, putting a hand to her chest. "He set the house on fire."

A small flame could quickly grow into a raging blaze, spreading unbelievably fast in a matter of seconds. In a few short minutes, the place could be filled with smoke that was just as deadly as the fire itself.

But what part of the house? Is that why he targeted the cameras? Bo spun back to the monitors and checked the system.

A steady seventy-two degrees Fahrenheit in every room of the house. He had an addressable smart multisensor system that registered multiple fire phenomena, such as heat and smoke. It combined inputs from several sensors and processed them using an algorithm built into the circuitry.

The sensors weren't picking up any heat, but according to the system, the smoke originated from the back of the house.

"Bo, we have to get out of here."

He shoved out from behind the desk and hurried toward the back of the house. The white smoke was thick and dense. He took a deeper whiff, noting a sulfury scent. Almost like the odor left in the air after fireworks were set off.

It wasn't fire that he smelled and the smoke was white, not black. Bo should've recognized it sooner. A smoke grenade had been set off. Most likely near the fresh air intake of the HVAC unit.

He swore under his breath. The intake wasn't even necessary for the HVAC to run properly. The only reason he installed the four-inch steel duct that led from the outside to the air return was to pass the home inspection.

Nora coughed, putting an arm up over her mouth and nose. "We have to get out of here."

"It's not a fire!" he said over the blaring alarm, hacking on the smoke as well. They still needed to leave. "He popped a smoke grenade to flush you out of the house since he can't get inside."

Gagging, she stared up at him. "He's out there some- where waiting. Waiting for me to show myself."

"Yes." It all made sense. Blacking out the cameras. Trig- gering more sensors in the woods again to draw Bo out. Then that tricky devil was probably going to loop back around and wait for Nora to run out of the house. Pan- icked. Distracted. Thinking the house was on fire. "Go grab our coats."

"But we can't go out there if he's expecting it. He might have a gun trained on the door, ready to shoot you." She clutched his chest. "We can't."

"We have to." It might not be a fire, but they still needed fresh air. "Trust me. Get our coats," he said tersely, and she took off down the hall.

Bo silenced his phone. He assumed that monster would be perched near the front of the house, but the odds were good that he might be lurking near the back as well. Or even hidden in the woods where he had a view of both doors.

That left them one viable option.

Bo jumped up, snatching the handle in the ceiling for the pull-down stairs that led up to the rooftop deck. He ex- tended the aluminum staircase and locked it in place. Hur- rying to the top, he entered the code for the digital lock. He drew his weapon, grabbed the lever, turned it and pushed up on the door.

But it didn't budge. Stuck. Layers of snow and ice must have weighed it down, jamming it.

Nora came to the bottom of the stairs, standing in her coat and holding his. More smoke pumped into the house. He choked, trying not to breathe in too much of the smoke.

He propelled himself up, surging with the momentum, and threw his shoulder up against the hatch door. Once. Twice. A third time and it gave way. He shoved hard, flipping it open.

A blast of wet wind and snow whooshed down on them. He beckoned to her to follow him.

As Bo climbed out onto the snow-covered deck, freezing wind slapped him. Shivering from the icy cold, he reached down and helped her step up and out.

Slamming the hatch door closed, he took his coat from her and threw it on. Going up to the roof was the best way out of the house, but it also made them visible targets. "Get dow—"

Bullets pinged off the railing in the howling wind. Bo lunged, wrapping his arms around Nora and taking her down to the floor of the deck. More gunfire came from the west. The same side of the shooter's original approach.

Covering her with his body to shield her from the incoming shots, he kept her head down, his arms wrapped around her.

"He's not shooting at me," she said.

Bo realized she was right. This man had murdered five women—that they knew of—and not once had he used a bullet to do it. If he had wanted to shoot Nora, he could've already done so. Whatever his ultimate plan for her, it involved a knife. Not a gun.

"Stay down," he ordered, and she nodded.

He crawled over to the generator that provided some cover while angry flurries whipped around him. Hunkered low, he peered around the side.

Muzzle flashes came from the western tree line near the house.

There he was.

Bo wished he had his Heckler & Koch SL8 rifle. Accurate. Smooth operation. Shot great at a distance. But he was happy to have something. The only problem was that he might not hit the shooter at that range. Bo got down and maneuvered to the side of the generator. Lying in the two-foot-deep snow, he aimed, lining up the sights. He drew in a breath, caressed the trigger, released his breath slowly and took the shot.

Bark spat from a tree and the shadow that had been standing right by it ducked out of sight.

Bo opened fire on the area. Snowy branches fell. Pine needles flew in the air.

A shadow darted between the trees, vanishing into the depths of the woods.

Gunfire erupted deep in the west quadrant. Muzzle flashes, coming from two different directions, converged on one area.

It must've been Tak and Eli zeroing in. But had the gunman been fast enough to make it that deep into the woods?

His phone buzzed with an incoming call. He glanced at the screen. It was Tak.

"Yeah," Bo answered.

"We got him."

Bo peered back into the darkness of the woods. He estimated that it was about four hundred yards from the tree line to the point in the woods where his friends had closed in on the assailant. Less than a quarter of a mile. In a flat-out sprint, in the snow, someone could do it in two minutes. Possibly one and a half. "Are you sure?"

"Eli's got him in zip ties and I just ripped off his ski mask. Mr. Goatee."

"Haul him into the police station. I'll call Logan and Autumn." What role she'd play, he wasn't sure, only that he should update her and ask her to join them. She might be helpful during an interrogation or to support Nora. "We'll meet you there," he said and hung up.

Just to be sure, Bo scanned the trees again for any sign of movement. He climbed to his feet and brushed off the snow from his legs. Scrutinizing the now quiet woods, he waited for relief that didn't come.

Bo helped Nora up. As she dusted the snow from her clothes, he locked the hatch.

Then they used the outdoor ladder along the back of the house. Keeping his weapon drawn and his head on a swivel, he moved quickly to his truck and got her safely inside. He jumped behind the wheel, cranked the engine and set his gun on the console, within easy reach.

Pulling out without incident, he brought up Logan's number in the menu on the dash and called him on Bluetooth. The entire time, the feeling that something was off wouldn't go away.

Chapter Fifteen

"Do you recognize him?" Logan asked Nora.

She stared through the one-way glass at the man hand-cuffed to a table in the interrogation room. Goatee. Meaty hands. Strong physique. Slight bruises under his eyes. Swollen nose with gauze packed in his nostrils and dressing on the outside. "He might've been the man who attacked me at the church. I can't say for certain because he had a stocking pulled over his head, covering his face. But I do recognize him from one of my open houses. Early November. I remember him because he hovered, but didn't really seem interested in the house."

Logan and Bo exchanged a glance, and in the back of the room, Eli and Tak whispered. She wondered what they were thinking.

"The police can see if his DNA is a match to what they already have from the incident," Bo said, standing beside her. "But do you recognize him from Cold Harbor?"

Nora took another look at him and racked her brain. She'd spent a decade trying not to remember the town and everyone in it, including her family. But Pa, Spencer and Rosa were the ones she'd truly missed and had never been able to forget.

The man in the other room was someone she couldn't place in her hometown with any certainty. "He has the right build of the guy who attacked me, but I don't know if I've ever seen him in Cold Harbor."

"That's okay," Autumn said, standing on the other side of her. "No one expects you to remember every single person you might have encountered."

Nora was glad that Bo had asked her to come.

"We ran his fingerprints." Logan looked down at a file in his hands. "His name is Louis Ames. Age fifty-two. Has a rap sheet as long as my arm. Petty theft. Shoplifting. Medicaid fraud. Disorderly conduct. Criminal trespassing. Simple assault. All misdemeanors. A repeat offender. But none of his offenses have been violent. He's done several stints in county jails in a hundred-mile radius as well as the state prison three times."

A shudder ran through Nora. "The state prison outside of Cold Harbor."

Autumn put a hand on her shoulder. "Do you want me to get your coat for you?"

They'd left their belongings in the bull pen at Logan's desk. Nora shook her head. "No, thank you." She wasn't shivering from the cold.

"Was Ames free or locked up at the time of the Yuletide murders?" Bo asked.

"Free." Logan glanced back at the file. "He was released two months beforehand."

"It can't just be a coincidence." Bo folded his arms. "Two months before Nora's friends are stabbed to death, that guy is set free from the state prison. Is it located twenty minutes outside of Cold Harbor?" he asked, and Nora nodded. "He's also the one who attacked her at the church, trespassed on my property and shot at us."

"We haven't confirmed that his DNA is a match to that of her assailant's at the food pantry," Logan pointed out. "With the goatee and the broken nose, he's probably our guy for that. But the only gun Tak and Eli found him carrying was an air rifle filled with paintballs."

"No live ammo on him," Tak said.

"True," Eli agreed, "but that doesn't mean he didn't ditch another gun and ammo in the woods."

"Has Ames been incarcerated at the state prison since then?" Autumn asked.

"Yes." Nodding, Logan flipped through the paperwork. "Two more times. The last was earlier this year. He did six months and was released in March."

"Well, let's go in there and talk to him." Bo gestured at the room on the other side of the glass. "Let's apply a little pressure and see if he cracks."

"When you question him," Autumn said, "refer to Nora and her slain friends as girls. Children. See how he reacts. Whether he naturally talks about her that way himself."

"Why?" Logan asked.

"The killer's desire to play children's games with Nora—Hide and Seek, Sharks and Minnows, Santa Says—it's more than a power dynamic for him. My theory is that he once viewed her that way, as a child, and may still."

"That makes him even more twisted," Bo said. "Wanting to harm children."

"On the note card, the Santa is holding a book of deeds. I believe, in the killer's eyes, Nora is naughty. Maybe because she refuses to play his game. It's something you should test while questioning him."

"All right." Logan headed to the door.

"I need to be in there with you," Bo said. "I know you

have a job to do, but so do I. Our goals are aligned, but our priorities aren't the same."

"Yes, they are."

"If that were true," Bo said, "there wouldn't have been a need to send Nora to IPS."

Logan considered it and finally gave a curt nod. "Fine. We'll do it together. Just remember it's being recorded. I know at IPS you only answer to Chance, but I've got a boss."

"I might threaten to push it in there, but don't worry. I'd never do anything that could get you suspended or fired."

"Why does that not make me feel relieved?"

The detective had to follow the strict rule of the law. The same law that prevented him from protecting Nora.

But Bo and the others at IPS would do whatever was necessary to keep her safe.

LOGAN SET A cup of coffee down in front of Louis Ames as they took their seats at the table across from him. He dropped a few packets of creamer and sugar in front of the guy.

"Thanks." Ames tore the packets opened, dumped them all in and stirred the hot coffee with his grimy finger. Then he took long gulps of the hot drink.

"Want to tell me what you were doing out there tonight on private property?" Logan asked.

"Just a prank." Ames shrugged. "No big deal."

"Trespassing and vandalism *is* a big deal," Logan said.

Bo put his forearms on the table and clasped his hands. "Attempted murder is an even bigger deal."

Ames shuttered his gaze and drank more coffee.

No doubt stalling.

"You're looking at some serious time," Logan said. "Did

you know you could get fifty years for attempted homicide, with an additional ten years for the use of a deadly weapon?"

"I don't know what you're talking about," Ames snapped. "Did you find a gun with bullets on me?" The man's beady eyes shifted between them. "I don't think so. You can cut the hogwash. You pigs got nothing on me besides a stupid prank." He drained his cup. "Can I get another coffee and a sandwich this time?"

Logan pulled an evidence bag from his pocket. With a handkerchief, he picked up the cup and dropped it in the bag. "Now we've got your DNA. I'm betting it's going to match the forensic evidence collected after Nora Santana was violently assaulted at the Methodist church yesterday evening. You bled on her when she broke your nose. You made the mistake of picking up a knife during that altercation. When this comes back as a positive match," he said, shaking the bag, "I'm going to charge you with aggravated assault. Then I'm going to put together a case on how you've been stalking Nora Santana. Terrorizing that *girl*."

"Is that how you get your sick kicks? By stalking and terrorizing young girls?" Bo asked.

Ames's beady eyes flared wide with alarm, and they had his full attention now. "No, of course not! Young girl? That woman is a real estate agent. How young could she possibly be?"

"Stalking and terrorizing wasn't enough for you, was it?" Logan took out pictures of Mrs. Moore and Amanda Collins from the file and threw them on the table "Then you murdered her neighbor and coworker. Like you murdered those innocent girls in Cold Harbor ten years ago."

"Hold on!" Ames reared back in his chair. A look of horror wrestled with one of disgust on his face. "I didn't murder anybody! Do you hear me? I may be a thief and a fraud but I'm no killer."

"Unfortunately for you," Bo said, "that's not how any of this looks."

"The public is eager to blame someone for those brutal deaths." Logan crossed his arms over his chest. "I'm happy to throw you to the wolves after your DNA comes back from the assault. And considering your mile-long rap sheet, the judge is not going to go easy on you. Unless…"

Ames gulped. "Unless what?"

Bo leaned forward. "Unless you can give us a better explanation."

"Okay. Listen, I went home one day and found an envelope waiting for me *in* my apartment. On the kitchen counter. It had my name written on it. Inside the envelope was a hundred bucks and a burner phone."

Logan tapped a finger on his notepad. "When was this?"

"Two days before Halloween."

Very precise. "How can you be so sure?" Bo wondered.

"Because it was right after that shooting on Main Street and the person paying me was interested in the woman who was shot but survived. Nora Santana."

Greasy unease slid through Bo's gut. "You got a hundred bucks and a burner. Then what?"

"Then it rang. I answered it. Some guy, or maybe a woman, was on the other end. I couldn't tell for sure because the voice was disguised. By, like, a machine. But I think it was a dude."

"What did the person say?" Bo asked.

"They asked me if I wanted more money. I said, *hell yeah*. They gave me instructions. Every time I did something they asked me to do, I received another envelope with more cash."

"What sort of things?" Bo stared hard at the man. "Start at the beginning and don't leave anything out."

"First it was only following her without getting too close. Once I was told to clean myself up, put on nice clothes and go to an open house she was hosting. The person left something in the envelope that looked like a USB drive but smaller. I was supposed to get her purse, lift her cell phone and insert that drive thingy until it turned green. Then I had to put her phone back without her knowing. That was easy-peasy because she left it sitting on the kitchen counter."

Bo stifled a groan. "Why? What did the USB drive do to her phone?"

Ames shoved a hand through his disheveled hair that looked like it hadn't been washed in weeks. "I don't know. Didn't ask that because I didn't care."

The man after Nora used Ames to surveil her and possibly hack her phone. With some kind of malware?

"Did you ever deliver any notes or gift boxes?" Bo asked.

"No." Ames shook his head. "I was never given anything physical like a gift to give to her or anybody. But I was told to give her a message."

Logan jotted things down even though the interview was being recorded. "A message?"

"Yeah. I was instructed to give her a message when she was at the church."

Bo lifted a palm. "The person on the phone knew in advance that she was going to be at the church?"

"Sure did," Ames said, nodding. "The man, or woman, told me that she was being protected, but that they were going to distract her bodyguard. The big Black guy." Ames looked at Bo. "The bodyguard being you."

Bo gritted his teeth. "Were you told how I'd be distracted?"

"Nope. I asked. He said that I didn't have a need to know. Only that when you weren't focused on the girl. Oh—" Ames straightened "—that's what he always called her. The *girl*. That when you weren't focused on the girl that I had to get to her some kind of way. Not to hurt the girl. Just scare her. Give her the message. He didn't say anything about her hurting me though. She broke my fricking nose."

Logan set his pen down. "Tell us the message."

"He made me memorize it." Closing his eyes, Ames thought for a moment. "Get rid of him and go home alone. If you don't, more will die. More minnows will bleed." He opened his eyes. "That was it. Kind of weird. I had to look up what the heck a minnow was."

A surge of anger rushed through Bo, but he sat back and clenched his hands under the table. "What happened tonight?"

"An air rifle was waiting at my apartment close to dinnertime. Loaded with paintball cartridges. And a map. I got a call and I was told to be at some coordinates in the woods at one in the morning. Sharp. All I had to do was hit the cameras with paint. They were marked on the map. Then I was supposed to go back out the same way I came in."

Bo put a hand flat on the table. "Who was shooting at us?"

"I have no idea."

"You didn't see anyone else?" Logan asked, setting down his pen.

"Nope. No one other than those two fellows who tackled me to the ground, shoved a gun in my face and zip tied me like a hog."

Bo tried to wrap his head around the intricacies of what Ames told them. Setting aside his disappointment and ire that this wasn't their guy and this nightmare wasn't close to being over, he honed in on a gap that needed filling. "You were instructed to follow Nora."

"Yeah, and to keep a log of the things she did, the folks she dealt with, and to pass it along during the calls."

"Why?"

Ames shrugged again. "I told you I don't know."

Bo didn't buy that this man was completely clueless. Ames was a desperate criminal. A criminal smart enough not to get convicted of a felony. Smart enough to be curious. To ask questions. To press for answers even when they were readily given.

"Why didn't this guy follow her himself? And why did he pick you of all people to do it?" Narrowing his eyes, Bo clenched his hand and pounded his fist on the cold metal, making Ames flinch. "And if you tell me that you don't know one more time, we're going to turn off the cameras. The good cop over here is going to leave the room. Then I'm going to ask you again. A different way. One you won't like. I might start by smacking you in your broken nose. And I won't worry about losing my badge because I don't have one."

Eyes big as saucers and sweat beading along his brow, Ames hesitated.

Logan stood. "I guess I'll duck out now."

The chain connected to the handcuffs and table jangled when Ames raised his palms. "Wait. I asked the person why me and refused to work for him until I knew. He told me it was because he knew I needed money and had the right skill set. He knew I'm used to scoping out people and things. Have quick fingers for lifting a phone. Could be mean when necessary. That I'd be willing to deliver some weirdo message and scare that chick."

"And why didn't he follow her himself?"

"I asked that, too. He's not from here. Doesn't live in Bitterroot Falls. Once he let it slip that he had a three-hour drive to get here. He needed someone local. Who could have eyes on her with a phone call."

Cold Harbor was a three-hour drive from Bitterroot Falls. Every thread of this web led back to Nora's home-town, where this nightmare started.

They needed to go there for answers if they ever wanted to stop this guy.

Chapter Sixteen

Sitting at the conference table, Nora found it hard to believe that the last time she was in this room was three days ago.

In such a short amount of time, she'd endured more than she had over the past three years. She'd lost a neighbor and a colleague at the hands of a relentless serial killer, been attacked by a petty criminal and been smoked out of the safe house.

But she'd also opened herself up to putting her life in someone else's hands. As well as her heart.

She looked up at Bo, who sat across the table from her. Their eyes met, and something in her chest stirred, her thighs tingling, and she felt that irresistible pull toward him—like no one else in the world existed.

Even when they were in a room full of people.

Eli opened the conference room door and stuck his head in the room. "Bo, can I have a word with you in the hall before we start the meeting?"

"Chance is already patched in on speaker. It'll have to wait until afterward."

"If I may," Autumn said, "since you two mentioned that whatever issue you're having is both a personal and professional matter, perhaps it should be discussed with the entire group."

Bo and Eli both averted their gazes, each grumbling some protest.

"This doesn't need to take up the time of the entire group," Bo said.

"There's a client present." Eli shifted his weight, clinging to the door handle. "Bo and I can discuss it later."

Leaning back and angling the chair, Autumn plastered on a plastic expression. "With all due respect, if your discussion involves the client, then it should be had with her present. Does it involve Nora?"

Eli stepped into the room and shut the door. "Yes, it does, but it's a matter of protocol."

Nora stiffened and glanced at Bo for some idea about the problem, but he wouldn't look at her.

"I disagree," Autumn said. "I'm not sure how you're used to operating, but I believe transparency is essential."

Eli shook his head. "It's not your call to make."

"You're right," Chance said over the phone. "It's mine. I agree with Autumn. What's the issue?"

They sat in silence for a long moment that seemed to grow even quieter with each beat of Nora's heart.

"I'm sorry, man. I didn't intend to do it like this." Clasping his hands behind his back like a dutiful soldier—or rather airman—Eli hung his head. "But the fact remains that Bo has gotten intimately involved with Nora. It goes against protocol, could endanger the client and could jeopardize the reputation of IPS."

Nora tried and failed not to squirm in her seat.

"Whatever may have happened between the two of you, was it consensual, Nora?" Autumn asked.

Her cheeks burned like someone had set her face on fire. She could only imagine the embarrassment that Bo must've felt. "Yes. Of course, everything has been consensual. Nothing happened that I didn't encourage or welcome or initiate. Bo has discussed a similar concern with me and frankly, I commend his professionalism and restraint."

The corners of his mouth perked, and she hoped the hint of satisfaction in Bo's expression wasn't her imagination.

"This is my fault." Chance sighed over the phone. "Initially, Bo refused to take this case because of his level of attraction to Nora. I was the one who insisted because she requested him and they already had an established rapport. I thought it was for the best."

"I didn't see a problem with their relationship." Tak picked up his mug of coffee and took a swallow. "Bo offered to be replaced at the hospital and Nora shot down the idea. Quite strongly."

"My professional opinion is that Bo's presence has had a positive effect on Nora's well-being." Autumn spoke to the group but looked at her.

"Regardless, my apologies, Nora," Chance said, "if this has in any way compromised your safety."

"No, no, please. It hasn't. If Bo hadn't agreed to be my bodyguard, I would've run again." Instead of standing her ground and facing this head-on. "This wasn't a mistake. Not for me." When she looked up, Bo was staring at her.

In his eyes, she saw heat and affection and the determination to stay her protector. It wasn't a mistake for him either. She smiled at him, and the grin that spread across his face filled her with warmth.

"Am I the last one to know?" Eli finally took a seat.

Tak nodded. "Always late to the party."

"Moving on to more pressing business," Chance said. "Did you figure out what this guy loaded on her phone?"

"Spyware." Bo sat forward, turning his focus to the speakerphone. "It's allowed him to track her and eavesdrop. Not only on her phone calls, but on any conversation when the phone was nearby."

Since Bo discovered that her phone had been hacked, they'd been careful about anything they said with it around. Before the meeting, he had her leave it in her purse in his office.

"We believe that's how he knew what security measures to expect at Bo's house," Tak said. "Regarding the cameras and sensors."

"And how he tracked her there to begin with," Bo added. "It also explains the convenient timing of him dropping off the package for Nora when the pizza was dropped off. This guy used the delivery as cover."

"Any reason for us to think that he might have picked up on the fact we know about the spyware on her phone?" Chance asked.

"No." Bo shook his head. "Logan is holding the low-level criminal that the killer enlisted to help him orchestrate all this for seventy-two hours before charging him for assault, trespassing and vandalism. After that he'll be moved to the county jail. He won't be talking to anyone."

"We should use this to our advantage," Chance said. "Feed him the information that we want him to know. Flush him out and bait him into a trap. But how?"

"The killer is a three-hour drive away according to Louis Ames," Bo said. "I think the key is to go back to Cold Harbor."

Eli scratched his jaw. "In the report you wrote up after your conversation with Detective Gagliardi, you mentioned that Nora's father, Jamal Banks, is in Bull River. That's a three-hour drive from here, too."

"What does my dad have to do with this?" Nora shifted

in her seat toward him. "The police never suspected him of anything."

"They never investigated him," Eli said gently. "There's also a connection between Banks and Louis Ames."

Anger percolated and she wasn't sure why. "What connection is that?"

"The state prison. Gagliardi told Bo that your dad used to work there as a corrections officer. Granted, it could've been before Ames ever set foot in that prison, but we should reconcile the dates and check out his alibi for the night of the Yuletide murders and the two here in Bitterroot Falls."

The memories she had of her father were all wonderful. Sparse but wonderful. Her mother had always referred to him as a good man. One who had been hurt by their divorce and by her moving on. But there had never been a negative word about him.

"Since you guys are done with the security system upgrade for the other client," Chance said, "Eli, I want you to go to Bull River to check out Banks. Let's do our due diligence on this. Autumn, do you have a profile on this guy?"

"It's not as complete as I'd like, but I'll share what I have thus far. I reached out to a contact of mine in Los Angeles. She's a nose. A sensory evaluator. A professional smeller. I sent her samples of the scent from the box. She identified a series of notes: cashmeran, leather, cloves, pink pepper and juniper. The strange thing is she's not convinced that it's cologne. She thinks it's tobacco. She just received the sample and is still working on it, trying to identify what type and the brand. Also, I scanned the holiday card the killer has been leaving for Nora and did a search for the images. Got a hit on Instagram for the artist who designed and drew the border. She lives in Billings. The woman posted the image of the border in her gallery as part of her portfolio."

Tak sat up like that was the first interesting thing he'd heard. "You contacted her?"

"I did." Autumn nodded. "The person who commissioned her did so through her website. They never actually met. The person provided a description of what he wanted. It reminded her of the European version of Saint Nicholas, where children's deeds are judged. An angel will bring presents or sweets to good kids and Krampus, a devil or monster, comes for the bad ones. She received cash payment in the mail and was told to send the cards to an address in Cold Harbor. To a house on Appleway Road, five blocks from the Howard residence."

Nora's heart skipped a beat. "I don't understand. You found him?"

Autumn frowned. "Not quite. The address was for a Roger Zielinski."

"Mr. Z?" Nora shook her head in confusion. "It can't possibly be him. He's blind. Must be in his late eighties by now."

"He's ninety-two," Autumn said.

"Before I left Cold Harbor, he was already a frail recluse. I can't imagine what condition he's in now."

"Which made him the perfect person to exploit," Bo said. "Easy to go through his mail and take a package without Mr. Zielinski knowing."

"As I told the rest of the team last night, I believe the killer views Nora as a kid. Take his desire to play children's games with her. His usage of Santa. The way he refers to her as a girl. It's most likely because he knew her as one and, I think, once thought of her fondly."

"Fondly," Eli scoffed. "Are you serious? He's trying to kill her."

"He didn't just give her coal. He left sugarplums for her as well. I think his view of her is multifaceted. The note cards being delivered to Roger Zielinski ten years ago does confirm that he lived close by in your neighborhood. That's probably why he disguised his voice. He doesn't want you to recognize him. Not until he's ready for you to know his identity. Probably when he's about to punish you."

It was one thing to think of this man as a faceless, nameless monster, but to realize this was someone she had known well, since she was a child, made her skin crawl. She rubbed her arms to make the feeling go away.

"Are you okay with me continuing?" Autumn asked her. "If you need a break or want to step out of the room—"

"I'm fine. Please, go on."

"Any idea why he might've looked at you or the other girls as naughty?" Autumn asked. "I'm not putting this on you in any way. This could be his demonization of young females for no reason at all, other than the fact you weren't born boys. I just want to make sure we're not missing anything."

"Nothing I can think of. I was a good kid. Never did drugs or drank alcohol. I was well mannered. Got excellent grades. Don't get me wrong—I wasn't perfect. I went through a phase where I cut school sometimes, talked back to my parents, didn't always do my chores. Normal teen stuff." Honestly, she'd started skipping school and sassing her parents as early as seventh grade. Her pa had blamed it on hormones. But after her mom died, she followed all the rules as a way to honor her memory.

"The killer is most likely in Cold Harbor," Autumn said. "That's not to say that we shouldn't completely rule out

Banks since the police didn't investigate him and it's not a far drive. However, I think the odds are high that the man we're looking for is white. Not Black. As for age, during the Yuletide murders, he was most likely in his midtwenties to midforties, but I can't narrow it down without knowing if those were his first kills. I do know that he derives gratification from exerting control over Nora. That's why the first game was Santa Says, and it made him so angry when she refused to play. He believes that she deserves to be punished. Perhaps, in his mind, by the devil himself."

"I think we need to go to Cold Harbor as soon as possible to finish this," Bo said. "If we don't, you may never be safe, Nora. But it's your call."

"I'm worried about going back home," Nora admitted. "I don't want to antagonize him. Make things worse. There are people I love who could be targeted."

"Going to Cold Harbor could make him feel backed into a corner." Autumn looked around the room and let that sank in. "It could push him to take a drastic step he wouldn't otherwise consider. On the flip side, the excitement of having her so close again could also cause him to make a mistake. Especially if we make it time-sensitive somehow. Create a sense of urgency in him."

"We need to look at laying a trap there for him," Chance said, "where he feels that he has the upper hand—that he can win. Then we might be able to keep his focus squarely on you, Nora."

His focus and all the danger. She would take on both if it ensured that no one else she cared about was hurt. "It's time I went back home." Faced her demons. Figuratively and literally.

"I'll need backup to cover Nora properly." Propping his elbows on the table, Bo clasped his hands. "I have no doubt that this guy has researched IPS and knows everyone's face. He'll easily spot us."

"Sure, he knows your faces," Chance said. "But not the faces of every IPS agent. We have other offices. Let me talk to Rip. I'm confident I can have some people in Cold Harbor no later than tomorrow morning."

"We can bait him by using the phone he bugged." Autumn rolled a pen between her fingers and looked around as she spoke, like she was thinking out loud. "But I wish there was an organic way to get the town talking about the fact that you're there. The frenzy of chatter around him could push him to slip up."

An idea came to her. "Tomorrow is Sunday. If things are the same as when I lived there, half the town will be at church. I could make an appearance. It would get everyone at the service talking and news will spread faster than wildfire."

"It can work." Bo nodded. "We should go up tonight, which means I'll need backup sooner than the morning. I can ask Winter and Declan. See if they're available. And Jackson might be free. He had to take vacation days to get out of a WITSEC detail so he can attend the engagement party next weekend."

"Who's Jackson?" Nora asked.

"Logan's brother," Bo explained. "He's a US marshal and lives in Missoula."

"Winter is too high-profile," Chance said. "She was the face briefing the media about the mass shooting. If this guy saw Nora during media coverage, I guarantee you that he knows Winter also. Still, check with Declan and I think Jackson is a good idea, too."

"I should go, too," Autumn said. "He'll see me as a target before he thinks of me as a threat. To this guy, women are vulnerable, prey, easy to pick off. But if I'm there, gauging reactions, speaking to people, I might be able to pinpoint who it is."

"Agreed," Chance said. "If we can ID this guy and nail him before we have to use Nora as bait, that would be ideal."

Nora's mouth went dry. She picked up the glass of water and took a sip. This was happening. The possibilities and pitfalls whirled in her head. "So, what's the plan? How do we catch this guy?"

Chapter Seventeen

Glancing in the rearview mirror, Bo checked to see if the car was still behind them. The van was a Ford based on the shape of the frame and pattern of the headlights, but the vehicle stayed too far back in the darkness for him to make out a license plate or see the driver. Getting behind the van proved impossible. Every time Bo had slowed down, so had the other vehicle.

Plenty of other cars were on the road. Yet, that dark-colored van was too similar to the one that had shown up at his house for him to readily dismiss it.

He looked over at Nora. Her head was against the window and she stared outside. Deliberately exposing her to danger set his nerves on edge. There was no other way, and this was better than her running or trying to deal with a cold-blooded murderer on her own. Being by her side, facing this monster together, was crucial for him. As though every moment before this one had led him here. For this purpose. He'd do anything to give her the freedom to live on her terms and without fear.

His mind kept replaying the image of Amanda Collins's body but instead he saw Nora lying there. Bloody and butchered.

Fingers tightening on the steering wheel, he forced the reel of death from his head.

Nora was sitting beside him. Very much alive. He just had to keep her that way.

This was the most important mission of his life. He had to get it right. No matter what.

The plan they had hatched was risky. Jackson and Declan were both available on short notice and would arrive later that evening around the same time as Autumn. Given Nora's concern for her loved ones and Autumn's belief that the killer would likely target a female, the IPS personnel Chance had enlisted—already en route from Spokane— would be assigned to keep a close eye on her sister, Rosa, and old best friend, Savannah. If the killer went after them to use them as leverage against Nora, capable, well-trained individuals would be at the ready to intervene.

So long as everyone did their part without any deviations, they had a good shot at pulling this off and getting justice that was long overdue.

"Are you all right?" he asked without worrying their conversation was being monitored.

Music played and her phone was in the backseat, locked in a dead box. At first, they had considered removing the battery and putting the phone in a Faraday pouch that blocked all signals. But in addition to protecting them from hacking and eavesdropping, it would also prevent the man hunting Nora from tracking her. They couldn't tip their hands.

The next best solution was using the dead box. The GPS and Bluetooth still functioned, but no sound would register while the phone was in there.

Prior to shoving her phone in the box, they had a conversation for the benefit of the eavesdropper that she needed to try to sleep and should stow her gun and phone in the back on the drive.

"I'm nervous," Nora said. "About popping up on my family out of the blue after being gone for a decade. It doesn't feel fair to them. Putting them through that kind of shock and emotional upheaval. In public. I know where Rosa lives. I followed her once. Maybe we could stop there on the way to the B&B and we can get reacquainted privately."

He reached over and took her hand. "We hashed out a solid strategy. To keep everyone safe—Rosa and Savannah—and protect you, too, we have to stick to the plan. It'll be hours before the others arrive. They need time to scope out the lay of the town and get into place discreetly. Seeing anyone tonight jeopardizes the plan."

From the corner of his eye, he glimpsed her nod slowly, like she was considering the situation.

"You're right," she said. "I know. Stick to the plan. I'm sorry."

"Nora, you don't have to apologize for anything."

She took in a big breath and let it out on a shudder. "I think I'll have quite a lot to apologize for to my family."

Provided her pa or brother weren't behind this.

"If I make it through this," she added in a whisper.

"No ifs. *When* you make it through this, you'll be able to see your family whenever you want. As much as you want. You can put this nightmare behind you. Maybe you'll even want to move back to Cold Harbor permanently. The point is you'll be free to choose. To move on." He desperately wanted to give her that. She deserved nothing less than a fresh start.

Nora swallowed hard. "Bitterroot Falls is my home now. I don't want to move on from the town." She interlaced their fingers and squeezed his hand. "Or from you."

His heart swelled at the words and the way she looked at him with such warmth in her eyes. "I'm happy to hear it."

He brought their joined hands to his lips and kissed her knuckles before lowering it to the center console.

He didn't want her to leave, but if that's what she chose to do, he'd have to break his rule about having a long-distance relationship. Maybe even relocate with her.

Whoa. Wanting to follow a woman he'd only known a couple of months, only spent a few days with, sounded absurdly dramatic when Bo was anything but.

Maybe he needed to have his head examined.

At the sign for Cold Harbor, he switched on his signal and took the turnoff. Flicking a gaze up to the rearview mirror, he spotted the van changing lanes and exiting, too. After Bo turned left at the end of the off-ramp and headed to the B&B, he watched the van turn right.

"Thank you, Bo. I've needed you more than I first realized."

"You're welcome," he said brusquely. "But with or without me, you can do this." She just shouldn't have to do it alone.

"I don't know about that."

"Are you kidding me? You've made it ten years without me or anyone else. You were smart enough to learn self-defense, which staved him off in your dorm room, and you defended yourself against a man who was almost twice your size at the church. Sure, you've taken protective measures, keeping others at a distance, but you volunteer all over the place. Giving back to the community when you ask for nothing in return. You have the biggest heart and the bravest spirit." He wanted her generosity and affection for himself, but he wanted to give himself to her in return, to give her everything. As foreign as the feeling was, it made it no less true. "I have no doubt you can do this."

She smiled, so beautiful that it hurt, and something in his chest gave a little tumble.

Then he realized there was nothing wrong with his head.

It was simply falling in line behind the rest of him and leading the way was his heart.

NORA STARED AT herself in the mirror of the room's en suite bathroom, rigid with nerves. When Tak arranged lodging for everyone, he put Jackson, Declan and the IPS agents from Washington at the Roundup Motel in between Cold Harbor and the state prison. While she, Bo and Autumn would stay at the B&B on the edge of town.

It had been unspoken that Bo wasn't going to let Nora out of his sight, which meant one room. No one had questioned it. Tak had reserved the only small suite at the B&B with a sitting area and sofa.

Sharing a room didn't bother her. Wearing a frumpy T-shirt and baggy sweats did.

Given that she had packed a bag with the possibility of running at the forefront of her mind, her choice of clothing had been practical. She'd only thought about survival.

Not seduction.

Last night, Bo had been on the cusp of rejecting her, and after that mortifying group discussion in the office about their *relationship,* she was sure to meet further resistance. It would've been nice to wear something sexy to entice him.

Tipping her head back, she growled in frustration.

The plan the IPS team had created was indeed solid. But past experience taught her that the man after her always managed to be two steps ahead. She hoped everything worked perfectly, but in her gut, she had to account for the unforeseen factor that would invariably rear its ugly head.

By this time tomorrow, she might be dead. As long as

they got him, stopped that monster and made him pay for the lives he'd brutally taken, her sacrifice would be worth it.

But she didn't want to die without ever being truly touched, without acting on the desire she felt for Bo. If this was her last night—and she wasn't foolish enough to believe that it might not be—she wanted him to make love to her.

Plain and simple. Yet, getting him to do that might not be.

Leaving the phone on the bathroom floor, where the spy had undoubtedly listened to her shower, she opened the door and stepped into the bedroom. The sofa had been made up with a sheet, blanket and pillow, where he obviously intended to sleep.

The security chain was on, the dead bolt turned and a door stopper was wedged underneath the door.

Turning, she glanced at the bed and her heart started pounding again. Then she saw him standing by the window and her pounding heart fluttered.

Bo was leaning against the wall near the bed, arms folded, peeking out the side of the drawn curtains. He'd changed into navy lounge pants and a charcoal T-shirt that stretched tight across broad shoulders and sculpted muscles.

Her first instinct was to sit on the bed and talk to him. She feared if she did, he'd stay by the wall or retreat to the sofa.

Taking matters into her own hands, she strode over to him, slid her arms around his waist and pressed her cheek to his back, her palms flattening over his rock-hard stomach.

Bo tensed, his muscles flexing. He didn't push her away, which was good.

"Do you see anything outside for us to worry about?" she asked, softly.

"No. I was only checking to be on the safe side. All clear." He turned in her arms and lowered his to fall at his sides. "Big day tomorrow," he said, stopping short and glancing toward the bathroom. "Seeing your family. It's late. You should get some sleep."

She lifted up on the balls of her feet and leaned in to press a tentative kiss to his lips.

Wrapping his hands around her arms, he pushed her back gently.

"I don't want to sleep." She stared at him, searching his face for a hint of desire, but she only saw restraint.

"What do you want?"

"The same thing I asked for last night." She grabbed the hem of her shirt and pulled it over her head. Then she pushed her sweatpants down, stepped out of them and faced him, wearing nothing at all.

On a shudder, a harsh breath tore out of him as his gaze roamed over her.

Resisting the inclination to cover herself, she stood there, letting him take her in.

"You're perfect," he whispered, and she beamed. Then he tilted his head away from her.

Nora slid her palms up his chest and wrapped her arms around his neck, pressing her body against him. "Don't you want me?"

"Yes, of course I do."

"Then what's wrong? Why won't you touch me?"

He sighed and looked at her, his gaze intense and direct. "Why do you want this?"

Why?

A hundred different reasons rushed through her head

all at once, like a high-speed train without brakes, but she had no idea where to start. She only knew that mentioning the possibility of dying would not persuade him.

"Rosa and Savvy have full lives. With friends and family and love. With so many things I haven't had because I've been hiding, stuck in limbo. I want more good things to fill up my life." Good things worth fighting for. "Tonight, for a little while, I don't want to feel scared. I want to feel... *good*. When you kiss me, when you hold me, when you touch me, you make me feel good, Bo." Instead of drifting like a ghost, she felt grounded by him. Bo made her *feel*. Sexy. Desired. Smart. Brave. Useful. So many things that she was breathless thinking of it. This incredible man made her feel alive. "Is that wrong?"

"No, it's not." He put his arms around her, holding her close. "What I mean is, do you want this because of a primal urge? Because you want a physical release?" He huffed a heavy breath. "Would you want this if it were someone else here? Eli? Tak? There's no judgment either way. I've had meaningless sex before and I can give you something convenient. Casual. Feel free to use me anytime." He chuckled, the sound halfhearted, and flashed her a soft smile that didn't reach his eyes. "I just need to know. If another man was here protecting you, would you want him to make you feel good?"

Now she laughed, not that it was funny. "You haven't been listening." She caressed his cheek. "No, I don't want just anyone. I want you. I can let my guard down with you. Ever since you took me home from the hospital, I've trusted you. Maybe prematurely, but I felt that I could." Biting her bottom lip, she wondered if she should continue. But she needed him to know. "I want this because I... I'm falling for you," she whispered.

"Yeah?" A real smile this time. "Really?"

She nodded. "But if you only want meaningless and convenient—"

Bo cut her off in what began as a simple kiss. It heated as she opened to him. It became rough and hard and full of need. Shoving a hand in her hair, he groaned in her mouth, his hips doing a slow, grind against her. She curled her fingers in the soft cotton of his shirt, wanting to rip it from his body.

He broke away for a moment, only far enough to whisper against her lips, "I want you. This isn't meaningless or casual for me. Not by a long shot." He crushed his mouth to hers in another scorching kiss.

His arm swept under her legs, tucking her against him. Without breaking the kiss, he carried her to bed. The yearning flaring through her was consuming—a fire that burned deep inside.

Gently, he set her down, pressing his body on top of her. His hips ground against her, a groan rumbling from his chest. She skated her hands down his spine and cupped his backside, drawing the bulge between his legs to her pelvis.

But he shifted, changing position, stoking her frustration and her desire. His lips and hands were everywhere, caressing and kissing.

A moan escaped her, and she reared her head back when he sucked a sensitive nipple into his mouth.

"Too much?" he asked, brushing his lips over the hollow of her throat.

"No. Not nearly enough." She tugged on his shirt, and he helped her take it off him. She gripped his waistband and managed to push his pants to his hips before he grabbed a wrist, stopping her.

"We don't have to go all the way tonight. I can still make you feel good."

Eyes flashing dark and hot, his hand dove between her legs and she gasped, not prepared for the instant pleasure his deliberate touch brought. She writhed helplessly beneath him. His fingers explored her, teasing and stroking while he kissed the valley between her breasts. Whimpering, she bucked her hips up, rubbing against his palm, needing friction, wanting more of him. All of him.

"Please." Her breath hitched in her throat. "Please, Bo."

"Please, what?" he murmured across her breast, his tongue tickling her skin. "What do you want?"

"You. I want to…"

His thumb hit a hot button of nerves and sensation detonated inside her. Shuddering, she cried out against the wave of pleasure that was swift and sharp.

Turning on his side, he held her, kissing her throat and running his nose along her skin up to her jaw. "We can stop. I can do other things. We have options." The hard length of his arousal pressed against her thigh, and she ached for so much more. "I just need to know how far you want to go."

Rolling over to face him, she stared in his eyes, slipped her hands down his pants, cupped him, and he groaned. "All. The. Way."

A grin tugged at his mouth, and he was off the bed in a flash. Her heart and body throbbed in anticipation. He closed the bathroom door, turned on music, dug in his overnight bag and came back to bed with a box of condoms.

Laughing, they pulled back the covers and climbed under the sheets. He settled between her legs and looked down at her.

There was desire in his eyes, but also something much deeper.

"I need to get this out now. Beforehand. I don't want you to think it's because we made love."

He took a breath like he was gearing up to say something serious. If he hadn't grabbed the condoms, she would've been certain another rejection was coming her way.

"Nora, you're special to me. I've never felt so strongly about anyone. We have a connection. One I need to hold on to. One I don't want to live without." Then he smiled at her softly, full of affection, and that single look mended the fractured pieces of her heart.

Chapter Eighteen

At eleven o'clock on Sunday morning, Bo and Nora watched the church doors as they waited for the ten o'clock service to finally end. Once it did, people would congregate outside, and they would make their move.

He didn't care that they'd been parked on the far side of the lot for thirty minutes. Or that the service had run longer than expected.

They were ready to rock and roll. The players on his team were in place. Autumn was in her SUV beside them. Declan and two other IPS agents were somewhere in the vicinity, keeping a low profile, observing. Jackson was at the B&B where he'd camp out as backup. Bo had given Detective Gagliardi a heads-up about their little op since it was in her backyard and asked her to keep quiet about it. She agreed, provided they include her once it was time to reel the killer in.

Nora wore the necklace Bo had given her. A tracking device with audio capability was hidden inside the pendant. He was taking no chances.

Since her stalker knew about her Beretta, and would certainly plan for it, Bo had given her a pocketknife and a Ruger LCP. Lightweight at less than ten ounces and compact with a length of only five inches, the backup gun was easy to conceal in the holster around her ankle. Despite the weapon's small size, it held seven rounds and packed a powerful punch.

He was even prepared to trade out his blue Toyota Tacoma for an all-wheel drive SUV.

With contingencies mapped out and every base covered, he allowed himself a few minutes to simply breathe. Just until those church doors opened.

He allowed two words to repeat in his head.

Mine.

She's mine.

He glanced over at Nora sitting in the passenger's seat and couldn't believe his luck. She was so beautiful. Kind yet tough. Caring and generous. As if all of that weren't enough, when they'd made love last night, she'd been perfect. Better than any fantasy. Tight and hot and just as hungry for him as he'd been for her. Like she'd been made for him.

He'd brought her to the brink and pushed her over the edge. With his fingers. With his mouth. Joining as one as he'd taken her, made love to her, and she had taken him, eyes closed, head thrown back, spasming around him until he had collapsed, boneless, burying his face in her hair.

It was pure pleasure, but it had gone deeper than the physical. It was proof that this thing between them was right.

Mine.

She was his and he was hers. For the first time, he'd found someone worth fighting for in every way.

Her eyes lifted, meeting his, and she smiled at him, but then she looked back at the church and the joy on her face faded.

Something was wrong.

He didn't expect her to be happy to involve her family in their plan, but she'd been acting differently since they left the B&B. Off somehow. Like a wall had gone up between them.

"Nervous?" he asked, not able to voice the real question running through his head because her phone was in her purse and the spyware was active.

She only nodded.

The church doors swung open, redirecting his attention across the parking lot.

Bo had gone over the Facebook pages of Nora's family and friends and some of the townsfolk who had a social media presence, making it easy to spot them as they emerged from the church.

People began filing out. Keith Graham and his wife, Sandy, were the first ones to shake the minister's hand. The former mayor was ten years older than his wife, though the age gap looked larger. Speaking to the minister, they wore amiable expressions, but when they went down the stairs to the walkway, tension between them became apparent, and their conversation ceased.

The temperature was mild, in the high forties, and there wasn't much wind. No reason why folks wouldn't stand around and socialize a bit.

Once a handful of individuals had made their way to the bottom of the stairs, Sandy Graham peeled away from her husband, leaving him alone, and eagerly chatted with others. The older man interlaced his gloved hands and stood there as though this was routine.

Spencer waltzed out of the church, carrying a toddler with a head full of dark ringlets. Savvy was by his side.

In the passenger's seat, Nora stiffened, wringing her hands.

As Spencer and Savvy spoke with the minister, Savvy's father, Terry, limped over to join them. Graying with a weathered face, Terry used a sturdy wood cane with a brass embossed collar. The handle was slightly curved at the end, making it easy to hook on a table or the crook of one's elbow. Slowly, he hobbled behind Spencer and Savvy, needing to take the stairs one step at a time.

In one of Savvy's online posts, she'd mentioned her brother Dylan's promotion to foreman in the coal mine and how they'd be able to help their father, who was scraping by on his disability checks.

Each vile gift box that Nora received contained a piece of coal. It occurred to Bo that the police had never questioned Dylan or any of the people at the party he supposedly attended without his good friend Spencer. Even if Dylan had gone, how simple would it have been to sneak out and blend back in later?

Where was Dylan now? Bo didn't spot him in the crowd. A no-show?

Rosa sauntered outside and Nora leaned forward, putting her hands on the dash. The two women bore a distinct resemblance. They had the same heart-shaped face and amber-colored eyes. The younger sister was shorter than Nora's five-foot-seven-inch frame—even with chunky winter boots—and had dark straight hair rather than wild curls.

The man with his arm around her shoulders was the new husband who Nora had never met. Behind them, Frank Howard hovered. Nora's pa looked uncomfortable for a moment, sweeping a hand through his silvered ebony hair. When it was his turn to step in front of the minister, he looked ready to shake his hand and move along.

"Okay." Bo turned to Nora. "This is it."

She sat there, quiet, gazing across the lot at the church.

"Don't you want to meet Rosa's husband? Hold your niece? See your family?" he asked. She still didn't respond. "Remember why we're here. So you can find answers. This is the only way."

"This isn't the only way," she snapped.

What was she doing?

Autumn got out of her car, came up to the driver's side window and held her hands out, silently asking the same question.

"If we're going to do this," Bo said, "we have ten minutes before they disperse and go home."

"I want to leave. Drive."

PULLING HER WOOL coat closed, Autumn tugged the purple scarf wrapped around her neck higher to cover her chin. She knocked on the window and waited.

Shoulders sagging, Nora picked up Bo's cell phone and gestured for him to unlock it. He did. She opened his texts and started a new message but didn't select a recipient.

Send Autumn back to Bitterroot. She's a friend. Makes her vulnerable. A liability. Now! Please!

What about going to the church? Speaking to your family? What happened to the plan? he replied.

Nora pointed to her message. "You and Autumn think I should be here in Cold Harbor. This isn't the way I want to handle things. I don't like the pressure. From either of you." Again, she gestured to the message.

Scrubbing a hand over his jaw, Bo turned to the window. Rolled it down. "I want you to go back to the office. You're not needed here," he said.

"What changed?" she asked, carefully.

Quickly, he weighed what to say. "I don't answer to you. It's the other way around. Go back to Bitterroot Falls."

Autumn drew her brows together in confusion. *Really leave?* she mouthed.

He nodded, once.

Pursing her lips together, Autumn spun on her heel, got into her car and drove off.

"Satisfied?" Rolling up the window, Bo shifted to Nora and took his phone from her. "Pressure cut in half."

He typed a message.

What are you doing? Stick to the plan.

Holding the phone low, he showed her the screen.

She read it and looked up at him. "I'm not satisfied. I don't want the pressure cut in half. I want it down to zero. Completely eliminated. Take me back to the B&B."

Narrowing his eyes, he stared at her, trying to pull an answer from her.

She snatched the phone from his hand, shoved it into the cup holder and faced forward. "Please. Take me."

"Are you sure?"

"I'm positive that I don't want to go out there and risk getting anyone else hurt." She glanced at him. "Your way isn't the only way. Trust me," she said, her eyes imploring him.

Bo threw the gear of his truck in Drive, wheeled out of the lot and hit the main road.

He hated this. Not being able to talk freely with her to understand what she was thinking. Find out why she was deviating from a plan after they had gone through painstaking efforts to make it work.

They drove in silence. Ten minutes without a word exchanged until he pulled up in front of the B&B.

Reaching over, he took her hand. He wasn't sure in what direction her changes were going. The best thing he could do was follow her lead. "Nora, you're an IPS client, first and foremost. But you're also my friend." Such a tame word that didn't scratch the true surface of what she meant to him. "I care about you and want to help you. I thought reconnecting with your family—getting questions answered, finding out what you've missed in their lives—would get you closer to what you ultimately want."

"It isn't necessary to drag my family into this. I want to see them, which makes me selfish. Last night you gave me something special that I needed. Thank you," she said, giving his hand a small squeeze before snatching it free of his grip. She looked out the window. "But it was simply sex. Nothing more. We shouldn't confuse hormones with something else. It'll only make this harder."

"What harder?" he asked, trying to decide how much of this they'd discussed in advance and how much of it was coming from a different place he was struggling to grasp.

"You and Autumn think you know what's best for me, but you don't. I never should've come to you and IPS." Her tone was deadly serious. "I never should have come back to Cold Harbor. It was a mistake. The only thing I can do is something I should've done four days ago. *Run.* Wipe away everything that's Nora Santana. My business. My charity work. Leave it all behind. My house. My car. My phone. Disappear and stay gone for good. Start over somewhere else as someone else."

Some elements he recognized, but the rest of what she was saying was sending him into a tailspin. "And your family?"

"Seeing my family will only hurt them. They don't want me to dig up painful memories that they'd rather forget. I have to let them go." Her jaw trembled, cheek quivering, and she pressed her lips together in a hard line. "The same way I have to let *you* go."

Bo reeled back in his seat. "Don't do this." *Don't go rogue.*

"This is the only way. I purchased an airline ticket. Later tonight, I'll fly out of Missoula. I don't want you to follow me. Not into the B&B and not to the airport."

"You can't be serious. I have to go inside to get my stuff. We can sit down and talk this through."

"I'll ask the owner of the bed and breakfast to mail you your things. I'll pay for it. Just get out of here and go back to your life."

"Nora, I can't leave you like this. I won't."

"You have to. Because I'm a bad omen. Anyone who gets close to me dies and I don't want that for you." Sucking in a deep breath, she looked at him, meeting his gaze, and held it. "Bo, you're fired. I don't want anything else to do with IPS." Tears welled in her eyes but she hiked her chin up. "If you don't leave me alone, I'll call the police. I hope you can understand this is for the best." She hopped out of the truck and slammed the door shut behind her.

NORA MARCHED UP the B&B porch steps without a single glance back at Bo. She strode through the foyer and caught sight of a man in the front sitting room. Blond and handsome, he looked like a younger, broodier version of Logan. Her only guess was that he was Jackson.

He made no eye contact with her, and she did her best to minimize any overt focus on him.

She hurried up to the third floor, went into the small suite and locked the door.

Plunking down on the bed, she wrung her hands. One thing she'd learned over the years of running and starting a new life was that the best lies were half-truths. Every word about her family had come from the pain in her heart.

She worried her presence would only resurrect ugly memories of death. That she'd stir up unwelcome emotions. That her presence would cause more harm than good. Endangering them wasn't an option. She wasn't going to play games with their lives for the sake of exciting a despicable killer.

Nora also wasn't willing to put Autumn in harm's way. They'd become friends and Nora wasn't going to paint a bull's-eye on the back of anyone she cared about. Not even Bo.

There was no need. None whatsoever.

The man stalking her was spying on her, and he already knew she was in Cold Harbor. The plan had been to spend the day with her family. Try to get some answers and piece together this deadly puzzle.

Then fight with Bo. Mention leaving her hometown and Montana for good in the morning—though she'd pushed up that timeline by twelve hours. The IPS team had stressed the importance of creating a sense of urgency. To her, this was a job well done.

Next, she needed to go back to the bed and breakfast alone.

And wait.

Wait for that monster to take the bait and show himself.

In the event he didn't come for her today, where this could be finished one way or another, she had told Bo another hard truth.

Running might be her only choice to protect everyone else. Otherwise, there was nothing to stop him taking more lives to coerce her into playing one of his games. So, she had purchased an airline ticket from Missoula to Seattle. From there, she'd take a ferry to Alaska. Reinvent herself in the last frontier. Go off the grid if necessary. That was surely the perfect place to do it.

Abandoning the life that she'd started building in Bitterroot Falls and walking away from Bo would devastate her.

But she'd make any sacrifice for the people she loved. They'd only been together a few days, shared one passionate night, yet it felt like she'd known him for years. Every time she thought of him, she saw him as a part of the future life she wanted.

She took a deep breath, held it and exhaled.

For now, she would follow the IPS plan. With modifications.

It was impossible to know how long she would be waiting. The last departure out of the Missoula airport was eight o'clock tonight. With an hour and a half drive to get there, plus time to check in, if the man who'd been obsessed with her for a decade was coming for her, he'd have to make a move no later than 5:00 p.m.

The only question was, did he need the cover of darkness or was he bold enough to maneuver in the light of day?

In less than three hours, she had her answer when her cell phone rang. A random number she didn't recognize.

This was it.

The last game she was ever going to play with him.

Winner takes it all.

Chapter Nineteen

Bo sat behind the wheel of a Subaru SUV with tinted windows that he had exchanged with Tak, who had taken his truck.

Parked on the side street of the intersection that faced the B&B, he stayed seated low, wearing shades and a cowboy hat because it blended in more than a ball cap. In one ear he had comms to speak with the team. An earbud was in the other, connected to his laptop, which he used to monitor the device hidden in Nora's necklace.

Declan and Detective Gagliardi were stationed on the road parallel to the one the bed and breakfast was on, and Jackson was inside the house, where he could cover both the front and back entrance.

Bo only wished he'd been able to have a candid conversation with Nora before they'd separated. The things she'd said to him hadn't all been for the sake of a pretense. The tears in her eyes had been real.

Did she really intend to leave? Disappear and start over somewhere new without him?

A cell phone rang. Not his.

Dropping his gaze to the laptop screen, he saw that it was Nora's.

"Look alive," he said over comms. "She's got action."

Bo turned up the volume and prayed she put the call on speaker so he could hear both ends of the conversation.

"Hello," she answered.

"Sweet Nora." The voice was digitized and crystal clear through the phone's speaker.

If Bo could've kissed her, he would have.

"You came home," the voice said, "and you got rid of him. Good girl."

Clenching a fist, Bo scanned the area for any other parked cars that hadn't been there earlier, any vehicles cruising or anyone lurking.

"Ready to finish playing?" the voice asked.

"What do I get if I am?"

"Peace of mind. I won't harm anyone else you care about. Not if you play. Are you ready?"

A moment of hesitation. "Yes," she said.

"Santa says, go out the back door of the bed and breakfast. Beyond the yard, there's a forest. Take the trail on foot and don't stop until I tell you. No coat. No purse. No gun. If you're followed, I'll know and there will be fatal consequences for someone you care about. If you hang up, there will be consequences. If you stop before I say so, you won't make it in time."

"In time for what?" Tension raised the pitch of her voice.

"To finish this round of Santa Says. Then we'll have to play a new game. A very bloody game."

"No, please. Don't hurt anyone else. I'll do it."

"Good girl. Santa says, run, Nora. Go now."

Bo tapped his earpiece. "Jackson, hang back and give her space. Three minutes. Four tops."

"I might lose her if I do."

Bo swore, his gut burning over having to make a choice.

Over wanting to pick her over everyone else when she would beg him to choose differently. "We risk the chance of him seeing you and someone else paying the price with their life." Nora would never forgive herself or him. Maybe he could still protect her without jeopardizing anyone else. "We'll track her via GPS and tail her at a distance by car." He was already moving, readying to drive the perimeter of the forest until he came across a road that cut through. At the same time, he was trying to bring up a map.

"She's out the back door," the youngest Powell said. "Those woods stretch for miles. I don't know where they could lead or if you'll be able to reach her destination by car. And she's fast. Really, really fast."

"The woods lead to a lake, the quarry and coal mines," Gagliardi said, coming over comms. "If she steps foot inside those mines, kiss your GPS coverage good-bye. You won't be able to track her, and you may never find her. Not alive, anyway."

By not following her on foot, he might be trading her life to save someone else's.

Nora might hate herself and hate him, too, if there was more innocent blood shed because he made the wrong choice. But he'd take her hatred over her death. The gamble of her being led or dragged into the coal mine was too great.

Bo would sooner play Russian roulette with his own life. He couldn't bear it if he lost her. *Choosing you, Nora, can't be wrong.*

"Follow her, Jackson. Just try to stay out of sight."

KEEP GOING. Don't slow down. Don't stop!

Nora was gasping for air, panting, her mind whirling as she tried to anticipate what surprise might come next. With no time to strategize, all she could do was run.

Her thoughts were racing as she kept sprinting, even as her body protested. Her shoulder ached now, a throb that spread down to her hand. She tucked her left arm, pressing it against her torso, and only pumped with her right arm to boost her momentum.

A cold wind whipped through the snow-covered trees, cutting through her and slapping her face. She shivered so badly, she had difficulty thinking straight. Perhaps that was the point. To have her too cold, too tired, and in too much pain to fight back.

One thing at a time. Put one foot in front of the other. One move, then a countermove.

She just had to run until he told her to stop. Her legs were strong, and so were her lungs. They would carry her through this. Ignoring the bite of pain in her shoulder, she stayed on the trail as he instructed.

"Go toward the trees with the yellow ribbons tied around the trunks," the voice said.

Past a cluster of evergreens, she spotted the ribbons. Silky streamers bright as the sun billowing in the wind. More than a quarter of a mile away.

Her lungs were on fire, but she could do it.

CRANKING THE WHEEL HARD, Bo made a right turn that had the tires screeching as he left the paved road and hit the dirt trail that ran through the forest.

A glance at the laptop screen told him he was going the correct way. She was headed straight for the road and would hit it farther down.

It occurred to him that someone else might be on the road. A road that led to the coal mines. His heart skipped a beat. The man they were after might be there waiting to intercept her. And if he got her into a car—

Bo smothered the thought. He didn't want to go there. Nora understood the danger of being moved to another location. Being forced to run wasn't much better. But there was a big difference between traveling on foot and by car. The distance could grow exponentially within a matter of minutes. Seconds.

What if Bo was spotted on the road? Would that endanger her? Would she suffer consequences?

Slowing down, he triangulated, looking at where he was in relation to her current position and where she was headed. He could reach her on foot from here if he ran quickly, but he'd have to leave his laptop and rely on the others to be his eyes and ears, updating him on her progress. He couldn't afford to miss her. Not by a second.

"I'm going on foot the rest of the way," Bo said, pulling over as far off the road as possible. "I don't want the car to be seen." He hopped out of the SUV and shut the door quietly, not wanting to make any noise that would draw attention.

"Jackson, what's your status? Do you have eyes on Nora?" Bo left the well-worn path, ducked in between trees and took off deeper into the woods.

"Negative." Jackson huffed, sounding winded. "But I see the yellow ribbons."

Look for the yellow ribbons, Bo reminded himself.

KEEP MOVING! She groaned through the discomfort of her shoulder and the burn in her chest. *Almost there!*

One of the yellow ribbons was almost within reach. But she still didn't have a plan. She had to outsmart him, outmaneuver him.

Somehow.

Overpowering him was impossible at this point. Inside, she was shredded. Totally spent. She used what little she

had left in the tank to push onward to a tree with a yellow ribbon.

"Stop!" the voice commanded

Nora halted. Gasping, she tipped her head back and
raked in as much air as possible.

"Walk to the center of the trail."

Heart on the verge of bursting from her chest, she
slogged forward like he demanded.

"Stop."

She stood still, trying to recover. The physical toll of
sprinting in the cold with no coat on was too much, sap-
ping her mentally, too.

Looking around, she spotted a van parked a hundred
yards down the trail. Was he inside it?

"Lift your sweater up and turn around," the voice said,
"so that I can be sure you're not carrying a weapon."

Nora grabbed the hem of her sweater and pulled it up,
stopping short of exposing her bra, and spun in a full circle.

"Drop the phone."

She released it from her grasp, letting it hit the cold ground.

Then someone wearing a ski mask stepped out from behind a tree in the woods on the other side of the trail. He
held up a gun, aimed it at her and approached her slowly.

Panic seized her roiling gut as she raised both palms.

Once he reached the trail, he dug into his pocket and took
out a pair of flex cuffs—disposable zip tie handcuffs—and
tossed them at her feet. "Put them on," he said, still using
the digitized voice, "and tighten them with your teeth."

Not happening. "I don't think so." She could finally
breathe again.

He reached toward his back, pulled something from
under his black sweater and held it out for her to see.

A purple cashmere scarf.

Autumn's.

"If you don't, our game ends, and I'll play a different one with your friend. The psychologist."

Terror sliced her down to her core. Not for herself, but for Autumn.

Squeezing her eyes shut a second, Nora shook her head. This monster kept besting her. Outwitting her at every turn. She'd sensed that Autumn might be in danger and she'd been right.

Why did Nora agree to let her come to Cold Harbor in the first place?

Now, he had her. A good, kind woman who had only tried to help her through this mess.

Nora wanted to scream, attack this sick animal and beat him to a pulp. But what had he done to Autumn?

"Is she hurt?" Nora asked.

"I left her undamaged. For now. If you want her to stay that way, put on the cuffs."

Clenching her jaw to keep her teeth from chattering, Nora swallowed the hot bitterness that filled her mouth. She bent down, picked up the cuffs and slipped them on her wrists.

"Tighten them."

She yanked each strap with her teeth until the plastic straps tightened, digging into her skin. "Show me your face. Some part of you wants me to know who you are and why you're punishing me. So, let me see who you are."

He stepped closer until he was within arm's reach. Sticking his hand under the mask, he peeled off the voice digitizer that had been affixed to his throat and tossed it down. Then, slowly, he pulled off the mask.

Nora rocked back on her heels, her mouth falling open in disbelief. "You?"

Bo's PHONE BUZZED. Incoming call over comms. Whoever it was wanted to speak to the entire team. Tapping the earpiece twice to connect, he didn't slow.

"It's me," Autumn said. "I'm here."

"Where?" He wanted to ask if she was back in Bitterroot Falls, but he saved his breath, needing it for the run.

"Cold Harbor. I never left."

If he had the lung capacity to curse without slowing down, he would've. The one thing Nora had wanted was for Autumn to leave and stay safe. Instead, she had defied an order.

"Why not?" Declan said, asking the question that was on the tip of Bo's tongue. "This killer only targets women. Women close to Nora. That makes you a potential target."

"Stop. I'm fine. I stayed to talk to Rosa and Savvy. I had a feeling that they might know more than they realized. Questions about the case led nowhere. A dead end. I showed them the note card and they'd never seen the drawings. But I brought a sample of the seat cushion from Nora's car that still had that smell of cologne or tobacco trapped in it."

"And?" Bo managed to say.

Spotting yellow streamers up ahead in the distance, he slowed down. He was too close now to go tramping along.

"Savvy recognized it. Pipe tobacco."

"Whose?" Three of them asked at once.

"Terry Watts."

NORA WAS REELING in terrified shock.

"Hands up. High in the air," Mr. Watts said, and she raised them.

Stepping even closer, he patted her down, starting with her breasts.

Her heart sank. Bo had given her extra weapons to defend herself and he was about to find them.

The pocketknife first. He pulled it from her pocket.

Her only hope now was that he was tracking her.

Terry Watts tsked at her like she was a child or a dog and tossed the blade to the ground. "Naughty, naughty, Nora."

"Why are you doing this?"

"Twelve stab wounds. The card with Santa and Krampus." He stroked down one of her legs. "You really don't remember, do you?"

"Remember what?"

Down the other leg. His hand stopped on the gun holstered around her ankle. "The lives you destroyed." With his gun aimed at her midsection, he yanked up her pant leg and unstrapped the holster. He tossed it back in the woods. "Walk to the van," he said, gesturing for her to move.

She lowered her hands. Taking her time, giving Bo a chance to reach her, she took slow, deliberate steps. "What are you talking about?"

"It was the week before Christmas break. That day you skipped school along with Jessica, Alice and Dana. You went back to your house. Saw your Pa and—"

"My mom." They were being intimate with the bedroom door open, thinking no one was home because the kids were supposed to be at school. Nora had only glimpsed them before skedaddling out of the house with the others. A few days later, her mother yelled at her about a skirt she was wearing. How short it was—almost indecent. Nora snapped, said things she regretted, told her mom that she wasn't going to grow up to be *loose*. Would never bring boys to the house in the middle of the day to have sex the way her mom and pa had. Nora had been a silly, rude twelve-year-old to speak that way.

Twelve. They had all been twelve. Her, Jessica, Alice and Dana.

Twelve stab wounds.

"No. It wasn't your mother. It was my wife. Peggy. Your mom didn't know about the affair. Neither did I. Not until you told her inadvertently." He shoved the gun in her face. "You caused that car accident, you know. We all went out to dinner. Luisa had been tense, acting weird. It wasn't until we all got in the car and Peggy and Frank sat in the back that she brought it up. That you four, rotten twelve-year-old girls had played hooky from school and caught them. Frank and I started arguing. Luisa got distracted. Only for a split second. For the wrong second. And hit that truck."

"Oh, my God." Nora lurched forward, sick to her stomach. "I never had any idea."

"Your pa didn't want you to know. Didn't want you to carry that on your shoulders. But it's your burden to bear." He stopped as they reached the van. "That argument, that accident, changed my life. I didn't think I'd ever fully recover. I did. But then Peggy got sick and needed full-time care. I pretended that I was still injured so I could look after her. Do you know what that's like? To love someone so much and to hate them for betraying you, but to be stuck tending to them, watching them slowly wither away?"

Nora swallowed around the lump in her throat. "I'm so sorry, Mr. Watts."

"It's too late for apologies. You need to pay for what you did."

"I didn't know. If I had, I never would have said anything to my mom."

"If only you and Alice and Jessica and Dana had been good girls." Mr. Watts reached behind his back again and this time his hand came up with a boning knife. "If only you had gone to school that day like you were supposed to." He lowered the gun in his right hand and raised the knife in his left. "Then you never would have found out. Luisa and I wouldn't have either. Our lives wouldn't have been destroyed. Your mother would still be alive. And I could have tended to Peggy for four years without hating her. You wretched girl!"

Nora kicked his leg, hoping that it wasn't fully healed, and interlocked her fingers. She batted his arm with her clasped hands, knocking him into the side of the van. She whirled around and sprinted toward a tree, praying she could duck behind it for cover before he took aim and squeezed the trigger.

A gunshot blasted the air, chilling her down to the marrow in her bones. She froze, waiting for the pain. But no agony followed.

Bo darted out of the woods and rushed toward her. Holding out his arms, she ran to him. It wasn't until he held her that she realized she was shivering.

She looked over her shoulder.

Terry Watts was on the ground, eyes open, dead.

Jackson Powell burst from the woods and hurried to the body. He knelt down and checked for a pulse, then picked up his gun.

"It's over," Bo said, brushing his lips across her forehead. "He's never going to hurt you, or anyone else, ever again."

Chapter Twenty

Six days later...

They were all gathered at Chance and Winter's house. The luxury ranch home was enormous, with eye-catching amenities and high-end decor that would exceed any real estate agent's expectations. Set on one thousand pristine acres, the swanky retreat was the perfect spot for Summer Stratton and Logan Powell's engagement party.

Sitting on Bo's lap on the sofa, Nora leaned against him as he slid his arms around her, holding her close. The spacious living room was packed with Strattons and Powells, most from out of town, as well as friends and plenty of people from Bitterroot Falls.

Nora soaked in the festive atmosphere and, to her surprise, the holiday spirit, too. With Christmas less than a week away, the house was decked out in decorations and string lights. Presents were piled under the tree. Lively music played in the background while everyone chatted, ate and danced. A spirited debate continued over where to hold the nuptials. The Powells wanted Wyoming, on their large ranch, where they had dreamed all their children would be married. The Strattons wanted Texas, where they had lots of relatives who wanted to attend. The newly engaged couple wanted to stay out of it, choosing to dance and kiss.

The love-fueled discussion reminded Nora what it was like for things to be normal, to be around family. It seemed hard to believe that just six short days ago, she had finally faced her demons and almost died. If not for Bo and Jackson racing to her aid, she would be dead. The incredible man who was holding her now had taken the shot that saved her.

So much had come to light with Terry Watts finally paying for what he had done. Answers to her questions had surfaced. All these years, her pa had been hiding the fact that she had discovered his affair. He'd been plagued with such shame at having cheated on her mother. A short-lived dalliance during a difficult time in their marriage. One he regretted so much he'd tried to drown it in booze. But he had never wanted her to feel responsible for any of the fallout. Especially not for the horrible accident that had killed her mother.

On the night of the Yuletide murders, Spencer had lied to the police about being home. Instead of watching movies in his room or going to the party with Dylan, he had been with Savvy. He'd had a crush on her, way back then, but knew he had to wait until she was older to act on his feelings. However, when he found out she had the flu, he'd brought her soup and watched a movie in her room to keep her company, not caring if he got sick.

They later connected the dots that years ago, in Cold Harbor, Terry had arrested Ames. Terry must have seen Ames again in Bitterroot Falls and decided to use the ex-convict to help carry out his plan.

A deadly plan that had nearly succeeded.

Renewed relief washed over Nora as she tightened her arm around Bo and pressed her cheek to his.

No more living in fear. No more running. No more hiding. No more pushing people away to protect them.

It was still surreal.

"You want to dance?" Bo asked with a smile that made her heart flutter.

"Sure."

They rose together. He set her down on her feet and twirled her while keeping a steady hand on her so that she didn't fall.

She wrapped her arms around his neck and his hands went to her waist to pull her tight to him. Leaning down, he kissed her softly and she tingled. Bo understood her and accepted her. After fighting to survive for so long, suppressing her opinions and desires in order to blend in, he encouraged her to stand out, to tell him what she wanted even if it caused an argument. He made her believe that no matter what, they could work it out.

Every night, whether they were at his house or hers, they talked for hours about everything. Made love and talked some more. They were healing each other, and Nora felt herself changing as she opened up about the things she kept locked away inside her.

Bo pulled his lips from hers and caressed her cheek. "You know how much I love you."

Hearing the words still made her warm all over.

No matter what she did or said, he loved her, and the power of that love left her in awe. "I know."

"If you ever need a break, want to explore other options since you never had a chance to before—"

She rose on the balls of her feet and silenced him with a kiss. Before she'd become involved with him, she hadn't relied on anyone. Had never truly trusted anyone. To have another person love her, body and soul, was a remarkable thing that she didn't take for granted.

For the first time in forever, she was filled with optimism for the future. For a future with him. "I keep telling you—I want *you*," she said. "I love you. In fact, I was thinking that maybe in the spring, I'd put my house up for sale. We're together all the time anyway." Aside from work, they were inseparable.

"Okay."

She smiled. "That's all? Okay?" No hesitation?

"Yeah. You're the person I need to hold on to. I just didn't want to hold on too tightly."

"Hold on as tightly as you want. I'm not fragile. I won't break. Just don't let go."

"The brave, strong woman I know is anything but fragile." He placed a tender kiss on her lips. "And I'll never let go." His smile was soft and only for her.

Life was beautiful. Nora looked around at all the beaming faces, absorbing the joy that overflowed in the room. She'd not only found friends and family in these fearless people who fought for her, but she'd also found something in Bitterroot Falls that she'd been too scared to think possible. Love and a home—where she was going to build a life with Bo.

* * * * *

COMING SOON!

We really hope you enjoyed reading this book.
If you're looking for more romance
be sure to head to the shops when
new books are available on

Thursday 18th December

MILLS & BOON

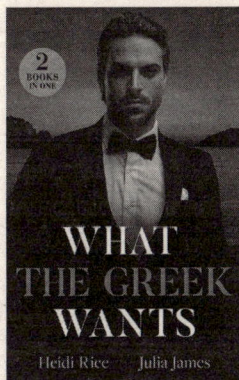

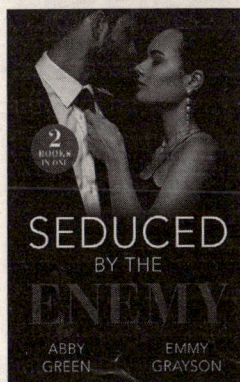

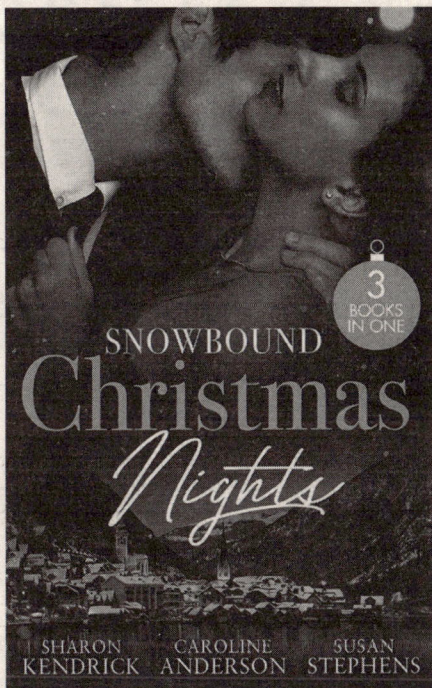

LET'S TALK
Romance

For exclusive extracts, competitions and special offers, find us online:

⬤ MillsandBoon

✕ @MillsandBoon

⬤ @MillsandBoonUK

♪ @MillsandBoonUK

Get in touch on 01413 063 232